SECULARISM

OTHER BOOKS BY THE AUTHOR

Good Governance: Never on India's Radar (2014)
The God Who Failed: An Assessment of Jawaharlal Nehru's Leadership (2014)
India's Parliamentary Democracy on Trial (2011)
The Judiciary and Governance in India (2008)
The Holocaust of Indian Partition: An Inquest (2006)
Public Accountability and Transparency:
The Imperatives of Good Governance (2003)
The Changing Times: A Commentary on Current Affairs (2000)
Unfinished Innings: Recollections and Reflections of a Civil Servant (1996)
Rural Employment Strategy: A Quest in the Wilderness (1990)
Public Expenditures in Maharashtra: A Case For Expenditure Strategy (1989)
Industrial Dispersal Policies (1978)

SECULARISM
INDIA AT A CROSSROADS

MADHAV GODBOLE

RUPA

Published by
Rupa Publications India Pvt. Ltd 2016
7/16, Ansari Road, Daryaganj
New Delhi 110002

Sales centres:
Allahabad Bengaluru Chennai
Hyderabad Jaipur Kathmandu
Kolkata Mumbai

Copyright © Madhav Godbole 2016

All rights reserved.
No part of this publication may be reproduced, transmitted,
or stored in a retrieval system, in any form or by any means,
electronic, mechanical, photocopying, recording or otherwise,
without the prior permission of the publisher.

The views and opinions expressed in this book are the author's own and the
facts are as reported by him/her which have been verified to the extent possible,
and the publishers are not in any way liable for the same.

ISBN: 978-81-291-3762-3

First impression 2016

10 9 8 7 6 5 4 3 2 1

The moral right of the author has been asserted.

Printed at Replika Press Pvt. Ltd, India

This book is sold subject to the condition that it shall not,
by way of trade or otherwise, be lent, resold, hired out, or otherwise
circulated, without the publisher's prior consent, in any form of
binding or cover other than that in which it is published.

For my grandchildren
Aditi, Manan, Gaayatri and Taarini
and
their generation who may be called upon to choose
between
India as a Hindu Rashtra and a secular nation.

Contents

Preface	ix
Introduction	1
1. India's Secularism—Defining the Indefinable	30
2. The Minority Syndrome	70
3. Are These Signposts of Secularism?—I	118
4. Are These Signposts of Secularism?—II	219
5. An Increasingly Unsecular Society	286
6. The Way Ahead	329
Appendix I	381
Appendix II	384
Appendix III	388
Appendix IV	392
Abbreviations	394
Bibliography	397
Acknowledgements	415
Index	417

PREFACE

At a panel discussion in Hyderabad, Karri Sriram, one of the exponents of Information Technology, aptly summed up his assessment of the Modi government's first year in office: 'The login name for the Modi government is development, but the password is Hindu.'

In every sense, the year 2014 has been a watershed since Independence. Intolerance has been a hallmark of India for several years but the driving force was not Hindutva, as it is now. Article 1 of the Constitution specifies the name and territory of the Union of India as 'India, that is Bharat'. The Rashtriya Swayamsevak Sangh (RSS) would like this to be changed to 'Bharat'. A private member's bill has been moved in the Lok Sabha to substitute the word 'India' with 'Hindustan'. The 'two-nation theory' ascribed to M.A. Jinnah was, in fact, first propounded by V.D. Savarkar, though he did not want the country to be divided. He wanted Muslims to continue to stay on as second-class or lesser citizens in a Hindu Rashtra. The concept of secularism itself is being questioned by the RSS, the Bharatiya Janata Party (BJP) and their constituent organizations. The amendment of the Constitution during the Emergency in 1976, by which the word 'secular' was included in the Preamble to the Constitution, is also being questioned. The Constitution has left the word 'secular' undefined. It is argued by the BJP that the true meaning of secularism is *panth nirapeksha* (neutral to sect), and not *dharma nirapeksha* (neutral to religion).

There is a perceptible unease in civil society regarding these disturbing trends. The President of India, Pranab Mukherjee, has publicly expressed his anxiety, more than once. This is also true of the Vice-President of India, Hamid Ansari. Writers, artists and intellectuals have protested by doing what they can, and returned the awards received by them over the years. The response of the government has been unbelievably shocking, to put it mildly, with Minister of State (Independent Charge) for Culture and Tourism Mahesh Sharma saying, 'Let them stop writing.'

I have also been struck by the ambivalence of the Constitution regarding secularism. In spite of repeated efforts by some Constituent Assembly members, the founding fathers did not agree to describe the Constitution as secular, though it contained several features of a secular state. The inclusion of the provision pertaining to a uniform civil code as a mere directive principle of state policy—not as a fundamental right—in spite of a demand by several members, leaves one perplexed. Equally difficult to appreciate is the provision of Article 48 which, though innocuously titled, 'Organization of agriculture and animal husbandry', effectively calls for 'prohibiting the slaughter of cows and calves and other milch and draught cattle'. After having achieved the important objectives of abolition of separate communal electorates and reservation of seats in the legislatures according to the percentage of minorities, in the name of compromise arrived at with the minorities, the founding fathers gave in to a number of their other demands.

It is interesting to note that all important decisions regarding the provisions of the Constitution were taken by the Congress party in its party meetings and were merely formalized by the Constituent Assembly. Several members, including Minister of Law and Justice Dr B.R. Ambedkar, alluded to this in their speeches in the Assembly. I have extracted and referred to those statements in this book.

One question which has bothered me is: What have we done about our secularism? Religion, which is supposed to be a private and personal matter, is present everywhere in our public life. More so after the BJP's coming to power at the Centre, on its own strength, in 2014. Right since Independence, Parliament has been made the *dharma sansad* (religious forum), mostly in respect of the Hindu religion. A number of important temples have been taken over by state governments or are being managed by trusts under their supervision. The high courts and the Supreme Court have taken on the responsibility of interpreting the Hindu (and Jain) religion, including the questions: What is religion? Which customs and practices can and cannot be segregated as strictly pertaining to religion? The Madras High Court has gone so far as to prescribe a dress code for going to temples. But the fundamental tenet of secularism laid down by the apex court, namely, the separation of religion from politics, has remained a distant dream. A stage has been reached where even the Supreme Court has started entertaining doubts as to how long India will continue to be a secular nation. It is a travesty that this doubt should arise when the apex court itself has declared secularism as a part of the basic structure of the Constitution.

It is against this background that I have written this book. I sincerely believe that India is at a crossroads. It is being called upon to choose between its largely secular governance till now and the Hindu Rashtra (nation) ideology. If India opts for the former—which I am sure it will do—it will also have to decide how to ensure that it will be truly secular. I have tried to look at the relevant issues as objectively and apolitically as possible. I have no political ideology to promote. I sincerely believe that India has no option but to be a secular nation. In doing so, it will have to give up considerable political and ideological baggage, and look at issues as rationally as possible.

The thrust of the book is on the operationalization of secularism, keeping in view the experience so far. Inevitably, fresh thought will have to be given to a number of constitutional and statutory provisions discussed in this book. When the stakes are as high as the survival of the country, nothing need be considered sacrosanct. As Thomas Jefferson, the eminent American statesman who played a big part in the making of the American Constitution, said: 'We may consider each generation as a distinct nation, with a right, by the will of the majority, to bind themselves, but none to bind the succeeding generation, more than the inhabitants of another country.' I hope the suggestions contained in the book will be considered in this light.

The names of places have been retained as they were at the time, e.g., Bombay, Calcutta or Madras. The discussion in the book is confined to only religious minorities and does not cover linguistic, racial and caste minorities. Some portions of the text have been italicized to invite the reader's attention. Reference to the source is given at the end of the quotation in the bracket with the name of the publication/author, year of publication, and page number(s). In the Constituent Assembly/Parliament proceedings, the number(s) denote column(s).

INTRODUCTION

The danger to India, mark you, is not Communism. It is Hindu right-wing communalism.

—Jawaharlal Nehru's talk to officers of the Indian Foreign Service in 1959

This chapter discusses:

- Hindutva ideology—its origin and rapid spread;
- A many-sided assessment of India's secularism; and
- The portents for the future.

Nehru's assessment of the future danger to India, made over fifty-seven years ago, is highly significant and remarkably accurate. But, unfortunately, the Congress party, during his seventeen-year-long tenure as prime minister[1] and later, during the term of his daughter Indira Gandhi and his grandson Rajiv Gandhi as prime minister, and during the Congress rule even thereafter, did not address this threat seriously. In fact, with their policies, they alienated the Hindus and drove them, willingly, and in most cases, unwillingly, into the Bharatiya Janata Party (BJP) fold.

This is borne out by the fact that the central government's Intelligence Bureau (IB)—which kept tabs on all political happenings in the country and particularly the activities of political parties and organizations opposed to the government—totally overlooked the threat posed by the rightist ideology. This was amply evident during the massive agitation

---

[1] Radha Rajan, for example, considers Nehru to be 'acutely hostile to everything Hindu'. (Rajan 2009: 1)

launched by the BJP in the 1980s and 1990s for building a Ram temple in Ayodhya. After the shocking demolition of the Babri Masjid on 6 December 1992, the question arose of banning some communal organizations. It was found that the IB had not built up any worthwhile record of the activities of these organizations. Concerted efforts had to be made by the Ministry of Home Affairs (I was home secretary at the time) to compile data from the state governments, spending literally five–six sleepless nights in the office.

Fali S. Nariman, the noted senior advocate of the Supreme Court, in his lecture organized by the National Commission for Minorities (NCM) on 12 September 2014, opened his speech with the following observations:

> The elections in April–May 2014 this year have put a strong majoritarian government in power at the Centre. I welcome it. Whilst I welcome a single-party majority government, I also fear it. I fear it because of past experience with a majoritarian government in the 1960s and 1970s, when the then-all-Congress government had unjustifiably imposed the internal Emergency of June 1975. And rode roughshod over the liberties of citizens. I cannot forget it nor can I condone it. Traditionally, Hinduism has been the most tolerant of all Indian faiths. But recurrent instances of religious tension fanned by fanaticism and hate-speech have shown that the Hindu tradition of tolerance is showing signs of strain. And let me say this frankly—my apprehension is that Hinduism is somehow changing its benign faith because, and only because, it is believed and proudly proclaimed by a few (and not contradicted by those at the top) that it is because of their faith and belief that Hindus have been now put in the driving seat of governance. (Nariman 2014: 1–2)

Hindutva Ideology: Its Origin and Rapid Spread

It would be pertinent to begin this discussion with Swami Vivekananda's address at the Parliament of Religions in Chicago on 11 September 1893. I wish to invite the attention of readers to how far we have come in discussing religion from its Vedic concepts. Vivekananda had eloquently stated:

I am proud to belong to a religion which has taught the world both tolerance and universal acceptance. *We not only believe in universal toleration, but we accept all religions as true.* I am proud to belong to a nation which has sheltered the persecuted and the refugees of all religions and all nations of the earth…I will quote to you, brethren, a few lines from a hymn which I remember to have repeated from my earliest boyhood, which is every day repeated by millions of human beings: 'As the different streams having their sources in different places all mingle their water in the sea, so, O Lord, the different paths which men take through different tendencies, various though they appear, crooked or straight, all lead to Thee.' The present convention…is in itself a vindication, a declaration to the world of the wonderful doctrine preached in the Gita: '*Whoever comes to Me, through whatever form, I reach him; all men are struggling through paths which in the end lead to Me.*' Sectarianism, bigotry and its horrible descendant—fanaticism—have long possessed this beautiful earth. They have filled the earth with violence, drenched it often and often with human blood, destroyed civilization and sent whole nations to despair. *Had it not been for these horrible demons, human society would be far more advanced than it is now.* (*The Complete Works of Swami Vivekananda*, Vol. 1, 1989: 3–4)

The BJP's[2] rise in India's electoral politics has been meteoric. In 1951, it had a vote share of just 3.06 per cent of the total. Soon after the termination of the Emergency, it increased to as much as 41.3 per cent in 1977. Thereafter, it declined to 11.4 per cent in 1989 and touched a high of 25.6 per cent in 1998. It again declined to 22.2 per cent in 2004, but went up steeply in 2014 when it got, for the first time ever, a clear majority of seats in the Lok Sabha. This trend is also borne out by the number of seats won by the BJP in those years. In 1951, it won only three seats while, in 1998 and 1999, it had as many as 182 seats. This number came down to 138 seats in 2004, but went up steeply to

---

[2]Before 1971, the BJP was known as the Bharatiya Jana Sangh (BJS) or the Jan Sangh (JS). In the 1977 and 1980 general elections, the BJS contested the elections in coalition with some other political parties.

282 in 2014. As can be seen, something important was at work during those years which enabled the BJP to consolidate its position to such a striking level. To some extent, it was also due to the decline of the hegemony of the Congress party.

It is generally recognized that the term 'Hindu' emerged as a geographical nomenclature and implied a geographical identity of the people living across the Sindhu or the Indus river. Vinayak Damodar Savarkar stated that the religion of the majority of the Hindus could be best denoted by the ancient accepted appellation, the *sanatan dharma* or the *Vaidic dharma*. He wrote:

> ... In the case of some of our Mohammedan or Christian countrymen who had originally been forcibly converted to a non-Hindu religion and who consequently have inherited along with Hindus, a common Fatherland and a greater part of the wealth of a common culture—language, law, customs, folklore and history—are not and cannot be recognized as Hindus...Their Holy Land is far off in Arabia or Palestine. Their mythology and Godmen, ideas and heroes are not the children of this soil... A Hindu... is he who looks upon the land that extends from Sindu to Sindu—from the Indus to the Seas—as the land of his forefathers, his Fatherland (*pitribhu*).' (Savarkar 1923: 107, 113, 115)

Nehru always had serious concerns about the working of the RSS. In his letter to chief ministers dated 7 December 1947, Nehru invited their attention to the increasing activities of the RSS. He wrote:

> We have a great deal of evidence to show that the RSS is an organization which is in the nature of a private army and which is definitely proceeding on the strictest Nazi lines, even following the technique of organization. It is not our desire to interfere with civil liberties. But training in arms of large numbers of persons with the obvious intention of using them is not something that can be encouraged...It is desirable for provincial governments to keep a watchful eye and to take such action as they may deem necessary. (Guha 2010: 330–31)

Donald Smith, in his book, *India as a Secular State* (1963), went into the various facets of India's secularism. It is considered an authoritative assessment of the subject and has even been quoted by the Supreme Court. It is interesting to see that he had specifically commented on the communalism in the Congress. He wrote:

> It would be a great error to assume that the forces of Hindu communalism find expression only in the Hindu Mahasabha, RSS, and Jan Sangh. Almost from its inception, the Congress has contained elements sympathetic to the communalist viewpoint, and we have already noted the close association of the Hindu Mahasabha with the Congress during the period 1924–1926. Some Hindu Mahasabhaites retained their Congress membership well into the 1930s...It was only in 1938 that the working committee declared that...the Hindu Mahasabha and the Muslim League were to be regarded as communal organizations...The communalist sentiment within the Congress has come to the surface over such issues as the Hindu Code Bill, proposals to ban cow slaughter, the question of foreign Christian missionaries, and the treatment of the Muslim minority...It would be foolish indeed to assume that his [Nehru's] deep convictions regarding the secular state are shared by all his fellow Congressmen. Probably the majority at the present time does fully accept the secular state, only a tiny minority (secretly) rejects it, but a substantial minority merely acquiesces in the present policy and would be willing to go in a different direction. Nehru declared that from his own inquiries, it appeared that local Congress leaders made no attempt at all to calm the communal frenzy which seized Jabalpur and other cities and towns of Madhya Pradesh during the riots of February 1961. They simply sat in their houses like 'purdah ladies' while the situation deteriorated. This lack of positive conviction about secularism, and the willingness to stand by passively in the presence of communalist disruption are serious defects. The Congress parliamentary party resolved in April 1961: 'Those Congressmen who by their acts or inaction in an emergency support directly or indirectly communalistic activities are not worthy of remaining in the Congress.' It is difficult to think of any potential successor

to Nehru who is likely to take an equally strong stand on the question of secularism.

Smith also invited attention to the fact that, while spurning all association with the Hindu Mahasabha or the Jan Sangh and opposing them bitterly, the Congress made special arrangements with Sikh and Muslim communal parties, which clothed them with a certain respectability. (Smith 1963: 479–81)

M.J. Akbar's assessment was not very different. He succinctly wrote that the growing communalism in the country worried Nehru. After Partition, Nehru made it his primary concern to try to make Muslims feel equal and secure: *he regarded the perennial threat of Hindu dominance as a major danger to the unity of India, a unity which could survive only through a commitment to secularism.* What worried him even more than the official Hindu revivalist parties—the Hindu Mahasabha or the Jan Sangh—was the possibility of Gandhi's Congress being usurped by such elements. *He would not drive this element out of the Congress, for that would only drive it into the Jan Sangh.* But he kept them under a strong check. (Akbar 1988: 580)

While addressing a public meeting organized by the Delhi State Congress Committee on 6 September 1951, Nehru made his position clear on the *Hindu Rashtra*. He said:

> It may sound very nice to some people to hear it said that we will create a Hindu Rashtra, etc. I cannot understand what it means. Hindus are in a majority in this country and whatever they wish will be done. But the moment you talk of a Hindu Rashtra you speak in a language which no other country except one can comprehend and that country is Pakistan because it is familiar with this concept. They can immediately justify their creation of an Islamic nation by pointing out to the world that we are doing something similar. Hindu Rashtra can only mean one thing and that is that you leave the modern way and get into a narrow, old-fashioned way of thinking, and fragment India into pieces. Those who are not Hindus will be reduced in status. You may say patronizingly that you will look after the Muslims or Christians or others as in Pakistan they say that they will look after the Hindus. Do you think any race or

individual will accept for long the claim that they are looked after while we sit above them? (Gopal and Iyengar, Vol. 1, 2003: 186)

In his book, *Thoughts on Pakistan*, Ambedkar drew attention to the fact that Savarkar's definition of the term 'Hindu' was designed to serve two purposes: first, to exclude from it Muslims, Christians, Parsis and Jews by introducing the recognition of India as a holy land in the qualifications required for being a Hindu. Second, to include Buddhists, Jains, Sikhs, and other religions, by not insisting upon belief in the sanctity of the Vedas as one of the qualifications. The scheme had some very important features. One was the categorical assertion that Hindus were a nation by themselves. This, of course, meant that the Muslims were a separate nation by themselves. That this was his view, Savarkar did not leave to be inferred… speaking at the Hindu Mahasabha session held in Ahmedabad in 1937, he said:

> Several infantile politicians commit the serious mistake in supposing that India is already welded into a harmonious nation, or that it could be welded thus for the mere wish to do so. These, our well-meaning but unthinking friends, take their dreams for realistics. That is why they are impatient of communal tangles and attribute them to communal organizations. *But the solid fact is that the so-called communal questions are but a legacy handed down to us through centuries of a cultural, religious and national antagonisms between the Hindus and the Muslims.* When time is ripe you can solve them; but you cannot suppress them by merely refusing recognition of them. It is safer to diagnose and treat deep-seated disease than to ignore it. Let us bravely face unpleasant facts as they are. *India cannot be assumed today to be a Unitarian and homogeneous nation, but on the contrary, these are two separate nations in the main, the Hindus and the Muslims in India.*

Ambedkar emphasized that:

> Strange as it may appear, Mr Savarkar and Mr Jinnah, instead of being opposed to each other on the one nation versus two nations issue, are in complete agreement about it…Mr Jinnah says that

India should be cut up into two, Pakistan and Hindustan, the Muslim nation to occupy Pakistan and the Hindu nation to occupy Hindustan. Mr Savarkar on the other hand insists that, although there are two nations in India, India shall not be divided into two parts, one for Muslims and the other for Hindus; that the two nations shall dwell in one country and shall live under the mantle of one single Constitution; *that the Constitution shall be such that the Hindu nation will be enabled to occupy a predominant position that is due to it and the Muslim nation made to live in the position of subordinate co-operation with the Hindu nation.* (Ambedkar 1941: 136–38)

The two-nation theory, which culminated in the creation of Pakistan, was propounded by Mohammad Ali Jinnah in 1939. But in reality, Savarkar was the first to propound it. He described it in his book, *Hindutva*, in 1923 and later in his presidential address to the Hindu Mahasabha on 30 December 1937: 'There are two nations in the main: the Hindus and the Moslems in India'. A year later, in 1938, he said: 'The Hindus are the nation in India—in Hindustan—and the Moslem minority a community'. Rajagopalachari had suggested, as far back as 1942, that Pakistan should be conceded. (Tahmankar 1970: 272)

In 1925, M.R. Jayakar invited Savarkar to speak at a public meeting at Vedanta Ashram. A.G. Noorani quoted from M.R. Jayakar's *The Story of My Life* (Vol. II: 541):

... Savarkar, the Hindu Sabha leader, made an extraordinary speech, the main theme of which was that, until we are a free nation, we must not think of practising soft virtues like humility, self-surrender or forgiveness. On the contrary, we must, during our subjection, develop sturdy habits of hatred, retaliation, vindictiveness and such other features. In other words, we must postpone, until we are free, the virtues inculcated by our religion.

In a detailed critique of Hindutva, Dr B.R. Ambedkar showed that Savarkar's definition of a Hindu—which forms the basis of Hindutva—has 'been framed with great care and caution'. A Hindu is one who regards India as both his Fatherland (*pitrubhoomi*) as well as his Holy Land (*punyabhoomi*).

> It is designed to serve two purposes which Mr Savarkar has in view. First, to exclude from it Muslims, Christians, Parsees and Jews by prescribing the recognition of India as a Holy Land as a qualification for being a Hindu. Secondly, to include Buddhists, Jains, Sikhs, etc., by not insisting upon belief in the sanctity of the Vedas as an element in the qualifications. (Noorani 2002: 25–26)

Savarkar was the first person to bring out clearly the distinction between Hindutva and Hinduism. He had to coin some new words, such as 'Hindutva', 'Hinduness', 'Hindudom', in order to express the totality of the cultural, historical and, above all, the national aspect along with the religious one, which marks the Hindu people as a whole.
He wrote:

> Here it is enough to point out that Hindutva is not identical with what is vaguely indicated by the term Hinduism. By an 'ism' it is generally meant a theory or a code more or less based on spiritual or religious dogma or system...Had not linguistic usage stood in our way then 'Hinduness' would have certainly been a better word than Hinduism as a near parallel to Hindutva. (Savarkar 1923: iv, 4)

After Gandhiji's shocking assassination, the RSS and some other organizations were banned by the central government. After some time, Vallabhbhai Patel suggested the lifting of the ban on the RSS. Nehru wrote to him saying:

> The RSS have a definite ideology which is entirely opposed to that of the government and the Congress. They definitely oppose the idea of a secular state...If at this juncture we remove the ban on the RSS and continue it on other groups, this will be widely interpreted as our encouraging certain fascist elements in India.

When the matter of lifting the ban came up again in 1949, Nehru agreed with Patel that the ban on the RSS and the detention without trial of thousands of its members could not continue indefinitely. In July 1949, after M.S. Golwalkar accepted Patel's conditions, he and the other RSS détenus were released and the ban on the organization lifted. The conditions were that the RSS should adopt a written and published Constitution, restrict itself to culture, forswear violence and secrecy, profess loyalty to India's flag and Constitution and provide for a democratic organization. (Gandhi 1990: 496–97)

In view of the powerful role being played by the RSS in recent years, particularly after the Lok Sabha elections in 2014, it would be enlightening to examine the extent to which the RSS is abiding by these conditions. It is significant to note that, for the first time, the top leaders of the RSS held a meeting with Prime Minister Modi and his cabinet colleagues to review the functioning of the government in September 2015. No one was going to be deceived any longer by the pretence of the RSS being just a cultural organization.

S. Radhakrishnan commented that: 'Hinduism is a movement, not a position; a process and not a result; a growing tradition, not a fixed revelation.' Mahatma Gandhi stated: 'Hinduism is a relentless pursuit after truth'. (Jagmohan 2010: 183)

K.R. Malkani was of the view that: *India cannot be rebuilt good and strong on the basis of a colourless and tasteless secularism;* it will have to be revived on the basis of its own rich and inclusive culture, what Sri Aurobindo calls 'the larger Hinduism'. That is what Hindutva is all about. (Malkani 1993: 152)

Writing about 'Hindutva and Secularism', M.S. Golwalkar, who was the *sarsanghachalak* (chief) of the RSS[3] for thirty-three years, stated:

> An untenable argument is being repeated *ad nauseam* that the concept of Hindu Rashtra is opposed to the idea of secularism. First of all, *this idea of secularism, born in the West, is out of place in our country*...it is in line with the idea of Hindu Rashtra, and provides equal opportunities to all religions to carry out their activities as per their practices, and prevents any effort of one religion to attack another religion. *Then, it would be better to define the state as*

---

[3] As compared to the Hindu Mahasabha, the RSS has allowed a gradual and natural flow of non-Hindus into the RSS. Malkani has given the details of these in his book, *The RSS Story*. (Malkani 1980: 99–100)

'multi-religious' rather than 'secular'...Our concept of the state has always been secular. (Golwalkar 2008: 179–80)

Interestingly, Golwalkar was won over to the cause of a Hindu nation by a prominent Congress leader, Madan Mohan Malaviya... Golwalkar regarded Savarkar's 'Hindutva' as a great scientific book which fulfilled the need of a textbook on Hindu nationalism. He followed in Savarkar's footsteps while putting forward his ideas about a Hindu nation in a highly controversial booklet, 'We or Our Nationhood Defined' (1939), which included a foreword by a prominent Congress leader and member of the central legislature, M.S. Aney. This booklet, indeed, determined the future direction of the concept of Hindu nationalism and nation as advocated by the RSS. (Islam 2006: 11, 14)

The RSS, which professes to be only a cultural organization, has been quite vocal on a number of political issues. As the publication, *RSS Resolves*, brought out by the Karnataka Branch of the RSS in 1983, shows, the resolutions passed by the organization cover diverse areas, such as national policies; the Sangh, government and political groups; communal and subversive threats; national integration; external aggression/policy; national calamities; elections and Emergency heroes. Of course, the pretence of its being only a cultural organization has been exposed in recent months with the RSS doing back-seat driving on a number of policies pertaining to the BJP-ruled states and the Centre.

By now, it has been accepted that the Jammu and Kashmir problem which has troubled India all these years has been largely due to mishandling by Jawaharlal Nehru. Permitting that state to have a separate Constitution, a separate flag and a chief minister designated as prime minister were matters which caused concern even in the 1950s but, due to the hegemony of the Congress party, hardly any opposition was publicly voiced. It is therefore significant that a joint agitation was launched by the Jan Sangh, the Hindu Mahasabha. and the Ram Rajya Parishad in 1953 under the leadership of S.P. Mookerjee.[4] The slogans raised in the agitation were also

---

[4] Shyama Prasad Mukherjee

significant: *Ek Desh Mein Do Pradhan, Do Bidhan, Do Nishan Nahi Chalega* (Two prime ministers, two constitutions, two national flags will not be allowed in one country). (Das 2000: 197)

Kanungo pointed out:

> According to the RSS, the Muslim invaders were not only plunderers, they were also religious fanatics. Marxist historians, on the other hand, argue that, though these invaders were plunderers, their sole aim was to loot and plunder the invaded land, irrespective of the faith of those who inhabited it...Thus the perception of the RSS on the issue of Hinduism's encounter with Islam varies greatly from that of the Marxist and secular historians. While RSS historians magnify the religious divide out of proportion, Marxist and secular historians excessively emphasize the ethnic, racial and cultural aspects of the encounter, ignoring the religious part. (Kanungo 2003: 99, 101)

In 1952, the RSS launched a massive movement in support of cow protection. In a month-long campaign, workers collected 1.75 crore signatures all over the country, urging an immediate and complete ban on cow slaughter. Among the signatories were lakhs of Muslims. Fazal Ali, the governor of Orissa and former judge of the Supreme Court, publicly associated himself with the demand. (Malkani 1980: 61)

The RSS passed at least four resolutions—in 1952, 1958, 1960 and 1966—on the protection of cows and banning cow slaughter. In 1960, it proposed that the government should undertake a Constitution amendment for the purpose. A country-wide agitation was launched by the Sarvadaliya Goraksha Mahabhiyan Samiti for a 'total and unreserved ban on the slaughter of cow-species'. It was alleged that, though the government had accepted in principle the need for banning cow slaughter, it had not taken any concrete steps in this direction.

In a resolution passed in 1970, the RSS countered the government's baseless charges against it as 'patently false and mischievous propaganda'. It said that the physical training which was being imparted to its members was not meant to equip them for violent and destructive activities.

In its 1979 resolution, it urged its considered opinion that 'proselytization and secularism are incompatible. Proselytization, which implies the concept of superiority of one's religion and the inferiority of all others, is the very antithesis of secularism... It is most unfortunate that the Christian missionaries should have started a virulent campaign against such a welcome measure (the Freedom of Religion Bill 1978 proposed by O.P. Tyagi), which ensures the freedom of all religions equally.' The resolution urged the central government and all members of Parliament to give whole-hearted support to the bill and to expedite its passage.

In its 1983 resolution, the RSS criticized the Tamil Nadu government's ban on the Hindu conference which was to be held at Nagercoil on 13 February 1983. It alleged that the state government's action was prompted by certain fanatical Christian sections. (*RSS Resolves*, 1983: 4, 12, 22, 54, 66–68, 91–92, 118–19)

A Many-Sided Assessment of India's Secularism

In his book, *Pakistan or the Partition of India*, Dr Ambedkar wrote: 'Islam does not recognize territorial affinities. Its affinities are social and religious and therefore extra-territorial...This is the basis of Pan-Islamism.' (Malkani 1993: 182)

During the course of the Khilafat movement, Indian Muslims began to feel that they were a part of a brotherhood of Muslims living in different countries. That, necessarily though subconsciously, created a sense of extra-territorial loyalty to the Muslim brotherhood, which transcended loyalty to the country in which Indian Muslims lived as citizens. This is further borne out by the agitation launched by the Muslims in India after the famous Al-Aqsa Mosque at Jerusalem was damaged. Justice P.B. Gajendragadkar has written that, on this occasion, processions were taken out in many important cities in India, which were reminiscent of the spirit which had overwhelmed the Muslim masses during the days of the Khilafat agitation. He has quoted from the *Times of India* (30 August 1969: 5) about the procession which had been taken out in Bombay the previous day:

The news item was titled, 'Mammoth City Morcha Demands Jehad'. It read: 'We demand Jehad.' These three words told the feelings of Muslims in Bombay who came out into the streets on Friday to express their anger and shock at the Al-Aqsa incident. Nearly 3,00,000 Muslims marched through the streets in a two-mile-long procession carrying banners which demanded Jehad. Nearly everything about the march was different from the usual *morcha*s seen in the city. First, the march was singularly 'unorganized'. People just pored [*sic*] out into the roads and walked. Policemen were content to stand on the sidelines and watch them as they marched in a disciplined way… (Gajendragadkar 1971: 147–48)

Though Patel seldom talked of secularism, he was no proponent of Hindu rule. In February 1949, he spoke of 'Hindu Raj' as 'that mad idea' (Gandhi 1990: 497)

It is important to note the warning given by Ambedkar in the Constituent Assembly on 25 November 1949. He emphasized that it would not be enough to have mere political democracy:

We must make our political democracy a social democracy as well. Political democracy cannot last unless there lies at the base of it social democracy. What does social democracy mean? It means a way of life which recognizes liberty, equality and fraternity as the principles of life. These principles…are not to be treated as separate items in a trinity. They form a union of trinity in the sense that, to divorce one from the other is to defeat the very purpose of democracy.' (*Constituent Assembly of India Debates* [henceforth *CAD*] Vols X–XII, Book 5, 2009: 979).

It will be amply evident that the future of secularism will continue to be in a precarious condition till these basic requirements are fulfilled.

Abdullahi Ahmed An-Na'im emphasized that:

The core deficiency of Nehru's secularism was precisely that it lacked substantive authority, since it did not emerge as a result of negotiations, contestation, and discussion among different religious and secular viewpoints within Indian communities. He has quoted Bilgrami (1994) as saying: 'Secularism just never got the chance to emerge out of a creative dialogue between these different communities.' (An-Na'im 2008: 166)

In a letter to Nehru dated 12 August 1950, Vallabhbhai Patel wrote:

> I do not recognize any Islamic culture or any Hindu culture. I do not recognize that there is any book in the world which has said the last word on what man should be. Neither the Veda nor the Quran is the last word for me in human thought...My leading thought in politics is an all-round unity in the country as far as it can be achieved with unavoidable and necessary diversities being kept within proper limits. *I have openly advocated Hindu–Muslim marriages and, as you know, caste orthodoxy has played little part in my life.*

M.A. Karandikar, in his book, *Islam in India's Transition to Modernity*, has referred to 'the most vitriolic attack on India's secularism' by Syed Badrudduja on the floor of Parliament on 28 April 1966 when he said:

> 'Secularism is a snare and a delusion, it is a fraud and a deception... Secularism! Thy name is hypocrisy, thy name is treachery, thy name is corruption, thy name is bribery, thy name is nepotism and favouritism, thy name is filth and abomination, thy name is wanton encroachment upon the fundamental rights of the citizens...thy name is exploitation of the minorities particularly of the religious Muslim minority, spoliation and ruination of the Muslim minority' etc. etc. The shocked Union home minister [Gulzarilal Nanda] exclaimed, 'I wonder how in a few minutes in a single speech one could pour so much venom.' (Karandikar 1968: 323)

It would be useful to remember what L.K. Advani stated in the Lok Sabha on 6 December 1993, the first anniversary of the demolition of the Babri Masjid:

> In 1947, Pakistan had declared itself a theocratic state. If India had done something similar, the world may not have blamed her. But those who understand the history and culture and tradition

of this country would not have accepted it. Therefore, I say that *theocracy is alien to Indian tradition and culture.* We cannot become a theocratic state. *This country is secular because of its culture and history and tradition and that is principally because it is a Hindu country.*

As for the future of secularism, Asghar Ali Engineer, a Muslim intellectual, in his article, 'Secularism in India—A Minority Perspective', stated that it would not be correct to reply in the negative. 'There is definite hope for a secular future...Certain institutions of Indian democracy like the Supreme Court of India have proved to be a strong pillar for protecting democracy and democratic values, including secularism...The functioning of secular democracy in India for the last 61 years has generated a strong base which will be very difficult to tamper with.' (Siam-Heng 2010: 182)

In the compilation of his blog posts, L.K. Advani quoted Mark Tully, the well-known BBC journalist who has spent many years in India:

'In one of the several conversations I have had with one of India's leading Islamic scholars, Maulana Wahiduddin Khan, he said to me, "I am a Muslim, Islam is my religion, but I honour other religions. *I also believe Muslims enjoy far better conditions in India than in any Islamic country.* In Islamic countries they either have peace or freedom, in India they have both."'... [Tully added] 'When I first came to India... I thought there was only one way to God and that was Christianity. It's India's tolerance, its secularism that has changed my belief.' (Advani 2011: 10–11)

But, this was long before the BJP came to power at the Centre in 2014.

Fareed Zakaria, editor of *Newsweek International*, emphasized that Hinduism is not a religion in the 'Abrahamic' sense of the word. He wrote:

Every sect and every sub-sect of Hinduism worships its own god, goddess or holy creature. Every family forges its own distinct version of Hinduism. You can pay your respects to some beliefs, and not to others. You can be a vegetarian or eat meat. You can pray or not pray. None of these choices determines whether you are a Hindu. There is no heresy or apostasy, because there is no core set of beliefs, no doctrine, and no commandments.

Zakaria argues that *it is this non-doctrinaire character that gives Hinduism its absorptive and assimilative power.* (Advani 2011: 68)

As compared to the aggressive stance of Hindu rightist groups and organizations at present, M.S. Golwalkar had asserted: 'Hindus did not need any certificate of secularism. *We are the most secular people on earth.* India had allowed Muslims and Christians to build their religious places long before Muslims or Christians came to rule India. Parsis, fleeing religious persecution in their homeland, had been given refuge in India.' (Malkani 1980: 103)

However, Rajeev Bhargava, in the introduction to his book, *Secularism and Its Critics*, took an entirely opposite view that, on the face of it, secularism has performed

> ...rather poorly. There is perhaps as much, if not greater, religious bigotry today as before. Religious minorities continue to feel disadvantaged and often face discrimination. The scale and intensity of religious conflict does not seem to have declined: if anything it has proliferated, touching people who have never known it before. The verdict against secularism appears unequivocal; it failed to realize the objectives for which it was devised. (Bhargava 1998: 1)

This is clearly an extreme, one-sided view. First, Bhargava has perhaps in mind only the Muslim minority, for there is no evidence to show that other minorities have such a grievance. Serious issues also need to be raised, as has been done in this book, whether Muslims need to be recognized as a minority in India any longer.

Pralay Kanungo stated:

> The RSS calls its own brand of secularism as true or 'positive secularism'. What are its salient features? First, the RSS consistently clarifies that the Hindu Rashtra does not advocate a theocratic state. This could be believed, as the RSS is aware of its impracticability.

Therefore, it would rather prefer to have a stake in which Hindus would enjoy a hegemonic role. It is very unlikely that in a Hindu Rashtra the laws of the state would conform to this or that *samhit*... The ideology of Hindu Rashtra shows a scant regard for the pluralist cultural traditions of Hinduism. The RSS stands for a mono-cultural Hinduism...The attack on the Sahmat exhibition makes it clear that Hindu Rashtra recognizes only one Ramayana, not many ramayanas. The burning down of M.F. Hussain's [sic] paintings suggests that the iconography of Hinduism is too sacrosanct to be creatively interpreted, especially by a non-Hindu. The assault on Deepa Mehta's films, *Fire* and *Water,* warns that every cultural expression must conform to the tenets of Hindutva. (Kanungo 2003: 124, 280)

Y.B. Chavan, who held the portfolios of Minister of Defence, Minister of Home Affairs and Minister of Finance during his exceptionally long tenure as a central minister, stated in an interview with Jayant Lele in the early 1970s: 'I think secularism will become more and more strong. Some of these aggressive tendencies that are there, they will go, not merely because I have faith in it...What is going on today are merely aberrations, I consider them aberrations.' (Pawar 2015: 526).

But India has changed drastically since then.

Meghnad Desai, in his essay, 'Hindutva's March Halted? Choices for the BJP after the 2004 Defeat', written after the most unexpected debacle of the BJP in the 2004 Lok Sabha elections, reflected the general mood in the country that the Hindutva forces were not likely to make a return in the near future. He wrote:

> Had the BJP–NDA coalition won, there was little doubt that the BJP would have become the natural party of power, much like the INC [Indian National Congress] used to be in the first 40 years after Independence. It would have moved into hegemonic position... School textbooks would have forever changed children's views of Indian history, and minorities would have had to come to terms with a precarious state of existence, henceforth under suspicion of their loyalty...Five more years would have given the BJP ideologues a real stranglehold on history and social science disciplines.

Desai predicted:

> The reality is that neither of the two largest national parties—INC or BJP—can by itself come to power...India's politics is becoming more fragmented, more devolved and less majoritarian...*The defeat in the 2004 general election puts the BJP at a crossroads. It has to reconcile itself to never coming to power as a single party and hence implementing its Hindutva dream by stealth or not at all. In any case, a Hindutva-based India remains a distant prospect.* (Adeney 2005: 254, 258, 263)

Within less than a decade, Meghnad Desai was in for a shock when, in the 2014 elections, the BJP came back to power on its own with a clear majority. This is a clear pointer to the success of the BJP in reasserting its Hindutva ideology and its appeal to the masses across the country. This was no doubt partly due to Narendra Modi's extraordinary oratorical skills and his emphasis on development agenda. But the basic appeal of the BJP ideology cannot be lost sight of. With its success, the BJP has placed India and its secularism at a crossroads.

The declining percentage of the Hindu population and the increase in that of the Muslim population have always been a subject of intense debate and anxiety among certain sections of Hindus. The census figures show that, in 1881, Hindus were 75.09 per cent of the total while Muslims were 19.97 per cent. The percentage of Hindus declined to 69.46 per cent in 1941, when Muslims were 24.28 per cent of the total. The census of 1951, which was held after the Partition of the country, was a watershed. In that year, Hindus were 84.98 per cent while Muslims were 9.91 per cent. The pattern of decline in the Hindu population and increase in the Muslim population has continued and, in 2011, the percentage of Hindus came down to 79.5 while that of Muslims increased to 14.5. This has led to yet another controversy and added a new facet to the communal question.

Abdul Shaban mentioned that the growth rate of the Muslim population in the country has been relatively higher than that of the Hindu population. The observed national trend has been an increase of around 1 per cent in the share of the Muslim population every decade since 1961. This higher growth rate—which emerges mainly from the poverty and economic deprivation of the community—has often been interpreted adversely and seen as a strategy by Muslims to overtake the Hindus numerically.

Shaban emphasized that Muslims, who are generally given a monolithic identity in day-to-day discourses, are an extremely divided community on the basis of caste, sect and region. In fact, the term 'Hindu' used today for signifying the majority religious community in India was once used to denote a geographic region, and even Muslims and Christians were referred to as Hindus.

Shaban also quoted Amartya Sen who wrote:

> In fact, seeing Hinduism as a unified religion is a comparatively recent development. The term 'Hindu' was traditionally used mainly as a signifier of location and country, rather than of any homogenous religious belief. The word derives from the river Indus or 'Sindhu'...and the name of the river is also the source of the word 'India' itself. The Persians and the Greeks saw India as the land around and beyond the Indus, and Hindus were the native people of the land. *Muslims from India were at one stage called 'Hindavi' Muslims, in Persian as well as Arabic, and there are plenty of references in early British documents to 'Hindoo Muslims' and 'Hindoo Christians' to distinguish them respectively from Muslims and Christians from outside India.* (Sen 2005: 310). (Shaban 2012: 2–4)

The problems of implementing secularism in India are by no means simple. On the one side, there is a strong Hindu rightist view which believes in the ideology of Hindu Rashtra. This ideology has gained strength after the dramatic success of the BJP in the 2014 Lok Sabha elections. As a result, voices, which had been muted till then on making India a Hindu Rashtra, have become strident. There are even demands that the word 'secular' should be removed from the Constitution. On the other side, there are equally strident conservative, orthodox and fundamentalist Muslims who would like to do everything possible to retain the separate identity of Muslims.

It is interesting to see that even a liberal Muslim intellectual, Asghar Ali Engineer, candidly stated that:

> *Islam is declared to be incompatible with secularism because in a secular state there is no place for divine laws, and secular laws are unacceptable to Islam.* Also it is believed that *in Islam religion and politics cannot be separated.* On these grounds, secularism is totally rejected by orthodox Muslims. They also think that secularism is atheistic, and atheism has no place whatsoever in Islam. Islam strongly emphasizes faith in Allah. These are some of the grounds which make orthodox Muslims uneasy with the very word secularism. Islam emphasizes life hereafter and secularism means only those matters which pertain to this world. There is no place for the world hereafter as far as secular philosophy is concerned. (Engineer 2003: 98)

Mushir-ul-Haq commented on the attitude of Indian Muslims towards the forces of secularization. He frankly stated:

> *Leaving aside a small section of Indian Muslims the majority is by no means secular*...it is 'religious-minded' in the sense that, in its outlook even on worldly life a majority of Muslims is guided by religion...the Muslim community in secular India is more concerned with its religious identity than is usually realized by others. Their ever-increasing interest in establishing religious schools (*madrasa*s), financially and administratively independent of the government, for imparting traditional Islamic education, their unquestioning reliance on the madrasa-educated ulema for religious guidance in almost every matter through the institution of *fatwa* (authoritative religious decrees) attest to the community's strong attachment to its religion...The ulema are less to be blamed for the Muslim resistance than the Indian intellectuals and leaders of public opinion. The latter, first, underestimated the hold of religion on the community, neglecting the need for establishing a line of communication with the ulema, and thus alienated themselves from the Muslim masses; second, they could not convince the Muslim community that secularism was not really antithetical to religion; and third, they did not try to learn what religion meant to Muslims. (Mushir-ul-Haq 1972: 1, 3–4)

Haq made these observations as far back as in 1972. Prima facie, while they still seem to be partly true, one only hopes that, over the years, the thinking of Muslims has undergone a change since it would have a significant impact on the success of secularism.

Gopal has written at length about the need to consider the present and the future of secularism in India in a historical perspective. They have emphasized the interaction of Hinduism and Islam as seen in music, dress and food (also architecture). They have added:

> Nor could the two religions evolve in India in isolation. An inscription of the year 1264 found in Junagadh, written in Sanskrit and issued by a group of Muslim traders, refers to Allah as Viswanatha. This strand strengthens with the development of the Sufi and Bhakti movements and the emergence of figures like Ramanand and Kabir...It is easy to find instances in the history of ancient and medieval India of the desecration or demolition of institutions of religious significance. But such actions were not the monopoly of the followers of any one particular religion. A Hindu ruler of the eleventh century, Harsha of Kashmir, melted images in Hindu temples, and a Hindu general cut down the Bo-tree in Bodhgaya. Shaivites and Vaishnavites, Hindus, Buddhists, and Jains, Sunnis and Shias quarrelled and frequently pillaged each other's shrines. When the Sikhs conquered Sirhind in 1764, they deliberately destroyed all buildings, including the mosques... Nor were such actions the result solely of mindless fanaticism. If Mahomed of Ghazni demolished the temple at Somnath, he also destroyed mosques in Central Asia...To establish authority in India over people of several faiths, rulers had perforce to keep religion in its place. A Maratha ruler built one of the five minarets of the *dargah* at Nagore. A Muslim ruler was the benefactor of the temple at Madurai, and the nawab of Arcot was the protector of temples at Chidambaram and Tirupati. Tipu Sultan of Mysore in 1793 bore all the expenses for the restoration of the *math* at Sringeri which had been destroyed by a Maratha chief. To this day there are shared traditions and ceremonials in the temples, mosques, and churches in south India. In these years, then, religion did not dominate public affairs but was at most one of several factors in a society with 'a

predominantly syncretic culture' and with no 'pervading sense of social separateness.' (Gopal in Raghavan 2013: 341–43)

Instances of composite culture are not rare even in today's India with its pronounced communal strife and tensions. Two such places in Maharashtra are Kurundwad town in Kolhapur district and Gotkhindi village in Walwa taluka in Sangli district where, each year, during the Ganapati festival, the Ganapati image is installed in five masjids in the former and one masjid in the latter.

Asghar Ali Engineer wrote that:

> The composite culture is far more widespread even today than is generally realized. This has been vividly brought out in a recent study conducted by the Anthropological Survey of India under the 'People of India Project'. According to its findings, Indian Muslims share a very high percentage (96.77) of material and cultural traits relating to ecology, economy and occupation with Hindus. The ratio of shared traits between Muslims and Sikhs is 89.95 per cent and that between Muslims and Buddhists is 91.95 per cent. (Engineer 2003: 76)

The assessment regarding the future of India's secularism has differed widely over the years. During the Nehru period, there was a great deal of optimism on the subject. D.E. Smith, professor of political sciences in Pennsylvania University, raised the question, 'Is India a secular state?', and gave a qualified answer, 'Yes.' He felt that, 'It is meaningful to speak of India as a secular state, despite the existence of the problems... India is a secular state in the same sense in which one can say that India is a democracy.' (Smith 1963: 499–500). Writing in 1963, Smith said:

> The political parties in India which directly challenge the secular state can claim but a microscopic amount of popular support. The Jan Sangh [predecessor of the BJP] is the only Hindu party which appears to have the potentiality for an important role on the national scene. But its total strength at present is represented by 14 seats out of 500 in the Lok Sabha. Outside of the communal parties there has been no movement of any significance to make India a

Hindu state...For India to reject the secular state, it will have to repudiate both Gandhi and Nehru...The Hindu communal parties affirm that *'the misconceived notion of secular democracy cannot inspire the masses'*. *The argument of this book is that the notion [of secularism] is well conceived and indeed vital to India's national development; but it cannot be denied that it lacks emotional appeal.* It is far too early to dismiss the possibility of a future Hindu state in India. However, it must be said that on the basis of the evidence now before us, the possibility does not appear a strong one. *The secular state has far more than an even chance of survival in India.* (Smith 1963: 495, 501)

India has come a long way since the time Smith made the above assessment. The stakes are much higher now and the time has come to address the real issues, if secularism is to survive.

Mohan Bhagwat, the *sarsanghachalak* of the RSS, has reiterated that, since India is a Hindu Rashtra, it will survive and prosper only if all Hindus unite. If Hindu society gets disrupted, it will endanger the whole country, Bhagwat said. (*Loksatta* 5 January 2015: 10)

The BJP general secretary, Ram Madhav, in an interview to Al Jazeera, reiterated the traditional RSS line that India, Pakistan and Bangladesh could re-unite through 'popular good-will' to form an 'Akhand Bharat'. (The *Indian Express* [henceforth *IE*] 27 December 2015: 1). This interview, given to the Al Jazeera TV channel, must have been telecast to the whole of Muslim world and raised doubts about the real intentions of the BJP (and the RSS) government in Delhi. It also needs to be noted that Madhav is not just a functionary of the RSS but an important office-bearer of the ruling BJP. Any talk of 'popular goodwill' bringing these countries together is a pipedream, and I sincerely hope it will remain so. In my book, *The Holocaust of Indian Partition— An Inquest* (2006), I argued that, even with the fore-knowledge about Jinnah being a dying man and not having long to live:

Nehru and Patel (must have) consciously worked for the partition of the country from mid-1946, keeping in view the larger concerns for the stability, unity, integrity, and social cohesion of India... *India is better-off with the partition* and in fact, if it had not been partitioned then, it would have led to continuous struggle for the creation of several Pakistans, whatever names they might have been given, apart from having to face unmitigated social, religious and political feuds and turmoil. The contribution of Nehru and Patel on this score must be remembered with gratitude. (Godbole 2006: 22)

The spread of Muslim terror and fundamentalism in both these countries has aggravated the problems in recent years and no one should seriously think of Akhand (united) Bharat, if the future of 'India, that is Bharat' is not to be compromised.

Till recently, Nepal was the only Hindu country in the world. The BJP and the RSS hoped that it would continue as such in the future as well. But, to their deep disappointment, Nepal has opted to become a secular country in its newly promulgated Constitution. Though some political parties in Nepal tried to reverse this decision, it was finally declared a secular nation. This was a significant omen from the point of view of India.

The Portents for the Future

> Dennis Dalton, in his essay, 'Gandhi and the Clash of Civilizations', referred to Samuel P. Huntington's article, 'The Clash of Civilizations?' published in *Foreign Affairs* (Summer 1993) about the coming world conflicts: 'The most important conflicts of the future will occur along the cultural fault lines separating civilizations from one another...differences among civilizations are not only real, they are basic. Civilizations are differentiated from each other by history, language, culture, tradition, and most important, religion... These differences are the product of centuries. They will not soon disappear.' (Nanda 1995: 408)

Huntington elaborated further on this by saying:

> A third possible source of Muslim–non-Muslim conflict involves what one statesman, in reference to his own country, termed the 'indigestibility' of Muslims. Indigestibility, however, works both ways: Muslim countries have problems with non-Muslim

> minorities comparable to those which non-Muslim countries have with Muslim minorities. Even more than Christianity, Islam is an absolutist faith. *It merges religion and politics…* [and] As a result, Confucians, Buddhists, Hindus, Western Christians, and Orthodox Christians have less difficulty adapting to and living with each other than any one of them has in adapting to and living with Muslims. (Huntington 1996: 264)

These differences have come to the fore in recent years in a number of countries in Europe on issues such as wearing the *burqa*, headscarf and *hijab*. These differences have got accentuated lately with the emergence of the Islamic State (IS). The terrorist attack in Paris on the satirical weekly, *Charlie Hebdo*, on 7 January 2015, and on 13 November 2015 in Paris and its suburb Saint-Denis, has brought these issues into prominence. Donald Trump, the Republican presidential candidate in the United States, has taken a very strident position and has demanded that a total ban should be imposed on the entry of Muslims into that country. Another Republican candidate, Ben Carson, has declared Muslims as unfit to be President of the United States and has underlined that their faith is inconsistent with American principles. The public reaction to the violence sponsored by the IS has also led to demands in a number of Western countries that no refugees should be permitted to settle in those countries.

In so far as India is concerned, according to one survey, 35 per cent of the people surveyed believed that there was no incompatibility between Islam and the West. However, if such a poll were to be undertaken today, in 2016, I am sure the results would be quite the opposite. Reference may also be made to the decision of the Supreme Court in July 2015 that candidates appearing for the MBBS entrance examination would not be permitted to wear a headscarf. 'Your faith won't disappear if you don't wear scarf (hijab) one day,' the Supreme Court told the applicant. (*IE* 25 July 2015:1).

The portents for the future are also difficult in view of the announcement in the manifesto of the Islamic State to expand its fight to India. (*IE* 3 December 2015: 1). The Islamic State has released a new twenty-two-minute Arabic- language documentary in which Indian jihadists have threatened a war on India to avenge the demolition of the Babri Masjid and the killings of Muslims in Kashmir, Gujarat and Muzaffarnagar. (*IE* 21 May 2016: 1) A number of recent news items have shown that educated young Muslims are attracted by the ideology of the IS, causing serious security concerns in the country. Interestingly, *The Atlantic*, in its July–August 2003 issue, had written about the 'Headlines over the Horizon', based on a study by Rand Corporation researchers. In so far as India was concerned, it included two possible headlines on the horizon: 'The Hindu–Muslim Divide' and 'The Indus Water Fight'.

A Christian school in Lucknow is in the news for preventing a Class IX student from attending classes because she wore a hijab. The authorities said that the school had a dress code. 'If somebody wants to wear a religious dress, they should seek admission in a madrasa or some such school.'

Article 48 of the Constitution, under which cow slaughter is sought to be prevented, is one of the directive principles of state policy. The Constituent Assembly did not agree to demands to make this a fundamental right... But, in today's Hindutva-dominated governance in the country, it has become so important as to over-ride the provisions of even the fundamental rights pertaining to secularism, and the right to practise any profession, or to carry on any occupation, trade or business under Article 19 (1) (g), turning the Constitution on its head.

I am confident that the agenda for effective operationalization of secularism as proposed in this book will go a long way towards making secularism a reality in India. But it must be stated that even the existing provisions of the Constitution and laws are not being implemented for want of political will. This is particularly disturbing in view of the exponential rise in Hindutva ideology and its increasing radicalism. All political parties and MPs/MLAs take an oath to 'bear true faith and allegiance to the Constitution of India as by law established' (Third Schedule). That means, among other things, adherence to secularism and the fundamental duties set out in Article 51A, which, *inter alia*, include: i) promoting harmony and the spirit of common brotherhood among all the people of India, transcending religious, linguistic and regional or sectional diversities; and ii) valuing and preserving the rich heritage of our composite culture. Action could be taken against political parties and Members of Parliament/Members of Legislative Assembly (MPs/MLAs) who have failed to abide by these obligations. The concerned political party could be derecognized. Even an issue of show-cause notices to this effect would be salutary. Attention has been invited in Chapter 6 to the neglect of sections 153A and 153B of the Indian Penal Code over the years. I am sure the establishment of a constitutional commission on secularism, as proposed in this book, would strengthen the hands of the concerned institutions to take effective action in the matter.

Reference must also be made to the larger context in which the issues pertaining to secularism need to be appreciated. The Pew Research Center, in its publication, *Religion and Public Life* (2 April 2015) has reported, *inter alia*, under the caption, 'The Future of World Religions: Population Growth Projections 2010–2050', that by 2050:

- The number of Muslims will nearly equal the number of Christians around the world;
- In Europe, Muslims will make up 10 per cent of the overall population; and
- India will retain a Hindu majority but also will have the largest Muslim population of any country in the world, surpassing Indonesia.

It is also estimated that the Hindu religion will be the third largest religion in the world. (*Sakal* 4 May 2016:11)

We also need to refer to the importance of 'soft power' in today's world. I believe that India has the potential for creating its own soft power by making a success of its secularism and creating a homogeneous society, comprising different religions, races, cultures and languages, of communal harmony which is at peace with itself and the world. In a strife-torn and troubled world, this can be its singular contribution.

In his book, *The Paradox of American Power*, Joseph S. Nye, while talking about the soft power of the United States, wrote that three types of countries are likely to gain soft power and succeed:

> Those whose dominant cultures and ideals are closer to prevailing global norms which now emphasize liberalism, pluralism, autonomy; those with the most accessed multiple channels of communication and thus [who exert] more influence over how issues are framed, and those whose credibility is enhanced by their domestic and international performance.

I believe that India has an excellent chance of establishing soft power of the first kind but even that would be difficult unless it pursued the policies of liberalism and pluralism for which it has been known all these years. The image of India as an intolerant society with fascist tendencies will negate a chance of India's being even a regional power, leave alone a superpower, in the years to come.

1

INDIA'S SECULARISM—DEFINING THE INDEFINABLE

It is said that we are a secular state. In fact, we suffer very often from a new disease which may be called 'secularitis'.

—Dr Shyama Prasad Mukherjee in Parliament on 17 September 1951

In this chapter, I propose to focus attention on:

- The composition of the Constituent Assembly;
- Anointing the Constitution as secular;
- Problems of defining secularism; and
- How the apex court has looked at secularism.

The Composition of the Constituent Assembly

It is essential to study the composition of the Constituent Assembly (CA) to understand the Constitution as it finally emerged from the deliberations of the Constituent Assembly. The Cabinet Mission, in its statement of 16 May 1946, had set out in detail the procedure regarding elections to the Constituent Assembly. The statement rejected the idea of elections based on adult franchise on the grounds that it would lead to a wholly unacceptable delay in the formulation of a new Constitution. The only practicable alternative, according to the statement, was to utilize the recently elected Provincial Legislative Assemblies as the election bodies.

The Congress party had a strength of 175 seats and its nominees—other than Congressmen—were thirty of whom one belonged to the Hindu Mahasabha. The Muslim League had a strength of seventy-three, while the Sikhs were four. The representatives of the princely states were to be ninety-three among others, making a total of 385.

> Significantly, important personalities, elected to the Constituent Assembly, comprised, among others: Frank Anthony, president in chief of the Anglo-Indian Association; Shyama Prasad Mukherjee,[1] president of the All India Hindu Mahasabha; Jagjivan Ram, president of the All India Depressed Classes League; and Hansa Mehta, president of the All India Women's Conference, who were nominated by the Congress party. The Constituent Assembly had 8 premiers of provinces, 10 ministers of provinces, 6 ex-premiers of provinces, 17 ex-ministers or ex-members of governors' executive councils, 4 ex-members of the Governor General's executive councils and so on. There were 15 women elected to the Constituent Assembly. (Rao, 1966: 287, 292, 295–97)

Several members of the Constituent Assembly criticized the Constitution during its drafting, on various scores. It is particularly disturbing that Arun Shourie, in his book, *Worshipping False Gods: Ambedkar, and the facts which have been erased* (1997), has belittled the role of Dr Ambedkar, who was chairman of the Drafting Committee. Ambedkar himself was self-effacing and had modestly stated that perhaps there were more deserving people in the Drafting Committee who could have been given this responsibility. But, having spent some time in going through the Constituent Assembly Debates in recent years, I have been impressed by Ambedkar's contribution to this gigantic task. T.T. Krishnamachari, who was a member of the Drafting Committee and later a minister in the Nehru cabinet, has candidly talked about it. In his speech in the Constituent Assembly on 5 November 1948, he stated:

---

[1]In the Constituent Assembly of India related papers and in the book published by Parliament on Mukherjee, the name is spelt as 'Syama' but keeping in view the spelling which is currently used, it is spelt as 'Shyama' in this book.

I am aware of the amount of work and enthusiasm that he has brought to bear on the work of drafting this Constitution. At the same time, I do realize that the amount of attention that was necessary for the purpose of drafting a Constitution so important to us at this moment has not been given to it by the Drafting Committee. The House is perhaps aware that of the seven members nominated by you [President of CA], one resigned from the House and was replaced. One died and was not replaced. One was away in America and his place was not filled up and another person was engaged in state affairs, and there was a void to that extent. One or two people were far away from Delhi and perhaps reasons of health did not permit them to attend. So it happened ultimately that the burden of drafting this Constitution fell on Dr Ambedkar and I have no doubt that we are grateful to him for having achieved this task in a manner which is undoubtedly commendable. (*CAD* Vol. XII, Book 2, 2009: 231)

Apart from this elucidation from one who saw the working of the Drafting Committee at close quarters, Ambedkar's interventions in all debates bring out his deep understanding of issues and careful analysis in support of the decisions taken. Scores of Constituent Assembly members, cutting across various shades of opinions, provinces and regions, time and again during the debates, whole-heartedly and unreservedly expressed their appreciation of Dr Ambedkar's contribution. I take this opportunity to set the record straight from a researcher's point of view in so far as it is concerned. It is not often that one comes across a statesman who is in command of a subject and has such a scholastic bent of mind. The making of the Constitution was inevitably a collective effort—as it would be in any country—and Ambedkar never claimed that he alone was its author.

With an overwhelming majority in the Constituent Assembly, the Congress members of the Assembly in general, and the Congress leaders in particular, discussed and settled all matters before the formal meetings of the Assembly. Therefore, Ambedkar was being truthful when he told the House that he had carried out the decisions of others. During the final sessions, several members spoke to the same effect. Saying that the Constitution was a compromise and 'has all the defects of a compromise', and that it would have been much better if the Draft Constitution had been considered by the committees. Shibban Lal Saksena told the Assembly:

> Under the procedure adopted, the Drafting Committee could not get the advantage of the free opinion of the whole House and the decisions of the Congress party alone became binding upon it. I personally feel that the Constitution has very much suffered on this account. Out of about 10,000 amendments which appeared on the Order Paper from time to time during the course of the last one year, I think this House had opportunity for discussing hardly a few hundreds. The rest were all guillotined inside the Congress party and were not moved in this House because the party did not accept them. *Congress party meetings became the meetings of the real Constituent Assembly, and this real Assembly became the mock Assembly where decisions arrived at the Congress party meetings were registered.* (CAD Vol. XI, 1949: 705)

On 21 November 1949, during his speech on the third draft of the Constitution, Syed Muhammad Sa'adulla, who was a member of the Drafting Committee, also graphically described its functioning. He stated:

> The Drafting Committee was not a free agency... We were only asked to dress the baby and the baby was nothing but the Objectives Resolution...[The Committee] had to take the environment and the circumstances prevailing in the country into consideration... Many sections of our Draft Constitution had to be recast as many as seven times. A draft section is prepared according to the best in each of the members of the Drafting Committee. It is scrutinized by the particular ministerial department of government. They criticize it and a fresh draft is made to meet their criticism or requirements. Then it is considered by the biggest bloc, the majority party in the House—*I refer to the Congress Parliamentary Party, who alone can give the imprimatur of adoption in the House*; and sometimes we found that they made their own recommendations which had to be put into the proper legal and constitutional shape by the

members of the Drafting Committee. (*CAD* Vols X–XII, Book 5, 2009: 733)

This was effectively corroborated by K. Santhanam when he said:

> Finally, the work of the Drafting Committee is, to my mind, beyond all praise…I should also mention that it was not only on the open floor of the House that the Constitution has been scrutinized, but much more severely during the Congress party meetings. I do not want to mention names, but a group of people in the Party took the greatest pains to scrutinize every clause and every article and a great deal of improvement was made during those meetings. But for their scrutiny, the Constitution would not have been as good as it is. (*CAD* Vol. XI, 1949: 720)

Ajit Prasad Jain, while speaking on the final draft of the Constitution on 22 November 1949, corroborated this functioning by saying:

> I am also very grateful to our Congress President—for some time our Mr Kripalani and later on our Honourable Pattabhi Sitaramayya. *As a Congress party man behind the scenes he had to conduct so many meetings and he conducted them so well that the Congress people could come together and produce a Constitution for the acceptance of the whole of this House in such a beautiful manner.* (*CAD* Vols X–XII, Book 5, 2009: 829)

Sardar Hukam Singh regretted that, though the Sikhs had readily agreed to doing away with separate electorates and the reservation on population basis in the legislatures, their reasonable demands for economic safeguards about services were overlooked. He said:

> On scrutiny it appears to be a very trivial thing. But it was a test case where the majority was on trial. It was said that it was a blot to acknowledge any religious minority; but the Anglo-Indians have been given safeguards in the Constitution. They are a religious as well as a racial minority according to the government's own publication. The entry about consideration of claims of Sikh community to services

would have disfigured the Constitution, we were told here; but a similar entry about the scheduled castes and scheduled tribes and the Anglo-Indians does not impair its beauty. The whole economy of the Sikh community depended upon agriculture and the army service. Lands have been left in Pakistan and their proportion in the army since the Partition has been greatly reduced and is being reduced every day. (*CAD* Vols X–XII, Book 5,2009: 752)

Ambedkar himself was much more forthright when he admitted:

The task of the Drafting Committee would have been a very difficult one if this Constituent Assembly had been merely a motley crowd, a tessellated pavement without cement, a black stone here and a white stone there, in which each member or each group was a law unto itself. There would have been nothing but chaos. This possibility of chaos was reduced to nil by the existence of the Congress party inside the Assembly which brought into its proceedings a sense of order and discipline. *It is because of the discipline of the Congress party that the Drafting Committee was able to pilot the Constitution in the Assembly with the sure knowledge as to the fate of each article and each amendment. The Congress party is, therefore, entitled to all the credit for the smooth sailing of the Draft Constitution in the Assembly.* (*CAD* Vol. XI, 1949: 974)

In view of the above position, I made serious attempts to access all published material pertaining to Congress party deliberations while framing the Constitution. I felt that these were as important as, if not more important than, the Constituent Assembly Debates, and would throw light on contentious issues, such as defining secularism, protection of minorities, right to propagation of religion or the ban on cow slaughter. But, unfortunately, my efforts did not succeed.

Reference must be made to the observations made by Ambedkar on 25 November 1949 when replying to the third reading of the Constitution. Ambedkar said that the condemnation of the Constitution came largely from two quarters—the Communist party and the Socialist party. He clarified that their condemnation was not because it was a bad Constitution. He said:

The Communist party wants a Constitution based upon the principle of the Dictatorship of the Proletariat. They condemn the Constitution because it is based upon parliamentary democracy. The Socialists want two things. The first thing they want is that if they come in power, the Constitution must give them the freedom to nationalize or socialize all private property without payment of compensation. The second thing that the Socialists want is that the fundamental rights mentioned in the Constitution must be absolute and without any limitations so that if their party fails to come into power, they would have the unfettered freedom not only to criticize, but also to overthrow the state. (*CAD* Vols X–XII, Book 5, 2009: 975)

It is important to note that, as far as the subject matter of this book, is concerned, neither of these parties had any reservations about declaring India a secular state. But, as far as their economic ideology is concerned, the less said the better. India is really fortunate that even Jawaharlal Nehru with his socialist leanings did not fall prey to their ideology which would have brought ruination to the country. India has suffered enough due to Nehruvian socialism.

Anointing the Constitution as Secular

The Draft Preamble came up for consideration in the Constituent Assembly on 17 October 1949. The objective of keeping the Draft Preamble for discussion to the last was to see that it was in conformity with the Constitution as accepted by the Assembly. The president of the Constituent Assembly, Dr Rajendra Prasad, said that, in some of the several amendments which had been received, the name of God was brought in in some form or another. In others, the name of Mahatma Gandhi was brought in. Dr Prasad suggested that neither God nor Mahatma Gandhi need be discussed in the House.

The amendment proposed by H.V. Kamath, for prefixing to the Preamble the words, 'In the name of God', evoked animated discussion and provided one of those rare occasions when the Assembly actually divided by a show of hands. The Ayes lost (41 to 68) eventually, after some of the opponents of the amendment had forcefully pleaded that the invocation of the name of God was inconsistent with the freedom of faith which was not only promised in the Preamble itself but was also guaranteed as a fundamental right. Shibban Lal Saksena and Pandit Govind Malaviya also moved similar amendments later in the day and strongly urged that there was nothing un-secular about them. (Rao 1968b: 130–31)

P.K. Sen, speaking on the final draft of the Constitution on 22 November 1949, said:

> It has often been referred to here as a blot on the Constitution namely, that all contact with God or religion has been as it were abandoned by it, as if it is a godless Constitution, as if by calling it a Secular Democratic Republic it has actually become secular or godless. I beg to submit that this is a misconception. We have not banished religion...It has banished religions, that is to say the conflict between one religion and another...if that comes to pass, when the nation realizes that, the word 'secular' may in due course even be removed from the Constitution. For then, it will be no longer necessary in the exigencies of the case in order to imply, in order to proclaim that there shall be no preference given to any religion, any faith, any belief, any form of worship, it has been found necessary to call it secular. (*CAD* Vols X–XII, Book 5, 2009: 831)

It is necessary to note that, particularly after the Lok Sabha elections of 2014—which brought the BJP to power at the Centre—efforts are already being made to question India's secularism. But, this is not due to the rightist Hindutva parties having realized the supreme wisdom of the ultimate unity of all religions. The alternative of Hindu Rashtra is being propagated to correct what is called a monumental historical wrong.

As seen earlier, there was considerable discussion in the Constituent Assembly on the use of the term 'secularism' in the Constitution. However, in spite of persistent efforts made by some members, this proposal was not agreed to, though several provisions of the Constitution made it abundantly clear that it was meant to be secular. It was only in 1976, when the Emergency was in force, most of the Opposition leaders were in jail, and Parliament was on its extended term that, without much discussion, the Constitution was amended to make an explicit mention in its Preamble that India is a secular nation.

Para 15 of the Congress party's election manifesto for the 1971 elections made a specific mention of the intention of the party to amend the Constitution suitably. The manifesto stated:

> The nation's progress cannot be halted. The spirit of democracy demands that the Constitution should enable the fulfilment of the needs and urges of the people. Our Constitution has earlier been amended in the interest of economic development. It will be our endeavour to seek such further constitutional remedies and amendments as are necessary to overcome the impediments in the path of social justice.
>
> The Congress party was returned to power with overwhelming majority—more than two-third. It was therefore claimed that it had full mandate of the people to make necessary changes in the Constitution. (Diwan 1978: 15, Footnote 24)

The Swaran Singh Committee, appointed by the Congress president to suggest amendments to the Constitution of India, submitted its report in 1976. One of its recommendations was that, 'The concepts of secularism and socialism should be clearly spelt out in the Constitution. It is accordingly recommended that the Preamble should be amended…' (*Swaran Singh Committee Report* 1976: 64). It was a bland recommendation without giving any justification.

Accordingly, the bill—the Forty-fourth Amendment to the Constitution—was introduced in the Lok Sabha on 25 October 1976. This was the longest amendment bill ever introduced. It comprised fifty-nine clauses and effectively sought to rewrite the Constitution. The bill contained so many highly controversial features that the amendment to the Preamble to the Constitution to incorporate the word 'secular' therein did not invite much attention. There was another reason for it. The Preamble was also to be amended to include the word 'socialist' to which the Congress party professed to have been committed. During the discussion, several members spoke to welcome the inclusion of the word 'socialist'.

Thus, the inclusion of the word 'secular'—which had not been agreed to by the Constituent Assembly while drafting the Constitution— found an easy passage in 1976. This was also due to the fact that most of the Opposition members were languishing in jail. As Kashyap pointed out:

> The police arrested 676 leading opponents of Smt. Indira Gandhi, including Morarji Desai, Raj Narain, Chandra Shekhar, Ram Dhan, Charan Singh, Jyoti Basu, A.B. Vajpayee, L.K. Advani and Nanaji Deshmukh, Samar Guha, Asoka Mehta, Piloo Mody and K.R. Malkani...President Ahmed issued an order on 27 June 1975 forbidding the detainees from invoking their constitutional rights to equal protection of the law, protection of life and personal liberty and protection against unwarranted arrest and detention, to obtain their release. An ordinance promulgated on 29 June amended the 1971 Maintenance of Internal Security Act to remove the requirement that a detainee must be informed of the reason for his detention within a specified period... Six Congress Members of Parliament, who had not attended the meetings of the parliamentary party which confirmed their faith in Mrs Indira Gandhi's leadership, were expelled from the party on 8 August...Press censorship was introduced on 26 June 1975 for the first time since India became independent[2]...Even the publication of parliamentary proceedings by newspapers was subjected to prior censorship...When Parliament met, government attitude came in for strong criticism...Erasmo de Sequeira said, 'If you pass this motion, then, just as democracy has become a mockery outside this House, Parliament itself will become a mockery within it'...The government proposed the suspension of normal rules of procedure...The government introduced on 4 August the Election Laws (Amendment) Bill, which was clearly intended to validate Mrs Indira Gandhi's election...The only opposition to the bill came from Mohan Dharia, who commented that the government was obviously 'steamrolling' the Amendment through, to solve Mrs Gandhi's legal

---

[2] Even judgments of high courts and the Supreme Court had to be submitted to the censor for approval before their publication.

problems. The bill passed through the Rajya Sabha on 6 August in an hour without anyone speaking against it, and received the president's assent the same day...During the period of the Fifth Lok Sabha as many as nineteen Constitution Amendment Bills were passed. This was by far the largest number of such bills passed by any Lok Sabha. These included some of the most important, comprehensive and controversial bills in the constitutional history of India. (Kashyap 1997: 34–38, 61–63)

The main criticism of the Forty-fourth Constitution (Amendment) Bill in both the Houses was that the inclusion of the word 'secular' in the Preamble to the Constitution would by itself hardly serve any purpose. (Kashyap 1997: 91)

Among the persons who were critical of this highly controversial Constitution amendment was Professor S.V. Kogekar, former principal of Fergusson College, Poona. In the R.R. Kale Memorial Lecture delivered in 1976, Kogekar stated that the proposed amendment to the Preamble:

...clearly shows that whatever may be the criticism voiced by some leaders in respect of the idea of 'the basic structure of the Constitution' the Congress party is keen on emphasizing that secularism is one of its basic elements. The provisions made in relation to religious freedom of all citizens and the absence of a state religion in the Constitution, as also the policies pursued by government so far and the decisions given by the courts on this question, clearly establish the secular character of the state. The inclusion of this word in the Preamble is therefore only a recognition of a fact. (Kogekar 1976: 13)

Granville Austin, in his book, *Working a Democratic Constitution—A History of the Indian Experience*, brought out that:

During the weeks the Swaran Singh Committee was at work, prominent citizens analysed its proposals and opposed many of them, critiques that the Emergency's censors allowed the press to publish. One group of prominent citizens, The National Committee for Review of the Constitution, established itself in mid-March in

Bombay and published its comprehensive critique late in May. Its committee's basic position was that any amendments by the current Parliament would be a 'Constitutional impropriety' because the Lok Sabah's [sic] regular five-year term had expired, and it had voted its own extension. Also, due to government restrictions on assembly and expression, 'there is no proper atmosphere...for the necessary and purposeful national debate.' (Austin 1999: 366)

H.R. Gokhale, the cabinet minister for Law and Justice, who was piloting the bill, was highly critical of the concept of the 'basic features' of the Constitution which had been devised by the Supreme Court. He said: 'First of all I do not agree, with much respect to the Supreme Court, that there is something like the basic features which could not be amended... *What is not defined cannot exist and it is incapable of being defined.*' (Kashyap 1997: 91).

If Gokhale's contention were to be accepted, the concept of secularism itself would come into serious difficulty. For, like the concept of basic features, all attempts to define the word 'secularism' have failed. According to Gokhale's contention, what is not defined cannot exist. It may be considered flippant but since, in the Indian context, secularism has not been defined, it cannot exist.

There was also a fear psychosis, in that people were worried about opposing any moves made by the government. With this background, much need not be made of the Indian Constitution having been pronounced as secular by the Indira Gandhi government.

Moving the bill, H.R. Gokhale said:

The objectives which we had always in view, namely, socialism and secularism, which we have tried to implement, will be more and more implemented [sic] and will be more accurately and correctly reflected in a basic part of our Constitution, namely, the Preamble. Let anyone say that 'socialism' or 'secularism' is incapable of definition. Well, if that argument were to be accepted, even 'democracy' in that sense is incapable of definition because, is it not understood in different ways in different countries? But we understand what kind of democracy we stand for. In the same way, what 'socialism' stands for and what 'secularism' stands for.

Therefore, these criticisms are really intended to divert the attention from the main focus. The main objective of the amendment of the Preamble to my mind, is a very important and fundamental feature of the present amendment bill to [sic] the Constitution.

Reference may be made to the comments made by a few members regarding the inclusion of the word 'secular' in the Preamble. Indrajit Gupta said:

> When the government itself has come forward to add the word 'secular', particularly here, I take it to mean something; I take it to mean that the secular aspect of our democracy requires to be strengthened; otherwise it is superfluous to introduce this word here...I take it that what we want to assure people of all faiths and communities and religions, particularly the minorities, is that on our part we mean to take some further action, legislative and others, to strengthen and secularize the content of our democracy. I do not know whether this is how the government has understood it; I should like the minister later on to explain the object; otherwise, we have already a secular state and we are not a theocratic or religious state like some neighbours of ours. I think this is the positive meaning; otherwise it is meaningless. So, it should be spelt out and explained in a way which will give some fresh assurance and confidence to the people of various communities and religions, especially minorities.

Needless to say, no such action was taken by the government.

Dinesh Chandra Goswami said:

> I find from the debates of the Constituent Assembly that in fact an amendment was moved by Shri K.T. Shah that in the Preamble the words 'secular and socialist' should be incorporated. One of the supporters was Shri H.V. Kamat....At that time, it was not possible on the part of the leadership to open up a new front in the country between the reactionaries and the progressive forces.

P.R. Shenoy said:

> Certain events in the country have made it necessary to lay emphasis on certain concepts like nationalism and secularism. No one requires any lessons on nationalism or secularism, but we see that events are taking place in the country which have necessitated that we should put emphasis on the words nationalism and secularism in our Constitution.

Jagannath Rao was effusive when he said: 'The Preamble is a golden epigram so nicely worded that the addition of these two words [socialist and secular] will make it all the more attractive. So, there should be no objection to the amendment to the Preamble....'

Perhaps the most important intervention was that of Swaran Singh. It may be recalled that the Congress president had appointed a committee under his chairmanship to suggest suitable amendments to the Constitution. The amendment to the Preamble to include the words 'secular' and 'socialist' was based on his report.[3] The committee was of the opinion that the concepts of secularism and socialism should be clearly spelt out in the Constitution. Swaran Singh said:

> I think both these words appear to be just two words but the meaning behind them is very vital for our country to grow from strength to strength...So far as secularism is concerned, I would at the very outset clarify that our secularism is not synonymous with the dictionary meaning of this word 'secular'...'Secular' now is a word which I think has become part of our Indian languages. You may go to the Punjab, to Gujarat, even to the south; when they make speeches in their languages they always use the word 'secular' because it has assumed a definite meaning and that meaning is that there will be equality before the eye of the law in our Constitution with regard

---

[3] C.M. Stephen, who had worked on this committee, stated in the Lok Sabha that, in the course of its deliberations, the committee had received 4000 memoranda from different sections of the people. It had travelled far and wide in the country and had held conferences with interested persons. It also had the benefit of the opinions of judges—sitting and retired. Following this, the Swaran Singh Committee submitted its report on 19 May 1976. (*LSD* Vol. 65, 26 October 1976: 62)

to people professing different religions. Not only that but more than that there is no element of any anti-religious feeling but it is really respect for all religions. It is this concept which is broadly accepted by our country as a whole and, therefore, we thought it necessary that it should find a place of pride in our preamble and we are adding that by this amendment...Certain consequential provisions had to be made to ensure that the concept of secularism is not eroded. It will be found that in the clause where the concept of duty is spelt out there are elements of both these concepts of secularism and of integrity in the list of duties, apart from other things. Then again in the new clause that is proposed to be added where anti-national activities are defined both these concepts have been mentioned and the intention is to see that the concept of secularism is strengthened and the country remains united.

K. Manoharan of the Dravida Munnetra Kazhagam (DMK) welcomed the proposed amendment. He said that, after the country gained Independence, the people knew that they were in for a secular state and not a theocratic state. Era Sezhiyan of the DMK was also highly critical of the Emergency and pointed out that there were several restrictions on the freedom of expression and free speech all over the country and, therefore, the real views of the people on this amendment were not really known. He hoped that the central government 'will create an early opportunity for such a full consideration and free debate of the various proposals to amend the Constitution'. He also questioned the mandate given by the people to amend the Constitution, as had been claimed by the government.

Jambuvant Dhote said that the Hindi translation of the word 'secular' which has been done as *dharmanirapeksha* was not correct. Nor was its translation into *nidharmee*. It should, in fact, be a country which respected all religions.

Frank Anthony said that he had certain misgivings about the rights of minorities, and unfortunately, some of them had not been allayed.

Intervening in the debate, Prime Minister Indira Gandhi said:

The founding fathers of our Constitution and of our country [sic] had intended Indian society to be secular and socialist. These are not new definitions. They have guided our laws all these years. All we are doing now is to incorporate them in the Constitution itself for they rightly deserve to be mentioned there. The specific mention of this fact in the Preamble will provide the frame of reference to all, to our people, to the government, to the judiciary and the world.

From this very discursive discussion, it can be seen that the real issues pertaining to the amendment to the Preamble to include the word 'secular' were not really addressed, except by Indrajit Gupta. As he rightly said, he hoped that this amendment was meant to strengthen the concept of secularism and 'we want is to assure the people of all faiths and communities and religions particularly the minorities [*sic*] that on our part we mean to take some further action, legislative and others, to strengthen and secularize the content of our democracy.' (*Lok Sabha Debates* [henceforth *LSD*] Vol. 65, 25 October 1976: 58–59, 78–79, 106–08, 122, 147, 155; 26 October: 15–17, 22–23, 47; 27 October: 145–46; 28 October: 70–71)

H.M. Seervai, a respected Supreme Court senior advocate and jurist, invited attention to this retrospective amendment to the Preamble and said it was 'historically false and would involve a patent contradiction'. He cited Sir Maurice Linford Gwyer, chief justice, who observed in *Bhola Prasad* (1942) F.C.R. 17:

> But we doubt very much whether a Preamble retrospectively inserted in 1940 in an Act passed twenty-five years before can be looked at by the court for the purpose of discovering what the true intention of the Legislature was at the earlier date. A Legislature can always enact that the law is and shall be deemed always to have been, such and such; but that is a wholly different thing from imputing to dead and gone legislators a particular intention merely because their successors at the present day think that they might or ought to have had it.

Seervai also emphasized that the word 'secular' was not precise and would itself require to be defined. 'Secular' may be opposed to 'religious' in the sense that a secular state can be an anti-religion state. *In this sense, the Constitution of India is not secular,* because the right to freedom of religion is a guaranteed fundamental right. The word 'secular' may mean that, as far as the State is concerned, it does not support any religion out of public funds, nor does it penalize the professing and practice of any religion or the right to manage religious institutions as provided in Articles 25 and 26. Seervai therefore stressed that good drafting required that ambiguous words not be put into a Preamble without reason and, as far as one could see, there was no reason for putting in the word 'secular'. He also pointed out that the 45th Amendment Bill (which became the 44th Amendment) had proposed an Amendment of Article 366 by inserting the definition of the word 'secular', to the effect, *that the word should mean a republic in which there was equal respect for all religions*. However, this Amendment was not accepted by the Council of States. Consequently, the word remained undefined. (Seervai 2011a: 276–77)

Justice R.A. Jahagirdar, in his article, 'Secularism in India—The Inconclusive Debate', has rightly emphasised that 'the concept of *Sarva Dharma Samabhava* has been rejected by the Parliament in its constituent capacity.' (*The Radical Humanist*, February 2016: 30)

Nani Palkhivala, one of the most outstanding senior advocates of the Supreme Court, was also highly critical of this amendment. He stated:

'The words "secular" and "integrity" can add nothing to the content of the Preamble. Anyone who had a sense of rhythm and style would know that the beauty of the Preamble, which is distinguished by economy of words, would be marred by the insertion of the three words [including the word "socialist"], all of which were unnecessary and one of which was misleadingly equivocal.' And, typical of Nani, he added that one may as well try to improve upon Shakespeare by changing 'the rest is silence' into 'the rest is complete, weird and baffling silence!' (Kamath 2007: 305)

Rajeev Dhavan invited attention to Frank Anthony's speech on the amendment, asking for further amendments to protect the minorities. Otherwise, Frank Anthony said, 'You destroy our schools, you destroy our religious rights and all our cultural freedoms'. Ibrahim Sulaiman Sait picked the cue from here. He was suspicious about the new secularism:

With the addition in the Preamble, the whole nation stands committed to the principle of secularism. Therefore, while declaring our country to be a secular and socialist state, care should be taken to see that this character of secularism completely emerges from the provisions of the Constitution and that the rights of the minorities are not only strengthened but also attempts are made very frankly, honestly and sincerely to see that the rights of the minorities are fully implemented... Our prime minister has said...'The Indian version of secularism was based on respect to all religions and not opposition to any religions.' (Dhavan 1978: 94)

Krishan Kant, one of the 'Young Turks', was highly critical of the democratic implications of the amendment. He said: 'The present Parliament, which has outlived its period of legitimacy and is hanging on the thin poisonous thread of the Emergency provisions of the Constitution, has no right to adopt practically a new Constitution'. (Dhavan 1978: 102)

Rajeev Dhavan put a somewhat novel interpretation on the political motive behind the amendment to the Preamble which I find difficult to accept. In any case, there was no evidence of it. He wrote:

These 'secular' plans had a very deeply disturbing political aspect. Many of India's millions of Muslims saw this secular programme as a planned attempt to make inroads into the Muslim social structure and persuade the Muslims to give up many of their customs. The focal point of the controversy was the demand for a uniform civil code—an object enshrined as one of the Directive Principles of State Policy—which would virtually abolish the personal law of the Muslims.

Dhavan added: 'All in all, there was a whispering suspicion that the new secularism might not continue to propagate a Gandhian tolerance to other religions. It was seen as inaugurating a new kind of ideological transplant of an allegedly scientific humanism.' (Dhavan 1978: 67, 95)

Unfortunately, in spite of all the unbridled powers which the government enjoyed during the Emergency—and which it often used to commit atrocities against the people—it did not take any action to strengthen secularism in the country. Looking at the manner in which the Forty-fourth Amendment to the Constitution was passed, the Indira Gandhi government—with its two-third majority in Parliament—could easily have amended the Constitution and enacted laws to ban communal political parties and to separate religion from politics. However, in the absence of any such action, the amendment to the Preamble was merely window dressing which did not serve any purpose.

The election manifesto of the Janata Party categorically stated:

> The authoritarian trends that had unfolded themselves over the past few years were embodied in the Forty-second Amendment which was bulldozed through Parliament. To call it an amendment is a misnomer. It is a betrayal of testament of faith that the founding fathers bequeathed to the people and it subverts the basic structure of the 1950 Constitution. (Diwan 1978: 15, Footnote 25).

When the Janata government came into power with a massive majority of 297 seats and 43 per cent of valid votes polled in 1977 (Kashyap 1997: 320), initially, there was a proposal to rescind the whole of the Forty-fourth Amendment. However, under pressure from the Congress party, this proposal was later given up, and selective amendments to the Constitution were initiated to delete the more controversial provisions of the Forty-fourth Amendment. Since this would have required a majority of two-thirds of the members present and voting in both Houses of Parliament, and since the Janata government did not have such a majority in the Upper House, a consensus had to be built up between the political parties, including the Congress. There was no controversy in regard to the term 'secular'. However, an effort was made to define the term 'secular' to mean 'equal respect to all religions'. Even this met with opposition from the Congress party in the Rajya Sabha and was, therefore, given up.

The Objects and Reasons of the Forty-fourth Amendment Bill, 1978, provided that:

> Certain changes in the Constitution which would have the effect of impairing *its secular or democratic character,* abridging or taking away fundamental rights prejudicing or impeding free and fair elections on the basis of adult suffrage and compromising the independence of the judiciary, can be made only if they are approved

by the people of India by a majority of votes at a referendum in which at least 51 per cent of the electorate participates. Article 368 is being amended to ensure this. (Kashyap 2004: 138)

Speaking in the Rajya Sabha on the Constitution (Forty-fifth Amendment) Bill, 1978, on 28 August 1978, Shanti Bhushan, Minister for Law and Justice, said:

> Another important provision in the bill is in regard to the amendment to the Constitution...Whenever there is a new innovation, howsoever valuable, there are bound to be some anxieties, some apprehensions, some doubts and so on...This is a very important safeguard which is sought to be introduced... There have been periods and this country has seen an enactment like the Constitution (Thirty-ninth Amendment) Bill being enacted in which certain functionaries were sought to be put completely above the law. This House has also seen the Constitution (Fortieth Amendment) Bill being passed because that part of the Thirty-ninth Amendment Bill was struck down by the Supreme Court and that bill was not proceeded with thereafter in the other House. But the bill had been passed by a House. That bill provided that important functionaries like the Prime Minister, the Speaker, the President, the Vice President and the Governors would be above the law whatever crimes they might commit...They would have a life-long immunity. If a person becomes Governor for a day, then he can get away with all the crimes that he might have committed during his past life. In other words, it means that those high functionaries must have a licence, a Constitutional right to commit those offences... they [Constitution-makers] could not envisage and I do not blame them that they could not envisage that there may come a time when two-third majority in the two Houses, in certain situations, in a certain atmosphere, in a certain period of time, might enact such a provision by making an amendment to the Constitution which might not really be in the interest of the people. And, therefore, the question was: Should there be a safeguard in the Constitution so that all these things which are sacred in the Constitution like democracy, adult franchise, like free and fair elections, like basic

freedoms, etc., before these things are destroyed, whether the people should have a voice?

Shanti Bhushan further said that a referendum could not be contemplated as an everyday measure. (*Rajya Sabha Debates* [henceforth *RSD*] Vol. 106.3, 28 August 1978, 62–64)

However, later, the Congress party went back on the earlier understanding and the proposal for effecting amendments by recourse to a referendum was given up. In retrospect, this turned out to be the fortuitous decision at least so far as the amendment to the Preamble was concerned. For, if a referendum were to be held on whether the word 'secular' should continue in the Preamble, I am not sure that in the prevailing situation in the country, the popular vote would be in its favour.

No one really knows what is meant by India's secularism. It is often described as equal respect for all religions (*sarva dharma samabhav*). However, according to Shreekant Sambrani, this definition is clearly flawed. In fact, K. Subrahmaniam (*Times of India* [henceforth *TOI*] 26 March 2002) and Swapan Dasgupta (*India Today* 8 April 2002) consider it to be a political expedient for creating vote banks. (*Economic & Political Weekly* [henceforth *EPW*] 6 April 2002: 1310)

Syed Shahabuddin, speaking on the Constitution Amendment Bill moved by Dr Laxminarayan Pandeya, stated:

> We have passed laws in this Parliament pertaining to a specific religious group. I am not against social reform. We passed the Hindu Code Bill. We have the Parsee Marriage Act. We have a Muslim Divorce Act. In my view all these, *if you take a very strict view of secularism, will not fall within the jurisdiction of a secular state. In our country the Parliament agrees to function as the 'Dharma Sansad'*. The Parliament agrees to function as the established Church because there is no other alternative available, or perhaps the followers of a particular religion recognize the authority of the State and come to the State for the purpose of promoting social reform; to get a legislative sanction and a seal of legitimacy on the reforms that they wished to introduce in the society... Secularism in my view in a multi-religious society can be defined in many ways.

He said that one definition, which was under discussion in the

Constitution (Eightieth Amendment) Bill, was that the State shall show equal respect to all religions. But this is not enough. He said that cognizance must be taken of the socio-political fact that there are bound to be situations of inter-religious conflicts. That was the real test of secularism. How would the State behave in an inter-religious situation, not only with regard to a particular religion but when the interests of two religious groups conflict or when there is a situation of disharmony? *Shahabuddin defined secularism as the equi-distance of the State towards all religions, as neutrality or non-alignment towards all religions. The State does not identify itself with any religion...*'In our country, not only every minister but even every prime minister goes about exhibiting his religious zeal, his multi-religious faith. He thinks that a visit to Ajmer Sharif will cancel a visit to Benares,' added Shahabuddin. (*LSD* Vol. 24, 1993: 320–22)

Problems of Defining Secularism

The Constitution gives somewhat mixed signals in regard to secularism. For example, Article 25 (2) (b) Explanation 1 reads: The wearing and carrying of *kirpan*s shall be deemed to be included in the profession of the Sikh religion.

It is noteworthy that the founding fathers of the Constitution had a liberal stance on secularism and did not consider any religious symbol as anti-secularism, as is being considered in respect of the wearing of burkha, hijab or headscarf by women, wearing a turban by a Sikh, or keeping a beard by a Muslim or a Sikh, in a number of countries in Europe and Canada.

But Article 48, pertaining to the ban on cow slaughter, though it is couched in scientific and modern terminology of 'organization of agriculture and animal husbandry on modern and scientific lines', and Article 290 A regarding the annual payment to certain Devaswom Funds out of the Consolidated Fund of the state of Kerala and the state of Madras, clearly militate against secularism. I have discussed some other major issues in this regard later in this book.

M.N. Roy, who was a great secularist, took pride in saying that the essence of secularism was not to give every citizen the option to choose which religion he wanted to follow, but the option to escape the bondage of religion altogether. He thought—as many Marxists continue to think—that religion was a drug, and human society could progress only when the human mind was released from its addiction to it. Indian secularism does not subscribe to this view... Indian secularism recognizes the fact that religion cannot always, or need not necessarily, be banished from human life. (Gajendragadkar in Sharma, 1966: 3).

I, too, do not believe that secularism of this extreme variety would have been acceptable to the country. I am sure the Constituent Assembly would have rejected it outright.

M.C. Chagla, former chief justice of the Bombay High Court, later, minister at the Centre, and India's ambassador to the United States, stated:

> As a legal concept, secularism means equality before the law, and no distinction between one citizen and another as far as the application of laws is concerned. It also means equality of opportunity and a refusal to classify citizens into first-class citizens and second-class citizens. But in my opinion, secularism is much more than that. Secularism is an attitude of the mind and a quality of the heart. It is a matter of temperament, of outlook, even of feeling...I believe that religion should never be allowed to intrude into public affairs. Every public question must be judged from the point of view of national interest. (Chagla 2000: 83–84)

Neera Chandhoke, in her book, *Beyond Secularism—The Rights of Religious Minorities,* rightly emphasized that:

> Despite the fact that the decade of the 1980s witnessed the onset of a richly textured and nuanced debate on secularism, till date, neither scholars nor political practitioners seem to be quite sure what secularism is about. Is it about erecting a 'wall of separation' between the state and religion and thereby devaluing religion? Is it about the State treating all religions as equal and thus validating religious identities?...Considering the pervasiveness of religious sensibilities in India, is secularism appropriate for the country? Has secularism, as practised in the country, proved capable of warding

off the communalization of Indian society and polity? (Jayal and Mehta 2010: 333)

Even Jawaharlal Nehru seemed ambivalent about the true meaning of secularism though he was responsible for firmly advocating its inclusion in the Constitution:

> It is perhaps not very easy even to find a good word for 'secular'. Some people think that it means something opposed to religion. That obviously is not correct. What it means is that it is a state which honours all faiths equally and gives them equal opportunities; that, as a state, it does not allow itself to be attached to one faith or religion, which then becomes the state religion.' (Gopal 1980: 330)

Justice B.N. Srikrishna, in his article, 'Skinning a Cat', emphasized that:

> The observations of the Supreme Court in the three 'Hindutva judgments'[4] on 'Hindutva' must be compared and contrasted with the definition of 'secularism' in the seminal judgment of *S.R. Bommai v. Union of India*, (1994) 3 SCC 1. In fact,...not only has the Supreme Court taken conflicting opinions on the meaning of 'secularism' and 'Hindutva' but even individual judges have vacillated in their own views from case to case. Indeed, such problems can only be avoided if judges avoid reference to ideological conceptions that defy definition by proper and accepted legal construction. (Srikrishna 2005: J-15, Footnote 59)

In the second V.M. Tarkunde Memorial Lecture on 'Secularism under Our Constitution', Justice B.N. Srikrishna stated that: Secularism, like paramountcy, is more easily identified as a concept, but most difficult to define. He pointed out that, in post-Independence India, Jawaharlal Nehru's idea of secularism as 'keeping the state politics and education separate from religion' and making religion a private matter for the

---

[4] *Ramesh Yeshwant Prabhoo v. Prabhakar Kashinath Kunte*, (1996) 1 SCC 130; *Manohar Joshi v. Nitin Bhaurao Patil*, (1996) 1 SCC 169; and *Ramchandra G. Kapse v. Haribansh Ramkakbal Singh*, (1996) 1 SCC 206.

individual, became dominant. Its natural corollary was 'equal respect for all faiths, and equal opportunities for those who profess any faith'. Srikrishna summarized the essential requisites of a secular state to imply the following:

- The State guarantees freedom of conscience in matters of religion to all citizens.
- There is no discrimination between individuals on grounds of religion. This would imply that there is equality before the law, and positions of authority are open to all.
- The State is not concerned with and, therefore, does not interfere in matters of religion.

Srikrishna quoted S.M. Seervai, the renowned Constitution lawyer, who had stated:

> The word secular is not precise and would itself require to be defined. Secular may be opposed to religious in the sense that a secular state can be an anti-religious state. In this sense, the Constitution of India is not secular, because the right to the freedom of religion is a guaranteed fundamental right...Good drafting would require that ambiguous words should not be put into a Preamble.

Srikrishna also referred to Professor Upendra Baxi's definition of secularism, according to which:

> The State by itself, shall not espouse or establish or practise any religion; public revenues will not be used to promote any religion; the State shall have the power to regulate any economic, financial or other secular activity associated with religious practice; the State shall have the power through the law to provide for social welfare and reform or the throwing open of the Hindu religious institutions of a public character to all classes and sections of Hindus; the practice of untouchability (in so far as it may be justified by Hindu religion) is constitutionally outlawed; every individual person will have, in that order, an equal right to freedom of conscience and religion; these rights are however subject to the power of the State

through law to impose restrictions on the ground of public order, morality and health; and these rights are further more subject to other fundamental rights in Part III. Baxi has argued that in this view of the matter, it is absolutely erroneous to say that secularism is a 'vacuous word' or a 'phantom concept'. (Srikrishna, *The Radical Humanist* October 2007: 10–13, 18–19)

In understanding the difficulties of the Constitution-makers while defining the term 'secular', it is necessary to take note of the anxiety of the Constituent Assembly to take steps to change a number of practices and customs which obtained in the country in the name of religion. This will be evident from the letter of Rajkumari Amrit Kaur to B.N. Rau, constitutional adviser, dated 31 March 1947, written on her own behalf and that of Hansa Mehta, in which she stated:

> As we are all aware there are several customs practised in the name of religion, e.g., *purdah*, child marriage, polygamy, unequal laws of inheritance, prevention of inter-caste marriages, dedication of girls to temples. We are naturally anxious that no clause in the fundamental rights shall make impossible future legislation for the purpose of wiping out these evils. As worded, clause 16 may even contradict or conflict with the provision abolishing the practice of untouchability. (Rao, 1967: 146)

Justice R.A. Jahagirdar, former judge of the Bombay High Court, in his article, 'Secularism Revisited', underlined that secularism cannot mean different things in different countries. He quoted Justice Gajendragadkar to say that 'the word "secular", like the word "religious", is amongst the richest of all words in its range of meaning. It is full of subtle shades, which involve internal contradictions, and of those contradictions, the conventional dictionary meaning can scarcely give a correct view.' Jahagirdar argued that discussion in India has been largely coloured by this view. He urged:

> I have great objection to this meaning given to the word secularism. In the first place it says that there is an Indian type of secularism; secondly it says, the word secularism contains internal contradictions;

and thirdly that you cannot understand the meaning of these contradictions because no dictionary can help you in this regard. In other words, the word secular has only subjective meaning and everyone can use it in any way one likes. I wish to demonstrate that:

- There is no such thing as Indian secularism and English secularism—there is only one secularism which has a universal meaning;
- There are no internal contradictions in the concept of secularism and if there are any contradictions, they are between secularism and non-secular practices;
- There is a well-established and widely accepted dictionary meaning which has stood unaltered for a period of nearly a century and a half since 1851, when George Holyoake coined that word and gave it an explicit meaning.

Jahagirdar quoted Professor Smith's definition of secularism as under:

'The secular state is a state which guarantees individual and corporate freedom of religion, deals with the individual as a citizen irrespective of his religion, is not constitutionally connected to a particular religion nor does it seek either to promote or interfere with religion.' However, Smith himself finds that there are several instances both in the Constitution and the laws which, contrary to his definition, have amounted to interference by the State in religious matters. Jahagirdar stated that his criticism of Smith's approach was that 'It sweeps away the basic and historical meaning of secularism. I say: Back to basics. You cannot have one meaning of secularism in one country and another meaning in another country. The proper name for Indian polity is probably what Dr Rafiq Zakaria called "accommodative pluralism".' According to Jahagirdar, 'If you accept "sarva dharma samabhav" as the foundation of the Indian Constitution, you cannot bring about any religious reform.' Jahagirdar believed that the Indian attempt at redefinition of secularism demanded from an Indian acceptance of the values of other religions while permitting him to practise his own religion. (*The Radical Humanist* February 2015 and March 2015: 24, 35–36)

In another article on secularism titled, 'Secularism in India—The Road Behind and the Road Ahead', Jahagirdar asserted:

> Since the definition of secularism given in the Forty-fourth Amendment Bill to mean 'sarva dharma samabhav' was rejected by the Rajya Sabha, constitutionally speaking, this meaning could not be ascribed to secularism. Secondly, equal respect for all religions was destructive of the basic concept of secularism. Regard for any religion was inconsistent with the principle of secularism which says that life must be guided by reason. Thirdly, the concept of 'sarva dharma samabhav' was a vague concept, full of contradictions. Acceptance of this concept would prevent the State from bringing about religious reforms where needed. Jahagirdar emphasized: 'I have not been able to find any single thread that runs through all religions. A secular state should exhibit indifference to religion and indeed should keep a vigilant distance from the politics of communalism and religions.' According to his interpretation, the provisions of the Constitution, in sum, prohibited the establishment of a theocratic state and prevented the State from either identifying itself [with] or favouring any religion or religious sect or denomination. Jahagirdar also felt that 'sarva dharma samabhav' could not provide a proper or clear guidance either to the individual or to the State. Importantly, Jahagirdar underlined that secularism operated at three levels: the State as secular; society as secular; and the individual as secular. The USA provides a classic example of a secular state, although its citizens and society are not secular. Probably this is so in France too, though the invasive presence of religion is not felt there. It needs to be noted that the census figures in France do not disclose the religious composition of citizenry. The UK is not secular for the reason that the Anglican Church is the official church. The monarch of England must join in communion with the Church of England. A Roman Catholic or a person who marries a Roman Catholic cannot be the monarch of England. Finally, Jahagirdar emphasized that *a secular state would not necessarily bring about a secular society. It is the secular individuals who would create a secular society.* (*The Radical Humanist*, December 2005: 12–14)

M.C. Setalvad, the first Attorney General of India, in the Vallabhbhai Patel Memorial Lecture delivered in 1965, stated:

> It is true that many of our leading men, including Nehru, have described India as a secular state. But Nehru himself stated as early as 1954 that the use of the word 'secular' to describe the nature of the Indian state was 'perhaps...not a very happy one' and that it was being used 'for want of a better word'. Dr Radhakrishnan has stated that 'The religious impartiality of the Indian State is not to be confused with secularism or atheism. Secularism as here defined is in accordance with the ancient religious traditions of India.'... Nevertheless, it cannot be said that the Indian State does not possess some important characteristics of a secular state. Instead of creating a wall of separation between the State and religion, it looks upon religion with benevolent neutrality and treats all of them equally. (Setalvad 1967: 21)

In his autobiography, *My Life—Law and Other Things*, Setalvad wrote:

> A secular state is not easy to define. According to the liberal democratic tradition of the West, the secular state is not hostile to religion, but holds itself neutral in matters of religion. Such a state is not moved by an active hostility to religion, as is to be found in the communist tradition. The secular state, of which the United States of America may be regarded as an example, guarantees 'individual and corporate freedom of religion, deals with the individual as a citizen irrespective of his religion, is not constitutionally connected to a particular religion, nor does it seek either to promote or interfere with religion.' The basic ideas would seem to be freedom of religion for the individual, the exclusion by the State of all considerations based on religion in dealing with its citizens, and the non-recognition by the State of any particular religion as the religion of the State. (Setalvad 1970: 556–57)

In 1989, Dr Shankar Dayal Sharma, the then-president of India, while delivering the Zakir Husain Memorial Lecture, stated: 'We in India understand secularism to denote sarva dharma samabhav, an approach to tolerance and understanding of the equality of all religions. This philosophical approach of understanding, co-existence and tolerance is the very spirit of our ancient thought.' (Apte 2005: 166)

A question is often raised as to why the definition of 'secular' as equal respect for all religions, incorporated in the Constitution Amendment bill in 1978, was not accepted. It is also pointed out that this bill was introduced by the first non-Congress government at the Centre since Independence, and it showed the commitment of the Janata party to the concept of secularism. It is argued that the reason for this was the apprehension of the secularists that such an acceptance would establish the superiority of Hinduism over the other religions with which they were keen to fraternize for political ends. In this context, we may recall the observation of C. Rajagopalachari, the first governor-general of Independent India and an astute statesman, who said, 'Justice to minority groups does not mean injustice to majority'. (Apte 2005: 171–72)

The above discussion proves that defining the word 'secular' has been impossible so far. The commonly accepted definitions—such as, *'sarva dharma samabhav'* and the State remaining equidistant from all religions—are fraught with difficulties. I do not believe that it is best to leave the word undefined, as one can never hold anyone responsible for going against its precepts if one does not know what the word means. In a sense, this has been the problem so far. Most people in public life—and political life in particular—claim to be secular, but their thinking, utterances and actions convey quite the opposite. I believe that, unless India commits itself to being a secular nation in unambiguous terms, its future will be in serious jeopardy. In the last chapter, 'The Way Ahead', I have, therefore, suggested that the word 'secular' be defined with as large a public consensus as possible.

How the Apex Court Has Looked at Secularism

Delivering his judgment in *Ziyauddin Burhanuddin Bukhari v. Brijmohan Ramdass Mehra & Ors* (1975 Suppl. SCR 281), Justice M.H. Beg said:

The secular state, rising above all differences of religion, attempts to secure the good of all its citizens irrespective of their religious beliefs and practices. It is neutral or impartial in extending its benefits to citizens of all castes and creeds. Maitland has pointed out that such a state has to ensure, through its laws, that the existence or exercise of political or civil right or the right or capacity to occupy any office or position under it or to perform any public duty connected with it does not depend upon the profession or practice of any particular religion.

Our Constitution and the laws framed thereunder leave citizens free to work out happy and harmonious relationships between their religious and the quite separable secular fields of law and politics. But they do not permit an unjustifiable invasion of what belongs to one sphere by what appertains really to another. It is for courts to determine in a case of dispute whether any sphere was or was not properly interfered with, in accordance with the Constitution, even by a purported law. (Kashyap 1994: 59)

Vikramjit Banerjee and Sumeet Malik, in their article, 'Changing Perceptions of Secularism', comprehensively brought out the changing interpretations of secularism by the Supreme Court over the years:

> The Court expressed its views on the secular nature of the Constitution for the first time in *Sardar Taheruddin Syedna Saheb v. State of Bombay (All India Reporter* [henceforth *AIR*] 1962 SC 853, 871), and stated that the principle of religious toleration emphasizes the secular nature of the Indian democracy. In *Kesavananda Bharati v. State of Kerala* ((1973) 4 SCC 225), the Court said that secularism was a part of the basic structure of the Constitution. In *Ahmedabad St. Xaviers College Society v. State of Gujarat* ((1974) 1 SCC 717), the Court indicated that *it was uncertain about its views on secularism.* Mathew and Chandrachud JJ felt that it was only by implication that the Constitution envisaged a secular state. They gave a new dimension to the concept by stating: 'The Constitution has not erected a rigid wall of separation between the Church and the State. It is only in a qualified sense that India can be said to be a secular state. *There are provisions in the Constitution which make*

one hesitate to characterize our State as secular. Secularism, in the context of our Constitution, means only an attitude of live and let live developing in the attitude of live and help live.' Banerjee and Malik emphasized that apparently this view implied a contradiction between the judicially construed concept of secularism and the concept evident in the text of the Constitution.

In *Ziyauddin Burhanuddin Bukhari v. Brijmohan Ramdass Mehra* ([1976] 2 SCC 17), the Court stated that secularism envisaged a cohesive, unified and casteless society. Further, 'caste poses a serious threat to secularism and a consequence to the integrity of the country.' This view seems to be an enlargement of the concept of secularism beyond merely religious differentiation. This seems to indicate that the Court is still not decided as to what exactly the term means.

In the landmark *S.R. Bommai v. Union of India* ([1994] 3 SCC 1), the Court declared in no uncertain terms that secularism was part of the basic structure of the Constitution. But a complication arose in formulating a definition. Ahmadi, J., stated that secularism is based on the 'principles of accommodation and tolerance'. In other words, an espousal of a 'soft secularism'. He tended to agree with the broadened definition adopted by the Court in *Indra Sawhney v. Union of India* ([1992] Supp [3] SCC 217). In *Bommai,* the Court ruled that religion and temporal activities do not mix. Freedom and tolerance of religion are only to the extent of permitting pursuit of a spiritual life that is different from the secular life. The latter falls in the domain of the affairs of the State. The Court further said that 'the encroachment of religion into secular activities is strictly prohibited'. Ramaswamy, J., in his separate opinion, declared that the State has the duty of ensuring secularism by law or by an executive order. He explained that programmes or principles evolved by political parties based on religion amount to recognizing religion as a part of political governance which the Constitution expressly prohibited. According to him, it was the duty of the Court to bring every errant political party in line if it goes against secular ideals, like casteism and religious antagonisms. His opinion reiterates the view that secularism includes anti-casteism, and presents the rigid stance of the Court.[5] Jeevan

---

[5]This rigid stance was diluted in later cases.

Reddy and Agrawal, J.J., broadly agreed with Ramaswamy, J. In fact, the judges went on to say that the concept of secularism in the Indian Constitution was in broad agreement with the US Constitution's First Amendment. They also expressed the view that the State has the power to legislate on religion, including personal laws under Article 44 and secular affairs of temples, mosques and other places of worship.[6] They went on to say that if a political party were even indirectly to espouse a religious cause it would be acting in an unconstitutional manner.

Within a year, in *Ismail Faruqui v. Union of India* ([1994] 6 SCC 360), the Court started diluting the active, positive concept of secularism based on scientific thinking it had advocated in the *Bommai* case. An indication of this trend had been laid in *R.C. Podayal* ([1994] Supp [1] SCC 324). Subsequently, in the *Ram Janma Bhoomi* case, the Court justified its concept of secularism by quoting extensively from Indian scriptures. Verma, J. (as he was then) quoted from the *Yajur Veda, Atharva Veda* and *Rig Veda* to justify its concept of secularism: '*sarva dharma samabhav*', that is, tolerance of all religions. This reasoning—of justifying secularism by religious scriptures—seems odd. The Court seems to have rejected the Western concept of secularism based on separation of the Church and the State as explained in *S.R. Bommai,* and gone back to equating secularism with tolerance. The Court also noted that the State had the power to take over any religious place, including a mosque. Though dissenting, Bharucha, J. supported the concept of absolute, positive and active secularism, more in tune with that spelt out in *S.R. Bommai*. Yet, even he accepted that secularism in India exists because of the tolerance of the Hindus who are the majority religion.

The confusion was compounded with the three cases known as the 'Hindutva Judgment', the major and crucial one being *Ramesh Yeshwant Prabhoo v. Prabhakar K. Kunte*, ([1996] 1 SCC 130). The opinion of Verma, J. indicates the shift made by the Court from its stance on secularism advocated in *S.R. Bommai*. Verma, J. made the Court shift from its earlier position and take a different stand on three major grounds:

1. The Court enunciated that a speech with a secular stance alleging discrimination against any particular religion and promising the

---

[6] The Court withdrew from both these commitments later.

removal of the imbalance cannot be treated as an appeal on the ground of religion, as its thrust is for promoting secularism.[7]
2. The Court again seemed to have turned away from the *Bommai* case and the 'constitutional duty' of the Court to get political parties in line with secularism, advising leaders to be only 'more circumspect and careful in the kind of language they use'. The Court further explained by stating that the statement, 'The first Hindu state will be established in Maharashtra', is by itself not an appeal for votes based on religious grounds, 'but the expression, at best, of such hope'.
3. The Court equated Hinduism and Hindutva with Indianization: 'The words "Hinduism" or "Hindutva" are not necessarily to be understood and construed narrowly, confined only to the strict Hindu religious practices, unrelated to the culture and ethos of the people of India, depicting the way of life of the Indian people.'

The Court went on to explain clearly what it had held in the Hindutva Judgments in a series of cases. In this context, it must be noted that the Court was not unanimous in its own stance. This is evident from the stand taken by some judges in a number of cases. In *Abhiram Singh v. C.D. Conmachen* ([1996] 3 SCC 665), Ramaswamy, J. recommended that the question be sent to a larger bench for consideration, but refrained from taking a different meaning of secularism.

Banerjee and Malik concluded by saying that the Court clearly had not moved an inch from its original perspective on secularism as enunciated in the early cases of the 1950s and 1960s. The Court, with minor deviations, had stuck to its original stance of secularism not being a wall between the Church and the State, but a sense of toleration between people of different religions through '*sarva dharma samabhav*'. The Court had deviated from this position for a while in *S.R. Bommai*, where it espoused secularism to mean 'a wall between the Church and the State'. The line of thinking of the Court seems to be best portrayed by the majority in the *Ram Janma Bhoomi* case—secularism is toleration based on tradition. The Hindutva Judgments are a logical conclusion from it, that is, recognition of the essential Hindu identity of tradition. Yet it seems, the Court stopped short in taking the line to its ultimate

---

[7] The Court's stand in the *Bommai* decision was different.

conclusion—that of Hindutva being synonymous with nationalism. (Banerjee and Malik 1998: 3–8)

Apte drew attention to the fact that B.P. Jeevan Reddy, J., in his judgment in the *Bommai* case, stated that:

> Secularism was more than a passive attitude of religious tolerance. It was a positive concept of equal treatment of all religions. However, Ahmadi, J. (as he was then) had observed: 'Notwithstanding the fact that the words "socialist" and "secular" were added in the Preamble to the Constitution in 1976 by the Forty-second Amendment, the concept of secularism was very much embedded in our constitutional philosophy. *The term "secular" has advisedly not been defined presumably because it is a very elastic term, not capable of a precise definition and perhaps best left undefined.* By this amendment, what was implicit was made explicit.' (Apte 2005: 382)

From time to time, the question of what is Hindu religion has come up for consideration before the Supreme Court. The Court stated, as far back as 1966:

> We find it difficult, if not impossible, to define Hindu religion or even adequately describe it. Unlike other religions in the world, the Hindu religion does not claim any one prophet; it does not worship any one God; it does not subscribe to any one dogma; it does not believe in any one philosophic concept; it does not follow any one set of religious rites or performances; in fact, it does not appear to satisfy the narrow traditional [for traditional read Western] features of any religion or creed. It may broadly be described as a way of life and nothing more.' (*AIR* 1966 SC 1127)

Reference must be made to another important judgment of the Supreme Court in *S.R. Bommai v. Union of India*, *AIR* 1994 SC 2092. While dealing, *inter alia*, with the case of the dismissal of the three state governments of Madhya Pradesh, Himachal Pradesh and Rajasthan by the Centre in 1992, Justice Sawant and Justice Kuldip Singh, who wrote the judgment, stated:

Secularism is one of the basic features of the Constitution. While freedom of religion is guaranteed to all persons in India, from the point of view of the State, the religion, faith or belief of a person is immaterial. To the State, all are equal and are entitled to be treated equally. In matters of State, religion has no place. *No political party can simultaneously be a religious party. Politics and religion cannot be mixed. Any State government which pursues unsecular policies or unsecular course of action acts contrary to the Constitutional mandate and renders itself amenable to action under Article 356.* There is no dissent or qualification or reservation by any of the other judges on this part of the judgment. Soli Sorabjee has rightly stated that 'the propositions are over-broadly stated'. (Journal Section (1994) 3 SCC: 30)

In the comprehensive article on the judgment, Justice H.R. Khanna, former judge of the Supreme Court, wrote: The decision of the Court in respect of the three states in question would have serious repercussions on the survival or coming into power of the BJP in any state...It would also warrant the dismissal of all BJP governments if and when they come into power in any state... Yet, ever since the commencement of the Constitution, we have had political parties like, Muslim League, Akali Dal and Hindu Mahasabha. Some of these parties like, Akali Dal have formed state governments, yet no one has so far thought of dismissing such government because of the label of the party or its allegiance or affinity to some religion...No judgment of the Supreme Court, in the opinion of the writer, can and should ignore the ground realities of political life in the country. Life of law, it is said, is not logic, but experience and, one may add, taking due cognizance of the political and social realities. Constitutional law cannot operate in a vacuum or choose to reside in some higher region cut off from the world of existing political and social realities. (*AIR* 1994 Journal Section: 156)

The judgments of the Supreme Court thus give diametrically opposite signals so far as secularism is concerned. In a decision given in 2005, the Court held that housing societies may exclude from membership people of different castes or communities, and frame their bye-laws in such a way that membership is restricted to a particular caste or creed. As *The Lawyers Collective* (April 2005) editorially commented, 'The implications of this judgment are horrendous. The consequences for religious groups are even more frightening.'

Writing on the background of the litigation pertaining to the ban on the entry of women in some temples such as Sabarimala, Ronojoy Sen of the National University of Singapore and a well-known author, has rightly underlined: It is unfortunate that the courts have become the arbiter of what constitutes true religion. Rajeev Dhavan and Fali Nariman have pointed out that the judges have "virtually assumed the theological authority to determine which tenets of faith are essental" to any 'faith'. This situation has arisen because the Indian state is the agent for the reform and management of Hinduism and its institutions. (*IE* 21 April 2016: 10)

It is a well-known fact that segregation in housing and educational institutions had a major influence on the thinking of religious groups and communities, and has been responsible for their feeling of alienation. Social unrest and riots are, in no small measure, due to such segregation.

Equally disturbing is the judgment of the Supreme Court in respect of the Bombay Prevention of Excommunication Act, 1949, which laid down that, 'Notwithstanding anything contained in any law, custom or usage for the time being in force to the contrary, no excommunication of a member of any community shall be valid and shall be of any effect.' The said Act came to be challenged by the head of the Dawoodi Bohra community. The Bombay High Court dismissed the petition but the Supreme Court (*Sardar Syedna Taher Saifuddin Saheb v. State of Bombay*, AIR 1962 SC 853) declared the said legislation as void, in spite of the fact that the Constitution has given freedom of conscience, faith and belief to every citizen. (*AIR* 1988 Journal Section: 6)

Chief Justice Sinha, in his minority judgment, held that:

The Act is intended to do away with all that mischief of treating a human being as a 'pariah' and of depriving him of his human dignity and of his right to follow the dictates of his own conscience. The Act is thus aimed at fulfilment of the individual liberty of conscience guaranteed by Article 25 (1) of the Constitution and not in derogation of it. Former Chief Justice of India, P.B.

Gajendragadkar, too has underlined that the judgment of the Bombay High Court which was acclaimed as a progressive judgment when it was delivered, unfortunately received a knock-out blow when the Supreme Court set it aside. He has stated that if he had sat on the Bench to hear the case, as was originally intended, he would have strived to uphold the judgment of the Bombay High Court. (Gajendragadkar 1982: 148)

It is unfortunate that the judgment has remained unchallenged so far.

The importance of the issues involved is underlined by the series of election petitions filed over the years, in which candidates had solicited votes on the basis of religion. In one such case pertaining to the election for the Santa Cruz Legislative Assembly constituency, for example, the Bombay High Court held that 'the voluminous oral as well as documentary evidence leaves no room for doubt that the plank of Hindutva/Hinduism/Hindu was used...The campaign was on the basis of appealing for votes on the basis of the first respondent's community and religion, that is, the Hindu community and religion, and that there had been an attempt to create enmity and hatred between different classes of citizens on the basis of religion, community and caste, particularly the Hindus and the Muslims. When the matter went in appeal to the Supreme Court (*Abhiram Singh v. C.D. Commachen and Ors*, 1996, 3 SCC 665), the three-judge bench had directed on 16 April 1996 that the case be placed before a larger bench of five judges 'and, if possible, at an early date so that all questions arising in the present appeal could be decided authoritatively and expeditiously.'

Unfortunately, the case is still pending.

In yet another case, *Ebrahim Sulaiman Sait v. M.C. Muhammad and Anr*, AIR 1980 SC 354, the Court observed, '*Reading the speech as a whole, it cannot be denied that its tone is communal, but in this country communal parties are allowed to function in politics.* That being so, how an appeal to the voters, such as the one made in the speech in question should be viewed in the context of corrupt practices mentioned in the Act, has been explained by Gajendragadkar C.J., speaking for the Court in *Kultar Singh v. Mukhtiar Singh*:

It is well known that there are several [political] parties in this country which subscribe to different political and economic ideologies, but their membership is confined to, or predominantly held by, members of particular communities or religions. *So long as law does not prohibit the formation of such parties and in fact recognizes them for the purpose of election and Parliamentary life, it would be necessary to remember that an appeal made by such candidates of such parties for votes may, if successful, lead to their election and in an indirect way, may conceivably be influenced by considerations of religion, race, caste, community or language. This infirmity cannot perhaps be avoided so long as parties are allowed to function and are recognized, though their composition may be predominantly based on membership of particular communities or religion.*

This helplessness of the highest court of the land is eloquent and has still not been addressed.

The dismissal of some election petitions by the Supreme Court on the tenuous distinction between the Hindu religion and Hindutva is problematic. Thus, in *Manohar Joshi v. Nitin Bhaurao Patil and Anr*, *AIR* 1996 SC 796, the Court held: 'The word "Hindutva" by itself does not invariably mean Hindu religion and it is the context and the manner of its use which is material for deciding the meaning of the word "Hindutva" in a particular text. It cannot be held that in the abstract the mere word "Hindutva" by itself invariably means Hindu religion.'

In *Dr Ramesh Yeshwant Prabhoo v. Prabhakar Kashinath Kunte*, *AIR* 1996 SC 1113, the Court held:

No precise meaning can be ascribed to the terms 'Hindu', 'Hindutva' and 'Hinduism'; and no meaning in the abstract can confine it to the narrow limits of religion alone, excluding the content of Indian culture and heritage. The term 'Hindutva' is related more to the way of life of the people in the subcontinent. It is difficult to say that the term 'Hindutva' or 'Hinduism' *per se*, in the abstract, can be assumed to mean and be equated with narrow fundamentalist Hindu religious bigotry, or be construed to fall within the prohibition in sub-section (3) and/or (3A) of section

123 of the R.P. (The Representation of the People) Act. Ordinarily 'Hindutva' is understood as a way of life or a state of mind and it is not to be equated with or understood as religious Hindu fundamentalism. *The word 'Hindutva' is used and understood as a synonym of 'Indianization', that is, development of a uniform culture by obliterating the differences between all the cultures co-existing in the country.* Considering the terms 'Hinduism' or 'Hindutva' *per se* as depicting hostility, enmity or intolerance towards other religious faiths or professing communalism, proceeds from an improper appreciation and perception of the true meaning of these expressions.

Needless to say, this philosophical discourse is hardly relevant in the emotionally charged atmosphere during electioneering. Muslims and persons of other religious denominations of minorities are hardly likely to subscribe or take kindly to the above interpretation. In fact, this interpretation is the very logic of the two-nation theory on which the Partition of the country had taken place. It would also evoke fears of obliterating the religious and cultural identities of the minorities in the country. Equally difficult to understand is the logic of the Court in its assertion that, 'A mere statement that the first Hindu state will be established in Maharashtra is by itself not an appeal for votes on the ground of his religion but the expression, at best, of such a hope.' The fact that all these election petitions were based on the speeches made by the leaders of the Shiv Sena and the BJP—whose political ideology is based on the furtherance of Hindu religion at any cost—also has an important bearing on the issues at hand. It is unfortunate that the tenets on which these judgments of the Supreme Court were based and which have such an important bearing on secularism have not been reviewed by a larger Constitution bench so far.

2

THE MINORITY SYNDROME

In the long run, it would be in the interest of all to forget that there is anything like a majority or a minority in the country and that in India, there is only one community.

— VALLABHBHAI PATEL IN THE CONSTITUENT ASSEMBLY

In this chapter we shall look at some critical questions:

- Who are the minorities?
- The minority fixation in India;
- The right to freedom of religion;
- Constitution-making—some salient features;
- Religious endowments; and
- The National Minorities Commission.

Who Are the Minorities?

During the British regime, the government of India gave recognition to the 'political importance' of Indian Muhammadans in its fifth dispatch dated 23 April 1919 to the Secretary of State. This and subsequent dispatches emphasized that *numbers of Muslims were not, and could never be, the only criterion in any discussion of the constitutional problem of India.* Their political importance was clearly recognized in the advice tendered in these dispatches that the census strength of the Muhammadans by no means corresponded to their political strength. (Khan 1928: 116–19).

This shows that building up and encouraging a separate identity for Muslims was a part of a well-thought-out policy of the British. No effort was ever made to recognize Indian society as a homogeneous society.

Writing in 1928, Shafaat Ahmad Khan extensively elucidated the importance of UP Muslims in the scheme of things, though their percentage in the total population of the province was only 14.28. However, they paid one-fourth of the total land revenue. Their organizing ability and executive capacity had been responsible for building up the kingdoms of Oudh, Rohilkhand and Jaunpur. He argued that, as a result, Muslims must be given special rights, such as separate electorates, effective representation in all services in government and local bodies, and in the cabinets of the central and provincial governments, an increase in grants-in–aid for various purposes, the safeguarding of their language, and providing support to their educational institutions.

In compliance with the directions contained in the Madras Congress Resolution, 1927, the Working Committee of the Congress convened an All-Parties Conference to draft a Swaraj Constitution for India. The first meeting of the conference was attended, among others, by representatives of the All-India Muslim League, the All India Hindu Mahasabha, the Central Khilafat Committee, the All India Conference of Indian Christians, the All-India States' People's Conference, the All-India Liberal Federation as well as the Congress. It was held in February 1928, at Delhi. The conference decided that the Constitution to be framed should provide for the establishment of a responsible government. Meeting again in May 1928, the conference appointed a small committee with Motilal Nehru as the chairman and seven other members, namely, Ali Imam, Tej Bahadur Sapru, M.S. Aney, Sardar Mangal Singh, Shuaib Qureshi, Subhas Chandra Bose and G.R. Pradhan, commissioning them 'to determine the principles of the Constitution of India'. The report was acclaimed by constitutional historians as…'the frankest attempt yet made by Indians to face squarely the difficulties of communalism'.

The Nehru Report, submitted in August 1928, *inter alia*, recommended that the fundamental rights should include 'freedom of conscience and the free profession and practice of religion…subject to public order or morality, (are) hereby guaranteed to every person'. It also laid down that:

> There shall be no state religion for the Commonwealth of India or for any province in the Commonwealth, nor shall the State either directly or indirectly endow any religion or give any preference or impose any disability on account of religious belief or religious status. No person attending any school receiving any state aid or other public money shall be compelled to attend the religious instruction that may be given in the school. No person shall by reason of his religion, caste or creed be prejudiced in any way in regard to public employment, office of power or honour and the exercise of any trade or calling.

The report appended a note to say, 'Notwithstanding anything to the contrary in Article IV the Sikhs are entitled to carry kirpans.' It also recommended that:

> 'There shall be joint mixed electorates throughout India for the House of Representatives and the provincial legislatures. There shall be no reservation of seats for the House of Representatives except for Muslims in provinces where they are in a minority and non-Muslims in the N.W.F.P. [North-West Frontier Province]. Such reservation will be in strict proportion to the Muslim population in every province where they are in a minority and in proportion to the non-Muslim population in N.W.F.P. The Muslims or non-Muslims, where reservation is allowed to them, shall have the right to contest additional seats... Reservation of seats where allowed shall be for a fixed period of ten years.' However, the report did not define the term 'minorities'. (Rao 1966: 58–60, 74–75)

It is interesting to see what Jawaharlal Nehru, in the article 'Can Indians Get Together?' published in *The New York Times Magazine* dated 19 July 1942, wrote about the Muslim problem in India. He stated:

> The real problem so often referred to is that of the Muslims. They are hardly a minority, as they number about 90,000,000 and it is difficult to see how even a majority can oppress them...It must be remembered that the problem of Indian minorities is entirely different from nationalities with entirely different racial, cultural and linguistic backgrounds. This is not so in India where, except for

a small handful of persons, there is no difference between Hindu and Muslim in race, culture or language. The vast majority of Muslims belong to the same stock as the Hindus and were converted to Islam. (Gopal and Iyengar Vol. II, 2003: 43)

The Sapru Committee, which was asked to suggest the framework for India's Constitution, following the long-established British policy, considered scheduled castes, Muslims, Sikhs, Indian Christians, and Anglo-Indians as minorities in its deliberations. The committee suggested that 'representation of these communities (and the Hindus) in the executives shall be, as far as possible, a reflection of their strength in the legislature.' (Sapru Committee 1945: XI)

The Sapru Committee recommended that ten per cent of the seats in the Union legislature should be reserved for special interests. The remainder would be distributed among the religious communities, which would also be represented on the Union executive. In the interest of national unity, it was proposed that Muslims be persuaded to opt for joint electorates with reserved seats. The committee recommended that the reservation of seats for religious minorities in the Central Assembly should be on par with that of the Hindus, despite the great disparity in population strength. Further, Articles 292 and 294 of the Draft Constitution provided for the reservation of seats in proportion to the population of religious minorities under joint electorates, in both the Central and the state legislatures. This provision was to be reviewed after ten years. Article 296 provided that the claims of religious minorities should be taken into consideration along with the consideration of merit and efficiency in appointment to public services. Article 299 provided for the appointment of special officers at the Centre and at the state level to report all matters relating to the safeguards provided for minorities. (Chandhoke 1999: 76–77)

Unfortunately, no thought was given by either the Nehru Committee or the Sapru Committee to define the term 'minority'. The founding fathers of the Constitution, too, followed this well-beaten path and did not think it necessary to define the term. A lot of the problems which India is facing today on this account, could have been avoided if the term had been defined rationally. Considerable litigation in the Supreme

Court, too, could have been avoided. For example, the Supreme Court, in the Kerala Education Bill matter, laid down a numerical test for defining a minority. As a result, Christians, who were at the time 22 per cent of the population in Kerala state and who may be well over 25 per cent now, were treated as a minority. There is a demand that Hindus in Punjab who may be over 40 per cent of the population of the state should be treated as a minority. The same is true of Hindus in Jammu and Kashmir who are clearly in a 'majority' in Jammu while Muslims are in the majority in the Valley. As I see, this whole concept of 'minority' needs to be considered afresh. This is particularly true in the case of India. But it being a sensitive and politically explosive subject, no political party is prepared even to entertain such a thought. However, any discussion on secularism will be incomplete unless this subject is addressed in a forthright manner.

Jawaharlal Nehru, in his speech at the All-India States' People's Conference at Udaipur on 1 January 1946, stated:

> The Congress did not want to compel any unit to join the Federation against its will. At the same time, the Congress was not prepared to make concessions to fissiparous tendencies and to demands which would disintegrate and ruin India...I would not oppose Muslims in the Punjab or Bengal if they voted for separation but none would allow them to drag the communities with them. (Rao 1966: Footnote on page 158)

Another important milestone was the Objectives Resolution moved by Jawaharlal Nehru and passed by the Constituent Assembly in January 1947. *Inter alia*, it stated: 'This Constituent Assembly declares its firm and solemn resolve to proclaim India as an Independent Sovereign Republic and to draw up for her future governance a Constitution *wherein adequate safeguards shall be provided for minorities,* backward and tribal areas and depressed and other backward classes...'

It needs to be noted that the Objectives Resolution did not define the word 'minorities'.

S. Radhakrishnan, in his eloquent speech in the Constituent Assembly, pointedly referred to the statement of Mr Churchill who, in the debate on India in the British Parliament, asked, 'His Majesty's Government to remember its obligations to the Muslims, numbering 90 million, who comprised the majority of the fighting elements of India.' (Rao 1967: 3–4, 14)

It can be seen that once again the British were up to their favourite game of 'divide and rule' by emphasizing their interests in safeguarding the Muslims in India.

On the eve of the meeting of the Constituent Assembly, V.K. John, MLC, wrote a letter to Vallabhbhai Patel on 7 December 1946, saying that:

> 'It was his view that the Indian Christian community should not ask for separate electorate or even joint electorates with reservation but ought to sync its identity with the general electorate. My opinion, so far as I know the mind of Indian Christians, is shared by a very large section of the community, particularly by the younger members of the community.' (Das Vol. 3, 1972: 50)

Govind Ballabh Pant, while moving a resolution on 24 January 1947 on the appointment of an advisory committee on fundamental rights, said that, out of the fifty members, only twelve would be representatives of the general sections, others would represent the minorities and the tribals and Excluded Areas. He said:

> The entire strength of this committee has been fixed in accordance with the wishes of one and each of every one of all the minorities in the House. It represents their complete agreement. We have subordinated every other consideration in order to secure contentment and satisfaction...We trust that in this committee every regard will be paid to the wishes of the different minorities and the decisions taken will be fully satisfactory to them...Let not the minorities look back to any outside power for the protection of their rights. This will never help them. Let not the lesson of history be lost. It is a lesson which should be burnt deep in the hearts and minds of all minorities that they can find their protection only from the people in whose midst they live and it is on the establishment of

mutual goodwill, mutual trust, cordiality and amity that the rights and interests not only of the majorities but also of the minorities depend. This lesson of history, I hope, will not be forgotten...There is the unwholesome, and to some extent the degrading, habit of thinking always in terms of communities and never in terms of citizens. (Rao 1967: 60–63)

Pant also emphasized that:

The question of minorities everywhere looms large in constitutional discussions. *Many a constitution has foundered on this rock.* A satisfactory solution of questions pertaining to minorities would ensure the health, vitality and strength of the free state of India that will come into existence as a result of our discussions here. The question of minorities cannot possibly be overrated. It has been used so far for creating strife, distrust and cleavage between the different sections of the Indian nation. Imperialism thrives on such strife. It is interested in fomenting such tendencies. So far, the minorities have been incited and have been influenced in a manner which has hampered the growth of cohesion and unity. But now it is necessary that a new chapter should start and we should all realize our responsibility. *Unless the minorities are fully satisfied, we cannot make any progress: we cannot even maintain peace in an undisturbed manner.* (Rao 1968b: 746)

As brought out earlier, the Constitution did not define the term 'minorities' anywhere. This is in spite of the fact that the word was in the parlance of the Congress party from the 1930s, if not earlier. Leaving words undefined in this manner in the Constitution has led to a spate of litigations right up to the Supreme Court level.

I have given in Appendix I, the 'Declaration on the Rights of Persons Belonging to National or Ethnic, Religious and Linguistic Minorities', adopted by the United Nations General Assembly Resolution 47/135 of 18 December 1992. Reading it, one can see that, though serious questions arise whether India's minorities fall in the category of minorities as commonly understood in UN parlance, provisions made for the protection and welfare of minorities in the Indian Constitution go well beyond what is considered ideal by the UN.

Even at the beginning of the deliberations in the Constituent Assembly, there were hopes that the Muslim League would not press its demand for the creation of Pakistan and would join the Constituent Assembly. However, once it became clear that Pakistan was in the offing, the view on the demands of minorities underwent some change. This was evident from the Report of the Advisory Committee on Minorities presented by Vallabhbhai Patel to the Constituent Assembly on 25 May 1949:

> We have felt bound to reject some of the proposals placed before us partly because, as in the case of reservation of seats in the cabinet, we felt that a rigid constitutional provision would have made parliamentary democracy unworkable and partly because, as in the case of electoral arrangements, we considered it necessary to harmonize the special claims of minorities with the development of a healthy national life. We wish to make it clear, however, that our general approach to the whole problem of minorities is that the State should be run, that they should stop feeling oppressed by the mere fact that they are minorities and that, on the contrary, they should feel that they have as honourable a part to play in the national life as any other section of the community.

Rajkumari Amrit Kaur, in her memorandum submitted to the minorities committee on 20 March 1947, had, *inter alia*, urged that:

> The primary duty of the committee…is to suggest such ways and means as will help to eradicate the evil of separation rather than expedients or palliatives which might, in the long run, only contribute to its perpetuation…No minority should demand any safeguards but should be brave enough to rely solely on the goodwill of the majority and its own inherent moral strength. Nevertheless, it is up to the majority communities to inspire the necessary confidence in the minorities so as to enable them to adopt this attitude. The larger responsibility is really theirs…In drawing up a code of fundamental rights there should also be drawn up a code of duties of citizens. Rights should really follow duties, a wise axiom which is lost sight

of in the maze of fear and suspicion in which today we live and move and have our being. (Rao 1967: 309, 311–12)

It may be noted that it was only in 1976, a full twenty-six years after the adoption of the Constitution, that Article 51A on fundamental duties was incorporated by the Constitution (Forty-second Amendment) Act.

Reference may be made to the important observation of B.R. Ambedkar: 'Among the many problems the Constituent Assembly has to face, there are two which are admittedly most difficult. One is the problem of minorities and the other is the problem of the Indian states.' (Shourie 1997: 431)

The discussion in this book brings out how true this assessment was, at least in so far as the minorities were concerned.

The Sub-committee of the Constituent Assembly on Minorities issued a questionnaire prepared by K.M. Munshi to solicit the views of the members on six points as under:

1. What should be the nature and scope of the safeguards for a minority in the new Constitution?
2. What should be the political safeguards for a minority: (a) at the Centre; (b) in the provinces?
3. What should be the economic safeguards for a minority: (a) at the Centre; (b) in the provinces?
4. What should be the religious, educational and cultural safeguards for a minority?
5. What machinery should be set up to ensure that the safeguards are effective?
6. How is it proposed that the safeguards should be eliminated, in what time and under what circumstances? (Rao 1968b: 748)

Interestingly enough, the main question as to who should be recognized as minorities was neither posed nor ever answered clearly. The elimination of safeguards was considered by the Constituent Assembly only in respect of scheduled castes but not for any other minorities. Thus, for example, the Constitution does not envisage the elimination of safeguards in respect of minority educational institutions and their management. Needless to say, such a questionnaire was an open invitation for the minorities and their supporters to put forward their often questionable demands.

A.C. Hepburn, in his book, *Minorities in History*, has talked about two definitions of minorities. In the first 'American-type' definition, he has relied on the definition put forward by the American sociologist Louis Wirth, who wrote that a minority was:

> A group of people who, because of their physical or cultural characteristics, are singled out from the others in the society in which they live for differential and unequal treatment, and who therefore regard themselves as objects of collective discrimination. The existence of such a minority implies the existence of a corresponding dominant group with higher social status and greater privileges. The second definition which Hepburn has termed 'European-type' definition states, 'those non-dominant groups in a population which possess and wish to preserve ethnic, religious or linguistic traditions or characteristics markedly different from those of the rest of the population. (Hepburn 1978: 1–2)

Strictly speaking, neither of these two definitions can be said to apply to the minorities in India.

Myron Weiner, in the article 'India's Minorities: Who Are They? What Do They Want?' stated:

> At a conference several years ago, a prominent Indian journalist referred to India as a 'Hindu island in an Islamic sea'. In the same vein, Theodore Wright quotes a Hindu writer as saying that 'it is taken for granted that the Hindus are a majority…But to say so is totally wrong. The vast mass of people that are called Hindus are a vast congeries of sub-caste minorities[1]…Whereas the Muslims form the actual majority. These quotes highlight the point that minority and majority status is a matter of self-ascription as well as objective definition. What is a majority from one perspective is a minority

---

[1] According to the Anthropological Survey of India, more than 4000 distinct communities inhabit India. Their identity and cultural profile is shaped by their environment, language, occupational status and religion. (Marie Lall in Adeney 2005: 157)

from another.² Giving some instances, Weiner has highlighted that until recently most Indians did not regard Sikhs as a minority. Today, they are so regarded and they clearly see themselves as a minority. But in the Punjab it is the Hindus who consider themselves a minority. Similarly, Jains are India's oldest religious minority, but the Jains are unobtrusive, politically quietistic, and so intertwined with Hindus that they are often regarded as simply another kind of Hindus rather than a distinctive minority. Muslims are India's largest religious minority, but in Jammu and Kashmir it is the Hindus who regard themselves as a minority. (Chatterjee 1997: 460–61)

A madrasa in Ghazipur district filed a case against the rejection of its request for a grant-in-aid by the state government. The Allahabad High Court, by its judgment in April 2007, declared that Muslims could not be treated as a religious minority in UP. The state government was planning to go in appeal over the decision. (*Sakal* 6 April 2007: 1)

Ambedkar highlighted in his book, *Thoughts on Pakistan*, that:

In Savarkar's scheme, 'A Muslim is to have no advantage which a Hindu does not have. Minority is to be no justification for privilege, and majority is to be no ground for penalty. The State will guarantee Muslim religion and Muslim culture.' Ambedkar observed: 'This alternative of Mr Savarkar to Pakistan has, about it, a frankness, boldness and definiteness which distinguishes it from the irritating vagueness and indefiniteness which characterizes the Congress declarations about minority rights.' (Ambedkar 1941: 138)

In so far as a separate national state for Muslims was concerned, Ambedkar underlined that 'It is also catching because it opens up the possibilities of realizing the Muslim idea of linking up all the Muslim kindred in one Islamic State and thus avert the danger of Muslims in different countries adopting the nationality of the country to which they belong and thereby bring about the

---

²Arundhati Roy, writer and activist, rightly stated, 'In a society as diverse as India, even the idea of a majority community has to be constructed.'

disintegration of the Islamic brotherhood³...A Mussalman must be really very stupid if he is not attracted by the glamour of this new destiny and be completely transformed in his view of the place of Mussalmans in the Indian cosmos. (Ambedkar 1941: 333)

A.M. Khusro, a leading educationist and intellectual, wrote feelingly:

> For the sake of simplicity—and notwithstanding the substantial racial intermixtures—if approximately 3 per cent of Indian Muslims are taken to be Syeds and Mirs (claiming to have descended from the Prophet and Imam Ali), and if, say, 5 per cent are of Moghal descent (Mirzas, Baigs) and if 7 per cent are of Pathan descent (Khans—not the titular ones), then about 15 per cent of Muslims are seen to be of non-Indian origin (like the Aryan arrivals of, say, from 2500 to 1500 B.C.). The rest of the Muslims, no less than 85 per cent of them, are ex-Hindus of purely Indian origin whose forefathers adopted Islam: and the treatment of these foreigners is as erroneous as would be the treatment of Brahmins, Kshatriyas and all Hindus of Aryan descent, as people of a non-Indian base. Thus, by far the vast majority of Muslims in this country are of Hindu origin and the prevailing biases of foreign origin have no truth in them—unless such blame applies to the Hindu Aryan arrivals as well. And the same is true of Indian Christians, all or nearly all of whom are of Indian origin, ex-Hindus who at some stage were converted to their present faith. (Dube 2004: 18)

The Concerned Citizens' Tribunal on Gujarat, 2002,[4] which went into the Godhra carnage, has highlighted that it is necessary to remember that Muslims and Christians in this country are as

---

[3] Sir Muhammad Iqbal strongly condemned nationalism in Muslims of any non-Muslim country, including Indian Muslims in the sense of an attachment to the mother country.
[4] The tribunal comprised Justice V.R. Krishna Iyer, retired judge, Supreme Court; Justice P.B. Sawant, retired judge, Supreme Court; Justice Hosbet Suresh, retired judge, Mumbai High Court; Advocate K.G. Kannabiran, president, PUCL (People's Union for Civil Liberties); Aruna Roy of Mazdoor Kisan Shakti Sangathan; and others. The tribunal submitted its report on 24 October 2002.

much of Indian origin as are the Hindus. About 95 per cent of
the Muslims and 99 per cent of the Christians of today are those
who were originally Hindus and had voluntarily embraced their
respective religions, even while the rest might have been converted
forcibly or under duress. The higher castes and the higher classes
embraced these religions to seek pelf, power and position under the
regimes of the time, while the lower castes, who formed the vast
majority did so to escape the tyranny and exploitation of the caste
system and the rituals prevalent in Hinduism. Faiths like Buddhism,
Jainism and Sikhism were born as revolts against this very tyranny,
inequality and inhumanity. (Concerned Citizens' Tribunal–Gujarat
[henceforth CCTG] 2002: 183)

Madhu Limaye underlined:

Minorities are generally defined by Western sociologists as groups
which (a) seem and are in a state of subordination to the dominant
group; (b) are the recipient of discriminatory treatment; and
(c) are excluded from full participation in the life and culture of the
country in which they live. In this sense neither the Muslims nor
the Christians nor the Sikhs here are really suppressed minorities.
(Limaye 1988: 39)

This assessment, coming as it does from a staunch committed socialist, and not from a believer in the RSS or the BJP ideology, emphasizes the need, as brought out emphatically elsewhere, for a rethink on the whole subject of minorities.

Karan Singh, a leading intellectual, who has held a number of important public offices over the years, also made the same point: 'It is true that Muslims are in a minority (except in Jammu and Kashmir and Lakshadweep), but it is a huge minority, larger than the population of most countries in the world.' (Singh 1995: 36)

Reference may be made to the speech of Vallabhbhai Patel at Lucknow which, at the time, was regarded as the centre of Muslim culture:

I am a true friend of the Muslims, although I am described as their
greatest enemy. I believe in plain speaking. I do not know how to

mince matters. I want to tell my Muslim countrymen frankly that mere declaration of loyalty to the Indian Union will not help them at this critical juncture. They must give practical proof of their loyalty. I want to ask Indian Muslims only one question. In the recent All-India Muslim Conference, why did you not open your mouth on Kashmir issue? Why did you not condemn the action of Pakistan? Your silence on these things create doubt in the minds of the people. As a friend of Muslims, I want to say that it is your duty now to sail in the same boat with other Indians, and sink or swim together...you cannot ride two horses. (Tahmankar 1970: 244–45)

It is interesting to note that the same questions about loyalty are being asked of minorities in Europe after the rise of the ISIS (Islamic State of Iraq and Syria) and the shocking terrorist attacks in Paris in 2015. Russians are asking the same question of their minorities. It will be recalled that M.A. Jinnah too, in his Independence Day speech, said that minorities in Pakistan must have complete loyalty to that state.

M.J. Akbar, a respected journalist and former editor of *The Sunday Guardian*, wrote in the foreword to Rafiq Zakaria's book (2004):

A minority is not a function of numbers, but a definition of empowerment. As long as Muslims felt that they were an important and even decisive element of the ruling group, they did not feel that they were a minority, a term that implicitly condemns a community to the margins. In his essay, 'Minority and Minorityism: The Challenge before Indian Muslims', M. J. Akbar again emphasized that minority and majority are not the function of numbers but a derivative of empowerment. Akbar underlined that 'It is possible to argue that the only genuine minority of this country are perhaps the Dalits because they had never enjoyed political or economic power until democracy released them from the vicious trap of history.' Significantly, Akbar added: 'This is where the good news lies for Indian Muslims, who, unlike Muslims in most parts of the world, live in an uninterrupted, and now uninterruptible, democracy. There are not many Muslim communities in the world which can claim this privilege or good fortune. (Shaban 2012: 26)

I agree with Akbar's analysis. Clearly the question of minorities cannot be considered in isolation. The founding fathers, like Vallabhbhai Patel and Ambedkar, had hoped that over a period of time the artificial distinctions of majority and minority would get eroded, and minorities would become a part of the mainstream of society. Unfortunately, in today's rabble-rousing politics, we are travelling in the opposite direction by relying on and strengthening identity politics.

Saral Jhingran in the article, 'Minorityism, Majorityism, and the Category of the Community' stated:

> *There are secularists like A.S. Abraham, who assert that 'minorityism' is inherent in secularism.* Abraham argued that minorities cannot be coerced to accept any social reforms, and their consent has to be painstakingly procured by the government. Other writers, like H.Y. Siddiqui, confuse secularism with making allowances for communalism in one form or the other. Jhingran invited attention to the fact that even scholars like Durga Das Basu have argued that minority rights and minority status weaken the nation's socio-political structure. Justice H.M. Beg, who was the then-chairman of Minorities Commission, was reported to have said, 'Naming commissions as being meant for minority communities is itself misleading and encourages divisiveness'. Jhingran urged that the need for the protection of the minorities should be weighed against the development of an egalitarian, democratic, secular, socio-political order or national integration. (Narain 1995: 110–12)

Muzaffar Hussain, in his book, *Insight into Minoritism*, emphasized that:

> The Christians and the Muslims residing in India are tinged in Indian culture because they are the original inhabitants of this country. Only their beliefs are alien and as far as their culture is concerned they are fully Indians. *Hence, the Christians and the Muslims can't be called minorities*...All over the world, minority status is granted to those classes only which migrated from abroad, hence it is not proper to designate the Muslims and the Christians as aliens... It is not justified to divide them into majority and minority. (Hussain 2004: 101)

Nariman, in his lecture on minorities in 2014, invited attention to the fact that in some countries there is no linguistic equivalent for the term 'minorities'. In an official communication to the U.N. Sub-Commission on Prevention of Discrimination and Protection of Minorities, the government of Thailand stated that the concept of minorities was unknown in that country. But in India, according to Nariman, with a written Constitution, there is no difficulty in knowing who are reckoned as minorities. For this purpose, Nariman relied only on Article 29 read with Article 30, which provides that any section of citizens of India residing in India or any part of the territory of India having a distinct religion, language, script or culture of their own are minorities with the right to conserve their religion, language, script and culture. He stressed that 'One culture was anathema to the Founding Fathers.' Nariman pointed out that, historically, societies have tried to solve problems posed by the presence of a minority group by adopting one of the following four methods: forceful suppression and eradication; coercive or hostile toleration; voluntary or involuntary assimilation or absorption; or affirmative action. (Nariman 2014: 3, 5–6)

Reference may be made to the reply dated 31 March 1947 submitted by M. Ruthnaswamy to the sub-committee on minorities of the Constituent Assembly. He stated that in India, Muslims, Sikhs, Indian Christians and Anglo-Indians are 'permanent minorities', and special and peculiar safeguards for the defence and protection of their rights and interests are required in addition to the safeguards required for political minorities. These permanent minorities would never be able, or hope to be able, to influence and carry the government of any day and therefore they required certain rights to be asserted and safeguarded. (Rao 1967: 314)

Looking to the political leverage which Muslims and Sikhs enjoy, the argument put forth by Ruthnaswamy seems to have become out of date now.

Theodore P. Wright Jr. stated that, 'The concept of Hindu majority is wrong and misleading as there are many castes, sub-castes in this vast society and at many places the Hindus are in minority. Such places are J&K, Punjab, Assam, Nagaland, Arunachal Pradesh, Meghalaya.' (Singh 2005: 108)

The Maharashtra government, in an affidavit filed in the Bombay High Court, said that the eating habits of a group of persons do not make that group a 'cultural minority' entitled to protection under Article 29. The petitioners had claimed to be members of a minority group which had been eating beef as a part of their culture. The Maharashtra government has contested this by saying that the concept of culture is far above issues like what one eats. If a food habit, that too not essential food, is considered to be a part of culture, there would be thousands of minority groups in the country on this basis alone. (*IE* 6 December 2015:1)

The Merriam-Webster Dictionary defines the word 'culture' as 'behaviour typical of a group or class'. It is difficult to agree with the contention of the Maharashtra government that food habits are not relevant to culture. If that were so, the Maharashtra government itself would not have widely advertised its food items such as *puran poli, modak, thalipeeth* in national and international festivals. Kashmiri, Gujarati, Parsi food items are special to the groups of people. In fact, opposition to eating beef is also considered to be a part of Hindu culture as propagated by the BJP and its rightist allies, though this is far from true.

The Minority Fixation in India

The obsession with minorities can be primarily traced to the deliberate policy of 'divide and rule' followed by the British. As a result, Indian leaders could not get away from the concept of minorities, as is evident from the number of committees appointed before Independence and during the making of the Constitution.

The origin of the cleavage between the two communities—Hindus and Muslims—can be traced back to the period immediately following the revolt of 1857. But official recognition of the theory that the two communities could not be expected to vote together for their common good was given when Lord Minto, the then viceroy of India, recommended to the Secretary of State in October 1908, that the Muslims should be granted separate electorates: 'The Indian Muhammadans are much more than a religious body. They form in fact an absolutely separate community, distinct by marriage, food and customs, and *claiming in many cases to belong to a race different from the Hindus.*' This represented the starting point of the series of developments which eventually led in 1947 to the Partition of India into two separate countries. Step by step the recognition of communal claims and communal interests became part of the basic policy of the British government in India.

> In February 1924, T. Rangachariar moved a resolution in the central legislative assembly, calling on the government to take the necessary steps for revising the Government of India Act of 1919 so as to secure for India full self-governing Dominion Status within the British Empire and autonomy to the provinces. The debate gave an opportunity to Motilal Nehru, as the leader of the Swaraj Party in the central legislative assembly, to clear the ground for India's progress towards the status of a Dominion. The minimum demand of his party (he declared) was the summoning 'at an early date of a representative Round Table Conference *to recommend, with due regard to the protection of the rights and interests of important minorities*, the scheme of a constitution of India'. (Rao 1968b: 9)

This shows that the interest and well-being of the minorities was central to the thinking of the Constitution-makers right from the start.

In 1932, the British Prime Minister Ramsay MacDonald gave what is known as the Communal Award. This award accorded representation through separate electorates to Muslims, Europeans, Sikhs, Indian Christians and Anglo-Indians. Seats were also reserved for the Marathas in selected general constituencies in Bombay. Apart from separate electorates, a special responsibility was imposed on the governors to safeguard the legitimate interests of the minorities. One of the principal demands in connection with safeguarding the minority rights was their claim for representation in public services. From 1925, the government of India had followed the policy of reserving a certain percentage of direct appointments to government service for the redress of communal inequalities. This policy was adopted mainly with the object of securing increased representation for Muslims in public services. In 1934, this policy was placed on a formal basis, 25 per cent of all posts to be filled by the direct recruitment of Indians being earmarked for Muslims and 8.5 per cent for other minority communities. Special quotas were fixed for Anglo-Indians in subordinate posts in the Railways, Posts and Telegraphs, and certain branches of the Customs services.

In putting forward their proposals, the Cabinet Mission had in mind what they described as the 'very real Muslim apprehension that their culture and political and social life might become submerged in a purely unitary India in which the Hindus with their greatly superior numbers might be a dominant element.' (Rao 1968b: 745)

It may be recalled that Rajkumari Amrit Kaur, member of the Constituent Assembly, was against providing safeguards of any kind for minorities. She stated: 'Privileges and safeguards really weaken those that demand them...Axiomatically there is no reason why the interests of any individual or community should not be safe in the hands of a good person or persons, irrespective of their personal religion.'

K.T. Shah, another prominent member of the Constituent Assembly cautioned that:

> The rights of communities based on religion or race would have to be defined with some care and precision, so as not only to meet all the just demands for safeguarding their religion and culture, but also to prevent any abuse of the rights guaranteed to minorities as against the rest of the community. The rights of minorities were not the obligations of the majority alone, but rather the guarantees of the entire community.' (Rao 1968b: 752–53)

Special mention may be made of the speech of Ambedkar, which laid emphasis on safeguards for minorities, while presenting the Draft Constitution to the Assembly:

> The Draft Constitution is also criticized because of the safeguards it provides for minorities. In this, the Drafting Committee has no responsibility. It follows the decisions of the Constituent Assembly. Speaking for myself I have no doubt that the Constituent Assembly has done wisely in providing such safeguards for minorities as it has done. In this country both the minorities and the majorities have followed a wrong path. *It is wrong for the majority to deny the existence of minorities. It is equally wrong for the minorities to perpetuate themselves.* A solution must be found which will serve

a double purpose. It must recognize the existence of minorities to start with. *It must also be such that it will enable majorities and minorities to merge someday into one. The solution proposed by the Constituent Assembly is to be welcomed because it is a solution which serves this two-fold purpose.* To diehards who have developed a kind of fanaticism against minority protection, I would like to say two things. One is that minorities are an explosive force which, if it erupts, can blow up the whole fabric of the state. The history of Europe bears ample and appalling testimony to this fact. The other is that the minorities in India have agreed to place their existence in the hands of the majority...They have loyally accepted the rule of the majority which is basically a communal majority and not a political majority. It is for the majority to realize its duty not to discriminate against minorities. Whether the minorities will continue or will vanish must depend upon this habit of the majority. *The moment the majority loses the habit of discriminating against the minority, the minorities can have no ground to exist. They will vanish.* (Rao 1968b: 766–67)

These fond hopes of Ambedkar have unfortunately been belied, particularly in the last few years. As a result, the problem of minorities has become more acute than ever.

H.V. Kamath, in his speech on 5 November 1948, contested the claim of Ambedkar that the minorities in India had loyally accepted the rule of the majority. Kamath underlined that, if minorities had really taken this stand, India's history would have been different and would not have resulted in the creation of Pakistan. Kamath recalled that in 1927, he, as a student, attended the Madras session of the Congress. Maulana Mahomed Ali and Pandit Malaviya were both present there. 'There was a question about safeguards and Pandit Malaviya made a moving speech that went straight to the heart. He said: 'What safeguards did you ask from the Secretary of State for India or from the government of India? We are here. What better safeguards do you want?' After that speech, Maulana Mahomad Ali came to the rostrum, embraced Pandit Malaviya and said: 'I do not want any safeguards. We want to live as Indians, as part of the Indian body-politic. We want no safeguards from the British government. Pandit Malaviya is our best safeguard.' If that spirit had continued to animate us, we would have remained as united India, a single country, a single state and a single nation. This being so, I fail to understand what Dr Ambedkar means by saying that no minority in India has taken this stand. (*CAD* Vol. VII, Book 2, 2009: 220)

Sardar Bhopinder Singh Man, in his speech on November 5, 1948, raised the problem of minorities. He emphasized that before Independence, there used to be a third power which always induced minorities to become unreasonable. He said: 'I regret that as a consequence, one important minority succumbed to this temptation and adopted an unreasonable attitude and got the country partitioned. But, this cannot be said regarding other minorities... Now when there is no third power and the days of the unreasonable attitude of the minorities has come to an end, the responsibility of the majority has increased.' (*CAD* Vol. VII, Book 2, 2009: 226)

Frank Anthony, in his speech on 5 November 1948, underlined that the achievement of the goal of real secular democracy would be the greatest guarantee of any minority section in the country. Importantly, he believed that '*In 10 years there will be no minority problem in this country.*' (*CAD* Vol. VII, Book 2, 2009: 229).

It is unfortunate that these genuine hopes of a prominent leader of one of the minorities have been totally belied even sixty-six years after the Constitution came into being. There are no indications either that such an objective can be achieved any time in the near future.

M. Ananthasayanam Ayyangar, speaking on the final reading of the Draft Constitution in the Constituent Assembly on November 18, 1949, highlighted that the minority problem could not have been solved easily but thanks to the integrity of the various religious and other minorities, the separate electorates through which the British government divided one community from another and ruled it, were given up. They gave up at the outset, separate electorates for joint electorates with reservation of seats but latterly, they have given up even the reservation. Thanks to their farsightedness it marks one more step in the unification of the country...It is now left to the majority community to show that whatever religion an individual may belong to, it is only his talents and spirit of service that will count...Similar sentiments were expressed by B.A. Mandloi. Pandit Thakur Das Bhargava, who specifically mentioned that though the minorities sub-committee had preponderance of members belonging to minorities, 'They could arrive at the unanimous decision that no separate electorate or reservation was needed by the minorities... The members of the depressed classes also said that they wanted reservation only for ten years.' (*CAD* Vols X–XII, Book 5, 2009: 661–62, 674, 684)

Hansa Mehta, speaking on the final draft of the Constitution on November 22, 1949, *inter alia* stated: 'The most difficult problem that we had to tackle was the problem of minorities. Nowhere in the Constitution have we defined minorities. We accepted the definition that was given to us by the last rulers. They created religious minorities, communal minorities in order to help their policy of divide and rule and that policy has culminated in the Partition of this country. We do not want any more partitions. What do the minorities want? What can be their claims? *The Constitution guarantees equal protection of law, equality of status, equality of opportunity; the Constitution guarantees religious rights. What more can the minorities ask for? If they want privileges, that is not in the spirit of democracy.* (*CAD* Vols X–XII, Book 5, 2009: 796)

Hansa Mehta referred to another important point. She said that, while discussing the question of minorities in the Committee on Fundamental Rights, 'We also raised another point. We were anxious to consider the abolition of purdah. It is an inhuman custom which exists in parts of India. Unfortunately, we were told that raising this question would hurt the religious susceptibilities of some people. As far as the Hindu religion is concerned it does not enjoin purdah. Islam does. But, I feel that Islam will be better [if] rid of this evil. *Any evil practised in the name of religion cannot be guaranteed by the Constitution* and I hope that our Muslim friends will remember that, if not now, later on, this question is bound to come up before the legislatures.' (*CAD* Vols X–XII, Book 5, 2009: 796)

This hope has not been realized. It is not very reassuring to say that the Constitution-makers were much more perceptive and visionary than our Parliament has been even sixty-six years later. In fact now, political masters are even afraid to raise and speak on these issues in the name of secularism.

A wrong impression has been created that there was practically unanimous support for the abolition of communal electorates and reservation of seats for all except scheduled castes and scheduled tribes. However, this is far from true. Three Muslim members expressed their opposition to Patel's motion and each of them suggested a different alternative. Muhammad Saadulla from Assam, a member of the Drafting Committee, wanted the continuance of reservation for a period of ten years. Though he was personally not enamoured of reservation, the Muslim members of his party in the Assam legislature had given him a unanimous mandate to claim reservation for the Muslims, and he felt that reservation would have a 'tremendous psychological effect' on the Muslim community. He also made the interesting statement that only four members of the Muslim community had been present at the meeting of the advisory committee on 11 May 1949 and that only one of them had supported the proposal for the abolition of reservations, thereby challenging Vallabhbhai Patel's claim of unanimity. Saadulla mentioned in particular that Abul Kalam Azad had been neutral on this issue. Muhammad Ismail from Madras had not only opposed the motion for abolition of reservations but had also wanted a reversion to the previous position of separate electorates. He moved an amendment that the Assembly should approve and confirm the reservation of seats on the population basis for Muslims and other minority communities in the central and provincial legislatures, and that these seats should be filled by members elected by constituencies of voters belonging to the respective communities. He had maintained that separate electorates were the only means of bringing about harmony among the people. Z.H. Lari urged the removal of reservations for all communities and suggested instead the introduction of a system of proportional representation and cumulative voting through multi-member constituencies.

In the Constituent Assembly too, opinion was not unanimous. B. Pocker Sahib and Chaudhri Khaliquzzaman supported an amendment in favour of separate electorates so far as Muslims were concerned. Two main arguments were put forward in support of such electorates. The first was that the Muslim community had enjoyed that privilege for over forty years and 'it would be a sad thing to give rise to the feeling among the Muslims...that they are being deprived of the benefit of this institution now and that they are being ignored and their voice stifled'. Pocker Sahib made the further point that the Assembly should accept the principle that 'the best man in the particular community should represent the views of that community, and this purpose cannot be served except by means of separate electorates'. Replying to the debate, Vallabhbhai Patel strongly opposed the demand for separate electorates for Muslims and dejectedly asked, after having created Pakistan, 'Do you still want the two-nation talk to be brought here also?...Can you show me one free country where there are separate electorates? If so, I shall be prepared to accept it. But in this unfortunate country, if this separate electorate is going to be persisted in, even after the division of the country, woe betide the country, it is not worth living in.' The amendments were negated. (Rao 1968b: 468–69, 772–73)

Kazi Syed Karemuddin, speaking on the final draft of the Constitution on 21 November 1949, said:

> I take pride that I was the first man to move for the abolition of the reservation of seats at the time of the second reading of this Constitution, but I had pleaded that there should be proportional representation. Proportional representation was not given and the abolition of the reservation of seats was granted. Now it is very clear that the privileges and rights which we had enjoyed for the last sixty years exist no more and we depend on the good sense of the majority in this country for our privileges.' (*CAD* Vols X–XII, Book 5, 2009: 724)

Maulana Hasrat Mohani, speaking in the Constituent Assembly on 4 November 1949, referred to Ambedkar's remarks that the majority party should be considerate towards the minority party. Mohani contested this by saying:

We do not want them [to be considerate]. You have provided in the Constitution that 14 per cent of the seats should be reserved for the Muslims [as the position was till then]. You still consider yourself 86 per cent and Muslims to be 14 per cent. So long as you have this communalism, nothing can be done. Why do you say that Muslims are in a minority? So long as you depict them in communal colours Muslims shall remain a minority...So long as the Constituent Assembly is not elected on non-communal basis, you have no right to get a Constitution passed by this Constituent Assembly... In reality you are doing all that the British government had been doing...You should hold fresh elections on non-communal basis, on the basis of joint electorates, and then whatever Constitution you frame will be acceptable to us. We regard the Constitution framed by you worthy of being consigned to the waste paper basket. (*CAD* Vol. VII, Book 2, 2009: 46–47)

Reference must also be made to the opposition expressed by Mahboob Ali Baig Sahib Bahadur and Z.H. Lari to interference in the personal laws of Muslims. They said that a specific provision should be made in the Constitution to safeguard their personal laws as any interference would go against the secular principles. (*CAD* Vol. VII, Book 2, 2009: 297)

It can thus be seen that even after the major event of Partition, there was no change in the thinking of the Muslims and they continued to press for the continuance of the catastrophic practice of separate electorates. This shatters the deliberately created myth of change of heart of the Muslims and their unanimous support to the abolition of communal electorates and reservations.

Against this background, it is refreshing to see the thinking of someone like M.C. Chagla who contributed so much to India's public life. Chagla wrote in his autobiography that when he went to the United States as ambassador, in his first press conference he was asked whether he was a Muslim. He bluntly responded by saying, 'When I meet an American I never ask him whether he is Protestant or a Catholic or a Jew. To me he is a citizen of the United States.' He said that he failed to understand why the same attitude was not taken when dealing with the people of India. He wrote:

The Muslims, or a large majority of them, were making a great mistake in continuously emphasizing their minority status. They should join the mainstream of national life. They should not forget that they are as much Indian as their Hindu fellow citizens...I have often strongly disagreed with the government policy of constantly harping upon minorities, minority status and minority rights. It comes in the way of national unity, and emphasizes the differences between the majority community and the minority... *Frank Anthony, the Anglo-Indian leader, was a very good speaker but... [was] suspicious to discover minority grievances where there were none.* (Chagla 2000: 83–84, 452)

Muzaffar Hussain invited attention to the Supreme Court judgment by which it was held that it was not mandatory to sing the National Anthem if the students considered it to be against their religious sentiments. He stated that the students of Kerala felt that the National Anthem was against their religion and the Muslims felt that the National Song *Vande Mataram* was against Islam. Hussain apprehended that, in such a situation, the National Anthem would be only for the majority [community]. (Hussain 2004: 100)

This is a disconcerting situation. Religious freedom under the Constitution should not be permitted to extend to even not recognizing the National Anthem. This can lead to a serious law-and-order situation as happened recently when a few spectators in a movie theatre in Mumbai did not stand up when the National Anthem was being played. As if there were not enough divisive forces in the country, yet another sensitive issue should not be permitted to become a plaything in the hands of political parties.

During the Punjab Agitation in the 1980s, a number of demands were put forth by the Sikhs. Some of them, which are pertinent to the subject of this book, are briefly brought out hereafter. Article 25 Explanation I states that the wearing and carrying of kirpans shall be deemed to be included in the professing of the Sikh religion. The Akali Dal demanded that Sikhs travelling by air should be permitted to carry kirpans on domestic as well as international flights. The White Paper on the Punjab Agitation issued by the government of India in July 1984 stated that:

Although the government had always respected the constitutional provision recognizing the carrying of kirpans by Sikhs, certain restrictions had been imposed on carrying kirpans on flights after the hijacking incident of September 1981. However, in deference to the sentiments of the Sikh community, instructions were issued in February 1983 permitting Sikh passengers on domestic flights to carry kirpans which did not exceed 22.8 cm (9 inches) in length and whose blade length did not exceed 15.24 cm (6 inches). The Akali Dal representatives agreed to this. As regards international flights, it was explained that Air India could not act independently as it was bound by international regulations and conventions about the carrying of weapons.

Even while negotiations were continuing on the various demands placed earlier by the Akali Dal before the government, it raised a completely new demand in January 1984, asking for an amendment of Article 25(2) (b)[5] of the Constitution, and almost simultaneously announced an agitation which included the burning and mutilation of copies of the Constitution of India... The SGPC (Shiromani Gurdwara Parbandhak Committee) president had constituted a twenty-one member committee of experts to suggest relevant amendments to Article 25. The White Paper stated that:

> Article 25(2) (b), far from weakening the distinct identity of the Sikh community, was in fact a recognition of that identity. Nevertheless, since doubts had been raised, the home minister issued a statement on 31 March 1984 that the government would be prepared to consult the SGPC and other representatives of the Sikh community, as well as legal experts, and undertake such legislation by way of amendment as may be necessary to remove such doubts. The

---

[5]Article 25. Freedom of conscience and free profession, practice and propagation of religion... (2) Nothing in this article shall affect the operation of any existing law or prevent the State from making any law; (b) providing for social welfare and reform or the throwing open of Hindu religious institutions of a public character to all classes and sections of Hindus...Explanation II – In sub-clause (b) of clause (2), the reference to Hindus shall be construed as including a reference to persons professing the Sikh, Jaina or Buddhist religion, and the reference to Hindu religious institutions shall be construed accordingly.

SGPC was also invited to send its suggestions or proposals in this regard in order to enable the government to give the matter further consideration. The Akali Dal leaders arrested in connection with the agitation for the amendment to Article 25 were released from jail so as to create a more congenial climate for a dialogue. The Akali Dal also sought to link the demand for the amendment of Article 25 with the idea of a separate personal law for the Sikhs. However, no proposals were given to the government for consideration, nor was it made clear as to what changes were wanted in the existing laws and for what reasons. (White Paper on the Punjab Agitation 1984: 9–10, 20–21)

The policies followed by so-called secular party governments to support even the unreasonable demands of Muslims have created an adverse opinion about secularism, including among those who are not favourably inclined towards the Hindu rightist ideology. For example, the stand taken by the United Progressive Alliance (UPA) government in the Supreme Court that shariat courts were no threat to the country's judicial system. In its affidavit, the central government even defended the '*jaziya* tax' imposed by Aurangzeb as a mere 'special tax' which non-Muslims had to pay for failing to render military service. (*IE* 4 November 2006: 7). Yet another instance of this short-sighted policy was the UPA government's proposal to allocate government funding according to the proportion of various religious communities. Due to legal difficulties and widespread opposition, the proposal had to be given up.

On 20 January 2014, the government of India met with a long-standing demand of the Jain community and declared Jains as India's sixth religious minority community after Muslims, Christians, Sikhs, Buddhists and Zoroastrians. Rajat Ghai, in his article, 'United by Dharma, Divided by Law', contested the treatment of Sikhs, Jains and Buddhists as being part of the Hindu religion. He argued for the need to have separate personal laws for these communities. (http://www.business-standard.com/article/opinion)

At present, only Sikhs have a separate marriage law of their own—the Anand Marriage Act. The Buddhists in Maharashtra also asked for a separate marriage law and the government of Maharashtra seemed to be favourably inclined, though a section of Buddhists headed by Prakash

Ambedkar opposed the move. The stand taken by the government of Maharashtra in the matter is also intriguing, keeping in view the unambiguous position of the BJP on an early enactment of a uniform civil code.

> The RSS and the BJP expressed their opposition in recent years to the setting up of a minorities commission at the Centre and in the states. Instead, they have been advocating that these responsibilities could be entrusted to the The National Human Rights Commission (NHRC) of India. However, Shyama Prasad Mukherjee, who later founded the Jan Sangh, suggested the setting up in each province of a minorities commission, consisting of the representatives of minorities, to advise on the protection of minority interests. He suggested the reservation of seats in legislatures for important minorities. He and Jairamdas Daulatram also sought the inclusion of representatives of minority communities in the council of ministers. (Rao 1968b: 753)

It can be seen how far the BJP has travelled from the position of S.P. Mukherjee.

Right to Freedom of Religion

Articles 25–28 pertaining to the right to freedom of religion and Articles 29–30 regarding cultural and educational rights of minorities are central to the discussion on the subject. Ambedkar had also expressly enjoined the State not to 'recognize any religion as the State religion'.

At the instance of Harnam Singh, 'the right to wear and carry kirpans' was recognized as part of the practice of the Sikh religion.[6] (Rao 1968b: 258). This is interesting in the context of the raging controversy in France in particular, and some other European countries, about permitting Muslim women to wear headscarfs and for Sikh men to wear turbans. It is striking how liberal the view of the Constitution-

---

[6]Sikhs have been enjoined by their religion to abjure tobacco and wear the five ks—*kesh* (long hair), *kangha* (a comb), *kuchha* (shorts), *kara* (a steel or iron amulet) and *kirpan* (a small steel dagger).

makers was on this subject even as far back as 1947–48.

Reference must be made to an important point made by Rajkumari Amrit Kaur regarding encouraging minorities to establish and administer educational institutions of their choice. She was highly perceptive in her objection that this would perpetuate communal institutions in the country. (Rao 1968b: 273 Footnote 1)

Commenting on the use of the term 'minorities' in the provision pertaining to the setting up of cultural and educational institutions, B.N. Rau, constitutional adviser, pointed out that:

> The term had not been defined anywhere in the Constitution and that the existing position was so vague that even the declaration of a particular language as the national language could be said to prejudice the interests of the minorities whose mother tongue happened to be different. A comprehensive definition of 'minorities' was difficult to frame. They might be based on religion, community or language; but *to leave a vague justiciable right to undefined minorities was also quite unsatisfactory. B.N. Rau therefore suggested for consideration whether the cultural and educational rights conferred by the provision should at all be made justiciable.* (Rao 1968b: 275)
>
> When the revised draft of the Constitution came up for discussion on 16 November 1949, T.T. Krishnamachari suggested in an amendment that the words, 'certain classes', be substituted for the word 'minorities' wherever it occurred. This was necessary, he pointed out, in view of the objections raised by some members to the use of the word 'minorities' in the heading of this Part and also the consequential use of this word elsewhere. The amendment was adopted by the Assembly, and the heading was changed to 'Special provisions relating to certain classes'. (Rao 1968b: 780).

It is interesting to see that some members raised objections even to the use of the word 'minorities'.

> Reference may be made to a suggestion made by Ambedkar which, unfortunately, did not receive any support. He suggested that a candidate belonging to a majority community should, before being

declared elected, get a minimum number of votes from among the minority communities in his constituency. This would amount to a minority exercising a sort of veto on the majority communities. As was to be expected, nobody except Ambedkar himself was in favour of the proposal. (Rao 1968b: 755–56)

I have suggested, in Chapter 6, a variant on the same point to say that it should be made incumbent on a candidate to get a minimum of 50 per cent plus one vote to be declared elected. This alternative has a further merit in that it gets away from the divisive concepts of 'majority' and 'minority' and takes a holistic view of the constituency.

The deep interest which the Congress party in general, and Vallabhbhai Patel in particular, had in promoting the interests of minorities can be seen from the fact that he requested K.C. Reddi, chief minister of Mysore State, on 30 November 1947, to ensure that a reasonable number of Christian representatives were sent to the Mysore Constituent Assembly. Patel wrote:

> I feel that the request is reasonable. It is in our own interests that we should give ample proof of consideration and regard for the minorities. We should see that the minorities feel a sense of security and confidence in the majority. From all these points of view, I hope you will examine the position and see that the Indian Christian community in your state is adequately represented in your Constituent Assembly. (Das Vol. 5, 1973: 419)

Vallabhbhai Patel, speaking at the first meeting of the Advisory Committee on 27 February 1947, stated:

> Often you must have heard in various debates in British Parliament [in relation to India]...that they have a special responsibility, a special obligation, for the protection of the interest of the minorities. They claim to have more special interest than we have. It is for us to prove that it is a bogus claim, a false claim, and that nobody can be more interested than us in India in the protection of our minorities...In this committee...we begin our work today with a determination and a desire to come to decisions not by majority

but by uniformity. Let us sink all our differences and look to one and one interest only, which is the interest of all of us—the interest of India as a whole. (Rao 1967: 66)

Constitution-making: Some Salient Features

Reference should be made to some special features of Constitution-making in India. In a memorandum on minorities submitted by Rajkumari Amrit Kaur to the Sub-committee on Minorities on 20 March 1947, she raised some very pertinent issues:

> I hold that every question in connection with the framing of a just and righteous Constitution for our country should be looked upon, by and large, from the point of view of a citizen. If this standpoint is fundamentally correct it follows that the primary duty of the committee appointed to look into the problem of minorities is to suggest such ways and means as will help to eradicate the evil of separatism rather than expedients or palliatives which might, in the long run, only contribute to its perpetuation...Privileges and safeguards really weaken those that demand them...I am of the opinion that no minority should demand any safeguards but should be brave enough to rely solely on the goodwill of the majority and its own inherent moral strength...It is a big tragedy that the task of framing the Constitution has come to us at the time when hatred and mistrust dominate the minds of men...While consistently holding that safeguards for minorities are wholly undesirable, I nevertheless fear that the appeal for a non-demand of all such will today be a lone cry. (Rao 1967: 309–11)

Amrit Kaur, in her letter to B.N. Rau written jointly with Hansa Mehta, dated 31 March 1947, made some important suggestions:

> ...there are several customs practised in the name of religion... We are naturally anxious that no clause in the fundamental rights shall make impossible future legislation for the purpose of wiping out these evils...Indeed we have a further fear that validity of

existing laws, such as the Sarda Act and the Widow Remarriage Act, may even be questioned...It would appear that section 299 of the Government of India Act is more progressive and fair enough and would therefore meet our purpose better. (Rao 1967: 146–47)

Though the Constitution of India recognizes Jains, Buddhists and Sikhs as part of the Hindu community, the question of whether they should be considered as Hindus has been raised from time to time. This was also brought up before the Rau Committee on Hindu law. The committee noted:

Evidence was tendered to us by a Buddhist Association in Madras that Buddhists do not wish to be governed by the Hindu law. This Association expressed a preference to be governed instead by the Burmese Buddhist Law. We are by no means satisfied that this preference is shared by Buddhists in general, especially in other parts of the country. The Hindu Law now applies to Buddhists and, in our opinion, should continue to do so. (Hindu Law Committee [henceforth HLC] 1947: 36)

Similarly, Jains contended before the Rau Committee that the Jain law differed in certain respects from the Hindu law and that there should be a separate code for the Jains. The committee had, however, stated:

We are not in favour of this course. The differences are admittedly not many and none of them can be considered to be of a fundamental character or more important than those which exist between members of one Hindu community and another. The present position is that the ordinary Hindu law applies to Jains in the absence of proof of any special custom or usage varying that law. (Paragraph 613 of Mulla's *Hindu Law*, 10th Edition.) We are accordingly of the opinion that the [Hindu] Code should apply to Jains also. (HLC 1947: 36)

The biggest concern of the Constituent Assembly was to ensure that communal electorates and weightages, which had led to a serious divide between Hindus and Muslims and to the eventual Partition of the country, were done away with under any circumstances. After achieving this aim, the Congress party was in a frame of mind to agree to several other demands of the minorities. These included the right to propagation, the setting up of minority educational institutions, giving them special protection and so on. Interestingly, the Sikhs too, demanded communal electorates and weightages, on the same lines as the Muslims.

In April 1949, the Jains represented that they should not be treated as Hindus for purposes of the Harijan Temple Entry Act. 1947. They requested that the government should issue a notification exempting Jains from the provisions of the Act. Vallabhbhai Patel wrote to B.G. Kher, prime minister of Bombay Province, to look into the matter. In his reply, Kher stated that:

> The Jain religion has never so far been accepted as distinctly separate from the Hindu religion in the same sense as Christianity or Parsee religion has been. The generally accepted view is that it is a dissenting sect of the Hindus like Buddhism or the Lingayat sect. Save in minor variations depending upon customs and usages, ordinarily Hindu law has all along been applied to Jains...The statement that there are no Harijans at all among the Jains is not generally accepted. As there are Harijans among Jains, it would be all the more necessary to remove the disabilities of those Harijans as well.
>
> Kher emphasized that one essential provision of the Bombay Harijan Temple Entry Act, 1947, was that the temple was thrown open to Harijans in the same manner and to the same extent as to any member of the Hindu community or any section thereof. Kher therefore said that it would not be possible to exempt the Jains from the purview of the Act. (Das 1974: 68–71)

Arun Shourie rightly urged, 'We are regressing back to our religious identities—more and more of us are once again looking upon ourselves as "Sikhs" or "Muslims" or "Hindus" rather than as Indians. Each is thus distancing himself from the other—the "Us" from "Them". Sikh fundamentalism has already taken its toll in blood. (Shourie 1993a: 22) The latest case of encouraging separate religious identity is of the Gujarat government giving minority status to the Jain community. (*IE* 8 May 2016: 5)

The virus of communalism and identity politics has seeped into the communities to such an extent that the Muslims were agitated because Aligarh Muslim University (AMU) was not being declared a minority institution. The Congress, as also the Janata government, had taken a principled position on the subject and had held that AMU was a national institution and was not meant only as a Muslim institution, just as Banaras Hindu University was not a Hindu institution. The question of recognizing AMU as a minority institution was even taken up in the Supreme Court. But the Court declared that, among other considerations, since AMU had not been established by the Muslims and since it was not meant only for Muslims, it could not claim to be a minority institution.

> A private member's bill, introduced by Triloki Singh, proposed that AMU should be 'deemed to have been established at the instance of Muslims of India'. In his speech in the Rajya Sabha on 28 July 1978, he said that it would be open to Parliament to pass a bill conferring minority character upon AMU. Its very name implied its Muslim character. It was not Calcutta University or Bombay University or Lucknow University. It was Aligarh Muslim University. (*RSD* Vol. 106.1, 1978: 241–42)
>
> Pratap Chandra Chunder, minister of education in the Janata government, underlined in the Rajya Sabha, on 1 December 1978, that the main thrust of the subject was the minority character of the university. Under Article 30 of the Constitution, a minority can establish an institution and has the right to administer it as well. The implication is that, in such an event, the government, or for that matter even Parliament, would not be in a position to interfere in the administration of the institution. In spite of the Supreme Court decision mentioned earlier, the matter was discussed in the Rajya Sabha for three full days. Finally, the government amended the AMU Act to give more autonomy to the university. (*RSD* Vol. 107.1, 1978: 138–47)

What is troubling is that, even in matters pertaining to well-established educational institutions of national importance, the religious identity of the institution, rather than its academic credentials, is considered its most important attribute.

The identity politics came to the fore once again when the Child Marriage Restraint (Amendment) Bill, 1978, was introduced in the Rajya Sabha by the Minister of Law, Shanti Bhushan. The Bill sought to amend the Child Marriage Restraint Act, 1929, and to make certain consequential amendments in the Indian Christian Marriage Act, 1872, and the Hindu Marriage Act, 1955.

Doubts were expressed about whether the provisions of the bill would be implemented at all, as had happened in the case of the 1929 Act. S.K. Vaishampayen underlined the 1971 census data to show that the 1929 Act had more or less remained on paper. He said:

> I will give the figures on child marriages between the ages of ten and fourteen among males. The figure (is) 1.5 million. In the same age group, the number of child marriages among girls is 3.7 million. The next age group is between the ages of fifteen and nineteen. Here, the figure for males is 4.3 million whereas among the girls the number of child marriages in this age group is 12.5 million. The figures are revealing. If you try to put all the figures together, then you will find that there are 22.1 million child marriages in our country...There are also instances where child marriages take place in certain parts of the country below the age of ten years.
>
> Hamid Ali Schamnad said:
>
> This enactment would firstly offend the sentiments and feelings of some of the people and minority Muslims...There should be an exemption clause...I quite agree that social reforms are necessary. I also agree that social problems are there in this country; but we cannot solve these social problems, or we cannot make people socially reformed by enactments.
>
> After long discussion, the bill was finally passed by the Rajya Sabha on 2 March 1978. (*RSD* Vol. 104.1, 1978: 131–35, 168, 222)

The outcome of the Adoption of Children Bill, 1972, introduced in the Rajya Sabha on 18 July 1978 by Minister of Law Shanti Bhushan, is eminently relevant for the discussion on India's secularism. The bill had been originally brought in by the Congress party and introduced in

1972. Thereafter, it was referred to the Joint Select Committee which approved the bill with some minor amendments. The then Minister of Law H.R. Gokhale, was a member of the Select Committee. In the meanwhile, Muslims are reported to have represented to the then Prime Minister Indira Gandhi that the bill would be against the personal law of the Muslims and would never be acceptable to them. Though not made public, the bill was kept in cold storage and it was resurrected only after the Janata government came to power.

Apart from the Muslim members, the bill was stoutly opposed by Congress party members. In fact, the vehemence of the opposition by the Congress party was striking. Shyam Lal Yadav urged that:

> The initiative for such changes should come from the Muslims only. Only then it can universally be accepted. It is in view of these considerations that the Congress party gave out an assurance that the Muslim Personal Law would not be touched unless the Muslims wanted it and that is why, I think, this bill was kept in cold storage for so many years. I do not know what has prompted this government now to bring it forward...

Yadav further said that the Constitution guaranteed secularism and equal respect for all religions. He challenged the government to hold a referendum on this matter among the Muslims. Shanti Bhushan countered Shyam Lal by saying that it was a bill prepared by his own party and most of the members of the Joint Select Committee were also from his party. Yadav quipped, 'I do not know why you are carrying this dead baby. Let it be buried.'

Mohammad Yunus Saleem urged that the bill should be withdrawn. Several other Muslim members expressed their strong opposition and said that if the bill was to be passed, Muslims should be exempted from it. They pressed:

> Thousands and thousands of representations have been made by way of letters, telegrams, resolutions and memoranda to the effect that the Muslims in India should be exempted from the purview of this bill. More than 1000 Muslim witnesses appeared before the committee to give their evidence in their individual and collective

capacities. Ulemas (Muslim scholars) of undisputed repute belonging to such scholastic orders as, Darul Uloom of Deoband, Nadwathul Ulema of Lucknow, Imarath Shariah of Bihar and Orissa, Jamiathul Ulema of India, appeared before the joint select committee. Muslim advocates turned up in a great number. Muslim ladies came forth to express their views. The Muslim Personal Law Board, though of late origin, also tendered its evidence. The Muslim evidence is altogether non-political in its character and deals with the issues from the religious point of view only. The summary of evidence circulated to us by the Law Department says that *99 per cent of the Muslim evidence is against the bill.*

Khurshed Alam Khan said:

Mrs Indira Gandhi had given us an assurance that the bill would not affect the fundamental rights or the Muslim personal law in any way...The scope of the bill has been enlarged...to cover all the communities...This is going to open the floodgate for the future and *this is the first step, as they say, towards a common civil code...* Among the Muslims adoption is not allowed by the Quranic law or the Muslim personal law... The institution of adoption is unknown to the Quranic laws...*We are very keen that we should be part of this country in all respects, but our separate identity must remain intact. We do not want any infringement of that identity; we do not want to lose our identity.*

Khan further emphasized:

We are minority community but we are not such an insignificant minority community that you can ignore us completely.

After extensive discussion lasting over two days, in his reply, Shanti Bhushan thoroughly exposed the Congress party for its role in first sponsoring the bill and later opposing it so vehemently. Finally, Shanti Bhushan concluded his speech by saying that 'In deference to the sentiments expressed by various Members from both the sides, I would like to move for leave to withdraw this bill.' (*RSD* Vol. 106.1, 1978:

231, 238, 242–43, 246, 289, 300–04 of 18 July 1978; 225–30 of 19 July 1978)

Successive governments at the Centre have pandered to the unjustified demands of Muslims, thereby confirming the impression amongst the Muslim community itself that it is the fundamentalists and rabid Muslims, rather than the liberal and progressive amongst them, who carry weight with the government. For example, Salman Rushdie's novel, *The Satanic Verses,* was banned because some Muslim extremists were offended by the references to Prophet Muhammad.

Religious Endowments

The question of the proper management of wakfs had been causing concern to the British government even before Independence. On 29 June 1927, the Legislative Council of the United Provinces passed a resolution recommending that the government 'appoint a committee to advise what effective steps should be taken for the better governance, administration and supervision of Muslim public and charitable Waqf.' The government resolution dated 30 January 1932 stated that the report of the committee had recommended:

> ...the 'formation of district Waqf committees and the setting up of a Protector of Auqaf with superintendents and power to appoint auditors designed to remedy such defects as its investigation of the present management of the Auqaf has brought to light. Although the committee has found a great deal of mismanagement, the conditions of many of the Auqaf unsatisfactory and a large number of mutawallis violating the duties that the law imposes on them, it has wisely and as a matter of principle refrained from going into the details of individual cases of maladministration except in so far as this has been necessary for elucidating the principles underlying its recommendations. (Muslim Public and Charitable Waqf Committee, United Provinces, 1932: 1–2)

In keeping with the policy of the British government of appeasing the Muslims, individual cases of maladministration were consciously overlooked.

After Independence, the government of India 'found that the administration of the Dargah Khwaja Saheb, Ajmer, one of the holiest Muslim shrines in India, and its temporal affairs have since a long time been seriously affected by factions and departure of majority of members of the Committee of Management after the Partition of India have nearly brought about a deadlock'. It was therefore decided to appoint a committee on 14 January 1949 and to make suitable recommendations in the matter. Among other things, the committee recommended that the future administration of the Dargah should be entrusted to a small high-powered committee of Muslims in place of the unwieldy committee of 25 members under the Act of 1936. The committee also recommended that persons who have any beneficial interest in the Dargah should be rigorously excluded from being appointed either to the high-powered committee or to the office of the manager. (Dargah Khwaja Saheb [Ajmer] Committee of Enquiry, 1949: 91–92)

The Muslim Wakfs Bill, 1952, was considered by the Select Committee of the House of the People which submitted its report in March 1954. The committee felt that, in order to give effect to its decisions, it would be more convenient to redraft the bill introduced by the government and accordingly, it had done so. However, it recommended that in four states, namely, West Bengal, Bihar, Uttar Pradesh and Delhi, there were already state Acts relating to wakfs. Therefore, it recommended that the proposed Central Act should not be applied to these states against the wishes of the state governments. There were two minutes of dissent to the report. The first, that of Mohan Lal Saksena, urged that, since the subject was in the Concurrent List and since at least ten states were opposed to any central enactment on the subject, the proposed Act should not be extended to the states. However, there should be no objection to a model central Act being enacted which the states could consider. Interestingly, the second minute of dissent, by Amjad Ali, was quite contrary to the above. Ali urged:

> In the light of experience gained, it is necessary to apply this piece of legislation to the whole of India and more fully in those places or states where there are more Wakfs in number. It is common

knowledge that Wakf properties wherever they obtained were being mismanaged or not properly managed, and in most cases Wakf property had gone into the hands of designing and unscrupulous persons who had considered them as their personal and private property... The need for better supervision and good governance of those Wakfs now existing and also for those that are to come, this piece of legislation should be made applicable to the whole of India without making any exceptions. (Select Committee, The Muslim Wakfs Bill, 1952, March 1954: i, viii–ix)

The Wakf Enquiry Committee was first constituted on 9 December 1970. However, the committee could not commence its work till January 1973 due to various reasons beyond its control. In view of the judgments of Rajasthan and Punjab High Courts which adversely affected the functioning of the Wakf Boards, the committee decided to give an interim report suggesting immediate remedial measures. The report also commented on the unauthorized occupation of Wakf properties and the unsatisfactory financial position of Wakf Boards and Wakf Institutions. (Wakf Enquiry Committee Interim Report, 1973: i, iii, 14–17)

During the discussion in the Rajya Sabha and the Lok Sabha on 23 July and 27 August 1984, respectively, when amendments to the Central Wakf Act were being discussed, the comments of Muslim MPs proved the seriousness of the mismanagement of the wakfs. While piloting the bill on 23 July, the law minister told the Rajya Sabha at some length and with some emphasis:

'But you have to admit, though I do not want to say it, our brothers, our Muslim brothers, our *mutawallis*, our board members are the ones who have done all this.' 'The anger you have', he told the Muslim members, 'the anger you have in your heart is very little against me, it is largely against your associates...You pointed out to what happened in Punjab, Haryana...Who were the members? Your Muslim brothers and mine.' The bitter truth is that unfortunately, no reform movement has arisen among Muslims to set the Wakfs right. (Shourie 1993a: 278–79)

Rajya Sabha Joint Parliamentary Committee on Wakf had

comprehensively studied the problems of management of Wakfs and after carrying out a survey of Wakfs, once again noticed a number of common failings. These included encroachment of Wakf properties, pathetic condition of finances of Wakf Boards, Wakf matters under adjudication and Wakf tribunals, Wakf properties and problems with the Archaeological Survey of India, need for a new approach in leasing of Wakf properties, need for empowering Central Wakf Council, etc. The report had also appended a list of ten reports presented by the earlier Joint Parliamentary Committees on the functioning of Wakf Boards and eight reports presented by the present committee. (Joint Parliamentary Committee on Wakf, 2008: 167–207, 211–12)

The above details bring out the serious concerns which have been expressed from time to time regarding the functioning and management of wakfs. Unfortunately, adequate action has not been taken to remedy the situation.

In comparison, questions are often raised regarding the government's undue and excessive interference in matters pertaining to Hindu religious institutions. It is argued that this gross interference in the religious affairs of Hindus is a negation of the principles of secularism. As I have argued earlier, Indian secularism is *sui generis*. The Constitution has specifically empowered the government to look into the affairs of religious institutions whenever it is considered as a matter of public interest.

On 1 March 1960, the government of India appointed a high-level Hindu Religious Endowments Commission (1960–62). It comprised Dr C.P. Ramaswami Aiyar as chairman; Sankar Saran, retired judge, Allahabad High Court; Mahabir Prasad, Advocate General, Bihar; Swami Harinarayanan, general secretary, Bharat Sadhu Samaj; and P. Kameswara Rau, retired commissioner, Hindu Religious Endowments Board, Madras. Later, K. Venkataswami Naidu, advocate, Madras, and K.C. Sen, retired judge, Bombay High Court were appointed as additional members.

The report of the Commission proves how widespread the mismanagement, the defalcations and the lack of accountability were in a number of religious institutions in the country. Appendix xiii of the report of the Commission (pp. 382–89) has a state-wise list of alleged complaints against individuals or individual bodies brought to the notice of the Commission. The report brought out that (only) Andhra Pradesh (Telangana area), Gujarat, Maharashtra and Mysore (the area added from the old Hyderabad state) had enacted legislations for dealing not only with Hindu but also with Christian, Muslim, Jain and other endowments connected with non-Hindu religions. In the former state of Hyderabad, a large extent of which is now merged with the Andhra Pradesh state, all religious endowments (whether Hindu, Muslim or otherwise) came under the control of a body which, without interfering with the internal religious affairs of any institutions, provides for the proper management and utilization of the funds of temples, maths, wakfs and other such institutions.

The Commission stated that:

Certain important witnesses from Bombay, Hyderabad and other places, including representatives of the state governments concerned, have in their testimony before the Commission been emphatic in declaring that no difficulty has been or will be experienced in implementing comprehensive legislation which deals alike with Hindu, Muslim, Christian and other endowments, and certain other basic regulations in respect of them. These witnesses have stated that many advantages had accrued from uniform legislation dealing with all communities and not confined solely to Hindus... In fact, it may be added that several persons who have submitted memoranda as well as those who have tendered oral evidence have taken strong exception to an enquiry like ours which is conducted solely with the advertence to Hindu institutions. The gravamen of such complaints is that the enquiry seeks to discriminate between the Hindu community and other communities and to penalize it in contradistinction to other communities whose endowments are being left untouched...We are...of the opinion that we would be failing in our duty if this point of view and the strength of the feelings entertained in this regard were not brought to the notice of the government of India. In this connection we would like to invite attention to the provisions of Article 44 of the Constitution... In the light of the opinions expressed by the governments and the persons in charge of the practical administration of the laws in force in Hyderabad, Gujarat and Maharashtra, we take the view that there is no insuperable difficulty or complication in enabling a uniform type of legislation dealing with the religious endowments of all communities in India...The legislation recommended by us relates to topics which appertain to the Concurrent List.

The Commission also recommended certain amendments to the Constitution, so as to avoid unnecessary litigation under Article 26, elucidating the following points:

- That all temples, maths and other institutions to which the public resort as of right or by tradition or custom for the purpose of worship, religious training or performing or discharging vows and/or institutions that accept gifts, donations and offerings from the members of the public without the right to refuse such offerings should be treated as public trust in the sense that the public or a section thereof are interested in and have the right to enforce their proper administration and management.
- The fact that the management of either the temple or the math is in the hands of persons or groups historically connected with the foundation of the institution or in the hands of persons who claim to have acquired proprietary or other vested interests in the image or the temple associated with an image can make no difference with regard to the essential character of the institution.
- Gifts and offerings can never be private property in the ordinary sense of the term although a portion of the income or accumulation of the math properties may be utilized for the maintenance and proper dignity and traditional status of the head of the math...(Report of the Hindu Religious Endowments Commission (1960–62), 1962: 30, 146)

No action appears to have been taken on any of these recommendations. Like several other reports, this report too, appears to have been consigned to government archives.

V.M. Bachal, in his doctoral thesis, wrote:

The problems relating to the secular administration of endowments of all communities, Hindus and Muslims, are alike. The general principles as regards their management are also, more or less, the same. The approach adopted by the courts in interpreting legislation regarding these endowments is also the same. As recommended by the report of the Hindu Religious Endowments Commission, there should be 'no insuperable difficulty or complication in enacting a uniform legislation dealing with the religious endowments of all communities in India...Such legislation should of course incorporate such special provisions as may be considered necessary for the endowments of individual religions or communities.' (Bachal 1975: 215–16)

The Sachar Committee too had expressed concern at the mismanagement of Wakf properties. It suggested that The Public Premises (Eviction of Unauthorised Occupation) Act, 1971 should be applied to remove encroachments from Wakf properties, and arrears of rent, at market rates, should be recovered as arrears of land revenue. It also suggested that the exemption of Wakf properties from some enactments such as The Rent Control Act, The Land Reforms Act, The Agricultural Land Ceiling Act, The Indian Registration Act, Tenancy Act, etc., would serve the greater philanthropic purpose of Wakf properties. (GOI 2006: 234)

National Minorities Commission

It is significant to note that it was not the Congress government but the Janata government under Morarji Desai—of which the BJP was an important constituent—which set up the National Minorities Commission (NMC) by an executive order. Mohammad Yunus Saleem raised a discussion in the Rajya Sabha and pressed that:

'The formation of the Commission by an executive order would not solve the problem unless statutory sanctity is granted to the Commission.' Otherwise, he said, the recommendations of the Commission would not bind either the state governments or the Central government. Saleem raised this question again in the Rajya Sabha on 18 July 1978 saying that, in spite of the assurance given by the home minister in the consultative committee meeting that a suitable amendment would be introduced to amend the Constitution giving the Commission constitutional status, and though two sessions of Parliament had passed, no such bill had been introduced. (*RSD* Vol. 106.1, 1978: 217–22)

The government introduced the Constitution (Forty-sixth Amendment) Bill, 1978, to add Article 338-A to give constitutional status to the Minorities Commission. However, when brought before the Lok Sabha in May 1979, the bill fell through as it could not attract even a quorum in the House. (Kumar 1985: 238)

The NMC was empowered to:

- Look into specific complaints regarding the deprivation of rights and the safeguards of the minorities, and take up such matter with the authorities;
- Suggest appropriate measures in respect of any minority to be undertaken by the central government or the state governments.

The Objects and Reasons of the National Commission for Minorities Act stated:

> The main task of the Commission shall be to evaluate the progress of the development of minorities, monitor the working of the safeguards provided in the Constitution for the protection of the interests of minorities and in laws enacted by the Central government or state governments, besides looking into specific complaints regarding deprivation of rights and safeguards of the minorities.

In his lecture, which had been organized by the NMC, Fali Nariman expressed his dissatisfaction with its effectiveness in discharging its responsibilities. He stated:

> I do implore the Commission and its distinguished members to take steps as an independent commission *set up by Parliament and not controlled by government*, to actively move to safeguard the interests of the minorities. It is as important as giving educational facilities and improving the economic condition of the minorities

which the Commission and the government are rightly pursuing.

Those who indulge in hate speech must be prevented by court processes initiated at the instance of the Commission because that is the body that represents minorities in India. Whoever indulges in such hate speech or vilification (whatever the community to which they belong) they must be proceeded against and the proceeding must be widely publicized. It is only then that the confidence of the minorities in the NMC will get restored. I would respectfully suggest that if we minorities do not stand up for the rights of minorities and protest against such hate speeches and diatribes, how do we expect the government to do so?...The Commission is an independent statutory body. Its chairman is not a minister of government. And though it receives grant from the Central government *it is not expected to be a mere mouthpiece of that government.* (Nariman 2014: 7)

M.S. Golwalkar said that he would like the scope of the National Minorities Commission to be enlarged to make it a Human Rights Commission, so that any aggrieved section could approach it for redress. (Malkani 1980: 106)

The question of the neglect of the National Minorities Commission often figured in the media, as also in Parliament. For example, Nitish Kumar raised this subject in the Lok Sabha on 26 April 1993 and urged that the Commission be given a constitutional status:

Though the Commission had been set up about one year ago, yet the post of the chairman had been lying vacant. As a result the work of the Commission has come to a standstill. Even the annual report of the Commission for the financial year 1992–93 had not been submitted. The vacancy of the Parsee member was also lying vacant for the past several months. (*LSD* Vol. 21.1, 1993: 321)

This matter was raised once again on 13 May 1993 by Mohd. Khaleeur Rahman who said that, though the Commission had been given statutory recognition, a requisite notification had still not been issued and therefore it was functioning without any statutory powers. Rahman added: 'What is worse is that it has been functioning without a chairman since April 1992 and a Parsee member since November 1990...The trend of anti-secular forces has disturbed communal harmony and this can be checkmated only by a healthy and effective Minorities Commission.' (*RSD* Vol. 167.3, 1993: 436)

S. Ubaidur Rahman was highly critical of the working of the Commission. The National Minorities Commission had always remained a lame duck. According to him:

> It seemed 'to suffer from in-built inefficiencies compounded by ineffectiveness of the people who are at the helm...When Gujarat is burning for the last two months, the Commission not only failed in doing anything...but has also failed to condemn the government's siding with the marauders...Even a few days ago when the Gujarat pogrom was at its height the Commission was trying, though in vain, to rope in some disgruntled self-styled Muslim leader to sit with the RSS and talk what they want...Is there any need to continue with this farce and why should it continue?...It is not the case of the National Commission for Minorities alone, similar commissions in different states are also suffering from similar maladies. (http:// www. milligazette.com/Archives/01062002)
>
> Asghar Ali Engineer bluntly stated that the National Minorities Commission 'is hardly effective and has not succeeded in achieving its purpose. Its reports are not even tabled in Parliament and these reports are in no way binding to [*sic*] the government of India. The people do not even come to know when the NMC submitted its report and what are its contents. Its reports are not even properly publicized. (Engineer 2009: 190)

A sad commentary, indeed. Institution-building has never been India's strong point.

3

ARE THESE SIGNPOSTS OF SECULARISM?—I

The Hindu Code Bill will be a hundred times more beneficial to India than the Constitution. We are building a new society here and we are doing it by justice and law.

—Dr B.R. Ambedkar in the Constituent Assembly (Legislative)

I have been troubled by the way India has worked its secular Constitution, raising serious doubts about whether it is a secular nation. In this chapter, I have dealt with the following issues:

- Hindu Code—the cry of a religion in danger;
- Uniform civil code—time to make a beginning;
- The enactment of the Muslim Women (Protection of Rights on Divorce) Act;
- The propagation of religion;
- The protection of minority educational institutions; and
- The banning of cow slaughter.

We begin the discussion with the codification of the Hindu law and bring out a few important features of the initiative. One, it shows how necessary and overdue the reform was. Two, but for the strong support of Nehru and Ambedkar, it would have been impossible to bring it about so speedily. Three, it highlights the intense, persistent and vocal opposition to the reform from conservative Hindu elements. Four, it underlines that it would have been impossible to sustain the reform except for the insignificant but bold liberal element in Hindu society. Fifth, in spite of repeated suggestions, the reforms were not extended to Muslim and Christian personal laws. Finally, it shows the kind of efforts which will have to be made and the political will which will be necessary if a uniform civil code is to be made a reality in the foreseeable future.

Hindu Code—the Cry of a Religion in Danger

In the following discussion, I have traced the evolution of enactments pertaining to Hindu law. These show how far Hindu society has progressed over the years, in spite of stiff opposition from the highly organized conservative and orthodox elements in it.

> From Jawaharlal Nehru's article in *The Hindustan Times* dated 20 October 1940, it can be seen that Nehru was keen on bringing about a number of changes in Hindu law to bring it in consonance with modern thinking on the subject. He had written about the need for 'extension of the Civil Marriage Act to cover marriages between any two persons, to whatever religion they may belong, without any renunciation of religion, as at present. This will of necessity be optional.' Nehru had also talked about another desirable step to have records kept of all marriages. He had also written that divorce laws, especially for the Hindus, are a crying need. (Gopal and Iyengar Vol. I 2003: 39)

P.B. Gajendragadkar, former chief justice of India, in his article, 'Secularism: Its Implications for Law and Life in India', brought out how, over the years, Hindu law became rigid and inflexible:

> It was about 1868 that the Privy Council pronounced its judgment in the case of *Collector of Madura v. Moottoo Ramalinga*. By this judgment, the Privy Council advised the judges administering Hindu law in India to remember that *'under the Hindoo system of law, clear proof of usage will outweigh the written text of law'*; but custom which, according to the Privy Council, would

outweigh the written text of the law, had to be ancient, certain and reasonable; and in course of time, the test prescribed by judicial decisions for proving these three distinct constituents of a valid custom became so rigid and inflexible that custom which grew in society from time to time consistently with the change in the dictates of social conscience, failed to make any impact on the growth of Hindu law; and inevitably, the letter of the law, and particularly the opinions of commentators, began to play an exclusive and dominant role in the interpretation of Hindu law. (Gajendragadkar in Sharma 1966: 2).

The joint committee of the legislative assembly on the bill pertaining to Hindu law and relating to intestate succession submitted its report on 8 November 1943. Interestingly, *except for one Muslim member, S. Sultan Ahmed, all other members, who were Hindus, gave minutes of dissent!* Particular attention may be invited to the following observation of the committee: 'There is a body of opinion which still maintains that women as a class should be excluded from inheritance and should not be given absolute ownership over property they acquire either by inheritance or partition. In support of this opinion are urged (1) certain Vedic texts, (2) the general incompetence of women, (3) the evil of fragmentation of holdings and (4) the fear of the property being lost to the family.' The committee had suggested several amendments to the bill and had recommended that it should be republished for seeking public opinion. (Joint Committee on Intestate Succession, November 1943: 1, 6)

A bill for giving Hindu married women a right to separate residence and maintenance under certain circumstances was introduced in the central legislative assembly by Dr G.V. Deshmukh on 2 April 1946. The bill was objected to, among other points, on the ground that the bills on Hindu law were 'being rushed through very quickly in the Assembly'. A reference was made by P.B. Gole, member, to a 'very huge meeting in Old Delhi where many pundits and learned people from Benares were assembled...those people became afraid that there was some encroachment upon the old law and they thought that such legislation should not be pursued...in fact so far as this bill is concerned it was not circulated for public opinion at all.' The bill led to animated discussion before it was passed. (*Legislative Assembly Debates* [henceforth *LAD*] Vol. V, 1946: 3385–416)

I have referred to these deliberations to show how agitated the members were when questions arose pertaining to changing the social customs of Hindus.

On 15 November 1946, Dr G.V. Deshmukh introduced the Special Marriage Amendment Bill. The bill raised the question of whether 'the Hindu wife, the partner in Hindu marriage, is a sentient human being with ideas of human happiness and misery'. During the course of his speech, Deshmukh referred to the considerable opposition which was prevalent to the proposed Hindu Code. He said, 'When the committee was in Lahore, I read in the papers that about 10,000 people invaded the Town Hall.' Gole corrected him by saying, 'Not people; they were women'.

> Deshmukh said: I am very glad you have mentioned that. 10,000 women invaded the Town Hall and they did not agree to [sic] the Code Committee. I am particularly glad that my honourable friend, Mr Gole, has pointed out this incident, because it was Mr Gole and lawyers like him who brought forward the excuse that we should not do anything piecemeal and we should wait for the Hindu Code Committee...*women were instigated by Sanatanists and by orthodox persons and they were tempted [sic] to go and attack the places where the committee was meeting... I make bold to say on the floor of this house that all these women were instigated.*
>
> N.V. Gadgil said: We had heard that they were the instigators!
>
> Deshmukh replied: And not only that, but they were given wrong advice. I can frankly tell you what happened in Bombay. When this bill was sent round for their opinion, the women frankly admitted that they did not understand the legal implications of this measure. They approached some of these distinguished solicitors and lawyers who pointed out all these disadvantages and the women got so thoroughly frightened that they started making representations. (*LAD* Vol. VII–VIII, 1946: 1123, 1129)

I have given this somewhat lengthy quotation to bring out the atmosphere which prevailed when the Hindu Code was under discussion and amendments to the personal laws of Hindus were undertaken. It can be seen that the passage was by no means smooth or easy.

This is fully borne out by the report of the Hindu Law Committee under the chairmanship of Justice B.N. Rau which was submitted on 21 February 1947. The committee said that the public interest aroused by the Code surpassed its most sanguine expectations. The first edition of 1000 copies (of the report) was rapidly sold out and it was found necessary to reprint a fresh edition of 3000 copies. These, too, were exhausted quickly and there were two further reprints of 1000 copies each. In view of the great public interest aroused, the committee got the Code translated into various Indian languages, namely, Gujarati, Marathi, Hindi, Bengali, Tamil, Telugu, Malayalam, Kannada, Urdu, Gurumukhi, Sindhi and Oriya. In Bengal, where the demand for the translation was the greatest, the provincial government distributed more than 10,000 copies of the Bengali translation, free of cost, to various persons and institutions. The committee toured extensively and held sittings in Bombay, Poona, Delhi, Allahabad, Patna, Calcutta, Madras, Nagpur and Lahore. In all, the committee examined 121 individual witnesses and 102 associations, which were represented by 257 persons.

There were black flag demonstrations when the committee arrived in or passed through Allahabad, Calcutta, Nagpur, Amritsar and Lahore. There were also white flag demonstrations at Amritsar and Lahore, where supporters of the Code were present in large numbers. One of the committee members, Dr Dwarkanath Mitter, in his minute of dissent, opposed the codification of the Hindu law as well as the changes proposed in the draft code. In fact, he went to the extent of saying that he was 'definitely of opinion that there is no necessity for making monogamy a rule of law among Hindus.' Among the arguments advanced by others before the committee against making monogamy a rule of law was a shocking statement: 'Why should men be deprived of a vested right (of polygamy) which has been enjoyed by them for 3000 years?'

This, in spite of the fact that a legislation had been passed in Bombay Province prohibiting polygamy, and a member of the Madras Legislative Assembly had introduced a similar bill for the purpose. According to the committee, this showed that public opinion was rapidly changing in these matters. The committee found that in Bombay and Madras, particularly in Madras, the Code had a very favourable reception.

As was to be expected, there was a cross-section of progressive opinion which argued that the Code should apply uniformly, not just to Hindus, but also to Christians and Muslims. As has been the practice all these years, the Rau Committee decided to overlook this objection and did not address it.

The main objections to the codification of Hindu law were that the Code was *ultra vires* since the Hindu personal law was a religious law laid down by Hindu sages and scriptures. The second objection was that the Code posed a danger to the Hindu religion. It was also argued that the voting on the Code should be confined only to Hindus. Yet another objection was that it would be difficult to bring about uniformity in a vast country like India.

In his minute of dissent, Dr Mitter tabulated the evidence given before the committee which showed that, while seventy-five individuals and groups were in favour of monogamy, ninety-nine were against it. As regards divorce, seventy-eight were in favour of the proposed changes while 103 were against them.

> The Rau committee was of the view that 'hostility aroused by the Code was far less than that evoked by the Sarda Act for the prevention of child marriages.[1] The opposition to the Sarda Act has now died down, and it is now generally accepted to be a beneficial measure. The Deshmukh Act of 1937 against which the same sort of objections as have been advanced against this Code could have been and were advanced, has also been accepted by Hindu public opinion, including orthodox opinion. In the same way, we are confident that the revised draft Code appended to this report,

---

[1]Jawaharlal Nehru wrote: 'By a fluke, the Sarda Child Marriage Restraint Bill became law, but the subsequent history of this unhappy Act showed more than anything else how averse to enforcing any such measure the Government was...People rushed to take advantage of the intervening six months of grace which the Act very foolishly allowed. And then it was discovered that the Act was more or less of a joke and could be easily ignored without any steps being taken by Government.' (Nehru 1936: 382)

with such changes as the Legislature may make therein, will earn public approval.' (Report of the Hindu Law Committee 1947: 1–5, 12, 21, 38–39)

On 2 April 1947, Pandit Thakur Das Bhargava introduced the Child Marriage Restraint (Amendment) Bill. This bill was meant to amend the Child Marriage Restraint Act, 1929. Bhargava pointed out the enormity of the problem of child marriage which was 'eating into the very vitals of the nation'. He said that the first bill about child marriage had been thought about in 1924 but nothing had come of it till 1927, when another bill for the purpose was introduced. *When this bill was referred to the Select Committee, the Committee reported that it should be a general bill and should not be confined to Hindus alone.* After the 'thrilling speeches' of Pandit Madan Mohan Malaviya and Jinnah supporting the bill, the face of the bill was changed and it was made applicable to the whole of India. It was republished and then again referred to the Select Committee.

The provisions of the Child Marriage Restraint Act, 1929 were quite lenient. Citing the figures of the 1931 census, Bhargava said that 44,082 girls were married between the age of zero and one and there were 1515 widows aged one. Between the ages of one and two years, 63,954 girls were married and there were 1785 widows. Between the age of zero and five, there were 8,01,852 married girls and 30,880 widows. Unfortunately, the figures of the 1941 census were not available then. Bhargava quoted from the report of the Committee on Sati and Child Marriage, which observed:

> Let us compare the case of Sati which was prevented by legislation with the case of early maternity. Satis were few and far between.[2] They compelled attention by the enormity of the evil in individual cases by the intense agony of the burning widow and the terrible

---

[2]There were two not-so-distant incidents of sati—Deorala in Rajasthan in 1987, and Patna Tamoli in Madhya Pradesh in 2002. As *EPW* commented editorially, uprooting a barbaric practice like sati and making every incident of violence against women a public cause are the immediate tasks of all rights bodies and not only the women's movement. (*EPW* 17 August 2002: 3383–84)

shock they gave to human feelings. After all, they were cases only of individual suffering. The agony ended with the martyr and the incident had some compensation in the martyr being almost deified as an ideal *Hindu pativrata*. In the case of maternity, however, the evil is widespread and affects such a large number of women, *both amongst Hindus and Muslims*, as to necessitate redress. It is so extensive as to affect the whole framework of society. After going through the ordeal, if a woman survives to the age of 30, she is in many cases an old woman, almost a shadow of her former self. Her life is a long and lingering misery and she is a sacrifice at the altar of custom. The evil is so insidious in all the manifold aspects of social life that people have ceased to think of its shocking effects on the entire social fabric. In the case of Sati, the utter hideousness of the incident shocked the conscience; in this case, the familiarity of the evil blinds us to its ghastly results. If legislation was justified for preventing Sati, there is ample justification for legislation to prevent early maternity, both on the grounds of humanity and in furtherance of social justice.

Bhargava also highlighted the fact that the evil of pre-puberty consummation (of marriage) was prevalent in some parts of India. After a studied and disturbing speech, he moved the motion for referring the bill to the Select Committee.

Several members opposed the bill. For example, P.B. Gole quoted Pandit Madan Mohan Malaviya from his minute of dissent when the Child Marriage Restraint Act was on the anvil. Malaviya had said:

> In view of the fact that marriage is a religious sacrament among Hindus, in view of the belief which has prevailed on the question of the age for marriage among them for a very long time, to make marriage above the age of 12 and below the age of 14 punishable by law will be a violent interference with Hindu religion which I consider it my duty strongly to oppose. We must not forget that even in England the legal marriageable age for girls is 12 years.

Another member, N.V. Gadgil, said that when the Child Marriage Restraint Act, 1929 was passed:

The District Local Board elections were to be held in the district of Poona. Some of the Congress workers came to me and said, 'What have you done? We are sure to lose the elections, because the whole countryside is against you. How can our girls remain unmarried after they are 10 or 12? We will lose the election.'...I went round and I am glad to tell this house that we won all the 48 seats, although our opponents went about abusing me in particular as the villain of the piece. They said, *'This was the man who had tampered with our religion, he is now tampering with our social customs'*.

In his reply, Bhargava regretted 'the ignorance of the general public and even very prominent people about the actual prevalence of this bad custom in the country'. He said that the change in the country had not been significant since the time of the passing of the 1929 Act. After long discussion, the bill was finally referred to the Select Committee and simultaneously circulated for eliciting public opinion. (*LAD* Vol. 4, No. 1, 1947: 2864–67, 2877, 2888–89)

The tenor of this discussion shows the enormity of the problem on the one hand and the prevailing social atmosphere which was not ready for change unless special efforts were made and there was an enlightened leadership.

On 17 November 1947, B.R. Ambedkar moved a bill to amend and codify Hindu law. Naziruddin Ahmad said: 'I understand there has been a considerable amount of agitation among our Hindu friends over it and it is better we have a picture of the stage at which the bill is at present.' Ambedkar said that the bill had only just been introduced. R.V. Dhulekar said: *'In the new set-up we should have no Hindu Law and no Muslim Law. We should have a general law...'* Since this was only the introduction stage of the bill, there was no further discussion. (*Constituent Assembly of India [Legislative] Debates CALD* Vol. I, 1947: 41)

Even Rajendra Prasad, minister in the interim government and president of the Constituent Assembly, was strongly opposed to the Hindu Code initiatives. He wrote to Nehru on 21 July 1948:

A deputation of eight members of the Select Committee on the Hindu Code had represented to him that the proposed Code introduced some very fundamental and far-reaching changes in Hindu law as it had been accepted by a vast majority of Hindus. Rajendra Prasad further emphasized that 'the bill has never been considered at a meeting of the [Congress] Party...Fifteen members out of twenty have been attending the meetings of the Select Committee and the majority of them who came to see me feel that it would not be proper to rush this bill through the next session of the Assembly. Apart from the merits of the measure and apart from the considerations above mentioned, *my feeling is that a measure of such far-reaching consequences about which there is much difference of opinion, need not be passed by the Constituent Assembly sitting as a legislature.*' He also questioned the mandate and legislative competence of the Constituent Assembly to pass such a legislation.

Nehru replied to him the very next day and said that the Hindu Code Bill had been discussed repeatedly in the course of the previous year and a half. 'Few contemplated pieces of legislation have been so thoroughly thrashed out and publicly discussed... It has been considered by the Cabinet on more than one occasion. It has been considered by the Executive of the party certainly.' Nehru accepted that a large section of orthodox opinion was opposed to it and there was also no denying the point that socially progressive Hindus were anxious and eager for it. Nehru said personally he was entirely in favour of the general principles embodied in it. Concluding, Nehru asked, 'Are we to give up something that we consider right and on which so much labour has been spent, because some people object?'

Rajendra Prasad replied to Nehru on 24 July 1948 reiterating, 'I am definitely informed the matter has never been considered by the Party. The contemplated legislation is based on the report of the Committee which recorded evidence, and that evidence is overwhelmingly against the proposals contained in the bill... I am not aware that the bill, as proposed, has been subjected to any critical examination by the public at large on any extensive scale.' Prasad cautioned that the bill was bound to rouse bitter feelings and would have repercussions which may affect the chances of the Congress at the next election. He said, 'We have to weigh how it will be received by the vast bulk of the Hindu public against what foreigners outside India and those who call themselves "progressive" would say. My feeling is strong on the point that we shall be riding roughshod on the cherished sentiments of the vast bulk of our people.' He requested Nehru to reconsider the matter and not allow 'a major crisis to be created in the party and in the country'.

Nehru replied to Rajendra Prasad on 27 July 1948. It was obvious that Nehru had decided to go ahead with the Hindu Code Bill and said, 'The bill is before the Assembly and it is for the Assembly to consider it and decide this way or that way...It is perfectly true that the AICC [All India Congress Committee] or the Working Committee have not considered it. Nor is it in the election manifesto. Normally, such matters of legislation have not been considered by the Working Committee or the AICC...it is for the party to decide what they will do in this matter. At this stage even the Cabinet cannot thus go back on its decisions unless the party so directs it.'

Finally, in exasperation, Rajendra Prasad sent a written statement to Nehru with a request that it should be read at the meeting of the Congress party when it considered the Hindu Code Bill. He sent a copy of this statement to Vallabhbhai Patel on 31 July 1948. In his statement, Rajendra Prasad reiterated several points which he had made in his letters to Nehru earlier and also questioned the legislative competence of the Constituent Assembly to enact the Hindu Code. *Rajendra Prasad underlined that the passage of the bill would be tantamount to forcing a measure of a most fundamental character, introducing basic changes in their personal law,...in furtherance of the progressive ideas of a small, if not a microscopic minority, and all this is to be done without reference to the electorate* and by a legislature, which is competent only for drawing a Constitution but not elected with a view to effecting amendments in the personal law of the largest community in the country. (Das 1973: 399–404)

After prolonged discussions, the bill to amend and codify certain branches of Hindu law was referred to the Select Committee by the Constituent Assembly of India (Legislative) on 9 April 1948. Introducing the motion,

B.R. Ambedkar, Minister for Law, highlighted that the bill, aimed to codify the rules of Hindu law 'which are scattered in innumerable decisions of the High Courts and of the Privy Council, which formed a bewildering motley to the common man and give rise to constant litigation, seeks to codify the law relating to seven different matters'. These included rights of property of a deceased Hindu who has died intestate—male or female—without making a will; the order of succession among the heirs; marriage and divorce; adoption and guardianship, and so on.

The bill contained some fundamental and forward-looking changes. For example, women's rights to property were considerably enlarged; marriages were to be valid, irrespective of the caste or sub-caste of the parties entering into the marriage; the identity of *gotrapravara* was not to be a bar to a marriage; monogamy was prescribed as a rule; and provisions were made for dissolution of marriage. Ambedkar had specially highlighted some prominent features of the bill. First, the abolition of birthright and taking property by survivorship. Second, giving a half-share to the daughter. Third, the conversion of the woman's limited estate into an absolute estate. Fourth, the abolition of caste in the matter of marriage and adoption. Fifth, the principle of monogamy, and sixth, the principle of divorce.

> *A number of members spoke on the bill, most criticizing it.* Amongst the members who supported the bill was Hansa Mehta, whose progressive and forward-looking interventions in the Constituent Assembly debates were often in contrast with the views of several others. Mehta raised several questions indicating that women, and particularly herself, were not satisfied with some of the provisions contained in the bill relating to the rights of women. In the ideal sense, the bill did not come up to their expectations. In reply, Ambedkar urged that...much has been made of the fact that there is a great deal of public opinion which is opposed to this bill... this is hardly a question which we can decide by counting heads. This is not a question which we can decide in accordance with the opinion of the majority. When society is in a transitory stage, leaving the past, going to the future, there are bound to be opposing considerations; one pulling towards the past and one pulling towards the future, and the test that we can apply is no other than the test of one's

conscience. (*CALD* Vol. VI, 1948: 3629, 3633, 3652–53)

Naziruddin Ahmad, who supported the bill, emphasized that '*its provisions are largely in accord with the laws which prevail in my own community*... It is however with some amount of nervousness that I have risen to speak. When I find that sturdy members of the House who would have spoken against the bill have quailed before a powerful array of five distinguished members of the fair sex, ready to stand by their guns, little courage can I muster in giving out the views which I am charged to communicate.'

Begum Aizaz Rasul said that:

The provisions of the bill are no doubt extremely far-reaching and the provisions about marriage, divorce, inheritance and adoption that are being brought forward are extremely radical measures. It is an extremely important matter and the codification of Hindu law would certainly be looked upon as one of the most momentous pieces of legislation that has ever been brought forward in this House...That it is the status of the women of a country by which the society of the country is judged and *there is no doubt that the Hindu women were very backward in India. The Muslims have taken pride in the fact that the Shariat Law gives them great rights.*'
She however agreed that in many parts of India, Muslim women did not enjoy the rights given to them under the *Shariat*.

Begum Rasul said: '*I am glad that this piece of legislation... will put the Hindu women on a par with Muslim women as far as their rights are concerned.*' Rohini Kumar Chaudhuri felt that 'the title of the bill was a misnomer; it is not a Hindu Code but it should more appropriately have been called a Hindu Woman's Code'.

Reference must be made to the erudite speech of Hansa Mehta who, while supporting the bill, made a number of important observations. She felt that:

'The bill did not go far enough. A daughter who is recognized as heir inherits the property but she inherits half the share of the son. This violates the principle of equality... We therefore feel that the daughter should get an equal share in the property of her father with the son, and the son should also get an equal share in the property of his mother with the daughter...The husband can also inherit the property of his wife in the same way that the wife inherits the property of her husband...There should be law against fragmentation and the property should be sold if it goes below the prescribed limit. Or there could be collectivization of the land.'

She urged that the age of marriage could also be a condition of a valid marriage. She said that the Sarda Act should be made more drastic. She suggested that the mother should also be a co-guardian of the child with the father. She further suggested that the whole chapter in the Code on adoption should be scrapped. 'We are a secular state. We want to be a secular state. *Adoption in Hindu law is for religious purposes. Why should a secular state have anything to do with a religious custom?*...We have looked too much to the past. We must now look to the future.'

This was a remarkable intervention and showed how much ground still remained to be covered in the codification of Hindu law.

Replying to the debate, Ambedkar *inter alia* referred to the points made by Hansa Mehta and said: 'She must remember that this society is an inert society. The Hindu society has always believed that law-making is the function either of God or the *Smriti* and that Hindu society has no right to change the law...It is for the first time that we are persuading Hindu society to take this big step...' (CALD Vol. V, 1948: 3629, 3633, 3639–41, 3643–44, 3648–49, 3652)

The bill to amend and codify certain branches of Hindu law came up for discussion in the Constituent Assembly of India (Legislative) on 12 December 1949 after it had been considered by the Select Committee. The Deputy Speaker said:

The general discussion had begun as early as 24 February 1949. It continued on the 25th, 26th, 28th February, 1st March, 1st April and 2nd April. One honourable member had spoken for as much as six hours and eight minutes. He said that so far, six days nine hours and twenty minutes had been spent on this bill and still only fourteen members had spoken so far. Looking to the time which members have taken so far, we will have to sit nearly a year if all honourable members are to have a chance to speak.'

This highlights how controversial this bill was and how much resistance there was to enacting it.

It was a fiery debate by any standard. Right at the start, Pandit Bhargava protested that Prime Minister Nehru had said that this measure was a piece of simple and essential legislation. Bhargava said that neither of this was true:

> If you refer to previous occasions when social legislation like the Sarda Act and the Hindu Women's Right to Property Act was brought before this legislature, you would find what an amount of controversy they raised. Compared to those bills, this bill is enormously of great importance. It affects the entire structure of Hindu society. *This bill, if placed on the statute book... will result in the utter extinction of Hindu society,* not in the sense that 30 million Hindus will cease to exist, but that the distinctive features and characteristics of Hindu society will cease to continue...*The bill aims at the utter demolition of the entire structure and fabric of Hindu society.*

He further questioned the competence of the legislature in the matter and also said that nothing would happen if the bill were deferred till the new legislature came into being after general elections. He charged that the bill would lead to the destruction of the joint family system. Bhargava emphasized that:

> Every provision in this bill has got a stigma which is anti-Hindu and therefore cannot be acceptable to any Hindu....India of ours does not reside in urban towns like Allahabad and Delhi. *To me this bill is an insidious effort on the part of its sponsors to take the Hindus out of their Indian moorings and to launch them on foreign waters of Arabia and Jerusalem.* The real India lives in the 5 lakhs of villages. The life of the villagers is so intimately interwoven with the texture of their society that whatever modifications you might make by this piece of legislation, they will resist to the limit

of their might before you take away from them the time-honoured usage and customs to which they have been submitting as a matter of course for centuries.

K. Santhanam said that the Hindu Code was merely a continuation in the social sphere of the great Constitution that we had completed the other day in our capacity as a Constitution-making body. Santhanam emphasized that the bill sought to conserve as much of Hindu law as was consistent with modern needs and ideas, and it sought to change only where such change was necessary. He said that the bill had four aspects, namely, codification, unification, rationalization and reform. Santhanam emphasized that *providing one civil code for the entire country was not a disintegrating but a cementing process*. He said that one aspect which had evoked the greatest amount of opposition was a daughter's right to her father's property. He also underlined that *one great merit of this bill was that 'it takes away all legal sanction from the caste system. We abolished untouchability in the Constitution. Now we take the social reform further and take away all legal sanction for caste*. Here, in this bill, whether it is for a marriage or for any other purpose, all Hindus from the so-called untouchables up to the so-called Acharya Brahmins, all of them are one.' Shockingly, one member interjected, '*Without a caste, who is a Hindu?*' Santhanam countered: 'With the caste, a Hindu is a monster, according to me. In this country we want to establish a Hindu community without caste. Either we cease to be Hindus altogether or we establish Hinduism without caste. There is no alternative left for us.'

Lakshmi Kanta Maitra said that with the opposition which was building up for the bill, the stage for its clause-by-clause consideration would never come. Santhanam countered:

> There were people who were prophesying that the Constitution would never be passed; but we have passed it. In the same way, we are going to put this bill on the statute book. Though Sir B.N. Rau, who headed the committee on Hindu law was a Hindu, insinuations were cast by some that he was not a Hindu and therefore he could not be taken as an authority on matters pertaining to Hindu law.

Supporting the bill, H.V. Pataskar, who later became law minister in the

Nehru government, said that it was going to revolutionize the structure of Hindu society. He said that, under the Civil Marriage Act, any two Hindus belonging to any caste or community, without making a declaration that they did not belong to any religion, could get married. He said there was much agitation with respect to the question of inheritance but we had laid down equality of sexes as a principle in our Constitution. However, Pataskar questioned the need for keeping the provisions relating to adoption. He said adoption was a thing which was peculiar to Hindu law. In other societies, too, children were adopted, not for the purpose of continuing the family line, but only to satisfy the natural craving in any human being to have children and to rear them.

Pataskar also dealt with the question of formulating a uniform civil code as envisaged in Article 44 of the Constitution. He said:

> I would like you seriously to consider whether by enacting a measure like this only for the Hindus, we are advancing the cause of our progress towards that ideal. *I should think that we are going backward rather than forward*...What is to be welded in the interests of the security of our nation is not the welding of Hindus alone but all the citizens of this country. All the inhabitants of India should be welded into one...*The Code should apply to all citizens whether they are Hindus, Christians or Parsees or Muslims.* From that point of view, we are going exactly in the opposite direction...The present Hindu Code was conceived under different circumstances, and at a time when there was no ideal of having a uniform civil code. But since then, things have changed enormously and especially after Pakistan, it should be our endeavour to bring closer all the different elements in the country...One uniform civil code will further bring all the people together.

Pataskar went to the extent of saying that the present bill should not be proceeded with: 'It will serve no purpose. Therefore, *I appeal to my honourable friend the law minister to withdraw this bill, bring forward a uniform civil code regarding the matters covered by this bill applicable to all citizens alike...*'

The animated discussion continued for three full days, till the end of 14 December 1949.

Particular attention may be invited to the speech of Dr Bakshi Tek Chand, who traced the history of improvements made in Hindu law as a result of the efforts of social reformers. Chand said:

In 1829, sati was abolished under the inspiration of Ram Mohan Roy. As is well known, Chand underlined, 'It was argued at that time that sati was a part of Hindu religion. It was said that sati was one of the essential features of our dharma and any interference with it would be an attack on Hindu religion...This custom...was not a part of Hindu law. It was an innovation which has been introduced during the, what is called, the dark ages, or the medieval age.' After that, there was the 1850 Act for the removal of class disabilities so far as inheritance was concerned. Thereby, if a person or an heir changed his religion, his right of succession was not affected.

Then came the great reform in 1856 when the Widow Remarriage Act was passed. It was believed that Hindu religion did not permit the remarriage of widows. Under the leadership of Ishwar Chandra Vidyasagar and other leaders of that day, public opinion asserted itself and yet another Act was passed to do away with this great injustice under which Hindu women suffered.

Dr Chand asserted that Hindu religion had not come to an end by the enactment of these legislations. He said that there had been numerous other acts by which Hindu law was modified by Parliament or the Legislative Assembly of the day. There was a great deal of agitation in 1890 and 1891 when the Age of Consent Bill was introduced.

He continued: At that time too a cry was raised that it would be a gross interference with Hindu religion if a legislature consisting of Hindus, Muslims, Christians, and dominated by bureaucrats were to legislate in regard to a custom which had permitted intercourse with a child-wife below the age of twelve. *If you have any recollection of what appeared in the papers, even advanced papers like the Amrita Bazar Patrika, you will see in what kind of convulsion Hindu society was at that time.* But again the legislators persisted and that bill was passed, a bill which ultimately has culminated in the last session by almost unanimous vote of the House in further amending the bill which our friend Pandit Thakur Das Bhargava introduced and which, if I remember right was unanimously passed by all sides of the House. At that time none of our friends thought that this Assembly was not competent to legislate with regard to a matter which was considered to be an essential part of Hindu religion. Coming to more recent times, you will find that in 1916 the Indian legislature passed what is called The Dispensation of Property Act, an act which has had the effect of repealing the law which had been laid down by the Privy Council...After that came what is called The Removal of Disabilities Bill. Under certain texts of Hindu Law as enunciated by some of the *Smriti*s, if a person was suffering from a physical disability, if he was blind, if he was deaf and dumb, he was not entitled to inheritance.

After the passing of this act in 1928, persons suffering from physical defects were allowed to inherit in the same way as persons who were sound. This was another inroad into Hindu law. Another enactment of 1929 enabled certain classes of people to succeed to property who were earlier ruled by courts as not so entitled. When the Sarda Act came, it was argued that fixing a minimum age limit for marriage was an interference with Hindu religion. In spite of the opposition the law was passed. After that came what is known as the Deshmukh Bill. With this bill of 1937, a great change was effected in the Hindu law of succession. In 1946, a bill permitting marriage among *sagotra*s was passed by the legislature. Yet another enactment of far-reaching importance was passed in 1949 by which marriages between various castes of Hindus were declared valid. This was a very great step forward which permitted inter-caste marriages and which removed restrictions such as one must marry either in one's own sub-caste or, at any rate, in one's caste.

Bakshi Chand said that there was a very brief discussion on this bill at the first stage. The select committee was given only six days to consider this important bill. Select committee members wanted longer time for discussion but ultimately, the committee decided to proceed with the bill only on a majority of two. Chand urged that it was a most truncated and half-hearted measure and it would do the maximum mischief to Hindu society and the minimum of good to the members of the female sex. (*CALD* Vol. VI, 1949: 464–65, 468, 473–74, 475, 477–78, 480–84, 489–90, 590–91)

Kamala Chaudhri accorded support to the bill and said:

> It had been brought up before the House in conformity with the spirit of the time. She said that the bill contained a provision for prohibiting the right of polygamy which 'is at present exercised by religious-minded Hindus...With all humility, I would submit that I apprehend that this bill might be opposed by a majority of our brethren for the reason that some such ban is being imposed upon them that in the lifetime of their wives, they shall not be permitted to contract many marriages. But I do not find in it anything against religion...

Kameshwar Singh said that the consideration of the bill should be postponed till the wishes of the electorate were ascertained in the next general election as stated by Dr Rajendra Prasad. He said that the opposition to the bill was very strong.

> I belong to that class of people which considers the *Smriti*s and the school of interpretation...as sacrosanct; and the class to which I belong constitutes a large proportion of the total population of the country. We consider marriage, succession and the like as a part of our religious duty and obligations. To us these are much more than mere secular or social phenomena.

J.B. Kripalani said that he would support the bill and its broad principles. However, he further added, 'I do so because I do not want this government to resign upon a side issue, upon a social issue. I want it to resign on more substantial, political and economic issues.'

Intervening in the debate, Prime Minister Nehru said that the government would like to give as much time as possible to the discussion of this bill. He agreed to give one more day for the discussion of the bill. At the end of the day, the Deputy Speaker said that there were still thirty-four members who wanted to speak. He hoped that it would be possible to finish the discussion the next day. But with the filibustering which had been so characteristic of the discussion on this bill so far, it was most unlikely that the proposed time limit could be adhered to.

Looking to the highly adverse sex ratio in India at the time, it is interesting to see the observation of Lakshminarayan Sahu who, during his intervention said that '...The number of women in Utkal exceeds by 3 to 4 lakhs and when it is not possible to find out [sic] a match for their marriage, then they are married to a *sahada* tree.'

K.T. Shah was forceful in his argument:

> In a population of over 300 million, the income tax paying class numbered about 1 million, or with their dependents, about 3 to 4 million and that is less than 1 per cent of the total population who can possibly afford to have some property that can be divided... I see really no reason why on this subject any heat should be generated, as regards the recognition of equal rights of daughters and sons in the matter of division of patrimony.

Sardar Hukam Singh said:

> There is nothing of Hindu law that is being codified here. Provision for divorce is being taken from Christian countries and the law of inheritance from Muslim law. To me it is rather a misnomer to call it a codification of Hindu law.' Hukam Singh, who basically spoke as a representative of Sikhs, said that in the Sikh religion, customs and usages were most important. However, they had been considerably lowered in relevance in the proposed bill. He also believed that though Sikhs had all along been governed by Hindu law, now that changes therein were being brought from outside, Sikhs certainly had a grievance and felt that either their customs should be allowed to remain as they were or they should not necessarily be bound to revolve round the new wheel. For example, the new bill recognized only two kinds of marriages—sacramental and civil. There was however a third kind which is followed by Sikhs and this has been recognized by the passing of The Anand Marriage Validating Act, 1909. He said he was not sure whether this marriage would be recognized under the Hindu Code. He further emphasized that Sikhs would not be prepared to forego this form of marriage. He also had reservations pertaining to the provisions on divorce. He hoped that the current easy procedures for obtaining divorce would

not be changed and made more complicated and expensive. (*CALD* Vol. VI, 1949: 536, 541–42, 557–58, 605, 607–09)

Nehru initiated the discussion on the Hindu Code on 19 December 1949 by suggesting that:

> Since, in spite of best efforts, it would not be possible to find adequate time for further discussion of the bill, we may put an end to the present stage of consideration of this motion by adopting it, and then the House may permit the government to take those informal steps which I have indicated in regard to consultation about the various parts and clauses. That might be undertaken so that when the matter comes up again, as I hope, at the next session, it may have the support of a very great majority in this House and outside.
>
> The Speaker reminded the House that the motion had been debated for full nine days…Thirty-three speakers had taken part in it and thirty hours and twenty-eight minutes had been devoted to it. Replying to the debate, B.R. Ambedkar said that this bill sought to codify the Hindu law relating to eight matters, while there were five to which there had been no opposition whatsoever. One member interjected to say that this was because the government did not allow the members to speak. Ambedkar underlined: '*I have not the least doubt that unless Hindu law is not only codified but also modified so as to bring it in consonance with the provisions of Article 15, parts of the Hindu law will be declared to be void by the judiciary in view of Article 13.*' Ambedkar concluded by saying, 'This was in no sense a revolutionary measure. I say that this is not even a radical measure.'
>
> The two motions moved by Naziruddin Ahmad for circulation of the bill for obtaining further opinion thereon and for referring the bill to the select committee once again for a further report thereon, were negatived by the House. The House adopted a motion to take into consideration the bill as reported by the select committee. (*CALD* Vol. VI, 1949: 783–85, 790–92)

Dr Shyama Prasad Mukherjee who, at the age of thirty-four, became the youngest vice-chancellor of Calcutta University and later founded the Bharatiya Jana Sangh, spoke at length on the Hindu Code Bill in Parliament on 17 September 1951. He made an interesting proposition in the House:

> Pass the entire Hindu Code as it is; only make it optional. Those who want it can adopt it...I am prepared to admit, however much there may be opposition to the Code, that this represents a marvellous piece of work on the part of Dr Ambedkar...This is a most thorny subject and he has gone through the matter with as much ability as anyone could have. For that, *if he is prepared to accept an honorary degree to be conferred by Parliament, we are prepared to confer a degree on Dr Ambedkar*. But, *if you look upon it as a measure which has to be pushed down the throat of millions of Hindus who are opposed to it, I say that you will not be doing a service to the people of India*. (Lok Sabha Secretariat 1990: 96–97)

Subhash Kashyap, former secretary general of the Lok Sabha, brought out in the history of Parliament that:

> The Hindu Code Bill...was brought to the House [Provisional Parliament] twice but no progress could be made on both the occasions. When the bill was brought before the House on 5 February 1951, *of the 28 members who participated in the debate, as many as 23 opposed it...A fierce debate took place for five days on a clause of the bill which provided that the Bill would apply to Hindu community only.* Among the fourteen members who spoke at this stage, thirteen were against it. They argued that other communities also suffered from the evils which the bill sought to remove, but they were left out by the bill. *Declaring the bill as discriminatory, Naziruddin Ahmed, a member from West Bengal, wanted the bill to be extended to the Muslim community also*...In the course of debate, demand for a common civil code was also echoed. M.A. Ayyangar was of the opinion that legal measures had failed in reforming long-established social customs and that the bill awaited the same fate as was met by measures like the Child Marriage Restraint Act and Widow Remarriage Act.

The only member, it may be noted, who supported the bill at this stage was Raj Bahadur from Rajasthan...After a long but fruitless debate, further consideration of the bill was postponed till the next session...When the bill was taken up [again] for consideration on 17 September, 1951, similar arguments were extended by other members. Dr S.P. Mukherjee criticized Dr Ambedkar, who wanted to see the bill through at any cost, for trying to become a modern 'Manu' or 'Yajnavalkya'. Every clause of the bill was opposed as usual...

During the consideration of the bill, the attitude of members left Dr Ambedkar desperate and frustrated. He regretted the criticism of the Congress members who opposed the stand of their own party. Demand of the members to withdraw the bill and the voting pattern on clause 4 of the bill in which several Congress members voted against the exasperated Dr Ambedkar [sic]. Thereafter, the bill was never taken up by the Provisional Parliament. Dr Ambedkar resigned from the cabinet and wrote in his resignation letter: 'For a long time I have been thinking to resign my seat from the cabinet. The only thing that held me back was that it would be possible to give effect to the Hindu Code bill before the life of the present Parliament came to an end. I even agreed to break up the bill and restricted it to marriage and divorce in the fond hope that at least this much of our labour may bear fruit, but even this part of the bill has been killed. I see no purpose in my continuing to be a member of the cabinet. (Kashyap 1995: 22–23)

Thus ended this stormy chapter on the Hindu Code Bill. It must be said to the credit of Nehru that he persisted with this initiative in spite of such stout opposition and even from stalwarts like Dr Rajendra Prasad. To meet with the criticism that the Congress party did not have the popular mandate to carry out such drastic and revolutionary changes in the Hindu law, Nehru took this matter to the people in the general elections in 1952 and came back to power with a massive majority. With this mandate, he pursued the codification of the Hindu law by bringing forward separate legislations for the pointed attention of Parliament. This is in stark contrast to the leadership which has been holding sway in recent years. It once again brings out that, but for Nehru, Indian society would not have been as forward-looking and progressive as it is today. My only regret is that these reforms were not extended by Nehru to Muslims in spite of his unique and unequalled national stature.

Amrit Kaur, Hansa Mehta and M.R. Masani moved a motion in the Advisory Committee on Fundamental Rights that a clause based on Article 54 of the Swiss Constitution on the following lines: 'No impediments to marriage between citizens shall be based merely upon difference of religion' may be included. They had noted that the Special Marriage Act III of 1872, which governs civil marriages between Indians of different religious faiths, demands from both contracting parties the following solemn declaration: 'I do not profess the Christian, Jewish, Hindu, Muhammadan, Parsee, Buddhist, Sikh or Jain religion'.

They had argued that such an impediment to marriage between two Indians was a reflection on our claim to common nationhood. They had, therefore, urged that the incorporation in the Constitution of the proposed clause would render such a primitive law as at present prevails *ultra vires* of the Constitution. (Rao 1967: 162–63)

This infirmity was done away with only in the enactment of the Hindu Code.

Speaking in the Lok Sabha on 14 September 1954 on the Special Marriage Bill, Nehru emphasized:

> The rigidity that we have seen in the last many generations is not an original feature of Hindu society; it is a later development. I do submit that this extreme reverence shown to what is called personal new law seems to me completely misplaced, whether it is the Hindu personal law or the Muslim personal law or any other. In fact, it means that you are extending the sphere of religion to all kinds of minor and temporary and changing situations in society. (Gopal and Iyengar 2003: 141)

When The Hindu Succession Bill, 1954, was before the Rajya Sabha, it was referred to the joint committee which presented its report on 19 September 1955. The committee held as many as 16 sittings. The report of the committee contained 11 minutes of dissent which shows the extent of dissidence within the committee on this issue. The bill was later passed by Parliament but it showed that the question of codification of Hindu law continued to be highly divisive. (Joint Committee on Hindu Succession Bill 1954, 1955: vii–xxxv)

When the Hindu Succession Act was passed by Parliament, Nehru was so happy that he wrote to all the chief ministers on 10 May 1956 and said, 'This bill and the Hindu Marriage Act have a peculiar significance, not only because of the changes they bring about but chiefly because they have pulled out Hindu law from the ruts in which it had got stuck and given it a new dynamism. In that sense, the passage of this legislation marks an epoch in India.' (Gopal and Iyengar Vol. II. 2003: 143)

The question of the minimum age of marriage continued to agitate people in the 1970s. Suggestions were made in 1976 that it should be raised to twenty-one years for both men and women. A private member's bill was also introduced in that year suggesting that the marriage age should be the same as the voting age under the Representation of the People's Act. However the government decided that it should be fifteen years for girls and eighteen years for boys—the same as under the Child Marriage Restraint Act. (*LSD* Vol. 62, 1976: 11, 13)

It can be seen that ideas pertaining to personal laws change as society changes and inevitably there is a demand for reviewing them.

The Hindu Adoptions and Maintenance Bill, 1956, as reported by the Select Committee, came up for discussion in the Rajya Sabha on 27 November 1956. The animated discussion continued for three days and was marked by the quoting of Hindu scriptures by both sides—those who supported the bill and those who opposed it. During the discussion, as expected, a question was raised by one of the members, H.P. Saksena, as to when the government envisaged bringing about a code applicable to all communities residing in India. H.V. Pataskar, Minister for Legal Affairs, replied: 'We hope to do it as early as we can.'

India is still awaiting that day.

The bill was generally welcomed as the last chapter in the codification of Hindu law. In his speech, Jaswant Singh highlighted the fact that: 'According to our Hindu religious scriptures and our religious notions, the very *raison d'être* of adoption is that a genuine Hindu and a real Hindu who believes in rebirth feels that if he has no son of his own and he has to attain *moksha*, there must be somebody after him to do *pindadan*...'

In reply to a question, Jaswant Singh further said that, 'When there are no more men living on the face of this earth, only then a woman can give *pinda*'.

I am giving these quotations to show the mindset of the law-givers at the time. Jaswant Singh also raised the question of the need for a common law for all communities. He said:

> When the government feels itself to be a secular government and when our state is a secular state under the Constitution, why should a particular community be selected and their religious feelings be hurt? We have got fundamental objections for enacting this law only for the Hindus, not covering other communities and religions which live in this country. (*RSD* Vol. 15, 1956: 787, 795, 810–11, 814)

The Hindu Code enactments have gone some way towards improving the rights and status of Hindu women but the task is still incomplete on several points. It is more so since Muslim women are not covered by these major changes. One can only imagine what the social and other changes in India would have been if these reforms had been extended to Muslim women as well.

I am quoting below extracts from the speech of Veena Varma because the points made therein are as valid today as they were when she made them. Speaking on International Women's Day on 8 March 1993 in the Rajya Sabha, Veena Varma invited attention to some salient points:

> Females are discriminated against not only throughout life but even before birth and are subject of exploitation and indignities at every stage during childhood, adolescence, youth, old age and even death—deteriorating sex ratio, large-scale female foeticide, gross misuse of amniosynthesis tests (sex determination tests) and termination of pregnancies, a disproportionately high rate of infant mortality, and a still higher mortality rate in reproductive years in rural areas.
>
> She pleaded for compulsory registration of all marriages on the same lines as the registration of births. She also underlined that the status of women among Muslims was even more deplorable. It was

time that the minorities, especially the women among them, rose to the occasion and raised their voice for the enactment of a uniform civil code giving proprietary rights to women in their husband's property rather than mere *mehar*, a right which accrues only on being divorced. Varma underlined that the then Prime Minister P.V. Narasimha Rao, soon after he took over in 1991, had announced the constitution of two commissions—one to study the problems of women and improve their status and the other for women's rights. Unfortunately, no action had been taken thereon. (*RSD* Vol. 166.2, 1993: 488–91)

What J.B. Kripalani stated herein is fully borne out by the experience of the reforms in Hindu law.

> There are many customs and institutions among religious groups in India and elsewhere which need reform; but the majority stands against these and therefore, they cannot be brought about and the reformer feels helpless. *In history, reforms have been made possible through the efforts of gifted individuals or advanced minorities...* If the initiative of the individual reformer is to be pitched against the majority, at a particular period of time, no reform or reformer would have any chance of success. *The reformer and the revolutionary have very often to plough a lonely furrow.* They had always to resist the passions and prejudices of the majority. Sometimes they had to walk alone and even to suffer martyrdom.

Kripalani rightly stated that:

> If the removal of untouchability had been left to the will and vote of the orthodox Hindu majority, it may not have been possible to abolish it even though Gandhi had created a powerful opinion against it. If the reform of the Hindu Civil Code had been left to the majority opinion of the Hindu community, it would never have been effective. (Kripalani 2004: 930)

In contrast to what Dr Ambedkar had stated, P.B. Gajendragadkar, former chief justice of India, in his 'Reflections on Hindu Law' observed:

It is indeed a remarkable tribute to the Hindu genius that throughout its career spreading over 3 to 4 thousand years, Hindu law never lagged behind the social conscience, nor did it ever go far ahead of it. Unfortunately, this process of progressive adjustment which kept alive its threat of continuity and yet made suitable modifications in its structure was arrested during British rule...and so in many respects Hindu law came to be fossilized. The inevitable result was that, during British rule, the popular mind began to look upon Hindu law as based wholly on religion and lost sight of its essentially dynamic and progressive character...All social laws must be based on secular, rational and scientific considerations. The test must always be the test of social values. (Mahajan 1966: 301)

Gajendragadkar talked about the fossilization of Hindu law during the British regime but it has to be admitted that, as brought out above, a number of enactments for reform of the Hindu religious law were passed during the period, in spite of opposition from conservative and orthodox Hindus.

Uniform Civil Code—Time to Make a Beginning

Jawaharlal Nehru, in his article in *The Hindustan Times,* dated 20 October 1940, was quite clear in his mind even as far back as then that:

> A uniform civil code for the whole of India is essential. Yet I realize that this cannot be imposed on unwilling people. It should, therefore, be made optional to begin with, and individuals and groups may voluntarily accept it and come within its scope. The State should meanwhile carry on propaganda in its favour. (Gopal and Iyengar Vol. II. 2003: 39)

During the deliberations in the Constituent Assembly, M.R. Masani, Hansa Mehta and Amrit Kaur sent their note of dissent dated 14 April 1947 on the provision for uniform civil code being relegated to the directive principles of state policy, which could not be enforced in a court of law:

We are not satisfied with the acceptance of a uniform civil code as an ultimate social objective set out in clause 41 as determined by the majority of the sub-committee. One of the factors that has kept India back from advancing to nationhood has been the existence of personal laws based on religion which keep the nation divided into water-tight compartments in many aspects of life. We are of the view that a uniform civil code should be guaranteed to the Indian people within a period of 5 or 10 years in the same manner as the right to free and compulsory primary education has been guaranteed by clause 24 within 10 years. We therefore suggest that the Advisory Committee might transfer the clause regarding a uniform civil code from Chapter 2 to Chapter 1 after making suitable modifications in it. (Rao 1967: 162)

There was considerable opposition to this proposal. In fact, Muhammad Ismail Sahib moved an amendment on 23 November 1948, which provided that any group, section or community of people shall not be obliged to give up its personal law if it has such a law. He argued that the right to follow personal law was part of the way of life of those people who were following such laws; it was part of their religion and part of their culture. He also stated that the matter of retaining personal law was not new. There were precedents in European countries. Yugoslavia, for instance, under treaty obligations, was obliged to guarantee the rights of minorities.

He quoted the relevant rights of Muslims as follows:

'The Serb, Croat and Slovene State agrees to grant to the Mussulmans in the matter of family law and personal status provisions suitable for regulating these matters in accordance with the Mussulman usage.' He said that similar clauses obtained in several other European Constitutions also. But these referred to minorities while his amendment referred not to the minorities alone but to all people including the majority community. (*CAD* Vol. VII, Book 2, 2009 : 540–41)

On 23 November 1948, Naziruddin Ahmad also proposed adding a proviso to Article 35 (as it was then) to read:

Provided that the personal law of any community which has been guaranteed by the statute shall not be changed except with the previous approval of the community ascertained in such manner as the Union Legislature may determine by law.

Ahmad emphasized that: What the British in 175 years failed to do or was [sic] afraid to do, what the Muslims in the course of 500 years refrained from doing, we should not give power to the state to do all at once. I submit that we should proceed not in haste but with caution, with experience, with statesmanship and with sympathy. (*CAD* Vol. VII, Book 2, 2009: 541–43)

Mahboob Ali Baig Sahib Bahadur proposed on 23 November 1948, that a proviso should be added to read: 'Provided that nothing in this article shall affect the personal law of the citizen.' He said that the words 'uniform civil code' strictly do not cover the personal law of a citizen. However, to make the position abundantly clear, he had given an amendment as above. He added: 'As far as the Mussalmans are concerned, their laws of succession, inheritance, marriage and divorce are completely dependent upon their religion…(Marriage as a contract) is enjoined on the Mussalmans by the Quran and if it is not followed, a marriage is not a legal marriage at all. For 1350 years this law has been practised by Muslims and recognized by all authorities in all states…People seem to have very strange ideas about a secular state. People seem to think that under a secular state, there must be a common law observed by its citizens in all matters, including matters of their daily life, their language, their culture, their personal laws. This is not the correct way to look at the secular state…Citizens belonging to different communities must have the freedom to practise their own religion, observe their own life, and their personal laws should be applied to them.' (*CAD* Vol. VII, Book 2, 2009: 543–44)

Pocker Sahib Bahadur supported the amendment proposed by Muhammad Ismail Sahib to add a proviso to Article 35, referred to above. He said:

'One of the reasons why the Britisher, having conquered this country, has been able to carry on the administration of this country for the last 150 years and over, was that he gave a guarantee of following personal laws to each of the various communities in the country. That is one of the secrets of success...I ask whether, by the freedom we have obtained for this country, are we going to give up that freedom of conscience and that freedom of religious practices and that freedom of following one's own personal law, and try or aspire to impose upon the whole country one code of civil law?' He also questioned the authority of the Constituent Assembly to make such drastic changes in the personal laws without having a mandate for the purpose. (*CAD* Vol. VII, Book 2, 2009: 544–45)

Hussain Imam said:

India is too big a country with a large population so diversified that it is almost impossible to stamp them with one kind of anything... I feel that it is all right and a very desirable thing to have a uniform law, but at a very distant date. For that, we should first await the coming of that event when the whole of India has got educated, when mass illiteracy has been removed, when people have advanced, when their economic conditions are better, when each man is able to stand on his own legs and fight his own battles. Then you can have uniform laws...Secular state does not mean that it is anti-religious state. It means that it is not irreligious but [is] non-religious and as such there is a world of difference between irreligious and non-religious. (*CAD* Vol. VII, Book 2, 2009: 546)

On 6 December 1948, Muhammad Ismail Sahib and Pocker Sahib Bahadur jointly moved an amendment to the provisions of Article 19 (protection of certain rights regarding freedom of speech, and so on) again bringing up the question of protecting personal laws of Muslims: 'Nothing in this article shall affect the operation of any existing law or preclude the state from making any law—(a) regulating or restricting any economic, financial, political or other secular activity which may be associated with religious practice'. Muhammad Ismail Sahib said that he proposed to make it clear that so far as personal law was concerned, Article 19 would not affect the observance thereof by the people concerned.

Muhammad Ismail Sahib moved yet another amendment to Article 19 to state that:

After clause (2) of Article 19, the following new clause be added: '(3) nothing in clause (2) of this article shall affect the right of any citizen to follow the personal law of the group or the community to which he belongs or professes to belong'. Muhammad Ismail Sahib stressed that Ambedkar's reference to certain enactments concerning Muslim personal law, such as Wakf, shariat law and Muslim marriage law, did not abrogate the Muslim personal law at all. He said there was no revision and in all these cases what was done was that the Muslim personal law was elucidated and it was made clear that these laws shall apply to Muslims. Therefore, those enactments and legislations cannot be cited now as matters of precedence for us to do anything contravening the personal law of the people. K. Santhanam objected to these amendments saying that the question of UCC [uniform civil code] has already been discussed and settled separately and it cannot be reopened now. Ambedkar supported Santhanam's contention. However, the Vice-President of CA [Constituent Assembly] said: 'I do not know whether I am technically correct or not; but in view of the peculiar circumstances in which our Muslim brethren are placed, I am allowing Mr Muhammad Ismail Sahib to say what he has to say and to place his views before the House.' (*CAD* Vol. VII, Book 2, 2009: 829–31)

It can be seen that all five Muslim members who spoke, strongly opposed any interference in the Muslim personal law and, in fact, wanted a specific provision to be made for the purpose by adding a proviso to Article 44. They did not want to take the risk, at any time in the future, of steps being taken by the government to formulate a uniform civil code. Nor did they want Article 19 to extend to making any changes in the personal laws of Muslims.

In his speech, K.M. Munshi argued strongly that the particular clause which was now before the House had not been brought for discussion for the first time. It had been discussed in several committees and at several places before it came to the House. Munshi also contested the argument that the provision for a uniform civil code infringed the fundamental rights mentioned in Article 19. He underlined that the House had already accepted the principle that, if a religious practice followed up to then covered a secular activity or fell within the field of social reform or social welfare, it would be open to Parliament to make laws about it without infringing this fundamental right of a minority. Munshi also emphasized that, even if the provision for a uniform civil code in the directive principle were not made, it would still not stop Parliament in future from enacting a uniform civil code it. As stated earlier, Article 19 would not come in the way. He urged that Muslims should give up this 'isolationist outlook on life'. He further pointed out that the belief that personal law was part of religion had been perpetuated under British rule.

Alladi Krishnaswami Ayyar said a civil code runs into 'every department of civil relations to the law of contracts, to the law of property, to the law of succession, to the law of marriage and similar matters. How can there be any objection to the general statement here that the state would endeavour to secure a uniform civil code throughout India?' He invited attention to the second objection that religion was in danger. In fact, the article in question actually aimed at amity and not its destruction. He said that when the British introduced one criminal law in the country for all citizens, the Muslims had not objected. Similarly, when the law of contracts was introduced, no such objections had been raised. Ayyar asked whether different personal laws were perpetuated in France, in Germany, in Italy and in all the countries of Europe. He appealed to the House to approve the article unanimously.

In a studied and hard-hitting response to the debate, Ambedkar said he could not accept any of the amendments moved in the House. He refuted the various arguments put forth against the uniform civil code. He also challenged the contention of the Muslim members that the Muslim personal law was immutable and uniform through the whole of India. He said:

> 'Up to 1935, the North-West Frontier Province (NWFP) was not subject to the shariat law. It followed the Hindu law in the matter of succession and in other matters so much so that it was in 1939 that the Central Legislature had come into the field to abrogate the application of Hindu law to the Muslims of the NWFP and to apply the shariat law to them... Apart from the NWFP, up till 1937, in the rest of India, in various parts such as the United Provinces,

the Central Provinces and Bombay, the Muslims to a large extent were governed by Hindu law in the matter of succession. In order to bring them on the plane of uniformity with regard to the other Muslims who observed the shariat law, the Legislature had to intervene in 1937 and to pass an enactment applying the shariat law to the rest of India...In North Malabar, the Marumakkathayam Law applied to all—not only to Hindus but also to Muslims... it is therefore no use making a categorical statement that the Muslim law has been an immutable law which they have been following from ancient times.' Ambedkar also reassured the Muslims that in the initial stage, the application of UCC could be purely voluntary, as was done in the case of the Shariat Act of 1937. (*CAD* Vol. VII, Book 2, 2009: 546–52)

All amendments moved by Muslim members were negatived by the House. Unfortunately, all the forceful and articulate submissions made by three eminent legal luminaries, namely, Munshi, Ayyar and Ambedkar, fell on deaf ears.

While moving the motion for the introduction of the Draft Constitution, Ambedkar made an important observation. He said:

Care is taken to eliminate all diversity from laws which are the basis of civic and corporate life. The great Codes of Civil and Criminal Laws, such as the Civil Procedure Code, the Penal Code, the Criminal Procedure Code, the Evidence Act, Transfer of Property Act, Laws of Marriage, Divorce and Inheritance, are either [*sic*] placed in the Concurrent List so that the necessary uniformity can always be preserved without impairing the federal system. (Rodrigues 2002: 483)

Justice Gajendragadkar, in his memorial lecture on 'Secularism and the Constitution of India', referred to the question and answers which took place in Parliament on this subject. Commenting on the proposal of some members that a uniform civil code be enacted:

Mr Nehru: Well, I should like a civil code which applies to everybody, but...

Mr [Shankarrao] More: What hinders?
Mr Nehru: Wisdom hinders.
Mr More: Not wisdom but reaction hinders.
Mr Nehru: The honourable member is perfectly entitled to his view on the subject. If he or anybody else brings a civil code bill, it will have my extreme sympathy [sic]. But I confess I do not think that at the present moment the time is ripe in India for me to try to push it through. I want to prepare the ground for it, and this kind of thing is one method of preparing the ground.
Gajendragadkar wrote: It will thus be clear that Nehru thought that when Parliament took the first step of secularizing the personal law governing Hindus, it will have set in motion a revolutionary movement and that, in course of time, as a result of education and propaganda, the next inevitable step could be taken and Article 44 would then be fully implemented. (Gajendragadkar 1971: 124–25)

Any perceptive observer would agree that a golden opportunity was lost by the Congress party in not pursuing this point to its logical conclusion and not undertaking the exercise of formulating the uniform civil code. In fact, this was the only time when such an effort would have been successful, just as the Constituent Assembly was successful in doing away with communal electorates and reservation of seats in the legislatures for minorities on the basis of population. This is in sharp contrast with the codification of Hindu law which was pursued so vigorously under the enlightened leadership of Jawaharlal Nehru and Ambedkar. This effort, too, had met with very stiff resistance from the conservative and orthodox elements in Hindu society on the grounds that Hindu religion was in danger, and it had also been opposed by important and influential leaders of the Congress party such as, Rajendra Prasad and P.D. Tandon. If only Nehru[3] had decided to take up the cause of UCC equally boldly, Indian Muslim society today would have looked altogether different. Unfortunately, lost opportunities like this never come again.

B.N. Tandon, joint secretary to Prime Minister Indira Gandhi, wrote in his memoirs that the prime minister was being swayed by conservative

---

[3] Vallabhbhai Patel humorously used to call Nehru 'Congress's only nationalist Muslim'. (Gandhi 1990: 504)

Muslim leaders though she was personally favourably inclined towards social reforms. He wrote:

> The PM had left a note for Prof. Dhar [principal secretary to the PM]. The note contained the summary of her discussion with Ismail Suleiman Sait, the leader of the Muslim League on the 9th [January 1975]. Prof. Dhar discussed that note with me and said that he was very upset at the League's communal approach. He has studied Muslim politics in detail and, in general, he is not happy with the government's policy towards Muslims. He says that *the pseudo-liberal Hindus who surround the PM and advise her to accept all sorts of demands of the Muslims would not be able to solve the problems of that community*. The need of the hour is that the Muslims should give up their tendency to insist on a separate identity and join the mainstream. Their demand that there should be no change in their personal law is misplaced. Sait has again demanded that the government should provide a legal guarantee that there would be no change in their personal law. But Prof. Dhar has written to her [the PM] saying that this is impossible because the Constitution does not permit it. (Tandon 2003: 149)

On 6 August 1993, Sumitra Mahajan—who is at present the Speaker of the Lok Sabha—moved a resolution in the Lok Sabha, and urged 'upon the government that in order to achieve the objectives enshrined in Article 44 of the Constitution and to promote the feelings of unity and brotherhood amongst all citizens of the country, a commission be constituted for framing a uniform civil code'. During the course of her speech, she referred to the speech of K.M. Munshi in the Constituent Assembly stating that 'religion must be restricted to the spheres which legitimately pertain to religion only. The rest of life must be regulated, unified and modified in such a manner that we may evolve, as early as possible, into a strong and consolidated nation.' She invited attention to the fact that, instead of enacting a uniform civil code, there had been talk of implementing the law of shariat. One minister in fact had had to resign on this issue. She urged that, looking to the complexities of the issue, it was essential to set up a commission.

As was to be expected, Mani Shankar Aiyar of the Congress party strongly opposed the motion. Particular attention may be invited to the manner in which he defended Rajiv Gandhi's decision in the Shah Bano case. Rajiv Gandhi had said that by no means could his actions be treated as active appeasement of the Muslim community. He (Rajiv Gandhi) said:

> If the argument is right, that the country is outraged, then it means, automatically, that all the Hindus do not support us, so I lose 85 per cent of my electorate. He said then, if it is right that the women of Islam are outraged, I lose 7.5 per cent of the rest which means I lose 92.5 per cent and if it is right that several male members of the Islamic community are outraged, then, I lose another 3 or 4 per cent. So, I get down to securing the support of 3 per cent for this act and secure the opposition of 97 per cent of Indians. How can it be called the politics of appeasement? He explained—and I [Mani Shankar Aiyar] stand by that position—that if you create a communal divide by taking a particular Supreme Court judgment and converting it into a Hindu–Muslim issue, then, any responsible government of this country has to say that even if I lose the support of 97 per cent of the electorate, I must do the right thing to keep this country together and the country was kept together. (*LSD* Vol. 23.2, 1993: 402–03, 410, 423–24)

This whole argument is so facetious and ludicrous that it hardly calls for any serious comment. But this is how an important issue of national importance has been stonewalled by the so-called secular parties all these years. Needless to say, Sumitra Mahajan's resolution was defeated and the situation on the implementation of Article 44 remained unchanged.

J.B. Kripalani said:

> Today, if the question of the [*sic*] abolition of polygamy among the Muslim community is left to majority vote, it cannot be abolished, however desirable the reform may be under the present circumstances. It is this prejudice of the Muslim community that stands in the way of a Common Civil Code for all Indians.

However, this is a rather simplistic reasoning which hardly does credit to the weighty arguments adduced against a uniform civil code. I have discussed these at some length later.

Golwalkar, the prime ideologue of the RSS, surprisingly was not insistent on a uniform civil code. While inaugurating the Deendayal Research Institute, New Delhi, on 20 August 1972, he went so far as to say that the Muslim law could continue separately, without being replaced by a uniform civil code. When asked whether uniformity of law would not promote national integration, he said:

> 'Not necessarily, India has always had infinite variety. And yet, for long stretches of time, we were a very strong and united nation. For unity we need harmony, not uniformity.' When asked whether Muslims were not resisting a uniform code just to maintain their separate entity, he said: 'I have no quarrel with any class, community or sect wanting to maintain its identity, so long as that identity does not detract from its patriotic feeling. I have a feeling that some people want a uniform civil code because they think that the right to marry four wives is causing a disproportionate increase in the Muslim population. I am afraid this is a negative approach to the problem...Our approach is entirely different. The Muslim is welcome to his way of life so long as he loves this country and its culture. I must say politicians are responsible for misleading the Muslims. It was the Congress which revived the Muslim League in Kerala and thus accentuated Muslim communalism throughout the country.' (Malkani 1980: 70–71)

It is interesting to note the assessment of someone as eminent as M.C. Chagla on this question. He wrote:

> Although the directive principles of State enjoins such a code [UCC], the government has refused to do anything about it on the plea that the minorities will resent any attempt at imposition. Unless they are agreeable it would not be fair and proper to make the law applicable to them. *I wholly and emphatically disagree with this view. The Constitution is binding on everyone, majority and minority; and if the Constitution contains a directive, that directive must be accepted and implemented.* Jawaharlal showed great strength and courage in getting the Hindu Reform Bill passed, but he accepted the policy of *laissez-faire* where the Muslims and

other minorities were concerned. I am horrified to find that in my country, while monogamy has been made the law for the Hindus, Muslims can still indulge in the luxury of polygamy. It is an insult to womanhood; and Muslim women, I know, resent this discrimination between Muslim women and Hindu women. (Chagla 2000: 85)

The detailed discussion on this subject brings out the opposition expressed by the Muslim members to even retaining Article 44 in the directive principles. In fact, there was a vociferous demand from the majority community that this provision should form part of the fundamental rights so that it would be justiciable and have a greater weightage than merely relegating it to the directive principles. Because of the opposition of the minorities and particularly the Muslims, this demand was not conceded by the Congress party. It is interesting to see that even after Partition, when the Muslims had lost political leverage, they were unrelenting so far as their demands—such as protecting their personal law, primacy of the Urdu language and maintaining independent identity—were concerned. The Congress party, too, was so jubilant at having been able to persuade the Muslims and the Christians to give up their separate electorates and reservation of seats on the basis of population in the legislatures, that it was prepared to concede all their other demands, such as relegating the uniform civil code to being just a directive principle and including the right to propagation of religion as a fundamental right.

Durga Das Basu has quoted Granville Austin as saying:

> The framing of the provision regarding a UCC provides an interesting aside to the [minority] sub-committee's work. In India, in 1947, despite the inroads on personal law during the British period, many Indians lived their lives untouched by secular law, whether civil or criminal. The idea of a common civil code, therefore, struck at the heart of custom of orthodoxy, Hindu, Muslim and Sikh. During the days when the [directive] principles were to be justiciable, Minoo Masani moved in a sub-committee meeting that it was the State's responsibility to establish a uniform code, in order to get rid of 'those water-tight compartments' as he called them. The members voted against the recommendation 5:4, on the ground that it was beyond the sub-committee's competence. Yet,

two days later, it had been decided to non-justiciable section of the rights [sic], where the clause should be put. The reason behind these actions was not, as it might first appear, the wish to avoid a clash with Hindu orthodoxy, but a sensitivity, particularly on Nehru's part, to the fears of the Muslims and the Sikhs. Had the provision been made in the [fundamental] rights, it would have been justiciable and perforce applicable equally to all communities. In the [directive] principles, action could be taken at the will of the Parliament in regard to one community—as happened with the Hindu Code Bill a few years later. That the sub-committee refused to make the clause justiciable largely to calm Muslim fears can be seen in a letter written to Patel, as chairman of the Advisory Committee in late July 1947 by Masani and Amrit Kaur and Mrs Mehta, who had supported Masani's initiative the previous March. The letter recalled the earlier rejection of their efforts and went on 'in view of the changes that have taken place since (meaning certainly Partition) and the keen desire that is now left for a more homogenous and closely knit Indian nation' was [sic] with the Advisory Committee again to consider the matter when it meets on 28th July 1947. Their efforts were unsuccessful, however, and the clause remained one in the directive principle. (Granville Austin *The Indian Constitution: Cornerstone of a Nation*, 9th impression, 2005, pp. 80–81 in Basu, Vol. 3, 2008: 4134–35)

It is evident that the Congress party did not want to press the issue of formulating a uniform civil code while the Constitution was under discussion. But, that was the only time when such a uniform civil code could have been adopted. As suggested by Dr Ambedkar, the code could have been made optional so as to reduce the opposition to it by any of the minorities. Ambedkar stated that (When a uniform civil code is formulated) it is perfectly possible that the future Parliament may make a provision by way of making a beginning that the code shall apply only to those who make a declaration that they are prepared to be bound by it, so that in the initial stage the application of the code may be purely voluntary.

The Supreme Court has repeatedly exhorted the government to take appropriate steps in the matter. The Court had observed in the

Shah Bano case that, 'piecemeal attempts by courts....to bridge the gap between personal laws cannot take the place of a uniform civil code. Justice for all is a far more satisfactory way of dispensing justice than is justice from case to case.'

Justice V.D. Tulzapurkar, the then judge of the Supreme Court, asserted:

> In the context of fighting the poison of communalism, the relevance of a uniform civil code cannot be disputed; in fact, it will provide a juristic solution to the communal problem by striking at its root cause. Nay, it will foster secular forces so essential in achieving social justice and common nationality. Since our Constitution envisages one society with one singular citizenship, it is highly desirable that one single set of civil laws should govern all its citizens...*A more glaring instance of an abject surrender to pressures exerted by fundamentalists, obscurantists and religious fanatics of the largest minority community in the country with electoral considerations in mind would be difficult to find. Does not ritualistic invocation or incantation of the principle of secularism in the face of such behaviour sound hypocritical? When the political will to strike at fundamentalism is lacking, secularism will always remain an unattainable ideal.* (Tulzapurkar 1987: 17–18)

In its judgment on the *Shah Bano* case ([1985] 2 SCC 556), the Supreme Court quoted Dr Tahir Mahmood from his book, *Muslim Personal Law* (1977 edition, p. 200–02), in which he had made a powerful plea for framing a uniform civil code for all citizens of India. He had said: 'In pursuance of the goal of secularism, the State must stop administering religion-based personal laws.' He wanted the lead to come from the majority community but we would think that, lead or no lead, the State must act. It would be useful to quote the appeal made by the author to the Muslim community:

> Instead of wasting their energies in exerting theological and political pressure in order to secure an 'immunity' for their traditional personal law from the State's legislative jurisdiction, the Muslims will do well to begin exploring and demonstrating how

the true Islamic laws, purged of their time-worn and anachronistic interpretations, can enrich the common civil code of India.

In the said judgment, the Supreme Court also referred to the report of the Commission on Marriage and Family Laws which had been appointed by the government of Pakistan by a resolution dated 4 August 1955. The commission had concluded thus: 'In the words of Allama Iqbal, "the question which is likely to confront Muslim countries in the near future, is whether the law of Islam is capable of evolution—a question which will require great intellectual effort, and is sure to be answered in the affirmative".' (pp. 573–74)

The Supreme Court has stated above that 'lead or no lead, the state must act'. As I have urged in this discussion, my view is somewhat different. Looking at the sensitiveness of the issue and its explosive political implications, it would be futile to expect any political party to take the lead in bringing a bill for a uniform civil code in Parliament. Even if such a bill were presented, it is not likely to have an easy passage. The best course would be, in contrast with the short-sighted policies followed so far, to encourage and strengthen the modern, liberal elements within the Muslim community to take a lead in the matter.

The apex court also asked the government to undertake legislation for the compulsory registration of marriages and adoption of children but this, too, has not been possible due to the resistance of Muslims, though such legislations are on the statute books in a number of Muslim countries.

Tahir Mahmood, in his article, 'Walking Away from the Code', said:

Indiscreetly using the word 'Hindu' in the titles and provisions of the four acts of 1955–56 has, for four different communities, violated the spirit of the Constitution...enacting separate laws for Sikhs or Buddhists is a step in the opposite direction and strengthens other communities' demand for the retention of their personal laws. *There is a better way to respond to the prevailing misgivings.* As the four communities governed by the 1955–56 acts are listed in their opening provisions, just delete the word 'Hindu' from their titles and in the inside provisions replace it with 'every person governed by this act'. With these innocuous changes, the acts should be perfectly acceptable to Buddhists and Sikhs. By making other changes necessary to completely secularize the four acts, these may, in fact, be developed as the framework for consultations on a UCC. But, then, who is interested in such a code? (*IE*, 20 October 2015: 9)

The Gujarat High Court ruled that, in the case of minor Muslim girls, the Prohibition of Child Marriage Act, 2006, will prevail over the provisions of Muslim personal laws. The court held that the religion of the contracting party did not matter. The court also said that those who have not allowed any change in the Muslim personal law, have done a great disservice to the community. (*IE* 26 September 2015: 7)

In another case, the Gujarat High Court held that Muslims could not be booked for the offence of polygamy under the IPC (Indian Penal Code) as it was permissible in the Islamic law. It observed, however, that polygamy 'is an exception and not a rule'. (*IE* 6 November 2015: 6)

Justice Srikrishna candidly observed:

In *Sarla Mudgal* (*Sarla Mudgal v. Union of India*, (1995) 3 SCC 635; 1955 SCC (Cri) 569), the Supreme Court made wide-ranging observations on the need to bring in a uniform civil code and directed the State to explain the steps it had taken towards the enactment of the same. *The question of a uniform civil code is undoubtedly an issue fraught with complex political fault lines involving minority rights, personal laws, women's rights, and so on*, and the Supreme Court observations not unexpectedly erupted into a major political issue. In a later case, the Supreme Court was forced to back down by explaining away its controversial observations in *Sarla Mudgal* as having been 'incidentally made' (*Ahmedabad Women's Action Group v. Union of India*, (1997) 3 SCC 573 at p. 582 (para 14), per Venkataswami, J.). *In other cases, judges have sought to incorporate ideologically grounded concepts, such as 'Hindutva' and 'Socialism', into their judgment with no credit whatsoever.* (Srikrishna 2005: J-15)

In 2015, the Supreme Court once again urged the government to take an early decision on enacting a uniform civil code. 'You must take a decision soon,' the Court requested. The Court was hearing a public interest litigation (PIL) seeking a waiver of the two-year mandatory separation period for a Christian couple before it could move court for divorce by mutual consent. The separation period is one year for other religions. The petitioner had argued that the two-year mandatory period was biased against the Christian community and was discriminatory. (*India Legal*, 15 November 2015: 22)

Attention must be drawn to the fact that the demand for a separate Sikh personal law is being revived by a section of Sikhs. As stated elsewhere, there is also a demand in Maharashtra that a separate marriage law should be enacted for Buddhists, though a section of the Ambedkarites, headed by Prakash Ambedkar, is opposed to the making of such a law. (*Loksatta*, 23 September 2015: 4) If Article 44 pertaining to the uniform civil code continues to remain in cold storage, it will be difficult to resist such demands.

In sharp contrast, a section of the Parsis have willingly decided to give up the traditional disposal of dead bodies in the 'Tower of Silence' and instead opted for burial or cremation of the dead. Some priests have agreed to perform the last rites in such cases. (*IE*, 17 August 2015: 1)

Looking at past experience, it is unlikely that even the BJP government at the Centre, with its declared commitment to enact a uniform civil code, would dare to take any initiative in the matter, looking to the vociferous opposition of the conservative, orthodox and fundamentalist elements among the Muslims, and the vote-bank politics of the so-called 'secular' political parties.

As can be seen from the comments of Maulana Mohammad Wali Rahmani, general secretary of the All India Muslim Personal Law Board (AIMPLB), the stand of the Muslims in 2015 is exactly the same as it had been of the Muslim members of the Constituent Assembly, referred to above. (*IE* 5 November 2015: 3)

Against the background of the ruling BJP and its constituent and allied organizations, such as the RSS, the Bajrang Dal, the Vishva Hindu Parishad (VHP) and the Shiv Sena, strongly supporting causes such as the ban on cow slaughter, on the grounds that they are a part of the Hindu religion, Hindus no longer have the moral right to press for enactment of the uniform civil code which is being opposed by the Muslims on the grounds that it would be against the precepts of the Quran and their religious culture.

It is also necessary to emphasize that, as brought out in the section on Hindu Code, the reform of Hindu law was possible mainly because of the reformist movement among Hindus. Unless such reformist leadership is encouraged to come up among the Muslims, any imposition of a uniform civil code from the outside would clearly be counter-productive and meet with stiff resistance. Fortunately, winds of change seem to be blowing. It is a move from Shah Bano (1985) to Shayara Bano (2016). Shayara Bano, a thirty-five-year-old sociology postgraduate and a mother of two, has approached the Supreme Court seeking not just justice in respect of termination of her marriage but a ban on triple *talaq*, polygamy and *halala*, the custom that mandates that if a woman wants to go back to her husband following divorce, she must first consummate her marriage with another man. Shayara's is the first attempt at raising wider, more fundamental issues. (*IE* 13 April 2016: 9) She has become the first Muslim woman to challenge a personal law practice, citing her fundamental rights. A high-level committee appointed by the UPA government to review the status of women in India has sought a ban on the practice of oral, unilateral and triple *talaq* or divorce, as well as polygamy. The Supreme Court has directed the government to produce the report in the Court. (*IE* 31 March 2016: 9)

First women *quazi*s in Uttar Pradesh have started working. One is a professor and the other a science graduate. One is a Shia, the other a Sunni. (*IE* 13 March 2016: 1) Two women claiming to be the first *quazi*s in Rajasthan have run into trouble with the clerics who claim that they cannot perform certain religious rituals. (*IE* 9 February 2016: 6)

Unfortunately, the experience of governance since Independence has been quite the contrary. B.N. Tandon, who was joint secretary to Prime Minister Indira Gandhi, wrote:

> Karan Singh, [the then-minister for Family Planning], spoke very clearly in the PAC [Political Affairs Committee of the Cabinet]. He courageously stated that one of the directive principles of our Constitution is that we should have a uniform civil code applicable to the whole country and yet even twenty-five years later we are

hesitant in considering the issue. *Whenever there is any discussion of social reforms we always exclude the Muslim community from its ambit. This is not only improper, but is also not in the interest of the Muslims. It amounts to encouraging their feelings of separateness and backwardness.* His statement had quite an impact but the PM twisted the discussion to her purpose and in the end no decision was taken. (Tandon 2006: 53)

Over the years, because of the conservative and fundamentalist views of the Muslim community, proposals such as the registration of marriages—which is statutorily binding in a number of Muslim countries—had to be given up. As brought out earlier, even the law on adoption could not be made applicable to Muslims. But the biggest and most prominent case of this kind was the *Shah Bano* case, in which even the Supreme Court decision on providing maintenance to a divorced wife was nullified by the Rajiv Gandhi government, which passed the Muslim Women (Protection of Rights on Divorce) Act, 1986. As seen earlier, liberal Muslim opinion, including that of Arif Mohammad Khan, the then minister of state, was overlooked to pander to the ultra-conservatives in the Muslim community. With these examples, any hopes of liberal reformists coming to the fore from within to amend the Muslim personal law and to do away with the gender biases therein is unlikely to succeed at any time in the near future.

It is important to note that, apparently, Muslim women too are keen that their personal laws should change with the times. An all-India survey by the Bharatiya Muslim Mahila Andolan revealed that 92.1 per cent of the surveyed Muslim women were opposed to oral talaq, a form of unilateral divorce that does not give room for reconciliation, while 91.2 per cent were against polygamy...*A majority of those surveyed were not aware about the All India Muslim Personal Law Board that works to protect Muslim personal law in the country...Several women's groups have been demanding that the Muslim personal law be codified so that it is not open to interpretations.* The clergy is against any tampering with Islamic laws. (*IE* 9 August 2015: 3)

The All India Muslim Personal Law Board has, however,

rejected the demand for change in the triple talaq system and has stated that what has happened in Pakistan, Bangladesh, Iran, Sudan and other countries, in terms of changes in the personal laws of Muslims has no relevance to India. (*Loksatta* 4 September 2015: 9)

At the same time, it must be noted that Muslim women's groups are against UCC 'if it does not guarantee freedom of religion'. The organization has claimed that, rather than a UCC, there is a need for 'gender-just reform in the Muslim personal law based on Quranic values of equality and justice in line with Article 25 of the Constitution of India'. (*IE* 17 October 2015: 3)

Questions are often asked whether it is possible to have one common civil code applying to different religions. One does not have to look too far to see that this is perfectly feasible. In Goa, Daman and Diu, during Portuguese rule, there was a common civil code of 1867 for the entire territory and there are no recorded instances of any difficulties in its implementation. It is important to note that, in Goa, neither the shariat nor the Hindu Code applies. It is the common Portuguese Civil Code which applies. Soli J. Sorabjee, senior Supreme Court advocate, wrote:

> The idea of uniform civil code in our Constitution still eludes us. Interestingly, this goal has been realized in Goa, Daman and Diu and there is uniformity in the application of personal laws. The Portuguese Civil Code, enacted in 1867, constitutes the basic substantive civil law and regulates, *inter alia*, matters relating to family, contracts, succession and property. The code has been adhered to and followed by all communities, Hindus and Muslims, who, barring rare exceptions, have not chosen to avail of those usages and customs of their communities which are expressly saved in the Code of Usages and Customs. The Code has been helpful in forging a cohesive and homogeneous society, and according to Justice Dr G.F. Couto, former judge of the Bombay High Court, it 'has enabled its citizens to live in peace and harmony, as well as to strengthen the basic unit of the society—the family—by safeguarding the interests of the children and the widows.' (*IE* 28 October 2007 in Godbole 2008: 105)

The All-India Muslim Personal Law Board has been at the forefront in opposing any move to bring about any changes in the personal laws of Muslims, howsoever justified they might be. For example, it had pressed for an exemption for Muslim girls from the Prohibition of Child Marriage Act which prohibited the marriage of a girl before she had attained the age of eighteen years. According to the Board, the shariat has laid down that a woman is of marriageable age as soon as she attains puberty. The Board had also decided not to endorse the bill seeking to make registration of all marriages compulsory. In September 2015, the Board rejected changes to the *talaq* system.

I have intentionally given, at the beginning of this chapter, the whole process of the enactment of the Hindu Code to show the resistance with which it met. The stiff opposition to a uniform civil code from the Muslims and the cry of the Muslim religion being in danger are no different from what they were during the passage of the Hindu Code. It is as if the Indian political system is hell-bent on not permitting the Muslims to reform in any way. This is particularly disturbing, considering the fact that Muslims already constitute over 14 per cent of the population and this percentage is likely to stabilize around 20 per cent in the next few years. Thus, if the uniform civil code is to become a reality, the demand for it will have to come from the Muslims themselves and the catalytic element for it will have to come from Indian society at large. Sadly, there is hardly any evidence of its realization so far. However, it is time the government made a move at least to begin the discussion on the uniform civil code in the Muslim community. This can be done by asking the Law Commission of India to take up the work of drafting a uniform civil code in consultation with all stake-holders, including the National Human Rights Commission (NHRC) and the minorities commissions at the state and the national levels.

The Enactment of the Muslim Women (Protection of Rights on Divorce) Act

The Supreme Court, in the *Shah Bano* case (*AIR* 1985 SC 945), had held that a divorced Muslim woman, so long as she has not remarried, is a wife for the purpose of section 125 of the CrPC (Code of Criminal Procedure). The statutory right, available to her under this section, is unaffected by the provisions of the personal law applicable to her. It further held that a Muslim husband is under a statutory obligation to provide maintenance beyond the period of *iddat* to his divorced wife, who is unable to maintain herself. The Court concluded that there was no conflict between the provisions of section 125 of the CrPC and the Muslim personal law. It held that *mehar* (dower) is not an amount which can be said to be paid to the wife in consideration of divorce.

After the Supreme Court decision in the *Shah Bano* case, orchestrated efforts were made by fundamentalist Muslims to organize protests all over the country.[4] This included a conference organized by the All-India Muslim Personal Law Committee in Muzaffarpur on 16–17 November 1985. Other related events were the stoning of a procession organized in favour of the Muslim personal law in Ahmednagar on 18 November 1985; more than 5,00,000 Muslims in Bombay marching to Mantralaya on 20 November 1985. Muslim business establishments in Bombay, from Colaba to Mulund and Churchgate to Borivali, were closed. A rally was organized by the Bombay Muslim Federation; a procession was taken out by the Muslim Majlis in Lucknow on 20 November 1985. On 24 November 1985, in Patna, the police had to fire a few rounds to quell a violent mob protesting against the Supreme Court judgment. Lakhs of Muslims marched to the Collectorate in Gaya to give a memorandum on 28 November 1985.

The day on which the Rajiv Gandhi government introduced the Muslim Women (Protection of Rights on Divorce) Bill in the Lok Sabha, Minister of State Arif Mohammad Khan resigned from the council of ministers. He complained to Rajiv Gandhi that, while the government had claimed to have consulted leaders of the Muslim community, it had given credence to the views of only the conservatives, and ignored the progressive and secular opinion within the community.

A statement was issued by leading figures in the Muslim intelligentsia urging the government to ensure that rights guaranteed by the

---

[4]Jeffery has brought out that, in Pakistan, revised legislation passed in 1961 as the Muslim Family Laws Ordinance, attempted to enhance the legal rights of Muslim women by reducing some of the most overtly discriminatory provisions of the 1937 shariat legislation. Implementation and enforcement, however, have remained partial at best. (Jeffery 2006: Footnote 3, p. 80)

Constitution to women were upheld. They demanded, 'That section 125 of the CrPC shall not be changed and the right of divorced Muslim women to claim maintenance from their husbands or former husbands shall be preserved.' They also stressed, 'That the exoneration of the husband from all responsibility for maintenance of divorced women is contrary to the provision and spirit of section 125 of the CrPC which is meant for indigent women and seeks to prevent destitution.' The statement was signed by 118 leading Muslims in various walks of life. (Engineer 1987: 215–17)

A memorandum was submitted to the prime minister by the Committee for the Protection of Rights of Muslim Women on 24 February 1986. The signatories were well-known Muslim leaders of public opinion in various fields. It stated:

> We believe that Muslim women have the right to maintenance—a right that they enjoy in several Muslim countries... The interpretation being put forward by a section of the Muslim religious leadership in India, on the other hand, expresses a backward-looking perspective... It is evident that those Muslims who have opposed the judgment [of the Supreme Court] have done so in the name of religion. They have used all the platforms available to them to reassert their weakening hold on Muslim public opinion, and have sought to exploit religion for sectional and communal political ends. They have taken advantage of the sense of insecurity among Muslims, caused by the persistence of communal riots and by discrimination in jobs and vocations...It is noteworthy that many important sections of Muslim public opinion, particularly among the educated and professional groups and segments, have supported the right to maintenance... *We call upon the government of India to ensure that the rights guaranteed by the Indian Constitution to women are upheld.* We emphasize this in relation to the Muslim women particularly, who have been subjected to discrimination for so long. *In our opinion, to deprive them of the rights guaranteed by secular laws would be a retrograde measure...* (Engineer 1987: 217–21)

Seema Mustafa, in her article in *The Telegraph* of 2 March 1986, pointed out that:

The government changed its mind in the period between the monsoon and winter sessions of Parliament. It decided to support the conservatives and Mr [Z.R.] Ansari, [Minister], was allowed over three hours [in Parliament] to argue that the Supreme Court judgment was against Islam... he not only reiterated the conservative opinion but also criticized the former Supreme Court chief justice, Mr Y.B. Chandrachud, in insulting language. Mr Ansari's speech was applauded by orthodox elements in the Muslim community. He was at [sic] one with Mr Banatwala and Mr Sulaiman Sait. (Engineer 1987: 113, 238)

Justice Srikrishna, too, was critical of the *Shah Bano* judgment. He stated:

Judicial activism has also extended to the use of authorities with political overtones for deciding cases—a wholly improper approach. For instance, in *Shah Bano (Mohd. Ahmed Khan v. Shah Bano Begum*, (1985) 2 SCC 556; 1985 SCC (Cri) 245), while the final order granting maintenance to a divorced Muslim woman is probably correct, the Supreme Court's approach of relying on unfamiliar non-legal sources (such as the *Holy Qur'an* itself)[5] and making sweeping generalizations, instead of narrow legal reasoning,[6] made the Court the target of unseemly political controversies. (Srikrishna 2005: J-16)

The bill encountered considerable opposition even from Congress MPs.

---

[5]This unfortunate approach was again repeated in *M. Ismail Faruqui (Dr) v. Union of India*, (1994) 6 SCC 360, when the Court this time, referred to Hindu scriptures, such as the Vedas, to justify a particular notion of 'secularism'. Indeed, reference to non-legal sources, especially religious texts, to embellish a judgment stylistically is one thing, but using them as a mode of arriving at a legal result is another.

[6]To arrive at the legal result, there was no need to interpret the shariat or the Holy Qur'an. This issue could simply have been decided by relying upon the provisions of the Code of Criminal Procedure, 1973, that the Court had anyway found to be secular in nature and therefore, directly applicable to the case. Reference to the Holy Qur'an was, in other words, wholly gratuitous and unnecessary for the disposal of the case.

Finally, the Congress party had to tell them that passing the bill was imperative as the prime minister's prestige was at stake. The passage of the bill was also unique in that a three-line whip had to be issued by the Congress party ordering its MPs, including Arif Mohammad Khan who had opposed it so vehemently, to vote for the bill. The bill was finally passed at a marathon sitting of the Lok Sabha on 5–6 May 1986 at 2.45 a.m.

Interestingly, under increasing clamour by Muslim fundamentalists, Shah Bano herself opposed the judgment of the Supreme Court. Replying to a question in an interview by Ajoy Bose, Justice Chandrachud, who had delivered the judgment, said:

> Review of a judgment is a remedy which an unsuccessful litigant may seek. Shah Bano, having succeeded in her appeal, would not be justified in asking for a review of the judgment...I have never known of a successful party asking for a review of a judgment in her own favour...*Courts can activate social reforms by removing obstacles which hamper social justice. But ultimately it is for society to implement the court's decisions in the spirit in which they were conceived*...Courts are the fortress of people's freedom and the foundations of this fortress must remain unshaken for the effective functioning of our democracy. (Engineer 1987: 80–82)

Engineer has frankly emphasized that *the passage of this act was a 'great setback to secularism and angered even committed secularists...When the Muslim Women's Bill was passed, Rajiv Gandhi, as a balancing act, got the Babri Masjid doors opened for Hindus to worship Ram Lalla...'* (Engineer, *EPW* 14 December 2002: 5050)

Perhaps the most strident critic of this bill was Upendra Baxi, a well-known academic and jurist. He called the bill:

> *A fraud on the Indian Constitution*. In legal parlance, this expression describes the behaviour of a legislature which, knowing fully well that it has no power to legislate on a subject matter, yet proceeds to make a law in such a way that the transgression appears to be within its power...*The present bill is a coup against the Constitution. It violates every single major provision of the Constitution.*

In sheer disgust, Baxi concluded by saying:

> Parliament, by passing this lawless law, will be merely testifying to the arrogance of power. If the Supreme Court acquiesces with this gesture of extraordinary defiance of the Constitution, it will cease to be both Supreme and a Court. (Baxi 1994: 89, 93–94)

He suggested that this was one case reeking with anti-constitutionalism where the Court, within its jurisdiction, could even direct Parliament to desist from passing the bill or the President to withhold his assent.

Sadly, this was a futile expression of the frustration of a reputed liberal but, finally, the law was held to be valid by the Supreme Court.

Flavia Agnes, who believed that the Muslim Women's Bill was grossly misunderstood as being anti-secular and unjust, wrote in her article, 'Redefining the Agenda of the Women's Movement within a Secular Framework':

> The Muslim Women's Bill, which deprived the Muslim women of their right to maintenance, was strongly criticized. But an earlier amendment of 1976 to a secular code—The Special Marriage Act, 1954—through which two Hindus marrying under this code were taken out of the purview of the secular code in matters of property rights, went unnoticed by the women's movement. The ambiguities of procedures of solemnizing the Hindu marriage which enables the Hindu male to contract a second marriage with relative impunity in spite of a progressive legislation, the lacunae within the laws concerning the property rights which deny the Hindu woman equal property rights and the sexist laws of guardianship and child custody, denial of right to matrimonial and ancestral home, etc., were seldom challenged, nor did they receive much publicity. So, by default, the women's movement contributed to the fiction popularized by the fundamentalists that the Hindu Code is the perfect family code which ought to be extended to other religious denominations in order to liberate women. (Narain 1995: 154)

In another article, 'Transgressing Boundaries of Gender and Identity', Flavia Agnes emphasized:

The Muslim Women's Act, 1986, has over time, advertently or inadvertently, bestowed upon Muslim women, a superior economic right, than the one enshrined in sec. 125 of the CrPC. But despite this, for well over a decade, the statute enacted amidst protest from human rights and women's groups, was viewed as a marker of Muslim appeasement and a defeat of secular principles within the Indian polity... Since 1988, the act was being positively interpreted by various high courts in the country by awarding substantial amounts as 'settlements'. (*EPW* 7 September 2002: 3695)

I find it difficult to agree with this argument. The question is not whether the Muslim Women's Act is more just than the provisions of the CrPC. The question is whether the directive principle of the Constitution laying down the enactment of the uniform civil code should have been undermined by passing such a law. Parliament clearly was not competent to pass such a law. But, with his two-third majority in the Lok Sabha, Rajiv Gandhi, like his mother Indira Gandhi, was not bothered in the least about constitutional proprieties.

The Propagation of Religion

All along, one of the contentious issues has been regarding religious conversions. It is interesting to see that Ambedkar's draft, *inter alia*, provided for freedom to preach and to convert. There was considerable discussion on this subject. The advisory committee, in its interim report on fundamental rights, suggested that conversion carried out by coercion or undue influence should not be recognized by law. This led to a heated discussion in the Constituent Assembly on 1 May 1947 and was referred back to the advisory committee. The committee felt that the clause enunciated a rather obvious doctrine and recommended that it be dropped altogether. The Sub-committee on Minorities considered this clause on 19 April 1947, and accepted the suggestion made by M. Ruthnaswamy that *certain religions, like Christianity and Islam, were proselytizing religions and that they should be permitted to propagate their faith*. The sub-committee accordingly recommended a redraft of the clause which not only restored the right to free practice of religion but also secured an additional right to propagate religion. (Rao 1968b: 258, and Footnote 4, 261)

This is unfortunate considering the many ramifications of the problem. Quite clearly, the Constituent Assembly was not inclined to displease the Muslims and the Christians. A great deal of controversy and confrontation between the communities could have been avoided over the years if this issue had been addressed boldly.

Rajkumari Amrit Kaur, in her note on the 'freedom of religion' clause sent on 20 April 1947, stated, *inter alia*:

> Since conversion by force or undue influence only is to be banned, it follows that conversion of an adult to any religion by reason of conviction will be permissible. *Freedom of religious worship, freedom of conscience and free profession of religion should really give to the individual and community all he or it needs*...To make the 'free practice of religion' a justiciable right is, I submit, an error and will defeat not only social progress but will keep alive communal strife." (Rao 1967: 213)

As in several other matters, these important submissions made by Amrit Kaur were not given adequate attention by the Constituent Assembly.

When the supplementary report on fundamental rights came up for discussion in the Constituent Assembly on 30 August 1947, Sardar Vallabhbhai Patel stated that this subject had been discussed by the committee. The committee had come to the conclusion that it was not necessary to include the question of conversion from one religion to another as a fundamental right. Patel said that conversion was 'illegal under the present law and it can be illegal at any time'.

M. Ananthasayanam Ayyangar said:

> It is unfortunate that religion is being utilized not for the purpose of saving one's soul, but for disintegrating society. Recently, after the announcement by the Cabinet Mission and later on by the British government, a number of conversions have taken place. It was said that power had been handed over to provincial governments who were in charge of these matters. This is dangerous. What has religion to do with a secular state? *Our minorities are communal minorities for which we have made provision.* Do you want an

opportunity to be given for numbers to be increased for the purpose of getting more seats in the legislatures?...*We should not allow conversion from one community to another. I therefore want that a positive fundamental right must be established that no conversion shall be allowed.*

Vallabhbhai Patel said that there is no difference of opinion on the merits of the case that forcible conversion should not be or cannot be recognized by law. On that principle there is no difference of opinion. The Assembly decided that the proposition that 'conversion from one religion to another brought about by coercion or undue influence shall not be recognized by law' should not be put in the fundamental rights. (*CAD* Vols IV–VI, 1947–48: 363–65)

In spite of sharp differences, the Sub-committee on Minorities of the Constituent Assembly finally agreed to the right 'freely to profess, practise and propagate religion'. This decision was carried by a majority of 10 to 5, the dissentients being Rajkumari Amrit Kaur, Jagjivan Ram, Pandit Govind Ballabh Pant, N.K.P. Salve and B.R. Ambedkar. (Rao, 1967: 205)

Speaking in the Constituent Assembly on 3 December 1948, *Tajamul Husain proposed an amendment that the words 'practise and propagate religion' should be substituted by the words 'and practise religion privately'*. Husain stressed that religion is a private affair between oneself and one's Creator and has nothing to do with others. He further said, 'This is a secular state, and should not have anything to do with religion. So I would request you to leave me alone, to practise and profess my own religion privately.' (*CAD* Vol. VII, Book 2, 2009: 81718)

K.T. Shah suggested on 3 December 1948 that:

A clear provision may be made in Article 19 that no propaganda in favour of any one religion, which is calculated to result in change of faith by the individuals affected, shall be allowed in any school or college or other educational institution, in any hospital or asylum or any other place or institution where persons of a tender age, or of unsound mind or body are liable to be exposed to undue influence from their teachers, nurses or physicians, keepers or guardians or any other person set in authority above them, and which is maintained wholly or partially from public revenues, or is in any way aided or protected by the government of the Union or of any state or public authority therein.

Shah stressed that there are religions which are professedly proselytizing. He said he only wanted to make sure that no undue influence would be exerted to make any person change his religion.

Lokanath Misra said that he was shocked to see that there was no other Constitution of any country in which the word 'propaganda' figured as a fundamental right relating to religion. He emphasized that propagation of religion brought India into this unfortunate state and India had had to be divided into Pakistan and India. Resuming his speech on 6 December 1948, Misra said:

> Our secular state is a slippery phrase, a device to bypass the ancient culture of the land...Do we really believe that religion can be divorced from life?...*This unjust generosity of tabooing religion and yet making propagation of religion a fundamental right is somewhat uncanny and dangerous*...If people should propagate their religion, let them do so. Only I crave, *let not the Constitution put it as a fundamental right and encourage it*...Drop the word 'propagate' in Article 19 at least. (*CAD* Vol. VII, Book 2, 2009: 822–24)

Lakshmi Kanta Maitra made a forceful representation on 6 December 1948 in favour of permitting propagation of religion. He said:

> The Indian Christian community...spend to the tune of nearly Rs 2 crores every year for educational uplift, medical relief and for sanitation, public health and the rest of it...If this vast amount... were utilized for purpose of seeking converts, then the Indian Christian community which comprises only 7 million could have gone up to 70 million...

This whole matter was discussed in the Advisory Council and it was passed there.

L. Krishnaswami Bharathi fully agreed with Pandit Maitra that the word 'propagate' should remain as it was. He invited attention to the fact that this matter:

> ...was thoroughly discussed at all stages in the Minorities Committee, and they came to the conclusion that this great Christian community which is willing and ready to assimilate itself with the general community which does not want reservation or other special privileges should be allowed to propagate its religion along with other religious communities in India.

K. Santhanam argued that propagation was merely freedom of expression which had already been guaranteed by Article 19. He said that this article had been very carefully drafted and the exceptions and qualifications therein were as important as the right it conferred. (*CAD* Vol. VII, Book 2, 2009: 831–35)

The impression one gets after reading the debate on this important subject of religious conversion was that it was cursory and reflected the known positions of the speakers. Most disappointing were the speeches of T.T. Krishnamachari and K.M. Munshi. The enormity of the problem of conversion was clearly side-stepped. From this point of view, the speech of K.M. Munshi was particularly disappointing. He said that the Christian missionaries had derived some advantage during the British regime but it was not likely to be available to them after Independence. This in itself is a questionable proposition in the light of experience over the years. Munshi was more concerned about the compromise arrived at in the Minorities Committee and did not want the atmosphere of harmony and confidence that had been created thereby to be disturbed in any way. He said, 'the word "propagate" should be maintained in this article in order that the compromise so laudably achieved by the Minorities Committee should not be disturbed.' Surprisingly, Dr Ambedkar had nothing to add on the subject. H.V. Kamath pleaded that, in fairness to the House, Ambedkar should reply to the points raised in the amendments and during the debate. The Vice-President regretted his inability to compel Ambedkar to give reasons for rejecting the various amendments.

Golwalkar, who headed the RSS for a long stretch of 33 years, was candid when he said: 'We Hindus believe that each individual can worship God in a form of his choice in his own way. All can attain Him—if the effort to attain be sincere and honest. And that is why Hinduism is not a proselytizing religion. The very idea of conversion starts with the assumption that mine is the only "true" way and all others must be converted to it.' One Maulvi said: 'But Hindus are taking to converting Muslims and Christians now.' Golwalkar said: 'There is no conversion to Hinduism. It is only giving an occasion for those who had been made to change their faith by force of circumstances in the past, to return to their ancestral faith...It is like home-coming.' (Malkani 1980: 71)

After his return from a visit to the Vatican, Nehru wrote to Ravi Shankar Shukla, chief minister of Madhya Pradesh, on 14 July 1955, that the Vatican secretary of state with whom Nehru had had a discussion, had specially mentioned that 'Unfortunately, conditions in Madhya Pradesh were not happy.' Nehru wrote:

> I am passing this on to you as, unfortunately, Madhya Pradesh is getting a bad reputation abroad in regard to the treatment of Christians, and especially Catholics. The External Affairs Ministry has received another complaint from Nagpur stating that Inspectors of Schools have been going to various Catholic schools with police escort and school registers have been seized from these private schools, presumably for the Enquiry Committee [the Niyogi committee]. This seems rather an odd way of proceeding... I hope that you will do something to get rid of this general impression that Catholics are being persecuted in Madhya Pradesh.'

On 1 August 1955, Shukla replied that the District Inspector of Schools, Raigarh, had conducted investigations into the complaints of changing Hindu names of newly admitted boys into Christian names during the summer vacation and the seized registers had been returned before the end of the vacation. Police constables had to be taken as a precaution against untoward incidents such as those which had taken place on earlier occasions. Shukla enclosed the report of the Director of Public

Instruction, E.W. Franklin, an Indian Christian, pointing out that if any injustice had been done, the missionaries would not have hesitated to bring this to his notice. (Jawaharlal Nehru Memorial Fund [henceforth JNMF] Vol. 29, 2001: 160–61, Footnotes 4 and 6).

Reference may be made to the findings of the Niyogi Committee on the activities of the Christian missionaries in Madhya Pradesh in 1956. The committee, appointed by the Madhya Pradesh government, was headed by Dr Justice Bhawani Shankar Niyogi, retired chief justice of the Nagpur High Court. The state government had received a number of representations from time to time that 'Christian missionaries, either forcibly or through fraud and temptations of monetary and other gain, were converting illiterate aboriginals and other backward people, thereby offending the feelings of non-Christians. It was also represented to the government that missions were being utilized directly or indirectly for purposes of political or extra-religious objectives.' The missionaries had repudiated these allegations and had asserted on the other hand that their activities were confined solely to religious propaganda and towards social, medical and educational work. The missionaries had further alleged that they were being harassed by non-Christian people and local officials. The committee had been asked to go into all these matters.

The committee made a series of recommendations, largely upholding that the activities of the missionaries were objectionable and needed to be curbed. Some of the more important recommendations of the committee were as follows:

- Those missionaries whose primary object is proselytization should be asked to withdraw. The large influx of foreign missionaries is undesirable and should be checked.
- The use of medical or other professional services as a direct means of making conversions should be prohibited by law.
- Any attempt by force or fraud, or threats of illicit means or grants of financial or other aid, or by fraudulent means or promises, or by moral and material assistance, or by taking advantage of any person's inexperience...so as to agree with the ideas or convictions of the proselytizing party should be absolutely prohibited.

- Religious institutions should not be permitted to engage in occupations like recruitment of labour for tea gardens.
- It is the primary duty of the government to conduct orphanages, as the State is the legal guardian of all minors who have no parents or natural guardians.
- An amendment of the Constitution of India may be sought, firstly to clarify that the right of propagation had been given only to the citizens of India and secondly, that it does not include conversion brought about by force, fraud or other illicit means.
- Suitable control on conversions brought about through illegal means should be imposed. If necessary, legislative measures should be enacted.
- Institutions in receipt of grants-in-aid or recognition from the government should be compulsorily inspected every quarter. (Government of Madhya Pradesh [henceforth GOMP] 1956: 163–65, 167–68)

The Niyogi Committee invited attention to the judgment of the Bombay High Court (*AIR* 1953, Bombay, p. 242) in which:

Chagla, chief justice, stated that religious freedom as contemplated by our Constitution in Articles 25 and 26 is not unrestricted freedom. *The religious freedom which has been safeguarded by the Constitution is religious freedom which must be envisaged in the context of a secular state. The freedom given is not an unrestricted freedom.*

In the same judgment, Justice Shah stated: The right, therefore, which is conferred by Article 25 is not an absolute or unfettered right of freedom of professing or practising or propagating religion, but it is subject to legislation by the State limiting or regulating any activity, economic, financial, political or secular, associated with religious practice. (GOMP 1956: 92–93)

Whatever may have been the justification when the Constitution was framed, it needs to be examined whether a review of this provision is called for in the light of the experience so far. Jawaharlal Nehru stated in his circular letter to the Pradesh Congress Committees on 5 August 1954:

Our Constitution is based on this secular perception and gives freedom to all religions, even freedom to proselyte. *Personally, I do not appreciate attempts at mass proselytization.* But that is a personal opinion of my own, and I have no business to thrust it on others. I can understand an individual changing his religion because of certain convictions. *I do not understand attempts at mass conversions,* which can have no business with individual or personal conviction and which have often behind them some political urge. (*Muslim India* August 2008: 12).

Attempts at conversion of scheduled castes (SCs), scheduled tribes (STs) and poorer sections of society by Christian missionaries has been one of the important factors for communal tensions and violence, as brought out in recent cases in Karnataka, Orissa, Kerala and Madhya Pradesh. The distribution of population of each religion by caste categories is particularly striking so far as Christians are concerned, as compared to the other religions. It shows that 9 per cent of the Christians are SCs, 32.8 per cent are STs, 24.8 per cent are OBCs (other backward classes) and 33.3 per cent are 'others'. *Thus, nearly 67 per cent of the Christian population is accounted for by SCs, STs and OBCs.* For Hindus, the corresponding figure is 74 per cent. Among Muslims, the preponderant percentage is that of OBCs (39.2 per cent). (Government of India [henceforth GOI] 2006: Table 1.2)

While large-scale conversions to Buddhism have also taken place, there has been no hostile reaction to it among Hindus in general and Hindu fundamentalists, in particular, since Buddhism is accepted as a stream of Hinduism. The time has come to examine seriously the wide-ranging implications of religious conversion of Hindus to other religions, and particularly its impact on social cohesion and public order. More importantly, the very concept of secularism is being increasingly questioned by Hindus due to the unrestricted freedom given to religious organizations to carry out conversions with monetary and other inducements.

The constitutional issues pertaining to conversion were examined by the Supreme Court as far back as 1977 in the context of the enactments of Madhya Pradesh and Orissa. (*Rev. Stanislaus v. State of Madhya Pradesh and Ors; State of Orissa and Ors v. Mrs Yulitha Hyde and Ors etc., AIR* 1977 SC 908.) The Court had held:

> What Article 25 (1) grants is not the right to convert another person to one's own religion…It has to be remembered that Article 25 (1) guarantees 'freedom of conscience' to every citizen, and not merely to the followers of any particular religion and that, in turn, postulates that *there is no fundamental right to convert another person to one's own religion because, if a person purposely undertakes the conversion of another person to his religion, as distinguished from his effort to transmit or spread the tenets of his religion, that would impinge on the 'freedom of conscience' guaranteed to all the citizens of the country.*

The Court also held that:

> If a thing 'disturbs the current of the life of the community, and does not merely affect an individual, it would amount to disturbance of the public order. Thus, if an attempt is made to raise communal passions, e.g., on the ground that someone has been 'forcibly' converted to another religion, it would, in all probability, give rise to an apprehension of a breach of public order, affecting the community at large…The two Acts [of Madhya Pradesh and Orissa] do not provide for the regulation of religion.'

The Court therefore upheld the validity of both the enactments prohibiting conversion by force, fraud, inducements, allurements, and so on.

> Apart from Orissa and Madhya Pradesh, over the years, several other states have passed anti-conversion laws. They include: Chhattisgarh (2000); Tamil Nadu (2002); Gujarat (2003); Himachal Pradesh (2006); and Rajasthan (2008). These laws were intended to stop conversion by force or inducements, or fraudulently. Some of the laws made it mandatory to seek prior permission from local authorities before undertaking conversion. (*IE* 13 December 2014: 5).

The central government has, however, failed to pass any central law or to take a clear stand in the matter and to lay down a policy on the subject. This has led to the public perception that the government would not like to displease the religious minorities in general and Christians in particular. This major irritant needs to be removed to restore the faith of the majority community in the concept of secularism. It would also help to ensure that public order is not adversely affected.

Dr M. Afzal Wani, in his article, 'Freedom of Conscience: Constitutional Foundations and Limits', referred to the observations of Justice K.K. Mathew: 'All considerations applicable to freedom of speech are applicable to the right to propagate. Even if Article 25 (1) did not include the right to propagate, the same would have been guaranteed by Article 19 (1) (a). This right to propagate one's idea is inherent in the concept of freedom of speech.' H.M. Seervai, well-known constitutional expert, in his book, *Constitutional Law of India*, severely criticized the above observation of Justice Mathew. He wrote:

> It is unfortunate that the legislative history of Article 25 was not brought to the attention of the Supreme Court...Article 25 (1) confers freedom of religion...a freedom not limited to the religion in which a person is born. Freedom of conscience harmonizes with this, for its presence in Article 25 (1) shows that our Constitution has adopted 'a system, which allows a free choice of religion'. The right to propagate religion gives a meaning to freedom of choice, for choice involves not only knowledge but an act of will. A person cannot choose if he does not know what choices are open to him. To propagate religion is not to impose knowledge and to spread it more widely, but to produce intellectual and moral conviction leading to action, namely the adoption of that religion...On his deciding to choose a particular religion which is being propagated with a view to its acceptance, and on his being prepared to comply with the requirements necessary to be a member of that religion, he has the freedom to be converted to that religion...Therefore, conversion does not in any way interfere with the freedom of conscience but it is a fulfilment of it and gives meaning to it.

Seervai claims that his view harmonizes with the legislative history of Article 25 (a) and the inclusion of the word 'propagate' in it. He is of the view that the Supreme Court judgment is clearly wrong, is productive of the greatest public mischief and ought to be overruled. (Wani 2000: 306)

After a comprehensive discussion, Dr Wani concluded that the solution to the problem of conversion lies in the literacy of the people, their training and better social status, and not in the deprivation of freedom of conscience. I find it difficult to agree with the above view. In fact, the erudite arguments in Seervai's comment as above are mostly academic and do not really hold good in respect of large-scale conversion of rural people and tribals. I, therefore, believe that it is high time the Constitution was amended to delete the word 'propagate' from Article 25.

Reference must be made to the decision of the Supreme Court in February 2015 that a person who reconverts from Christianity to Hinduism shall be entitled to reservation benefits if his forefathers belonged to the scheduled castes and the community accepts him after reconversion. (*IE* 27 February 2015: 1)

This will have a huge impact on the efforts at reconversion which are being pursued so vigorously by the RSS and its affiliate organizations.

Javed Jamil, in his article, 'Ghar Wapsi: A Ploy to Push Anti-conversion Bill and the Second Round of Privatization', argued that:

> The Ghar Wapsi movement is in fact a well thought out and well planned attempt at bringing a new law which would make conversion almost impossible...By making the Ghar Wapsi movement a big issue, they seek to force Christian and Muslim leaders to accept the anti-conversion bill. Already some Muslim panelists appearing on TV debates can be seen favouring the idea of the new Act. (*The Radical Humanist*, February 2015: 5)

Since considerable foreign funding is received by Christian missionaries, effective use could have been made of the Foreign Contribution (Regulation) Act (FCRA) to check the malpractices in conversion. Unfortunately, the original purpose and objectives for which FCRA was enacted have been totally lost sight of. Instead, FCRA has become a tool for the harassment of non-government organizations (NGOs) and other bodies doing development work.

Justice P.B. Gajendragadkar suggested:

Since conversion sometimes leads to complaints about the adoption of unfair, illegal or unworthy means or methods in bringing about conversion, it is desirable that the appropriate legislatures may consider the reasonableness and the feasibility of requiring all conversions to be registered before the prescribed authorities. Speaking for myself, I am inclined to think that concerted and deliberate attempts at conversion are inappropriate in a truly secular society. (Gajendragadkar 1971: 72)

Strictly speaking, the right to propagation cannot co-exist with secularism since the latter emphasizes that religion should be primarily a personal matter. As brought out earlier, it was due to the pressure of Christians and Muslims that this right was included as a fundamental right and spacious arguments were put forth by the representatives of the Congress party to support it. The judgments of the high courts and the Supreme Court have clearly established that the right to propagation must be interpreted within the framework of the concept of secularism, freedom of conscience, and free profession and practice of religion. The argument of Christians and Muslims that propagation of religion is a part of their religion can hardly be accepted as it can lead to serious problems of law and order. In recent months, the Ghar Wapsi movement launched by the BJP and its affiliated organizations has already created such problems in a number of states. In the process, it has also brought in controversy the much larger and important concept of secularism. If there has to be a trade-off, secularism will have to be treated as of higher priority, and nothing should be permitted to undermine it. It would, therefore, be best if the word 'propagation' were deleted from Article 25. If necessary, an advisory opinion of the Supreme Court may be sought under Article 143 of the Constitution.

The Protection of Minority Educational Institutions

Article 30 (1) of the Constitution states that 'All minorities, whether based on religion or language, shall have the right to establish and administer educational institutions of their choice.' While the right given to linguistic minorities is understandable, serious questions need to be asked regarding permitting religious minorities to establish and administer educational institutions of their choice, particularly in view of the large expansion of private sector educational institutions which have proliferated across the country.

Govind Ballabh Pant suggested that the rights recommended by the sub-committee could more appropriately be incorporated as directive principles which the legislature would keep in view but which would not be enforceable in a court of law. This was opposed by K.M. Munshi who said that the rights would lose all their efficacy if they were made non-justiciable. Ruthnaswamy and Sardar Ujjal Singh stated definitely that Pant's proposal would not be acceptable to the minorities. *Rajkumari Amrit Kaur was of the view that this provision would seek to perpetuate communal institutions in the country.*

Significantly, this is perhaps the only Article in which the word 'minorities' has been used. Commenting on the use of the term 'minorities' in the provision, constitutional adviser, B.N. Rau, pointed out that the term 'minorities' had not been defined anywhere in the Constitution, and that the existing position was so vague that even the declaration of a particular language as the national language could be said to prejudice the interests of minorities whose mother tongue happened to be different. A comprehensive definition of minorities was difficult to frame. It might be based on religion, community or language; but to leave a vague justifiable [sic] right to undefined minorities was also quite unsatisfactory. *B.N. Rau, therefore, suggested for consideration whether the cultural and educational rights... should at all be made justiciable.*

Particular attention might be invited to the comments made by Jayaprakash Narayan that '*the secularization of general education was necessary for the growth of a national outlook and unity.*' With this object in view, he suggested two amendments: (1) the cultural and educational rights guaranteed in the draft article should be confined only to linguistic minorities, and (2) *denominational and communal educational institutions should be forbidden except for the purpose of the study of religion and oriental learning.* Both the amendments, B.N. Rau remarked, involved questions of policy. Acceptance of the second amendment would adversely hit institutions established for the promotion of education among the Anglo-Indian community under special endowments...

Damodar Swarup Seth, moving an amendment on lines similar to those favoured by Jayaprakash Narayan, suggested that the only minorities to be recognized should be those based on language; *recognition of minorities based on religion or community was not in keeping with the secular character of the State.* Besides, if such minorities were recognized and granted the right to establish and administer educational institutions of their own, it would not only block the way to national unity but would also promote communalism and an anti-national outlook which had already produced disastrous results in the past.

Replying to the debate, Ambedkar pointed out that the term 'minority' was used not merely to indicate the minorities in the technical sense of the term but also to cover minorities in the cultural and linguistic sense...The Article intended to give protection in the matter of culture, language and script...Since the word 'minority' was capable of a narrow interpretation and the intention was to provide protection in the matter of culture, language and script in the wider sense, the Drafting Committee had dropped the word 'minority' and instead used the phrase 'any section of the citizens'. (Rao 1968b: 273–80)

Muzaffar Hussain emphasized that the sub-committee on minorities of the Constituent Assembly had submitted its report on 19 April 1947 itself. It meant that the outlines of Articles 29 and 30 were already prepared before the official announcement of granting freedom to the country. Though the Constitution had been formulated by Indians, it can't be said that they were not influenced by foreign ideas...Hussain invited attention to the case of Ramakrishna Mission which had been founded to strengthen Hindu society. He said that it was a matter of shame and concern that the Mission which is famous for Hinduism all over the world has started declaring itself as non-Hindu. The Left government in West Bengal harassed this Mission so much that it began to contemplate itself as a non-Hindu institution. The Leftists not only launched a move to make the institution economically weak but also started interfering in its educational activities...This one example is sufficient to show that minoritism can divide society to such an extent. (Hussain 2004: 99–101)

Attention may be invited to the judgment of the Gujarat High Court in the case of *Firdaus Amrut Higher Secondary School, Ahmedabad v. M.M. Dave* (*AIR* 1992 Gujarat 179), S.C.A. No. 5239 of 1986, dated 19 April 1991. The high court relied on the guidelines issued by the National Commission of Minorities for determining the minority status of educational institutions. These guidelines were circulated to all states. The guidelines were as follows:

- The benefit of Article 30 (1) can be claimed by a community only on proving that it is a religious or linguistic minority and that the educational institution was established by it.
- The Commission stated that *it is not always necessary that the objects for which a minority has established an educational institution must include the conservation of its language, script or culture.* Thus an institution will be a minority institution even if it imparts secular education…Simply because the objects for which the (educational) trust was established are of a general nature it could not be said that it was not a minority institution.
- An institution seeking recognition as a minority institution must fulfil the statutory requirements concerning the academic standards, qualifications of teachers and of the students seeking admission.
- Neither the state government nor the university can prescribe the medium of instruction to be followed by minority educational institutions.
- The minority educational institution must be free to induct competent and reputed individuals from other communities in the managing committee and the governing bodies. (*AIR* 1992 Gujarat 179)

The court also referred to the advisory opinion of the Supreme Court on *Kerala Education Bill*, 1957 (*AIR* 1958 SC 956) in which the Court stated that the real import of Article 29 (2) and Article 30 (1) seems to us to be that they clearly contemplate a minority institution with a sprinkling of outsiders admitted into it. (*AIR* 1992 Gujarat 179)

M.P. Jain pointed out that the Constitution uses the term 'minority' without defining it. He wrote:

> In the Kerala Education Bill, the Supreme Court opined that while it is easy to say that minority means a community which is numerically less than 50 per cent, the important question is 50 per cent of what? Should it be of the entire population of India, or of a state, or a part thereof? It is possible that the community may be a majority in a state but in a minority in the whole of India. A community may be concentrated in a part of a state and may thus be in majority there, though it may be in minority in the state as a whole. If a part of a state is to be taken, then the question is where to draw the line and what unit is to be taken into consideration—a district, town, a municipality or its wards.
>
> The Supreme Court did not decide this point definitively. However, it had come to be accepted that minority is to be determined only in relation to the particular legislation which is being challenged. Thus, if a state law extending to the whole of a state is in question, the minority must be determined with reference to the entire state population. In such a case, any community, linguistic or religious, which is numerically less than 50 per cent of the entire state population, will be regarded as a minority for purposes of Article 30 (1). Thus the Christian community being 22 per cent of the population in Kerala is a minority there.
>
> This view was altered in T.M. Pai's case (*T.M.A. Pai Foundation v. State of Karnataka* (2002) 8 SCC 481), where the view of the majority [of judges] was that the minority for the purpose of Article 30 cannot have different meanings depending upon who is legislating. (Jain 2010: 1343–44)

Reference may be made to the minority decision of the Supreme Court in the case of *St Stephen's College, etc. v. the University of Delhi, etc.* The Court made an important observation therein: 'We cannot overlook that religious fundamentalism and linguistic parochialism leads to fissiparous tendencies and obstructs the national unity as a whole. *It is necessary that minorities should join and be part and parcel of common stream of the country.*'

The Court emphasized that the fundamental right guaranteed by Article 30 (1) was not to be extended so as to encroach upon other fundamental rights or to go contrary to the intentions of the founding fathers. Thus, Articles 15 (4), 28 (3) and 29 (2) place express limitations on the right given to minorities in Article 30 (1). The Court also referred to the judgment of A.N. Ray, chief justice in the *Ahmedabad St. Xavier's College Society* case, that the best administration reveals no trace or colour of minority. A minority institution should shine in exemplary eclecticism in the administration of the institution. The best compliment that can be paid to a minority institution is that it does not rest on or proclaim its minority character. (*AIR* 1992 SC 1630)

Attention may be invited to some other observations of the Court in the *St Stephen's College Society* case:

1. The minorities do not stand to gain much from the general Bill of Rights or fundamental rights which are available only to individuals. The minorities require positive safeguards to preserve their minority interests which are also termed as group interests. The safeguards and group rights have been the part of our Constitution-making.
2. Establishment of minority educational institutions solely for the benefit of minorities is impermissible.
3. Educational institutions are not business houses. They do not generate wealth.
4. The right of the minorities to administer educational institutions does not prevent the making of reasonable regulations in respect of those institutions. The right to administration of institutions is subject to the regulatory power of the state. (*AIR* 1992 SC 1630)

During the discussion on the Constitution Forty-fourth Amendment Bill 1976, Frank Anthony, who was a nominated Anglo-Indian member of the Lok Sabha, spoke at length on minority rights and how they were being denuded over time. He charged that in various cases involving minority education in which he had appeared, he had noticed that, 'inevitably the majority of the judges are for the majority community. Some judges, not with any oblique motives but because of certain conditioning, don't have the understanding of the minority difficulties that other judges do and....they tend to ride down the content of the minority fundamental rights.' He urged that the minorities be given the special fundamental rights pertaining to their language and culture. He said:

> Article 14 cannot be attracted because you have given a special differential right to the minorities. Some judges have been questioning as to why the minorities alone should get this fundamental right. It is also being questioned whether in this day and age, the minorities should have fundamental rights at all. Efforts have been made to garrote the minority educational institutions and if they could, they would garrote their religious rights also and all that they have to do is to adopt this device and put it in the Ninth Schedule. You destroy our schools, you destroy our religious rights and all our cultural freedom. So what I am pleading for is: put in an amendment that Article 31B will not apply to the minority rights. (*LSD* Vol. 65, 1976: 16–17, 21)

Fali Nariman, in his lecture on minorities on 12 September 2014, expressed his uneasiness with the marked change in the way the Supreme Court had been pronouncing its judgments on cases related to Articles 29 and 30 of the Constitution. He stated that, before the 1990s, on almost every occasion on which the minorities had approached the Supreme Court complaining of state or central legislation or executive action as infringing on their fundamental rights, the challenge had been upheld. 'It was most heartening. The Supreme Court of India functioned as a super minorities commission as it was meant to. This was long before a minorities commission got established by law made by Parliament.'

In 1959, for example, the Supreme Court thwarted an attempt by the Communist-controlled government of Kerala to take over the management of Christian schools, contrary to Article 30. In an advisory opinion given by a bench of seven judges, it declared large parts of the Kerala Education Bill as unconstitutional. Even the judge who did not entirely agree with the majority judgment had said: 'But what is the policy behind Article 30 (1)? As I conceive it, it is that it should not be in the power of the majority in a state to destroy or to impair the rights of the minorities, religious or linguistic. That is a policy which permeates all modern constitutions, and its purpose is to encourage individuals to preserve and develop their own distinct culture.'

Minority educational institutions, however, did not receive the same favourable reception from the Supreme Court when Article 30 was invoked in the case of institutions of higher learning. At first, different benches of the Supreme Court wavered as to how much or how little autonomy should be conceded to such minority educational institutions. The cases shuttled from a bench of two justices, to a bench of five justices, then to a bench of seven justices on 19 March 1994 and were ultimately referred to a bench of eleven justices (in *T.M.A. Pai Foundation v. State of Karnataka*). While, earlier, the Supreme Court had decided in the *Kerala Education Bill* case (1958) that: 'The real import of Article 29 (2) and Article 30 (1) seems to us to be that they clearly contemplate a minority (educational) institution with a sprinkling of outsiders admitted into it.'

Nariman invited attention to the warning which was given by Chief Justice S.R. Das in the *Kerala Education Bill* case referred to above, that the fundamental right guaranteed by Article 30 to administer educational institutions would not include the right to 'maladminister' them. According to Nariman:

> The ultimate majority decision in *T.M.A. Pai Foundation* was not so much the result of a textual interpretation of the constitutional provisions as of the apprehension of the judges that treating the right of minorities under Article 30 as 'absolute' would totally negate the claim of the states to regulate the minority educational institutions especially in higher education. My plea to the judges that not suspicion, but only concrete allegations and proof of such allegations in individual cases could deprive minority educational institutions of their fundamental right...was invariably met with stony silence! ...*The decision in T.M.A. Pai was an unmitigated disaster for the minorities*...Article 30 has now been placed by court decision on a much lower pedestal than it was, or was intended to be. It has been equated only with a fundamental right guaranteed under Article 19 (1) (g) i.e., a mere right to an occupation (*running an educational institution the judges said is an 'occupation' like any other*). Even though the fundamental right under Article 30 had been expressly made not subject to any reasonable restrictions

at all, the bench of eleven judges, by majority, relegated this right to a right to an occupation guaranteed by Article 19 (1) (g) i.e., therefore subject to reasonable restrictions imposed by law in public interest i.e., subject to state regulation...Initially, when dealing with minority rights, courts in India had invariably conceptualized their role as that of a political party in opposition—until one of the political parties, BJP, in the early 1990s, characterized the policy of the Congress party (the ruling party in power at the Centre for more than 40 years) as an 'appeasement of the minorities'. The label stuck; 'minority' became and has become an unpopular word. (Nariman 2014: 8–13)

The experience of states in the implementation of Article 30 is quite striking. The National Commission for Minority Educational Institutions, which was established by an Ordinance in November 2004, is mandated to look into specific complaints regarding the deprivation or violation of rights of minorities to establish and administer educational institutions of their choice. The data put out by the Commission shows that, during the decade of 2005–15 (up to May 26), 11,017 minority status certificates were issued by the Commission. It is also seen that, from 2010 to 2014, the certificates issued each year were as many as 1122; 1656; 1966; 1670 and 1515, respectively. This shows the popularity of this concept.

The experience of Maharashtra as given below may be relevant in this context.

In a statement, minority affairs minister of Maharashtra, Eknath Khadse, has announced that ten minority educational institutions in South Mumbai had not admitted a single student of minority community in these institutions in the last three years and therefore a show-cause notice as to why their minority status should not be cancelled has been issued to them. The number of minority educational institutions in the state has been going up every year and currently there are 2490 such institutions in the state. Getting minority status gives such institutions considerable autonomy in their administration and they are able to give admissions liberally to the other students by charging donations. Strictly, unless an institution has minimum 51 per cent students belonging to minorities, it does not qualify as a minority educational institution. (*Loksatta* 12 June 2015: 2) The number of such institutions has further gone up to 2573 in 2016. (*Loksatta* 3 May 2016: 4)

The National Commission for Minority Educational Institutions is also reported to have decided to remove from the academic year starting in 2017 the restriction that minority institutions must have a minimum enrolment of 51 per cent minority community students. This is expected to lead to further commercialization of such institutions. The government of Maharashtra has given notices to seventy-nine minority institutions as to why they have denied admissions to minority students and have given admissions to general category students. (*Loksatta* 5 May 2016: 1)

The status of a minority educational institution has become attractive as it gives exemption to such an institution from reservation of 25 per cent seats for students of the below poverty line category as also government rules pertaining to recruitment of teaching and non-teaching staff, admissions and so on (*Sakal* 17 May 2016: 3)

The position in other states may not be very different.

A news item in *The Indian Express* pertains to the memoirs of Archbishop Emeritus Joseph Powathil and his article which refer to the stand taken by the youth and student wing of the Congress party in 1972 against minority-run educational institutions. However, realizing that it had alienated the Christians, Indira Gandhi intervened. Antony, a senior Congress leader from Kerala, has, however, said that the protest was not against minorities, but against the exploitation by education institute managements as well as for the rights of teachers and students, and he had no regrets about it. (*IE* 2 November 2015: 4)

It may be pertinent to refer to the observations of the Justice Ranganath Misra Commission for Religious and Linguistic Minorities as follows:

> As the meaning and scope of Article 30 of the Constitution has become quite uncertain, complicated and diluted due to its varied and sometimes conflicting judicial interpretations, we recommend that a comprehensive law should be enacted without delay to detail

all aspects of minorities' educational rights under that provision with a view to reinforcing its original dictates in letter and spirit.

The statute of the National Commission for Minority Educational Institutions should be amended to make it wide-based in its composition, powers, functions and responsibilities, and to enable it to work as the watchdog for a meticulous enforcement of all aspects of minorities' educational rights under the Constitution.

...by the force of judicial decisions, the minority intake in minority educational institutions has, in the interest of national integration, been restricted to about 50 per cent, thus virtually earmarking the remaining 50 per cent also for the majority community. (GOI 2007: 150)

Fali Nariman and Frank Anthony have expressed their uneasiness at the interpretation of Article 30 (1) by the Supreme Court and feel that these have diluted the rights of the minorities. However, I welcome these judgments. In considering whether there is justification to continue Article 30 (1) in its present form, it needs to be stated that the situation regarding the spread of private sector and corporate sector in the education field has made a qualitative difference. Quite often, educational institutions are now run as a business proposition. The admission of students is also based on diverse criteria including their capacity and willingness to pay donations. Further, it needs to be considered whether the group interests of minorities need to be encouraged and promoted even 68 years after Independence. Reference may be invited in this context to Justice H.R. Khanna's observations in the *St. Xavier's* case referred to above, in which he had observed: 'The object of Articles 25 to 30 was to preserve the rights of religious and linguistic minorities so as *to place them on a secure pedestal and withdraw them from the vicissitudes of political controversy.*' (Jain 2010: 1551)

The time has come to re-examine seriously whether placing minorities 'on a secure pedestal' is the best way to deal with the minority problem, in so far as Article 30 (1) is concerned.

The Supreme Court rightly held that such institutions cannot cater exclusively to the requirements of minorities. If this is so, there is hardly any justification for their continuance as minority institutions.

Attention may also be invited to the criteria laid down by the National Minorities Commission (NMC) for the recognition of institutions as minority institutions. One of them states that conservation of the language, script or culture of minorities need not be the objective of such an institution and it can even impart secular education. If this is to be the case, there is no reason why such an institution should be given recognition as a minority institution. Under Article 30 (1), minority institutions enjoy the right of administration, that is, autonomy in the appointment of teaching and non-teaching staff, including the right of choice to confine the selection purely to the members of the community; non-interference by the government in the composition of the governing bodies, and right of choice in admission to students, and so on. The autonomy given to these institutions in respect of their administration is thus strikingly wide as compared to that of non-minority institutions and, as a result, a number of institutions started by prominent Hindu organizations, such as the Ramakrishna Mission, Swaminarayan Sampradaya, Arya Samaj and others, have been asking for recognition as minority educational institutions.[7] This is a travesty and only brings out the unjustifiability of the very concept of minority educational institutions. As stated above, a number of Constituent Assembly members, such as Jayaprakash Narayan, Amrit Kaur and others, had opposed the provision. For whatever reasons it may have been agreed to at that time, there is certainly no justification to continue it any longer even in respect of linguistic minorities. Market forces should be permitted to operate subject to such restrictions as the government finds it necessary in the interest of improving educational and academic standards, keeping education within the reasonable reach of the students and proper and accountable management.

The Banning of Cow Slaughter

It would be pertinent to refer to Jawaharlal Nehru's thoughts on this

---

[7] Extended definition of a Hindu can be seen in section 2 of the Hindu Marriage Act which provides that the Act applies to any person who is a Hindu by religion in any of its forms or developments including a Vaishnava, a Lingayat or a follower of the Brahmo, Prarthana or Arya Samaj.

subject during his long public life. S. Gopal wrote:

> As Mayor [sic] of Allahabad in 1923, Nehru guided the Board to reject unanimously the suggestion to prohibit the slaughter of cattle; but his attitude was based not so much on any principle as on a feeling that this was not a matter calling for administrative intervention, for he had earlier suggested to the Hindus that they should request Muslims to stop cow-killing rather than fight them about it. (Gopal in Grover 1990: 208)

Prohibiting cow slaughter in a country which professes to be secular is difficult to understand. Nehru, in his letter to Dr Rajendra Prasad dated 7 August 1947, stated:

> Nobody can possibly doubt the widespread Hindu sentiment in favour of cow protection. At the same time there is something slightly spurious about the present agitation...This question should in any event be considered in its larger context of general planning... I do not think we can ignore the political aspect. India, in spite of its overwhelming Hindu population, is a composite country from the religious and other points of view...It does make a difference whether we try to think of India as a composite country or as a Hindu country...If any such step [of banning cow slaughter] is taken purely on grounds of Hindu sentiment, it means that the government of India is going to be carried on in a particular way, which thus far we have not done...*There is a very strong Hindu revivalist feeling in the country at the present moment. I am greatly distressed by it because it represents the narrowest communalism. It is the exact replica of the narrow Muslim communalism which we have tried to combat for so long*...I have felt often enough during the last few weeks, and have stated as much at our party meetings in the Constituent Assembly and elsewhere, that I find myself in total disagreement with this revivalist feeling, and in view of this difference of opinion *I am a poor representative of many of our people today. I felt honestly that it might be better for a truer representative to take my place*. (Gopal and Iyengar Vol. I, 2003: 159–60)

One is struck by Nehru's deep understanding of the issues in the larger context of the future of India as a secular nation.

> Article 19 (1) (g) specifically states that 'all citizens shall have the right to practise any profession, or to carry on any occupation, trade or business'. The test of reasonableness which must be applied to justify any prohibitions on the right as above should *inter alia* comprise the underlying purpose of the restriction imposed; evils sought to be remedied by the law, its extent and urgency; how far the restriction is or is not proportionate to the evil and prevailing conditions at the time. (Bakshi 1998: 30)
>
> The Supreme Court has held that the prohibition of cow slaughter cannot be considered an unreasonable restriction imposed upon the right conferred by Article 19 (1) (g). This is a questionable decision and needs to be reviewed if the objective is to 'organize agriculture and animal husbandry on modern and scientific lines… and…to take steps for preserving and improving the breeds…'. It needs to be examined whether this objective is going to be subserved by imposing a total ban on cow slaughter. The judgment of the Supreme Court itself in the *Hanif Qureshi* case (*AIR* 1958 SC 731) had convincingly brought out the various studies which suggested that total prohibition of cow slaughter would not be justified. Though, the later 2006 decision of the Supreme Court was quite the contrary and was given when UPA was in power, no thought was given by the government to file a revision application in the Supreme Court. Whatever may be the political rhetoric, the Congress party, after Jawaharlal Nehru's term as prime minister, has been in favour of banning cow slaughter. In the recent controversy in 2015 on lynching of a Muslim in Dadri in Uttar Pradesh on a mere rumour that he had beef in his house, Digvijay Singh, one of the vociferous general secretaries of AICC has declared that the Congress party is in favour of imposition of a total ban on cow slaughter. As Basu has brought out while only C.P. [Central Provinces] and Berar had an Animal Preservation Act, 1949, a number of other states such as U.P., Bihar, H.P., Orissa, Rajasthan and Punjab passed laws banning cow slaughter during 1955–58. (Basu, Vol. 3, 2008: 4169)

The latest entrant in this list was Maharashtra in 2015.

Shamsul Islam, who teaches in a college in Delhi, stated that Vivekananda, while speaking on the theme of 'Buddhistic India' at the Shakespeare Club, Pasadena, California on 2 February 1900, said: 'You will be astonished if I tell you that according to the old ceremonials, he is not a good Hindu who does not eat beef. On certain occasions he must sacrifice a bull and eat it.'

Islam has also brought out that other research works sponsored by the Ramakrishna Mission founded by Vivekananda himself corroborate this. C. Kunhan Raja, an authority on Vedic India, did not miss the fact of widespread beef-eating in ancient India:

> The Vedic Aryans, including the Brahmins, ate fish, meat and even beef. A distinguished guest was honoured with beef served at a meal. Although the Vedic Aryans ate beef, milch cows were not killed. One of the words that designated cow was *aghnya* that (which shall not be killed). But a guest was a *goghna* (one for whom a cow is killed). It is only bulls, barren cows and calves that were killed. (Islam 2011: 74)

In spite of this background, when the article pertaining to prohibiting the slaughter of cows and related issues came up for discussion in CA on 24 November 1948, Pandit Thakur Das Bhargava, who was the main proponent, spoke at length to show that it was essential that the slaughter of cows be prohibited not just on religious grounds but on economic grounds as well. He said that, during the reign of Babar, Humayun, Akbar, Jahangir and even Aurangzeb, cow slaughter was not practised in India; not because Muslims regarded it to be bad but because, from the economic point of view, it was unprofitable.

He said: 'In China, cow slaughter is a crime. It is banned in Afghanistan as well. A year ago, a similar law was passed in Burma; before that, under a certain law, only cattle above 14 years of age could be slaughtered. But eventually, the Burma government realized that this partial ban was not effective...In the present conditions in our country, cow-breeding is necessary not for milk supply alone, but also for the purposes of draught and transport. It is no wonder that people worship the cow in this land. But I do not appeal to you in the name of religion; I ask you to consider it in the light of economic requirements of the country.'

He referred to the observations of Mahatma Gandhi who had said that 'cow slaughter and manslaughter are, in my opinion, two sides of the same coin'. He also invited attention to an expert committee appointed by the government of India on the subject. The committee had unanimously decided that cattle slaughter should be banned...A cow, whether it be a milch cow or not, is a moving manure factory and so, as far as the cow is concerned, there can be no question of its being useless or useful. (*CAD* Vol. VII, Book 2, 2009: 569–70)

Seth Govind Das proposed that the words, 'and other useful cattle, especially milch cattle and of child-bearing age [calf-bearing age], young stocks and draught cattle be deleted and the following be added at the end: the word cow includes bulls, bullocks, young stock of genus cow'. He felt that the amendment moved by Pandit Bhargava prohibited the slaughter of cow and other useful cattle but unfit or useless cows could be slaughtered. Seth Govind Das said that, according to his amendment, slaughter of any cow would not be permitted.

He also emphasized one other point in so far as Muslims were concerned: 'I would like to see my country culturally unified even though we may follow different religions just as a Hindu and a Sikh or a Hindu and a Jain can live in the same family, in the same way a Hindu and a Muslim can also live in the same family. The Muslims should come forward to make it clear that their religion does not compulsorily enjoin on them the slaughter of the cow. I have studied a little of all the religions. I have read the life of Prophet Mohammad Sahib. The Prophet never took beef in his life. This is a historic fact...Bhargava pointed out just now, that from the time of Akbar to that of Aurangzeb, there was a ban on cow slaughter. I want to tell you what Babar, the first Moghul Emperor told Humayun. He said: "Refrain from cow slaughter to win the hearts of the people of Hindustan".' He further said that if cow slaughter is totally banned, the government will require money for the purpose. He added: 'The government should not raise before us the financial bogey so often raised by the British government.'

(*CAD* Vol. VII, Book 2, 2009: 572–73)

Shibban Lal Saksena supported the proposal for a complete ban on cow slaughter.

Ram Sahay, who had also tabled an amendment, said: 'I find here that a section of the House does not like this. I also do not like, on my part, to make any proposal that may not receive the unanimous acceptance of the House nor a proposal which may lead to the curtailment of the freedom of the provinces in this matter. Under the Directive Principles of State Policy, provinces will have the power to stop cow slaughter totally or partially. Though there is a ban in one form or another on the slaughter of cows in almost all countries of the world, yet I would not emphasize that fact before you.'

He urged Dr Ambedkar to accept the amendment moved by Bhargava. Shibban Lal Saksena said that there was a common misconception that India had too many cattle and that most of them were useless, and therefore, they must be slaughtered. He said that this was a totally wrong impression. He whole-heartedly supported the amendment of Seth Govind Das. R.V. Dhulekar strongly supported the banning of cow slaughter and said that either of the two amendments which had been put forward by Bhargava and Seth Govind Das should be accepted. (*CAD* Vol. VII, Book 2, 2009: 574–77)

Reference must be made to the usual practice followed by the Vice-President of CA to give an opportunity to people who held different views from the majority view. Accordingly, he invited Z.H. Lari to take the floor.

Lari was diplomatic when he said: 'I for one can say that this is a matter on which we will not stand in the way of the majority if the majority wants to proceed in a certain way, whatever may be our inclinations. We feel—we know that our religion does not necessarily say that we must sacrifice cow; it permits it...Let those who guide the destinies of the country, make or mar them, say definitely, "This is our view", and we will submit to it. We are not going to violate it...In view of what I have said, I would not oppose nor support any of the amendments.' (*CAD* Vol. VII, Book 2, 2009: 577–78)

Syed Muhammad Saiadulla said that, according to his religion, there ought to be no compulsion in the name of religion. *He said that he therefore would not like to use his veto if Hindu brethren wanted to place this matter in our Constitution from the religious point of view.* He however asked the question as to what is to be done about the huge number of uneconomic cattle that must be done away with before you can supplant them with a better breed. Saiadulla further emphasized that there were lakhs of Muslims who did not eat cow's flesh. He concluded by saying, 'In the name of economic front, I cannot lend my support to the motion moved by Pandit Bhargava. I am sorry that, for the reasons given already, I am compelled to oppose the amendment of Seth Govind Das.' *Ambedkar interjected to say that he would accept the amendment of Pandit Thakur Das Bhargava.* With the adoption of this amendment, the discussion was concluded. (*CAD* Vol. VII, Book 2, 2009: 578–81)

Only a few members took part in the discussion in the Constituent Assembly on 14 November 1949 on prohibiting the slaughter of cows. They were Shibban Lal Saksena, Pandit Thakur Das Bhargava and Brajeshwar Prasad. Saksena emphasized that the draft article did not say, 'That the State shall prohibit the slaughter of cows'.

He added that the article said, instead: 'It will take steps to improve the breeds of milch and draught cattle including cows, and for prohibiting their slaughter...This is a very substantial alteration and I do not think the Drafting Committee was authorized to make such an alteration on such a fundamental thing on which there were strong discussions and it was agreed to after a very prolonged debate. I do not think anyone has the authority to change things in this manner and to substitute the original. I appeal that the original should be kept.'

Pandit Thakur Das Bhargava was more forthright and he said:

'In dealing with this article I would first of all beg to remind the House that this article was fairly hotly debated in this House. This article has the sanction of the whole House and of the largest party in the Assembly...Previously it was a much stronger one, but ultimately it was drafted in this form...There is no reason why the Drafting Committee should tamper with the wording of such a section like this...Seth Govind Das moved an amendment from the religious point of view but it was not accepted. *My submission is that every word in this article is to my mind a sacred one, in this sense that it has got the imprint of the whole House.* Secondly, I submit that on the basis of this article, some of the provincial governments have taken action. They have gone further and prohibited the slaughter of cows. Therefore, when this article has practically been acted upon by some of the provinces, it is not fair now to tamper with it.' (CAD Vols X–XII, Book 5, 2009: 470–72)

The decision to ban cow slaughter must have been taken and the wording of Article 48 settled separately by the Congress party. This was, therefore, only a formality through which the Constituent Assembly went.

J.J.M. Nichols Roy, speaking on the final draft of the Constitution on 19 November 1949, had specifically raised serious questions regarding the provision for banning cow slaughter. He said:

I was wondering whether this provision would mean the prohibition of cow slaughter at all times and of every kind of cows and cattle. I thought in my own mind that this was not the meaning. If that be the meaning of this provision—which I do not think it is—it would place a terrible burden on the State. *Think of the millions of cows that will float around the country without any fodder, and sickly, and the amount of money that will be spent on them and the terrible burden it would be on any country.* Hundreds of them will die in the fields without being taken care of. It will not be economic at all for any state to prevent the slaughter of cows under all circumstances. I consider that this Article would only prevent the slaughter of cows which are milch cows and draught cattle, which will be of benefit to people. If it be otherwise, I consider that this would be a blot on this Constitution and an *oppression also to some of the people, especially to the hill people of Assam, who eat beef and who keep cattle for the sake of eating.* (CAD Vols X–XII, Book 5, 2009: 711)

Gopal rightly commented that Nehru did not oppose the listing of the banning of cow slaughter as one of the Directive Principles of State Policy, but he was clear in his mind to see that nothing came of it in practice. (Gopal in Grover 1990: 216)

It is unfortunate that the discussion on such a crucial subject was quite cursory and did not address the basic questions as to whether prohibiting cow slaughter would be in keeping with the basic tenets of secularism, and whether it would not contravene important provisions of fundamental rights, namely, among others, Articles 14, 19 (1) (g) and 25. As can be seen, the enactments of several state governments were later challenged on these grounds. The so-called scientific and economic arguments given for banning cow slaughter, too, did not stand closer scrutiny. Clearly, Article 48 was a political decision taken by the Congress party.

It must be mentioned that the mind-boggling problem of organizing cattle camps all over the country to look after stray and unproductive animals has not really been appreciated fully. Experience has shown that, whenever such cattle camps had to be organized even during the short period of scarcity or drought, it led to rampant corruption and mismanagement. This problem assumed worrying proportions during the severe 2015 drought in most of the Marathwada area of Maharashtra. Particularly after the statutory ban on cow slaughter, the farmers in scarcity areas cannot even dispose of their cattle as they used to do earlier, and they are left with no option but to leave such cattle unattended. As for urban and semi-urban areas, the stray cattle roaming on the streets have posed traffic hazards and obstruction for the last several years. This problem will get further aggravated in the years to come.

It would be pertinent to note the thinking of Mahatma Gandhi on cow slaughter:

> *The Hindu religion prohibits cow slaughter for the Hindus, not for the world.* The religious prohibition comes from within. Any imposition from without means compulsion. Such compulsion is repugnant to religion. *India is the land not only of the Hindus, but also of the Mussalmans, the Sikhs, the Parsees, the Christians and the Jews and all who claim to be Indian and are loyal to the Indian Union.* If they can prohibit cow slaughter in India on religious grounds, why cannot the Pakistan government prohibit, say, idol worship in Pakistan on similar grounds? I am not a temple-goer, but if I were prohibited from going to a temple in Pakistan, I would

make it a point to go there even at the risk of losing my head. *Just as shariat cannot be imposed on the non-Muslims, the Hindu law cannot be imposed on the non-Hindus.* (Shah 1969: 4)

Gandhi, in his prayer meeting of 25 July 1947, once again explained his position on cow slaughter. He said: '*In India no law can be made to ban cow slaughter*. I do not doubt that Hindus are forbidden [sic] the slaughter of cows. I have been long pledged to serve the cow but how can my religion also be the religion of the rest of the Indians? It will mean coercion against those Indians who are not Hindus.' (*The Radical Humanist*, October 2015: 27)

It is important to note that V.D. Savarkar, who was a staunch proponent of Hindutva, ridiculed the concept of protecting and worshipping the cow. He said that, from Vedic times, the cow was revered and protected only because of her contribution to the economic life of the community. (*Samagra Savarkar Vangmaya*, Vol. 6, 2000–01: 40–9)

A.B. Shah, an ardent rationalist, has written in his book, *Challenges to Secularism*, that the argument that in a democratic state the wishes of an overwhelming majority of its citizens ought to be respected and given statutory expression can be faulted at least on three points:

> First, democracy does not give the majority—even if it were 99 per cent strong—the right to act in a manner that either undermines democracy or interferes with the right of other groups to live in their own way. He further emphasized that, for about 300 years after the rise of Buddhism and Jainism, beef-eating was common in India. Not only does archaeological evidence support this view but there are also a number of statements in Hindu scriptures, such as *Brihad Aranyaka*, *Grihya Sutras*, which explicitly recommend beef-eating on certain occasions. Indeed, the whole tone and temper of life during the Vedic and Upanishad period seems to have been altogether different from what came to be the case after Buddhism and Jainism took root in Indian society. The situation became still worse after the rise of Shankar [Shankaracharya] and his highly sophisticated but world-negating philosophy. *Shah bluntly stated that those Hindus who today claim the support of religion in favour of their demand for a ban on cow slaughter are either ignorant*

or knowingly dishonest. If they want to justify their demand, the only course open to them is to say that they are opposed to cow slaughter, regardless of what their history says and that, being a majority community, they are going to see it accepted by the rest of the country.

This is precisely what the BJP and its affiliated organizations are trying to do since the BJP's coming to power in 2014.

> Second, there is no evidence that a majority of Hindus themselves really want cow slaughter to be banned…Even during the two decades after Independence, the Indian peasant has been selling dry cows to the butcher for the simple reason that he cannot afford to maintain them.[8] *Some years ago, a non-official resolution for a ban on cow slaughter was thrown out by the Legislative Assembly of what was then the Bombay State on the grounds that it would merely result in the slow death by starvation of about 50,000 animals every year in Maharashtra, and lead to an outbreak of epidemics.* Also, if an opinion poll were to be taken today of the peasants who are the most directly concerned with the problem, they would refuse to accept the responsibility for preserving cows which had ceased to be of economic value to them.
>
> Third, even if a majority of Hindus were to support this demand, how would it justify their imposing their own religious beliefs on others? That a number of Muslims have supported the demand for banning cow slaughter should not mislead one into believing that they are really happy over it.

If the Congress government at the Centre or any government at the state level succumbs to the pressure tactics of the revivalist movement in India, it may very well find that sooner than it imagined, it would have to give up all claims to secularism… If the Shankaracharya is obstinate and is likely to die as a result of a second fast, what should the government

---

[8]Due to the severe drought in Maharashtra in 2014–15, at several places drought-affected farmers expressed anxiety due to the imposition of a ban on cow slaughter in the state.

do?...It should call his bluff and take the necessary steps to ward off the exploitation of his possible death for political purposes.

A.B. Shah has also extensively quoted from Hindu Vedic scriptures to show that eating beef was well accepted in Indian society. He has stated that, in a number of verses in the *Rigveda,* the use of ox-hide in the preparation of *soma* is mentioned. The conclusion is obvious: Vedic Indians—they were not yet Hindus as the term is understood today—were fond of the intoxicating drink and did not regard ox-hide as impure. At *R.V. (Rigveda)* II. 7.5, it is apparently suggested that Vedic Indians were fond of roast beef. At *R.V.* VIII. 43.11, *agni* [fire] is described as 'fed on ox and cow', suggesting, like the preceding quotation, that cattle were sacrificed and roasted in fire.

It is true that at certain places in the *Rigveda,* the cow is referred to as *aghnya* (that which shall not be killed), but whenever this is done, the cow under reference is a milch cow and is so indicated by the use of adjectives like *payoduha* or *payobhir.* The Vedic people saw nothing wrong in killing barren and useless cows which are mentioned as *vasha* or *vehat.* Shah has also quoted from *Aiteriya Brahmana, Taiteriya Brahmana, Panchavinsha Brahmana, Shatapath Brahmana, Brihadaranyaka, Manusmriti* and *History of Dharmashastras* to show that beef-eating was quite common during the period. As for the Buddhist attitude to meat-eating, Shah has quoted from Mukandilal, a well-known authority on the subject, that for nearly 300 years after the rise of Buddhism, beef-eating was prevalent on a large scale in India. Even the monks were not averse to it... It was only when Brahminical supremacy was seriously threatened by the growing popularity of Buddhism that Indian society took to vegetarianism and total abjurement of intoxicating drinks...In the event, indiscriminate slaughter of cattle was replaced by equally indiscriminate preservation regardless of its implications for the economy... *Briefly put, the decision requires a clear choice between reason and passion.* (Shah 1969: 15–18, 24–26)

This issue came into prominence in 1955. Nehru was clear in his mind when he opposed the demand, even though some states were considering legislative measures for the purpose. Nehru wrote to chief ministers in his fortnightly letter dated 23 February 1955:

I should like to make it clear that, so far as the Central government is concerned, it considers any such legislation unwise and inexpedient. *Indeed, there is an apprehension that such legislation will really be not to the advantage of protecting our best cattle.* The mere fact of a continuing agitation should not make us adopt a course which is not the right one. I think we should go to the public and explain the position quite clearly... I am very anxious to protect our cattle wealth in the country and I have often written to you about it. But the way to do so is not by legislation to ban cow slaughter. (Parthasarathi 1985: 138)

In April 1955, Seth Govind Das introduced a bill to ban cow slaughter. Nehru opposed it and it was lost by a very big majority. Nehru wrote to the chief ministers:

I will resign rather than accept such a bill... We must concentrate on preventing completely the killing of any milch cow. This is the first essential step, and I hope that particular attention will be paid to this in some of our big cities... *We should not and cannot surrender to the agitational demand of some of the communal organizations which seek to exploit religion for political advantage.* I know that some people, including Congressmen, feel strongly on this subject. I appreciate their sentiment but not this approach. I spoke rather strongly on this subject, so that there might be no doubt left in the public mind about our general policy and approach to this important question. (Parthasarathi 1985: 144-5)

It is significant to note that, in spite of these strong views on the subject, Nehru did not speak a word in the Constituent Assembly when Article 48 came up for discussion.

Despite this evidence, the agitation for banning cow slaughter has continued over the years. On 7 November 1966, there was a major agitation by sadhus who protested in the close vicinity of Parliament, leading to a law-and-order problem and firing by the police. The Opposition parties brought parliamentary proceedings to a standstill.

Agitations for banning cow slaughter have been undertaken on a number of other occasions. Vinoba Bhave threatened to go on an indefinite fast on this subject from 1 January 1979. Earlier, in May 1976, he had announced that he would go on an indefinite fast from 11 September 1976. At that time, Om Mehta, Minister of State for Home, had given an assurance that the government would implement Article 48 of the Constitution and impose a total ban on cow slaughter in the country. Mehta also said that a complete prohibition of cow slaughter existed in Jammu and Kashmir, Haryana, Punjab, Rajasthan, Gujarat, Madhya Pradesh, Uttar Pradesh, Bihar, the Vidarbha area in Maharashtra, Karnataka, Orissa, and so on. After the government's assurance as above, Vinoba Bhave declared that he was satisfied and that he would not undertake the fast. (*RSD* Vol. 107.2, 1978: 214–18)

On 2 March 1979, Dr Ramji Singh moved a resolution seeking a ban on cow slaughter. The resolution said:

> This House directs the government to ensure total ban on the slaughter of cows of all ages and calves in consonance with the Directive Principle laid down in Article 48 of the Constitution... as well as necessitated by strong economic considerations based on the recommendations of the Cattle Preservation and Development Committee and the reported fast by Acharya Vinoba Bhave from 21 April 1979.

Participating in the resumed discussion on 16 March 1979, Samar Mukherjee did not favour a ban on cow slaughter as it would be against secularism, national integration and moreover, was not justified from the economic point of view. M.N. Govindan Nair pleaded that the religious feelings of a section of the population could not be the basis for banning cow slaughter. The resolution, he added, ran counter to the guidelines laid down by Gandhi on the question.

> On 26 April 1979, the prime minister [Morarji Desai] referred to the fast deterioration in the condition of Vinoba Bhave, and announced the decision of the government to bring forward a Constitution Amendment Bill transferring the entry regarding the preservation, protection and improvement of [live] stock from the State list to the Concurrent List. The Constitution (Fiftieth Amendment) Bill was accordingly introduced on 18 May 1979. (Kashyap 1997: 382–83)

However, this bill was not pursued and, therefore, lapsed in due course.

> Disregarding the unambiguous stand of Jawaharlal Nehru on the subject, and the Congress party's commitment to secularism, Digvijaya Singh, a senior Congress general secretary, has stated that Congress governments had banned cow slaughter in most states and that if the BJP brings a bill to ban cow slaughter in the whole country, Congress will support it. (*IE* 6 October 2015: 5)

D.N. Jha, a former professor and chair at the department of history in Delhi University, wrote in his article, 'Elusive holiness of the cow':

> The ritual killing of cattle was *de rigueur* among the Vedic people, who routinely sacrificed cattle and ate their flesh. The *Rigveda* frequently refers to the cooking of the flesh of animals, including that of the ox, as an offering to the gods, especially Indra. In most Vedic Yajnas, cattle were killed and their flesh eaten. Although some post-Vedic texts recommend the offering of animal effigies in lieu of livestock, *ancient Indians continued to kill cattle and eat beef*. The practice of cattle-killing on sacrificial and other occasions, attested to by a number of post-Vedic texts, possibly continued for centuries. (*IE* 7 October 2015: 10)

Donald Smith pointed out that a number of unsuccessful attempts had been made in Parliament to secure legislation which would implement Article 48 on an all-India basis. Bills were introduced by Nand Lal Sharma, U.N. Trivedi, Jhulan Sinha and Seth Govind Das. In the debate on Seth Govind Das's bill in 1955, Nehru had asserted that it was a matter for state governments and not Parliament to consider. Nehru firmly declared that he was prepared to stake his prime ministership on this issue. The House rejected the bill by a vote of ninety-five to twelve; two Congressmen, Purushottam Das Tandon and Thakur Das Bhargava, ignored the hastily issued Congress whip and voted for the measure to ban the cow slaughter. Smith emphasized that Nehru's success in staving off legislation on cow protection in Parliament 'has not at all been paralleled by developments in state assemblies'.

Smith also invited attention to Nehru's speech in 1958 before an assembly of students at Allahabad when he declared that he looked up to the cow as he did to the horse. Pandit Sita Ram, chairman of the UP Gausamvardhan Inquiry Committee, and Nehru's opponent in two general elections, took serious exception to this statement which struck him as being akin to blasphemy. He threatened to prosecute the prime minister under section 295 A of the CrPC for speaking 'with deliberate and malicious intention of outraging the religious feelings of the Hindus'. (*Manchester Guardian Weekly*, 3 November 1958)

Nehru was not prosecuted, but the incident illustrated the intensity of feeling aroused by devotion to the cow.

> Assuming that economic considerations have had relatively little to do with their [cow protection] enactment, *they must be viewed primarily as attempts to impose the taboos of one religion upon all citizens. They are certainly contrary to the spirit of secular state.* The cow protection legislation is undoubtedly the result of Hindu communalism; the coercive power of the state is pressed into the service of Hindu religion to the detriment or at least inconvenience of beef-eating Muslims and Christians [and Hindus] (Smith 1963: 485–86, 489)

Justice Gajendragadkar, former chief justice of India, wrote:

> The truth of the matter is that, in providing for a ban on the slaughter of cows and calves and other milch and draught cattle... the Constitution, in effect, treated the Hindu sentiment as both relevant and valid in laying down the directive principle. Of course, in considering the question as to whether the implementation of the said directive principle came into conflict with fundamental rights, it was observed by the Supreme Court that fundamental rights must prevail over the directive principles...The imposition of a total ban on slaughter of cows and all their progeny is basically a social and economic issue and therefore in the discussion of the merits of this issue and its ultimate decision, religious texts should be treated as irrelevant. We should consider the economics of the proposition, its feasibility and its reasonableness; but we should not allow religious doctrines to enter into this discussion.

If the advocates of a total ban on the slaughter of cows and all their progeny consider what the ultimate implications of their claim would be for non-Hindu citizens of India, they will realize that *their claim, in substance, amounts to converting the secular democracy of India into a theocratic state.* (Gajendragadkar 1971: 130–31)

The Maharashtra Animal Preservation (Amendment) Bill, 1995, was passed by the legislature when the Shiv Sena–BJP was in power. The governor had sent the bill to the government of India for obtaining the President's approval. It was only in February 2015, a full 20 years later, that the President's approval was conveyed to the state government. And this is not the only case of its kind. No wonder, as I have brought out later in Chapter 6, the states are upset with the high-handedness of the government of India in dealing with the states. This approval also came about because of pressure by the BJP–Shiv Sena government which had come back to power in the state, and the NDA has been in power at the Centre. The act provides for a five-year jail term and a fine of Rs 10, 000 for possession or sale of beef. (*IE* 3 March 2015: 1)

The Haryana government has unanimously passed a new law—Gauvansh Sanrakhan and Gosamvardhan Bill. Under it, the state police will have draconian new powers to protect cows. If you are eating, selling, storing even canned or processed beef products, imported from elsewhere, you will face a jail sentence longer than for manslaughter. Shekhar Gupta has highlighted that this is being done in a country where, as the Anthropological Survey's People of India Report (1993) noted, 88 per cent of the 4635 communities into which we can be classified, are meat-eating. (*India Today*, 30 March 2015: 20)

'With a widespread drought in several parts of Maharashtra, farmers are finding it difficult to dispose of their cattle due to the ban on the slaughter of animals introduced in the state.' (*Pune Newsline* of *IE* 22 December 2015: 1) 'A ruling party, BJP, MLA from the severely drought-affected Beed district in Maharashtra has criticised the government over its beef ban, saying it was not in the interest of farmers. "Why should you snatch away the poor's meal?" asked Bhimrao Dhonde who represents the Ashti constituency.' (*IE* 11 March 2016: 1)

There is also a severe shortage of fodder. In several cases, farmers have no choice but to leave their cattle as stray cattle, at the mercy of nature and people at large. Soon, the state governments may have to announce a minimum support price for cattle.

> In the last four years, the number of cases filed under the Uttar Pradesh Prevention of Cow Slaughter Act have almost doubled, as compared with the number of cases registered in 2011. According to the Uttar Pradesh Crime Record Bureau, UP registered a total of 2456 cases under the law prohibiting cow slaughter in 2011. The figure went up to 3655 in 2012, and 5012 in 2014. (*IE* 11 October 2015: 1)
>
> The Himachal Pradesh High Court has stated that secularism is one of the basic features of the Constitution and the people should not hurt the religious sentiments of each other. It has also directed the Centre to consider enacting a legislation to ban cow slaughter. Interestingly, the court has also directed the Centre to provide the necessary funds to the Himachal Pradesh government for housing and providing fodder to cows and stray cattle. (*IE* 15 October 2015: 7)
>
> But, the views about how secularism is to be looked at in this regard differ diametrically. As compared to the above view of the Himachal Pradesh High Court, Surjit Bhalla, in a well-argued article, stated, 'An Islamic or Jewish nation can prohibit the killing of pigs. A Hindu nation can prohibit the killing of cows. A secular nation can do neither.' (*IE* 10 October 2015: 9)

I entirely agree with Bhalla.

> Aroon Purie has rightly underlined that the narrow politics of propelling the cow agenda and ethnic vigilantism puts roadblocks on Prime Minister Modi's drive on development. The mandate given to this government in the General Election was for economic development, not for Hindu revivalism... Also, it should know that once you uncork the genie of religious tensions in a multicultural society like India, it is difficult to put it back. It will only hurtle

India towards an Age of Chaos. (*India Today*, 19 October 2015: 5)

Supreme Court Pronouncements

The enactments banning cow slaughter in the states of Bihar, UP, Bombay and MP came up for consideration in appeal before the Supreme Court in the *Mohd. Hanif Qureshi and Others* case (*AIR* 1958 SC 731). These enactments were challenged under Articles 14, 19 (1) (g) and 25. The Court pronounced its judgment on 23 April 1958. The Court *inter alia* noted that:

> The report of the Cattle Preservation and Development Committee did not recommend the immediate total ban on the slaughter of all cattle. They recommended the establishment of concentration camps, later on euphemistically called *gosadan*s, and though total ban was the ultimate objective, it did not, for the moment, prohibit the slaughter of animals over the age of 14 years and of animals of any age permanently unfit for work or breeding owing to age or deformity. In paragraph 134 of the Expert Committee's Report at page 63 it is stated clearly that the total ban on the slaughter of all cattle would not be in the best interest of the country as it is merely a negative and not a positive approach to the problem. They consider that a constructive approach to the problem will be to see that no useful animal is slaughtered and that the country's resources are fully harnessed to produce better and more efficient cattle. *Neither the First Five-Year Plan nor the Second Five-Year Plan accepted the idea of a total ban on the slaughter of cattle.* Indeed, according to the Second Five-Year Plan, a total ban will help the tendency for the number of surplus cattle to increase and, in their view, a total ban on the slaughter of all cows, calves and other milch and draught cattle will defeat the very object of the Directive Principles embodied in Article 48 of the Constitution... The Planning Commission considered that it would be impossible to establish enough of these gosadans and they reached the conclusion that, in defining the scope of the ban on the slaughter of cattle, the states should take a realistic view of the fodder resources available in the country, and the extent to which they can get the cooperation

of voluntary organizations to bear the main responsibility for maintaining unserviceable and unproductive cattle...On the basis of this well-documented and reasoned logic, the Supreme Court held that a total ban on the slaughter of the she-buffaloes, bulls and bullocks (cattle or buffalo) after they cease to be capable of yielding milk or of breeding or working as draught animals cannot be supported as reasonable in the interest of the general public. (*AIR* 1958 SC 731: 752–53, 755)

This subject came up for decision again in *Akhil Bharat Goseva Sangh v. State of Andhra Pradesh and Others*, and *Umesh and Others v. State of Karnataka and Others* ([2006] 4 SCC 162), decided on 29 March 2006. This judgment comes as a surprise for various reasons. The Court decided that the protection recommended by this part of the directive under Article 48 of the Constitution can no longer be said to be confined only to cows and calves and those animals which are presently capable of yielding milk or of doing work as draught cattle. The protection under Article 48 also extends to cattle which at one time were milch or draught but which have ceased to be as such. The Court reiterated its earlier decision in which it found that bulls and bullocks do not become useless by merely crossing a particular age...The increasing adoption of non-conventional energy sources like biogas plants justify the need for bulls and bullocks to live their full life in spite of their having ceased to be useful for the purpose of breeding and draught. The Court stated: '*The interpretation of Article 48 of the Constitution has now been widened and "milch and draught cattle" include cattle which have become permanently incapacitated to be used for milch and draught purposes*...It is directed that the state government [of Karnataka] maintain proper institutions for providing care and protection to the cattle... (pp. 202–04)

This subject came up once again before the Supreme Court in three appeals namely, *State of Gujarat v. Mirzapur Moti Kureshi Kassab Jamat, Ahmedabad, and Others; Shree Ahimsa Army Manav Kalyan Jeev Daya Charitable Trust v. Mirzapur Moti Kureshi Kassab Jamat, Ahmedabad, and Others;* and *Akhil Bharat Krishi Goseva Sangh v. Mirzapur Moti*

Kureshi Kassab Jamat, Ahmedabad, and Others. ([2005] 8 SCC 534) The appeals came up before a seven-judge bench and were decided on 26 October 2005. By a laboured decision, the Court reversed its earlier decision delivered on 23 April 1958 and held that Independent India was not even eleven years old then. Since then, the Indian economy has made much headway and gained a foothold internationally. The Court referred to the Report of the National Commission on Cattle submitted in July 2002, which revealed that the existing fodder resources of the country could sustain and meet with 51.92 per cent of the total requirements to sustain its livestock population. The Court also felt that a major part of the fallow land could be put under the plough for cultivating fodder crops and, if managed properly, the grass reservoirs of India could be developed. The Court found that, according to evidence on record, beef contributes only 1.3 per cent of the total meat consumption pattern of Indian society. Butchers are not prohibited from slaughtering animals other than the cattle belonging to cow progeny. Consequently, only a part of their activity has been prohibited. They could continue with their activity of slaughtering other animals. It is futile to think that meat originating from cow progeny could be the only staple food or protein diet for the poor. Further, a desirable diet and nutrition are not necessarily associated with a non-vegetarian diet and that, too, originating from slaughtering cow progeny. The Court also took note of the fact that the National Commission on Cattle has incorporated as many as seventeen recommendations for strengthening *goshala*s. The Court also took note of the fact that the state of Gujarat has made adequate provisions for the maintenance of *gosadans* and *goshalas*, and adequate fodder is available for the entire cattle population. Against this background, the Court said: 'We are unhesitatingly of the opinion that there is no apparent inconsistency between the directive principles which persuaded the state to pass the law and the fundamental rights canvassed before the high court by the writ petitioners.'

Justice A.K. Mathur's was the only dissenting judgment. He said, 'The basic question that arises in these petitions is whether there is need to overrule the earlier decisions which held the field right from 1958–96; whether the ground realities have materially changed so as to reverse the view held by successive Constitutional Benches of this Court or those decisions have ceased to have any relevance.' The judge held that the slaughtering of bulls and bullocks beyond the age of sixteen years constituted only 1.10 per cent of the total slaughtering taking place in the state. 'If this is the ratio of the slaughtering, I fail to understand how this legislation can advance the cause of the public at the expense of the denial of fundamental right of this class of persons (butchers).' He held that the earlier decisions of this Court had not become irrelevant in the present context. He further noted that he failed to understand how an animal, whose average age is said to be twelve to sixteen years could, at the age of sixteen years, produce the cow dung or urine which could offset the requirement of chemical fertilizers. Only well-built young bulls, not aged bulls, were used for the purpose of improving breeding. If the aged and weak bulls were allowed for mating purposes, the offspring would be of poor health and that would not be in the interests of the country. The judge therefore concluded that he did not think that it would be proper to reverse the view which has held good for a long spell of time from 1958 to 1996. There was no material change in ground realities warranting the reversal of earlier decisions.

I feel that, in the majority decision, reversing of such a long-held view of the Court, the implications of the total ban on cow slaughter on the crucial concept of secularism—which the Court had declared as a part of the basic structure of the Constitution—had not been touched. The fact remains that the question of the fundamental rights of not only the butchers but also of the general public in terms of their eating habits and preferences, was not addressed. It is unfortunate that no revision application was ever filed to review this decision.

Salman Khurshid, senior advocate in the Supreme Court and a former central minister, rightly observed:

> It will henceforth not be legally permissible to slaughter bullocks and bulls over 16 years of age. It is unclear whether the Court was motivated by legitimate religious sentiments of a large section of Indians (that it shares) or actually believed that a total ban on the slaughter of cow and its progeny (including bulls) would contribute to the advancement of India's agricultural economy. An unselfconscious religious approach would have been preferable. Be that as it may, the American School of Realists in jurisprudence would have been impressed by the fact that the six judges in majority

are reported to be vegetarians and the dissenting judge, originally a non-vegetarian, too has given up eating meat! The majority of six judges were persuaded to reverse *Hanif Qureshi* on the grounds that improved scientific practices and the growing demand for organic fertilizer as well as biogas called for change in the view taken in 1958. Furthermore, compassion towards animals that serve human beings in their younger days was to be encouraged. Why only bovine cattle qualify for this was not explained—compassion for a bull but not for a goat or a horse! Culling, as a scientific instrument of breed improvement, was not even considered. Justice A.K. Mathur's candid and transparent approach has much to commend itself to practical reason and scientific temper. (*The Pioneer* 21 February 2006); (Godbole 2008: 96–97)

This brief and disturbing history of banning cow slaughter shows that Jawaharlal Nehru was the only prime minister of independent India who boldly took a principled stand against the banning of cow slaughter. In retrospect, his assessment that the demand for prohibiting cow slaughter represents the narrowest of Hindu communalism has turned out to be absolutely correct. This is fully brought out by the manner in which this issue is being pursued and advocated after the landslide victory of the BJP in the 2014 Lok Sabha polls. The killing of a Muslim on the basis of a rumour of his having beef in his house in Dadri in Uttar Pradesh; the threat made by a BJP MLA to the chief minister of Karnataka, Siddaramayya, that he would be beheaded publicly unless he stopped eating beef; blackening the face in Delhi of an independent MLA from Jammu and Kashmir for having hosted a beef-party; the shameful pandemonium and fisticuffs seen in the Jammu and Kashmir Legislative Assembly; the beating up of a truck driver who was allegedly carrying cattle—all these incidents show the increasing and frightening militancy of the Hindutva brigade in the country. The demand for cow slaughter is no longer based on economic factors. It has become the flagship of Hindu rightist philosophy. Against this background, it is all the more necessary to consider seriously whether the demand for banning cow slaughter should be accepted at its face value. Steps need to be taken to request the Supreme Court for a review of its decision upholding a total ban on cow slaughter. It is time that Article 48 of the

Constitution was amended so as to delete the words 'and prohibiting the slaughter of cows and calves and other milch and draught cattle'. Alternately, the provisions of Article 48 as above can remain merely a guiding principle to be implemented voluntarily and to the extent to which society is ready.

4

ARE THESE SIGNPOSTS OF SECULARISM?—II

The truth is one, wise men describe it differently.

—RIGVEDA, 1.164.46

I propose to discuss in this chapter some more matters which raise doubts about India's commitment to secularism. They are:

- Non-separation of religion from politics;
- Babri Masjid demolition—a national shame;
- Major communal riots in the recent past—anti-Sikh riots in 1984; Bombay (it was not known as Mumbai at the time) riots in December 1992 and January 1993, and Gujarat riots in 2002;
- Communalism and communal violence.

Non-separation of Religion from Politics

India is a treasure trove of lost opportunities. It is important to note that the founding fathers and mothers of the Constitution had fully realized the importance of the separation of religion from politics. On 3 April 1948, Ananthasayanam Ayyangar moved a resolution for the purpose in the Constituent Assembly (Legislative):

> Whereas it is essential for the proper functioning of democracy and the growth of national unity and solidarity *that communalism should be eliminated from Indian life*, this Assembly is of opinion that no communal organization which, by its constitution or by the exercise of discretionary power vested in any of its officers or organs, admits to or excludes from its membership persons on grounds of religion, race and caste, or any of them, should be permitted to engage in any activities other than those essential for the *bona fide* religious and cultural needs of the community, and that *all steps, legislative and administrative, necessary to prevent such activities should be taken.*

Nehru welcomed the resolution and assured that the government:

> ...wished to do everything in their power to achieve the objective which lies behind this resolution...The only alternative is civil conflict. *We have seen as a matter of fact how far communalism in politics has led us*; all of us remember the grave dangers through which we have passed and the terrible consequences we have seen... Resolution mentions administrative and legislative measures to be taken to give effect to it. Exactly what those administrative and legislative measures might be, it is impossible to say straight off; it will require the closest scrutiny, certainly the legislative part of it...I should like to make it perfectly clear again that as far as the implementation of it is concerned, more especially in regard to the legislative aspect of it, it will have to be very carefully considered and will ultimately have to come before this House...I have no objection on behalf of the government to accept the addition of the words 'social and educational' which are mentioned in one of the amendments to this resolution. It would read: '... should be permitted to engage in any activities other than those essential for the *bona fide* religious, cultural, social and educational needs of the community...'

The resolution, as amended, was passed by the Constituent Assembly (Legislative) on 3 April 1948. (GOI 1949: 47–51). Nehru's assessment that the legislative aspects of the resolution would require the closest scrutiny and approval of Parliament has been fully borne out by the experience of the Constitution (Eightieth) Amendment Bill 1993, discussed later in this section.

> At the Jabalpur session of the AICC on 29 October 1967, the question of communal riots was discussed at great length. Attention may be invited to the demand made by several members to ban communal parties. Syed Mir Qasim strongly urged a ban on communal parties which were determined to destroy India's nationhood, democracy and secularism. Ahmed Bakhsh Sindhi supported this demand and also asked for action against newspapers which propagated communal views. The demand for a ban on all communal parties was supported by Sheel Bhadra Yajee and others. K.L. Nagappa Alva moved an amendment for a ban on communal parties. S.K. Patil, who moved the political resolution and was a prominent member of the Congress party, rejected the amendment for banning communal parties and said that *it was a delicate problem in as much as it would be difficult to decide whether a party was communal or not.* He further pointed out that the Bharatiya Jana Sangh (the predecessor of BJP) had many Muslims among its members and that there was nothing in its constitution that militated against communal harmony. Patil also said that the Muslim League had supported some Jan Sangh candidates during the elections. (Hassnain 1968: 130–34)

If any proof were required at all, this once again shows that the Congress party, which ruled India for over forty years since Independence, was never really serious about the separation of religion from politics and about banning communal parties.

Religion and politics have become totally indistinguishable in India. Arun Shourie wrote:

> For half a century, the Sikh leaders, solitary figures apart, have been rallying their followers around one cry alone, the paranoid cry, 'The Panth is in danger'...The fundamental tenet of Sikh politics in the last few years—'Politics is for Religion and Religion is for Politics'—and its basic feature in practice [has been] that, contrary to every

> principle of a secular state, contrary to specific laws, the funds, personnel, premises of religious foundations and places of worship would be used for politics. Politics and religion have thus become one...Bhindranwale had but carried to their logical conclusion the fundamental tenet of Sikh politics—'Politics is for Religion and Religion is for Politics'—and its basic practical feature, that of using the religious infrastructure for political purposes. (Shourie 1987: 127–28)

After the demolition of the Babri Masjid, India's reputation as a secular nation was in tatters. Statements made by the Narasimha Rao government that it had been impossible for the government to intervene and stop the demolition failed to carry any conviction. There was a strong view within the country that communalism must be dealt with sternly, if India's survival was not to be jeopardized.

On 12 March 1993, S.S. Ahluwalia, a Congress member, and now a minister of state in the Modi government, moved a private member's bill in the Rajya Sabha for the banning of communal political parties. He also launched a severe attack on the BJP for its communal activities and said that action needed to be taken against it. He said that action against communal propaganda was being taken only when the election process began but, thereafter, there were no restrictions on a political party or an elected representative. He said his bill was meant to deal with this question.

The bill defined a communal political party as a political party which uses religion for electoral gains and indulges in sectional appeal to serve its communal interests, and whose activities are against the national interests. The bill further provided: 'Notwithstanding anything contained in the Representation of the People Act [RPA] 1951 or any other law for the time being in force, all communal political parties in the country, State Legislatures and Parliament... are hereby banned and stand derecognized.'

> John F. Fernandes, lending his strong support to the bill, said that, like the Anti-Defection Act, this bill should also be put in the Tenth Schedule or, if necessary, it should be made the Eleventh Schedule to the Constitution. He said that secularism was the main binding force, the cementing force which had kept the country together. He

suggested that there should be a national debate to see whether the existing system should be overhauled. Since it was the end of the day, the Vice-Chairman suggested that Fernandes should continue his speech on the next private member's day. (*RSD* Vol. 166.3, 1993: 349–52)

At the next sitting, when the bill came up again for discussion, it received wide support, except from the BJP and right-wing parties like the Shiv Sena. John F. Fernandes, supporting the bill, said that the subject was important enough to be debated in a Constituent Assembly, if necessary. 'It is not that Parliament has no power to amend the Constitution but... we are politicians and we have our own interests... It was high time that we gave a thought to it and appointed a second Constituent Assembly of eminent personalities of this country.' Fernandes pleaded that the provisions of the Representation of the People Act (RPA), 1951 needed to be strengthened so that a person found guilty could be debarred, disenfranchised for life. He said that a candidate should not only owe allegiance to 'the Constitution when he files his nomination but he should also give one more affidavit saying that in no way would he or his party or his supporters be involved in inciting communal sentiments among the voters.'

O. Rajagopal, who opposed the bill, said that if the bill, by any chance, had been passed and if it had been implemented, Mahatma Gandhi would not have been allowed to carry on his political activity. Gandhi had used religious symbols, religious sentiments, to take his political ideas to the common people. Rajagopal said that Lokmanya Tilak had 'effectively made use of religious sentiments for the purpose of propagating political ideas, to take the ideas to the common people. This year, we are celebrating the centenary of his attempt to make Ganesh *Utsav* ... a national activity, a social activity.' He concluded by saying: 'So, instead of giving this name communal party, why not openly say, ban the BJP? That would be more honest.'

Jinendra Kumar Jain who, too, opposed the bill said, 'It connoted politics of escapism, of opportunism...People are not willing to buy that pseudo-secularism which has divided this country, which has kept large segments of the Indian population as blind vote-banks...The most communal party today is the Congress party.'

V. Narayana Samy, who supported the bill, said that though the Constitution and the RPA had provisions to the effect that religion should not be mixed with politics and political parties should not use the religious sentiments of the people for their political game, the political parties and their candidates during the time of elections had been fully utilizing communal sentiments for political advantage. He pointed out that 'mixing religion and politics is nothing but criminalization of politics'. Narayana Samy invited attention to the fact that the president of the Bajrang Dal, a banned organization, was still a member of the Lok Sabha. He asked whether his membership was to be retained. (*RSD* Vol. 167.1, 1993: 267–70, 290–91, 293, 296, 309, 311, 315, 318, 320, 324); (*RSD*, Vol. 168.2, 1993: 248–50)

Replying to the motion of thanks on the President's Address on 11 March 1993, Prime Minister P.V. Narasimha Rao, *inter alia*, underlined:

> The unfortunate attempt to bring in religion for political purposes and making it operate on the minds of the people...What has really increased during the last few years is its intensity and the deliberate attempt, the deliberation, the planned way in which it is being done. In the earlier days, maybe it was done in a sporadic manner here and there. But this is totally different. And this has to be combated with all our might if the nation is to survive. I would like to draw the attention of the honourable members to the Resolution which was tabled even as early as 1948 in the Constituent Assembly where this matter was clearly referred to.

The prime minister said that, over the years, several attempts had been made in this regard, and laws had been passed which, to some extent, had tried to mitigate this menace but it had not eliminated it. He said, 'Unless you eliminate it lock, stock and barrel, the tendency of this is only to grow. Any half-hearted measure will only make it grow. It will not control it. This has been the experience.' He said that some communal organizations and bodies had been banned from time to time and even their assets and monies had been confiscated. But this had not really worked. This was mainly because of the political advantage that religion can give to a particular party at the polls; this electoral advantage has been the real reason why we could not control communalism, why we could not control the entry of communal politics in the elections. This is the crux of the whole thing. He invited a public debate on this issue. The prime minister also said:

> We have come to the conclusion that the present provisions of the Constitution, electoral laws and other enactments are not adequate to meet a situation in which a political party takes upon itself directly or indirectly to take up specific or general religious issues. This is the lacuna...we have passed an Act which prevents this country, fortunately, from continuing its political life only on the basis of temples and mosques—which is the next temple, which is the next mosque we have to demolish—if that is the perpetual programme that this country has, then I think it will go to pieces and it will be the most backward country in the world, if at all, it remains a country. (*RSD* Vol. 166.2, 1993: 364–71)

Finally, on 29 July 1993, the government introduced the Constitution (Eightieth) Amendment Bill for the separation of religion from politics and the Representation of the People (Amendment) Bill. (Appendix II and III, respectively.)

At the very introduction stage, it met with stiff opposition. L.K. Advani thundered that if the bill became law, it would have very dangerous consequences for democracy and the fairness of elections. If it became law, Advani said, a returning officer for the elections would be vested with far greater discretionary authority than even the election commission or the high courts. It should be left to the high court to decide whether a particular candidate had violated this law. Advani also raised a number of other points against the bill.

George Fernandes opposed the bill on the grounds of legislative incompetence. He said:

> This is the most dangerous bill ever introduced in this august House. On the pretext of communalism, an attempt is being made...not only to murder democracy but also to change the basic structure of the Constitution and to deprive the suppressed, downtrodden and backward classes of the country of their Constitutional rights.

He also said several clauses of the bill would ruin the Constitution of India:

> Religion is connected with morality. We will not allow curbing of various rights enshrined in the Constitution in the name of religion... We lend all support to the government in checking communalism but we cannot tolerate curbing our rights.

Somnath Chatterjee said, 'We have been demanding such a bill, such a law, in this country'. He requested the home minister to agree to send the bill to the Select Committee.

Ram Vilas Paswan said that he would support the delinking of religion from politics but, in that guise, the rights of the weaker sections and backward classes could not be curbed. On behalf of the Janata Dal, he urged that the bill should not be introduced in this form.

Indrajit Gupta said that, while the principle of the bill was acceptable, he would not support various clauses of the bill. Many such clauses would have to be removed. He, too, suggested that the bill be sent to the Joint Select Committee.

Ibrahim Sulaiman Sait said that, while bringing the bill, the government had forgotten that 'we Muslims' were alive in this country.

> A grave and dangerous bill has been brought without consulting us...All our fundamental and constitutional rights are crushed...It is the Muslim League on which the first axe will fall...I am with you for protecting the secular principles of this country...I want the bill to go to a select committee.

Guman Mal Lodha challenged the legislative competence of the bill. He said that the apex court had said that nothing could be enacted which went against the basic nature of the Constitution. He said that all the leaders of different parties, including the Muslim League, the Janata Dal, the CPI (Communist Party of India), and other parties had described this particular piece of legislation as draconian. He urged that the two legislations should not be given legal sanction.

Ram Naik opposed the introduction of the bill on the grounds that the meaning of religion had not been understood properly. He said that the bill was incomplete.

Surya Narayan Yadav opposed the bill on the grounds that it sought to curb the fundamental rights of the masses. He suggested that the bill be withdrawn.

Replying to the discussion, S.B. Chavan, home minister, said that members were trying to interpret the provisions of the bill in their own way. He said that, if members agreed that a Joint Select Committee be appointed, he had no objection but, *only if the committee reported within a fortnight so that the bill could be passed during the current session.* After considerable persuasion, the minister finally agreed to refer the bill to a Select Committee but kept on insisting that the committee should submit its report within two weeks. (*LSD* Vol. 23.1, 1993: 512–37)

This was a classic case of bad handling and deliberate (or otherwise) mismanagement of a crucial piece of legislation. In fact, such important and sensitive amendments should not have been brought up without an all-party consultation. But perhaps the Congress party wanted to take the credit for having brought such an important legislation single-handedly in order to establish its credentials of firm commitment to secularism. But this was clearly counter-productive. Even the elementary precaution of the proper constitution of a Joint Select Committee had not been taken. Instead of the normal thirty-member committee, on 30 July 1993, Home Minister Chavan proposed a Joint Committee of only fifteen members, ten from the Lok Sabha and five from the Rajya Sabha. The committee was asked to submit a report by 16 August 1993. (*LSD* Vol. 23.1, 1993: 681–82)

On 3 August 1993, objections were raised that there was no precedent for appointing a Joint Committee of only fifteen members as suggested by the government. Atal Bihari Vajpayee said, 'The constitution of the committee is not merely a formality. If you are determined to set up this Joint Parliamentary Committee...we will be compelled to review our stance on the entire committee. Again, it is being asked to submit its report immediately.' He said that if the government was 'bent upon their arbitrariness, we will have to retaliate in our own way'. Accordingly, he moved suitable amendments for the purpose. (*LSD* Vol. 23.1, 1993: 539–45)

Later, on the same day, Home Minister Chavan moved a motion to constitute a Joint Committee comprising twenty members from the

Lok Sabha and ten from the Rajya Sabha. He, however, insisted that the committee submit a report by 16 August 1993, which was just twelve days away. (*LSD* Vol. 23.1, 1993: 613–14)

The report of the Joint Committee was placed on the table on 20 August 1993, along with the record of the evidence tendered before the Joint Committee. (*RSD* Vol. 168.3, 1993: 388)

Having seen the functioning of Parliament for quite some time, I am not aware of any other case in which a Joint Committee was asked to submit its report on any bill in less than two weeks' time. And particularly in the matter of such an important bill, it was totally inexcusable, unless the government had developed cold feet and did not really want to pursue this legislation.

Upendra Baxi, in his article, 'The Constitution (Eightieth) Amendment Bill: Politics as Religion', wrote:

> The joint committee report submitted on 20 August 1993 had important dissents (Satya Prakash Malaviya, M. Padmanabhan, George Fernandes, and a collective note by L.K. Advani, Jaswant Singh, Sikandar Bakht and Guman Mal Lodha). The joint committee, as a whole, was practically unanimous on the insertion of a new provision in part III of the Constitution (renumbered Article 24-A as against the proposed Article 29-A). The original formulation was: *'The State shall have equal respect for all religions'*. The committee added to this the provision: *'The State shall not profess, practise and propagate any religion'*. The BJP dissent note wondered about this 'additionality and its consequences in government institutions, and those in government'. It wondered whether the lighting of a lamp at state ceremonies became 'a constitutional embargo'. Would Doordarshan's coverage of Diwali, Id, Christmas or Guru Nanak Jayanti violate the Constitution? The BJP dissent note described this additionality as not only 'pseudo-secularist' but also 'anti-religion'.

The second proposal in the Amendment Bill was Article 35-A. It provided that Parliament could make a law: 'That any association or body of individuals be banned if it, by words, either spoken or written or by signs or by visible representations or otherwise, promotes or attempts to promote disharmony or feelings of enmity, hatred or ill-will between different classes or citizens of India:

i) On the grounds of religion or
ii) On the grounds of race, place of birth, residence, language, caste or community,

The report, by a majority, proposed the removal of clause (ii) above; only four BJP dissenters were vehemently opposed to the Amendment Bill and the majority's proposal for change. The Joint Committee dropped clause (c) of Article 35-A which excluded the jurisdiction of all courts except the Supreme Court over issues of banning such activity or associations or of forfeiture of their property or assets.

George Fernandes also opposed certain proposals on the grounds that 'They strike at the root of our democratic institutions and parliamentary democracy. In the long run, the amendments in Articles 102 and 191 may even pave the way for one-party democracy'. According to him, the potential for mischief was as grave as the perversion of the Weimar Constitution by Adolf Hitler.

The Joint Committee, by a majority, suggested the addition of clause 28-A to the Eightieth Amendment, empowering Parliament or state legislatures to ban associations or bodies if they promoted or attempted to promote, on the grounds of religion, disharmony or feelings of enmity or hatred or ill-will between different religious groups. This was rightly criticized as being anti-democratic, especially as it empowered state legislatures to ban associations. The BJP dissent note rightly characterized it as a body blow to the citizens' sacred right to form associations.

Baxi wrote: 'The gravamen of the BJP objection was that "what the government and its allies" (the latter being Marxists and pseudo-secularists) contemplate is not merely a rootless India but an amoral, even immoral India. This is understandable because of their paranoia over the resurgence of cultural nationalism...'

The proposed amendments to the RPA were also criticized on the grounds that they violated the principle of free and fair elections.

Prime Minister Narasimha Rao announced at the Congress parliamentary party meeting that if the constitutional amendment did not 'garner' support, the RPA bill would be considered at a special session of Parliament. Baxi wrote: *There are difficulties in taking the prime minister seriously, as it appears that the prime minister does not himself take the bill seriously*. He rightly emphasized:

> The argument of fear which says that if the bill were to be enacted, politics will come to an end and India will slide into authoritarianism is misconceived. It is true that a certain kind of politics will come to an end...What will undoubtedly take its place would be an agenda perversely ignored for four and a half long immiseration decades... We should all help the emergence of real politics which would displace the pseudo-politics which has dominated us for so long. (Narain 1995: 160–69)

Soli Sorabjee, who was otherwise supportive of the two bills, however, emphasized:

- The provision for disqualification of a person who, after election, 'makes use of religion' is seriously flawed. The infirmity lies in its vagueness and over-breadth. If an elected member decries the curse of materialism and advocates a return to the spiritual values embodied in all religions, would that be making use of religion? If so, the provision is patently arbitrary.
- The insertion of the new Article 28-A to the effect that the State shall have equal respect for all religions is unnecessary because respect to all religions is clearly guaranteed by Articles 14, 15 and 25 of our Constitution. The proposed clause conveys a wrong impression that hitherto there was no equal respect for all religions.
- What is most important, however, is the [need for a] stern enforcement of these laws, without which *these amendments will be another exercise in humbug and hypocrisy*.

The election commission is reported to have opposed the proposal for entrusting it with the responsibility of deregistering political parties for exploiting religion. The commission wanted the government to lay down clearly what would constitute a 'religious name', which would invite the deregistration of a party. The commission felt that if the matter were left vague it would open floodgates of litigation.

The media too was highly critical of the bills. Newspaper editorials used headings like, 'Clumsy and Insincere' (*TOI*), 'A Stupid Law' (*ET*), 'Not by Legislation' (*IE*), etc. The *Economic Times* (ET) said the proposed amendment was 'unnecessary and redundant' and 'impracticable'. The *Times of India* argued that the proposed legislation would lead to endless litigation making a mockery of the electoral process. The proposed laws seem to be only for the statute book. They provoke 'suspicions of incompetence or worse'. The *Indian Express* was of the view that the timing of the bills put the *bona fides* of the government under doubt. *Also, no legislation can really delink religion from politics as the issues involved are 'too complex'*. *Hindustan Times* said that the draft was unsatisfactory, the procedure for achieving the objectives was not fool-proof, fresh problems may arise in implementing the law and it was essential to 'move cautiously', otherwise the very purpose of legislation may be defeated. (Kashyap 1993: 55–56, 61–62)

It appears as if the word 'secularism' is destined to remain charmingly vague and undefined as successive attempts to define it have failed, first in the Constituent Assembly, and thereafter while including it in the Preamble in 1976, and finally in the Constitution Amendment Bill in 1993.

Madhu Limaye, an ardent secularist, rightly stated that it was not true that there was only minority communalism (communalism of Muslims and Sikhs); there was also the communalism of the majority. Limaye wrote:

> The RSS has been openly propagating for over 60 years the concept of Hindu Rashtra...Can the government be trusted to make proper use of this legislation? The fact is that even with all the safeguards mentioned...such a law will put enormous powers in the hands of the executive and the danger of its abuse under a government not known for its adherence to democratic norms is very great. On a balance of considerations, therefore, I cannot recommend it. (Limaye 1988: 38, 44)

In sharp contrast was the Constitution Amendment Bill introduced by Laxminarayan Pandeya on 30 July 1993, which ostensibly sought to safeguard the fundamental rights of citizens in matters of religion. The bill sought to amend Article 107 by adding a proviso as under:

> Provided that a bill which affects any religion, religious place of worship, religious endowment or religious institution, shall be deemed to have been passed by each House only if it is passed by a majority of the total membership of that House and by a majority of not less than two-thirds of the members of that House present and voting.

It was also suggested that a new article should be added as under:

> 111-A (1) Not withstanding anything in this Constitution, all laws in force in the territory of India, affecting any religion, religious place of worship, religious endowment or religious institution, which have come into force after the first day of July 1991 shall be void.
> (2) Any action taken under the provisions of any law which has been declared void under clause (1), shall not be called in question in any court on any ground and such action shall be deemed to have been taken in good faith.

The bill was taken up for consideration on 13 August 1993. Ramesh Chennithala opposed it, saying that it was ill-conceived and unconvincing. He said that the country was facing a major challenge of communalism. In such a situation, it was the bounden duty of the majority community to protect the minorities. Election campaigns were going on in the name of religion. During the elections, candidates were preaching religion. Candidates were selected on the basis of religion. He said India's image before the world was already tarnished after the 6 December (demolition of the Babri Masjid) incident. Chennithala concluded by saying that the bill was against the spirit of the Constitution and if it were passed, the country would be in great danger.

> Syed Shahabuddin strongly opposed the bill, saying the entire purpose of the bill could have been served by a one-line bill: To repeal The Places of Worship (Special Provisions) Act, 1991. He said the formulation of this bill was an exercise in deception. Tej

Narayan Singh opposed the bill by pointing out that there were people who wanted this country to be a Hindu state but he did not think it was possible. (*LSD* Vol. 24, 1993: 298, 305, 315, 329)

The intention clearly was to negate laws passed by the government for misuse of religious places or to stop the conversion of a religious place belonging to one religion to another religion. The discussion on this bill, which was resumed on 27 August 1993, was along party lines. While members of the BJP and its allies supported the bill, the other parties opposed it. (*LSD* Vol. 23.1, 1993: 693–95)

Chitta Basu, who opposed the bill, said that the date of 1 July 1991 had been deliberately proposed in the bill as perhaps the Places of Worship Act had been passed on that day. It provided that *status quo* should be maintained in all places of worship. If Dr Pandeya's bill was passed, such acts would stand repealed, and Mathura and other disputed places of worship would become the agenda of the party that he represented. He said: 'There are more than 3000 temples and mosques which are of disputed nature.' If the Places of Worship Act were repealed, then, what would happen to the country? Basu urged that the essence of secularism rested on two basic principles: the separation of religion from politics and the acceptance of religion as a purely and strictly private affair of an individual, having nothing to do with the State. He emphasized that the bill had been motivated by a desire to further divide, or increase the communal divide between the Hindus, the Muslims and the Christians. This was absolutely an aggressive majorityism.

Mohan Singh opposed the bill, saying that it was self-contradictory. He charged that the bill severely hit the freedom of religious faiths and the Indian secular structure. (*LSD* Vol. 25, 1993: 376–79, 390–01, 406–08)

As was to be expected, K.R. Malkani, a senior BJP leader, was vehemently opposed to the idea of the separation of religion from politics. His logic was:

> There are religions and religions. You could easily separate church from State in Europe because the church and its chief, the Pope, had come from outside and this church was trying to act as a super state. But how exactly do you separate religion from politics when

that religion is a native cultural growth, the very life-breath of the people? Also, you cannot separate religion from politics when that religion is not organized as a church and it is not interfering in affairs of state. In India, the role of religion in politics has traditionally been confined to a *rajarishi* who may only advise or warn...His presence only gives a welcome moral tone to the State. That was why Gandhi said, 'Politics bereft of religion is absolute dirt, even to be shunned'...For another reason also, religion cannot be divorced from politics in India. Politics revolves round nationalism, and culture is an essential component of nationalism. In India, *desh* and *dharma* are two sides of the same coin. (Malkani 1993: 148)

Unfortunately, Nehru failed to take any action, even administrative, on the resolution adopted by the CA during his long tenure of seventeen years. Perhaps this was the only time when this resolution could have been decisively acted upon. This was partly because Nehru failed to understand the importance of religion in public life in India. In fact, he was totally out of touch with the ground realities on the subject. And this was not the case only after Independence. Long before it, Nehru's statements on religion come as a surprise. For example, it was in 1936 that Nehru observed that the day on which India achieved her freedom, communal differences and jealousies would get solved. He had also stated: 'The communal problem was a wasteful diversion from the main campaign against the British and communal parties were giants with feet of clay, who would fade into nothingness in the light of reason once the British were pushed out'. 'All attempts at a political settlement of the communal problem were a waste of time'. (Grover 1990: 210–12)

The only other time when the ruling party had a two-third majority was when Indira Gandhi and Rajiv Gandhi were in power. But they too did not think it important to take action to segregate religion from politics. In fact, during the tenure of Indira Gandhi, 'A record number of Constitution Amendments—as many as 19—were passed during the fifth Lok Sabha period [1971–77].' (Kashyap 1997: 189)

Rajiv Gandhi actively encouraged communal politics, and India is paying a heavy price for the total neglect of this crucial problem.

B.N. Tandon, who worked as joint secretary to Prime Minister Indira Gandhi, wrote that she was prepared to join hands with any political party or organization in the interest of securing electoral gains. He wrote:

> The Lok Sabha elections are also due in a few months. So the PM has woken up to the need to get the Sikhs on her side. Before going to Jamaica she had asked Om Mehta [Minister of State for Home and her confidant] and the Congress president to speak to the Sikh leaders so that some understanding could be arrived at. In such matters, the PM has never been guided by any principles or rules. She has but one objective—to win the election somehow. She is not averse to any alliance if it will help her win—she has tied up with the Muslim League in Kerala, the Shiv Sena in Bombay and the Akalis in Punjab at different times. But for public consumption, she has always maintained that she is opposed to narrow communal parties. But this is not the reality. She had tied up with the Akalis once before and when they were no longer useful, she had terminated the alliance. Now she wants to enter into a fresh understanding. (Tandon 2003: 325)

It is pertinent to note that the Supreme Court categorically declared in the *S.R. Bommai v. Union of India (AIR 1994 SC 2113)* that:

> *Secularism is one of the basic features of the Constitution.* While freedom of religion is guaranteed to all persons in India, from the point of view of the State, the religion, faith or belief of a person is immaterial. To the State, all are equal and are entitled to be treated equally. In matters of State, religion has no place. *No political party can simultaneously be a religious party. Politics and religion cannot be mixed.* Any State government which pursues unsecular policies or unsecular course of action acts contrary to the Constitutional mandate and renders itself amenable [liable] to action under Article 356.

Justice H.R. Khanna, a legend among Supreme Court judges, who was superseded by Indira Gandhi for the post of chief justice of India during the Emergency, however, emphasized that:

> The decision in respect of the three states [upholding the dismissal of Madhya Pradesh, Rajasthan and Himachal Pradesh BJP governments] has in a way broadened the field of Presidential proclamation under Article 356 in as much as justification for such proclamation can be based not on concrete act of the state government but upon mere apprehension that it would not implement the order of the Central government...The decision of the Court in respect of the three states in question would have serious repercussions on the survival or coming into power of BJP in any state...ever since the commencement of the Constitution we have had political parties like Muslim League, Akali Dal[1] and Hindu Mahasabha. Some of those parties, like Akali Dal, have formed state governments, yet no one has so far thought of dismissing such government because of the label of the party or its allegiance or affinity to some religion...*No judgment of the Supreme Court, in the opinion of the writer, can or should ignore the ground realities of political life in the country.* (Khanna 1994: 155–56)

In fact, the bold effort in 1993 was to change these same ground realities. But, the Narasimha Rao government went about it in a clumsy manner, without making any effort to build a consensus among political parties and to create a pressure of public opinion and media in its favour. As a result, the bills were opposed from all sides—political parties, intelligentsia, the legal community, jurists and media. Many of the arguments raised against the bills did not make sense. Every such enactment gets tested, often repeatedly, in a court of law, and a case law develops over time to take care of the developing situation. It was futile to expect the BJP and its allies to support the bill but, with serious spade work, they could have been isolated and exposed as the main stumbling block in going ahead

---

[1] The primary membership of the Akali Dal is open only to one who belongs to the Sikh community. According to the Constitution of the Akali Dal, only one who is an *amritdhari* Sikh can be an office-bearer of the Akali Dal. (Vivekanandan 1995: 215)

with this crucial legislation. Equally importantly, the government should have desisted from excessively widening the field of the legislation, as many of the concerns pertaining to race, community, caste, language, and so on are already addressed in the Unlawful Activities (Prevention) Act. If necessary, that Act could have been amended suitably. The thrust of the 1993 amendments ought to have been restricted to eliminating the association between religion and politics. When faced with an all-round—often unjustified—opposition, the government developed cold feet and decided to withdraw the bills. One wonders whether the Congress party itself was serious about the issue or whether this was only a window-dressing to show that, though the Babri Masjid had been demolished under its watch, it was firmly committed to secularism.

In spite of what the Supreme Court had observed, at least four undeniably communal parties are ruling in India. The BJP, since 2014, is again ruling at the Centre and that too by securing a clear majority by itself; the Akali Dal is in power in Punjab; and the Shiv Sena, in coalition with the BJP, in Maharashtra. The Muslim League, too, has been in power in Kerala from time to time. The phenomenal rise of communal political parties and organizations during the last two decades,[2] in particular, underlines that the separation of religion from politics would sound the death knell for these parties and organizations, and they would oppose it tooth and nail. It would, therefore, be a miracle if any steps were taken in the matter in the foreseeable future. And unless this is done, any talk of India as a secular state will continue to be meaningless.

Babri Masjid Demolition—a National Shame

Jawaharlal Nehru and Vallabhbhai Patel were greatly troubled by the clandestine keeping of Ram Lalla idols in the Babri Masjid in January 1950. On 9 January 1950, Vallabhbhai Patel, deputy prime minister, wrote a letter to G.B. Pant, prime minister of the United Provinces, expressing his anxiety in the matter. Patel wrote:

> The prime minister has already sent to you a telegram expressing his

---

[2] The BJP's seats in the Lok Sabha increased from two in 1984 to eighty-six in 1989, 117 in 1991 and 282 in 2014.

concern over the developments in Ayodhya. I spoke to you about it in Lucknow. I feel that the controversy has been raised at a most inappropriate time, both from the point of view of the country at large and of your own province in particular. The wider communal issues have only been recently resolved to the mutual satisfaction of the various communities. So far as Muslims are concerned, they are just settling down to their new loyalties... It would be most unfortunate if we allowed any group advantage to be made on this issue... I feel that the issue is one which should be resolved amicably in a spirit of mutual toleration and good will between the two communities. I realize there is a great deal of sentiment behind the move which has taken place. At the same time, such matters can only be resolved peacefully if we take the willing consent of the Muslim community with us. There can be no question of resolving such disputes by force. In that case, the forces of law and order will have to maintain peace at all costs. (Durga Das Vol. 9, 1974: 310–11)

Jawaharlal Nehru also wrote to Pant on 17 April 1950:

These recent occurrences in the UP have greatly distressed me. Or perhaps this was a culmination of what I had been feeling for a long time... I have felt for a long time that the whole atmosphere of the UP has been changing for the worse from the communal point of view. *Indeed, the UP is becoming almost a foreign land for me. I do not fit in there... I have not been to the UP for a long time. That is partly due to the lack of time, but the real reason is that I hesitate to go there. I do not wish to come into conflict with my old colleagues and I feel terribly uncomfortable there,*[3] because I find that *communalism has invaded the minds and hearts of those who were the pillars of Congress in the past. It is a creeping paralysis and the patient does not even realize it.* All that occurred in Ayodhya

---

[3]One would have expected the highest-ranking leader of India at the time, Nehru, to take on these elements in the Congress party. This is in sharp contrast with Indira Gandhi's courage in opposing the 'old guard' in the Congress party. She did not think twice before even causing a split in the party in 1969 and reducing the ruling Congress party to a minority in the Lok Sabha.

in regard to the mosque and temples, and the hotel in Faizabad was bad enough. But the worst feature of it was that such things should take place and be approved by some of our own people... (Gopal and Iyengar Vol. 1, 2003: 184–85)

Pant replied on 22 April: I am ashamed of the atrocities that have been committed in some places in this province. Things seem to be gradually returning to normal but the fact that we could not prevent these deplorable happenings continues to oppress me. (Gopal and Iyengar Vol. 1, 2003: 185, Footnote 6)

M. Chalapathi Rao, former editor of *The National Herald* (1946–77), in his book, *Govind Ballabh Pant: His Life and Times* (1981), does not even mention the placement of Ram Lalla idols in the Babri Masjid or the fact that no action was taken by Pant, as prime minister, to have them removed. This shows an utter lack of sensitivity on a matter of such important national consequence.

It is a sad commentary on our governance and sense of priorities that this issue dragged on and finally led to the tragic demolition of the Babri Masjid on 6 December 1992.

Anticipating the BJP's strategy for communalizing issues pertaining to the mosques in Mathura, Varanasi and 3000 other places of worship across the country which had been allegedly converted by Muslims into mosques, and for launching agitations for the conversion of these places into temples, the central government had enacted the Places of Worship (Special Provisions) Act, 1991. It had barred conversion of places of worship.
Section 3 of the Act states:

> No person shall convert any place of worship of any religious denomination or any section thereof into a place of worship of a different section of the same religious denomination or of a different religious denomination or any section thereof. Section 4 states: The religious character of a place of worship existing on the 15th day of August 1947 shall continue to be the same as it existed on that day.

However, importantly, the Act did not apply to Ram Janmabhoomi–Babri Masjid (RJB-BM). Section 5 of the Act made it clear that,

'Nothing contained in this Act shall apply to the place of worship commonly known as Ram Janmabhoomi–Babri Masjid, situated in Ayodhya... and to any suit, appeal or other proceeding relating to the said place of worship.'

This was a political game perfectly played by the Congress party. On one hand, it could claim to be the most secular and on the other, it pandered to the majority Hindu opinion.

> The BJP government in UP, under Kalyan Singh as chief minister, flouted all its assurances given to the government of India, the National Integration Council (NIC), and the Supreme Court of India that all steps would be taken by the state government to protect Babri Masjid. In fact, Kalyan Singh had the temerity to threaten the Central government that if any action were taken to take possession of the Babri Masjid site, its protection could not be assured. The only logical step which the government of India could have taken was to impose President's rule under Article 356, and, in the interim, to take action under Article 355 of the Constitution [duty of the Union to protect states against external aggression and internal disturbance] to take possession of the Babri Masjid site and to protect it by deploying central paramilitary forces. A contingency plan was prepared by the Ministry of Home Affairs (MHA) for the purpose. It would have required approval of the Cabinet, but P.V. Narasimha Rao, who was the prime minister, was reluctant to take such a decision and to place the matter before the Cabinet. I was union home secretary at the time and had revealed the entire sordid and painful history of this period in an eighty-page chapter titled, 'The Ayodhya Debacle' in my memoir, *Unfinished Innings: Recollections and Reflections of a Civil Servant* (1996). (Godbole 1996: 332–418)

During the discussion in the Rajya Sabha on the motion of thanks on the President's Address on 11 March 1993, the question of the government's fulfilling its assurance of rebuilding the mosque was raised once again. In fact, some members even walked out of the House after raising the issue. Prime Minister P.V. Narasimha Rao said:

> Both a temple and a mosque will be constructed as said by Rashtrapatiji. We are in the process of setting up the trust. I did not elaborate it because there was no need. It was so clear from the [President's] Address. But it is good to go on record because people have raised it. There is no question of either going back or dragging our feet on that. But it should be appreciated that if a temple is being built, it is not like having a few engineers put there. We have to have certain authority in temple building, certain authority in mosque building. Now, all this takes a little time and a little effort to talk to people, sound them out and then put it together. It is not easy to put together an authoritative trust like this. (*RSD* Vol. 166.2, 1993: 391)

Speaking in the Lok Sabha in reply to the debate on the motion of thanks on the President's Address on 11 March 1993, Prime Minister Rao said:

> It is not for the first time that the need to avoid bringing religion into politics has figured in our discussions, in our thoughts, in this country. After Independence, this has been figuring time and again. During the debates in the Constituent Assembly, again, this figured very prominently and since then it has been figuring from time to time. We have tackled it to some extent...The time has come when we cannot afford any further tinkering with this problem. We have to decide it once and for all. We have to say that this country is going to be perpetually wedded to secularism and [*sic*] this country cannot exist, cannot survive without secularism.

He emphasized that:

> We have several provisions by which, to some extent...the bringing of religion into politics could be avoided, but it could not be eliminated. We found that the present provisions in the Constitution, electoral law and other enactments are not adequate...We cannot accept a religious device for political means.

Madan Lal Khurana asked why, in Mizoram, the Congress manifesto had stated that, if voted to power, the Congress party would form a

Christian government in the state. Rao had to admit that it was wrong, constitutionally wrong. He said that the relevant para was removed from the Congress manifesto. (*LSD* Vol. 19.1, 1993: 408–09, 411–13)

If any proof were required at all, this proves the hypocrisy behind the Congress party's attempt to seek to separate religion from politics.

> On 23 March 1993, the government introduced a bill to provide for the acquisition of sixty-seven acres of land at Ayodhya. It was intended that the acquired area—*excluding the area on which the disputed structure stood*—would be made available to two trusts which would be set up for constructing a Ram temple and a mosque, respectively, and for the planned development of the area. Speaking in the Lok Sabha, Union Home Minister S.B. Chavan stated: The bill would help in resolving the RJB–BM dispute, restoring confidence among the people of India and combating the forces of religious fanaticism and the misuse of religion for electoral and other such gains. (*LSD* Vol. 20.1, 1993: 463, 465)

The government also made a reference to the Supreme Court under Article 143 of the Constitution to seek its opinion on whether a temple had existed at Ayodhya before the construction of the Babri Masjid. (*M. Ismail Faruqui v. Union of India* (1994) 6 SCC 360). Special Reference 1 of 1993 was heard along with connected matters. Justice Srikrishna observed that the reference:

> ...fell in the second category where the matter cannot be resolved by reference to 'judicially manageable standards'. It would have in fact required the judges to opine on a point of archaeology rather than law, and thereby step on to a political minefield. The Supreme Court was perfectly correct in refusing to answer the reference. *In fact, such questions have arisen merely on account of the failure of the executive or the legislature to resolve their own political problems and these are attempts to pass the buck to the judiciary.* The Supreme Court should stoutly refuse the temptation to crown itself with political thorns. (Srikrishna 2005: J-14-5)

The Ministry of Home Affairs also advised against making such a reference but was over-ruled by the Cabinet Committee on Political Affairs (CCPA). (Godbole 1996: 408–09)

> Soon after the demolition of Babri Masjid, Prime Minister Narasimha Rao announced that the government would reconstruct Babri Masjid on the same spot. S.R. Bommai recalled this assurance in his speech in the Rajya Sabha on 6 December 1993—the first anniversary of the demolition of Babri Masjid—that 'a mosque would be built in the same place' and he inquired whether the government would fulfil that promise. (*RSD* Vol. 169.1, 1993: 527–28)

Ram Vilas Paswan, too, raised this matter in the Lok Sabha on 6 December 1993. He urged the government to make a reference to the Supreme Court under Article 138 (2) for an early final decision in the matter. He said that, though a year had elapsed since the demolition of the Babri Masjid, it was difficult to understand why the government 'is keeping mum'.

Ibrahim Sulaiman Sait said that on the same day the previous year, the Babri Masjid had been demolished. He added:

> That was the bleakest [sic] day in the history of this country and that tarnished the image of our country throughout the world and shattered the secular fabric of our Constitution. At that time, on the same day, the entire Muslim delegation met the prime minister. *The prime minister categorically and solemnly promised that the mosque would be constructed at the same spot. He stated that it would be rebuilt.* So far, it has not been done. Not only has the prime minister betrayed the nation by not constructing the mosque, but he has also not kept the promise made by him on 15 August. On 15 August 1992, he declared from the Red Fort and later on he also assured all the delegations that the mosque would be protected... Now, one year has passed but nothing has been done. On the other hand, there have been insults to injury by way of acquisition of the mosque site and the reference under Article 143 for the opinion of the Supreme Court. We want the mosque to be constructed immediately at the same spot and the reference to Supreme Court under Article 143 should be withdrawn. The order relating to the

acquisition of the mosque site should also be withdrawn. We must be given an assurance that the mosque would be rebuilt on the same spot. Thus, secularism would be re-established in this country and there will be communal harmony in the country.

Somnath Chatterjee wanted to know whether the prime minister would make a statement in the House as to what the government proposed to do 'either about construction or reconstruction at the site of Ayodhya. It is because he made certain commitments earlier and we do not know the fate of them now.'

Sultan Salahuddin Owaisi said: 'After the incident of December 6, the prime minister has given an assurance that the mosque will be constructed on the same place. One whole year has passed and nothing has been done in this regard. I would like to demand that the mosque should be constructed at the same place…The feelings of Muslims have been badly hurt in the country. It cannot be tolerated and we cannot remain meek spectators…'

Home Minister S.B. Chavan tried to argue like an advocate, hair-splitting words, in a court of law. Referring to the demand for reconstruction of the mosque,

Chavan said: 'What does reconstruction mean? I do not think the prime minister has said that the reconstruction is going to be at the same site.' Ebrahim Sait countered Chavan by saying, 'He [the prime minister] has said, it would be "rebuilt". Rebuild means what?' Chavan replied, 'That does not necessarily mean at the same site'. Chandra Shekhar countered Chavan by saying: 'This is a very serious matter. The prime minister made a statement which is known to the country and known to the whole world. It is totally unfair that that statement should be interpreted in this House by the home minister in a way which is beyond the understanding of everybody who heard that statement.' Sultan Owaisi said that the cassette of the TV telecast should be brought into the House. 'Then you will know what the prime minister has actually said… I would raise the issue of privilege.' Somnath Chatterjee supported Owaisi and said, 'Let the telecast or the broadcast of the prime minister be brought here.' Indrajit Gupta said: 'Let the record be consulted. He [the prime minister] did say that it will be constructed on the same site. Afterwards, he never refuted it.' L.K. Advani reiterated the stand of his party by saying, 'No one will object to the construction of the mosque if the Muslims of the country and the Muslims of Ayodhya would select a place far from the Ramjanmabhoomi.' Ebrahim Sait too reiterated the position of the Muslims and said, 'The mosque should be constructed where it was located earlier.' (*LSD* Vol. 26–27, 1993: 326–50)

Reference may be made in this context to my memoir, *Unfinished Innings*, in which I had recapitulated the sequence of events in this regard:

> One of the issues which caused deep embarrassment to the government was the announcement by the prime minister on 6 December that 'The government will see to it that the demolished structure is rebuilt'. Both Law Secretary Rao and I had argued [in the Cabinet Committee on Political Affairs] that the plain reading of this sentence would be that the demolished structure would be rebuilt at the same place. There was a subtle distinction between the words 'rebuild' and 'reconstruct'. But Naresh Chandra [Adviser on Ayodhya in PMO (Prime Minister's Office)] argued that this was not true and all that it meant was that it would be reconstructed elsewhere. The prime minister repeated this assurance of rebuilding the mosque on several occasions. (Godbole 1996: 403)

But, the government reneged and decided to construct both a temple and a mosque through two trusts, as written earlier. However, this did not fructify as there was no consensus on the subject. If the government had implemented the declaration made by Narasimha Rao about reconstructing the mosque at the same location, the government's commitment to secularism would have been fully established and acclaimed, but this was too much to expect.

Karan Singh pointed out:

> The direct physical assault on a place of worship and the subsequent

torching of Muslim houses at Ayodhya surely does not fit into the tradition of Vedanta...Having spent the better part of the last decade travelling around the world speaking on Vedanta, it is indeed shocking to see such a wave of hatred and aggressive behaviour suddenly overtaking sections of the Hindu community in some parts of the country. This attitude is well portrayed by one Swami Vamdev... [who] reportedly denounced the Constitution as 'anti-Hindu' and laid claim to the Jama Masjid because, according to him, it was built on the ruins of a Hindu temple! (Karan Singh 1995: 36)

It must be stated that several incidents of communal violence took place in the country in retaliation for the demolition of Babri Masjid. One such major communal episode was the series of powerful bomb explosions which occurred at 11 places in Bombay [as it was called then] on 12 March 1993 between 1320 and 1600 hours.[4] It is evident that commercially important and crowded places in the city were deliberately selected by the perpetrators of the crime with a view to causing a sense of fear and panic and inflicting maximum damage. By 14 March 1993, 235 persons were reported to have died and 1214 persons had received injuries. Of them, 59 were reported to be in critical condition. (*RSD* Vol. 166.3, 1993: 267–68)

This subject came up again in the Rajya Sabha on 22 March 1993. Persistent demands were made by members that the perpetrators of the crime should be brought to justice speedily, and Dawood Ibrahim, the mastermind, should be repatriated from Pakistan, or Dubai where he was reported to have been seen last. The interjection of Home Minister S.B. Chavan was as evasive as ever: 'I can only say that intelligence agencies are on the right lines. Please bear with us.' (*RSD* Vol. 166.4, 1993: 204–06)

---

[4]The serious communal riots in Mumbai in December 1992 and January 1993 were attributed mainly to the role played by communal parties. This has also been brought out in the report of the Srikrishna Commission. By comparison, the bomb blasts on 12 March 1993 were alleged to have been carried out at the instance of Dawood Ibrahim, a terrorist based in Pakistan, in retaliation for the demolition of the Babri Masjid.

It has been twenty-three years since then but India has not been able to get Dawood Ibrahim extradited. This is one of the most abject failures of its international diplomacy.

Several adjournment motions were pressed in the Lok Sabha on 15 March 1993, mainly to hold the government responsible for its failure in avoiding the bomb blasts. The government was blamed, among others, for the serious failure of its intelligence agencies. (*LSD* Vol. 19.2, 1993: 559, 654–58)

Immediately after the demolition of the Babri Masjid, the central government appointed a judicial commission of inquiry—the Liberhan Ayodhya Commission of Inquiry—on 16 December 1992. Like everything else pertaining to this issue, this commission too, made ignominious history by taking as many as seventeen years to complete the inquiry, submitting its report in June 2009. After such a prolonged labour, it had the distinction of not bringing out anything worthwhile in its findings. This shameful chapter was thus given a completely democratic burial.

Narasimha Rao, in his book, *Ayodhya 6 December 1992*, published posthumously (in accordance with the author's wishes, as stated in the Publisher's Note), wrote:

> *It is time to pause and think whom history will hold responsible for this complacency and its disastrous consequences*...I tried to explain all these things to my colleagues, but on their side also political and vote-earning considerations definitely prevailed and they had already made up their minds that one person was to be made historically responsible for the tragedy, in case the issue ended up in tragedy. If there had been success (as there definitely seemed to be, in the initial months) they would of course have readily shared the credit or appropriated it to themselves. *So they were playing either for success, or an alibi through a scapegoat in case of failure*! It was a perfect strategy. They could loudly proclaim later that the Muslim vote did not come to the Congress after the demolition of Babri Masjid solely because of me. (Rao 2006: 188)

In my article, 'Ayodhya and India's Mahabharat: Constitutional Issues and Proprieties', in the *Economic & Political Weekly*, I had extensively brought out how totally untenable Rao's arguments were that the Constitution's provisions could not have been used for taking pre-emptive action under Articles 355 and 356. I stated:

> ...It was not the Constitution which was found wanting as averred by Rao. It was the failure of the national leadership during this critical period. In this light, Rao's assertion that 'any prudent president or prime minister would not have gone ahead and clamped Article 356 under these circumstances' (p. 180) will not have many takers...The painful memories of the demolition of Babri Masjid, which signified *a monumental failure of governance* of the country, will linger for a long time. *Making the Constitution the scapegoat, as Rao has tried to do, will not take us anywhere...The tragedy showed how fragile the Constitution can be in such crisis situations.* It highlighted the weaknesses of the major pillars of democracy. But, this was due to the failure of political leadership at various levels. Almost all those responsible, in one way or another, for the tragedy, have got away. The foremost of them was Kalyan Singh [governor of Rajasthan at present] who incredibly got away with only a token punishment of one day's imprisonment and a fine of Rs 2000 for contempt of the highest court of the country. (*EPW* 27 May 2006: 2075–76)

It may be recalled that, immediately after the demolition of the Babri Masjid and before the central paramilitary forces could enter Ayodhya after the midnight of 7 December 1992, lakhs of *karsevak*s were milling around agitatedly, and had hurriedly constructed a small make-shift temple and installed Ram Lalla idols in it. Strictly, this structure was illegal but, due to possible law-and-order implications, it was permitted to continue. Since then, it has slowly acquired the status of a regular temple, in that, a *pooja* is performed, *darshan* for visiting devotees is permitted and, according to recent news reports, even a fireproof ceiling is being contemplated. I have no doubt that, slowly but surely, a Ram temple is thus taking shape.

The Supreme Court has permitted repairs to be carried out to the temporary structure and its vicinity. (*Loksatta* 11 August 2015: 4) The Court also directed that the temple should be maintained by the local authorities. (*India Legal* 31 August 2015: 73) The Divisional Commissioner, Faizabad, who is the receiver of the disputed RJB–BM site, has approached the Indian Institute of Technology, Roorkee, for a fireproof sheet to cover the make-shift temple in Ayodhya. (*IE* 18 August 2015: 1). A.G. Noorani was of the view that 'The make-shift temple erected there is legitimized by Parliament and the Supreme Court'. (Noorani 2014: 10)

Though the BJP has kept the Ram temple issue aside due to the opposition of its NDA (National Democratic Alliance) partners, the RSS—which is becoming increasingly assertive since Modi came to power—is not prepared to let go. Mohan Bhagwat, the *sarsanghachalak* (chief) of the RSS, declared on 3 December 2015 that the Ram temple would be definitely constructed during his lifetime. Welcoming Bhagwat's statement, the Shiv Sena demanded in the editorial of its mouthpiece, *Saamana*, that Bhagwat should now announce a date for the commencement of the construction of the Ram temple in Ayodhya to give an impetus to the issue. (*IE* 6 December 2015: 5).

On 20 December 2015, to set the ball rolling, the Vishva Hindu Parishad (VHP) did the *bhoomi-poojan* of the stones brought for the temple from Rajasthan by Mahant Nrutya Gopal Das. (*Loksatta* 21 December 2015: 3) The VHP Trust announced that the RSS would like the temple construction to start before the elections to the UP state legislature which are due in 2017.

In any other democratic country, a few heads would have rolled for this massive failure of governance but, in this vibrant democracy, no one has been held responsible.

It is interesting to note that P.V. Narasimha Rao was the union home minister when, as brought out in the following section, the anti-Sikh riots took place in Delhi. Now that the BJP is in power at the Centre, plans are afoot to rehabilitate the image of P.V. Narasimha Rao, who was considered an outcast by the Congress party. According to news reports, the NDA is keen on building a memorial for Rao in Delhi. The chief minister of Andhra Pradesh, Chandrababu Naidu, has demanded that the Bharat Ratna should be conferred posthumously on Rao, while the Telangana government is planning to include a chapter on Rao in the textbooks for schools in that state. (*India Today* 13 July 2015: 26) What more can one ask for?

Major Communal Riots in the Recent Past:

The Anti-Sikh Riots of 1984

These riots—following the shocking assassination of Indira Gandhi by her Sikh security personnel—in which over 3000 Sikhs were massacred, are yet another eternal shame for the country. Due to lack of political will and political interference, police investigations were tardy and hardly a few were found guilty by the Court.

Pranay Gupte, in his book, *India: The Challenge of Change* (1989), brought out the enormity of atrocities committed in Delhi during the period:

> While the actual property loss may never be known, many estimates suggest that between 31 October and 5 November [1984], more than $250 million worth of property was destroyed in Delhi alone. Investigators from the Delhi-based People's Union for Democratic Rights (PUDR) and the People's Union for Civil Liberties (PUCL)[5] found that the attacks against Delhi's Sikh community were hardly spontaneous expressions of grief and anger over Mrs Gandhi's assassination—as the Delhi authorities have asserted they were. Deliberate rumours were spread that Sikhs were distributing *mithai* [sweets] and lighting oil lamps to celebrate the demise of Mrs Gandhi; trains containing the bodies of hundreds of murdered Hindus were said to have arrived from Punjab at the Old Delhi station; and Delhi's water supply was said to have been poisoned by Sikhs.

The PUDR/PUCL reports, as for the second phase of rioting, said:

> We were told by local eye-witnesses that well-known Congress leaders and workers led and directed the arsonists and that local cadres of the Congress party identified the Sikh houses and shops... The orgy of destruction embraced a variety of property ranging from shops, factories, houses to gurdwaras and schools belonging to Sikhs. In all the affected spots, a calculated attempt to terrorize the people was evident in the common tendency among the assailants

---

[5] The reports titled, 'Who Are the Guilty?', were published under the signatures of Govind Mukhoty and Rajni Kothari.

to burn alive the Sikhs on public roads. Throughout the carnage, Delhi's policemen were either totally absent from the scene; or they stood by while mobs freely burnt Sikhs alive; or they themselves participated in the orgy of violence against the Sikhs.

P.V. Narasimha Rao, who was union home minister at the time, gave the assurance that the situation would be immediately brought under control. But he did not impose a curfew until two days later, and he belatedly called in the army to restore law and order. Even then, however, the violence against the Sikhs continued, aided and abetted by those in power.

The PUDR/PUCL reports make some dramatic points in their conclusion: the social and political consequences of the government's stance during the carnage, its deliberate inaction, and its callousness towards relief and rehabilitation are far-reaching. It is indeed a matter of grave concern that the government made no serious inquiries into the entire tragic episode, which seems to have been so well-planned and designed. It is curious that, for the several hours that the government had between the time of Mrs Gandhi's assassination and the official announcement of her death, no security arrangements were made for the victims. The riots were well-organized and were of unprecedented brutality. Several very disturbing questions arise that must be answered:

> Why did the government refuse to take cognizance of the reports of the looting and murders and to call in troops even after the military had been alerted? Why was there no joint control room set up, and who was responsible for not giving clear and specific instructions to the army on curbing violence and imposing a curfew? Who was responsible for the planned and deliberate police inaction and their often-active role in inciting the murders and the looting? Who was responsible for the planned and well-directed arson? Why were highly provocative slogans (such as *khoon ka badala khoon* [blood for blood]) allowed to be broadcast by Doordarshan during the televised transmissions depicting the mourning crowds at Teen Murti Bhavan, where Mrs Gandhi's body was kept on display [sic]? Why did the Congress party not set up an inquiry into the role of its members in the arson and looting? (Gupte 1989: 70–78)

P.C. Alexander, the then principal secretary to the prime minister, stated in his book, *My Years with Indira Gandhi*, that the responsibility for organizing both relief and protection in Delhi was taken over by the central government:

> I rushed back to the cabinet secretariat and informed the cabinet secretary about the blanket authority given by the PM for organizing relief and protection. The cabinet secretary immediately formed a special action group of senior officers representing the ministries...The Lt. Governor and the senior officers of the Delhi administration were not quite pleased that the central ministries and agencies were stepping into an area which they thought was their responsibility. But their views were ignored and they were asked from then on *to take instructions directly from the cabinet secretary on the action on all matters relating to relief and protection for the Sikhs.* (Godbole 1996: 327)

This would show that the overall responsibility for the lapses was directly that of the government of India and not of the Delhi administration.

The pogrom in Delhi was looked into by various commissions and committees. The citizen's commission comprised: S.M. Sikri, former chief justice of India; Badr-ud-din Tyabji, former commonwealth secretary and vice-chancellor, Aligarh Muslim University; Rajeshwar Dayal, former foreign secretary; Govind Narain, former governor of Karnataka, and home and defence secretary; and T.C.A. Srinivasavaradan, former home secretary. The commission submitted its report in January 1985. The commission observed:

> Many who came forward to relate their experiences and provide eye-witness accounts to the commission, have specifically and repeatedly named certain political leaders belonging to the ruling party. These included several MPs in the outgoing Parliament, members of the Delhi metropolitan council, and members of the municipal corporation...They have been accused of having instigated the violence, making arrangements for the supply of kerosene and other inflammable material and of identifying the houses of Sikhs.

The commission, *inter alia*, observed:

> We have referred to the utter failure and dereliction of duty of the police in Delhi. Some of them have been accused of instigating or even participating in the criminal acts committed during the fateful five days. Wherever such officials are found to have committed crimes, they should be prosecuted according to the law. Negligence or dereliction of duty calls for exemplary punishment after departmental inquiry. Where appropriate, recourse could be had to the proviso to Article 311 of the Constitution.[6]

After taking over as home secretary in the government of India in 1991, I decided to pursue the question of taking action against the guilty persons. The Delhi administration was keen that the cases against H.K.L. Bhagat, a former central minister, should be investigated by the Central Bureau of Investigation (CBI), due to the importance and political clout of the persons involved. For the same reasons, though ostensibly due to overwork, the CBI wanted to return the papers to the Delhi administration. After speaking to the home minister, I told the director, CBI, to take up investigation of these cases.

The case against Sajjan Kumar, MP, was referred by the Delhi administration in 1992 to the home ministry before filing a charge sheet. As the home minister wanted to consult the prime minister, the papers were sent to the PMO. The prime minister desired that the matter should be placed before the Cabinet Committee on Political Affairs (CCPA). A

---

[6] The proviso to Article 311 reads as follows: 'Provided that where it is proposed after such inquiry, to impose upon him any such penalty, such penalty may be imposed on the basis of the evidence adduced during such inquiry and it shall not be necessary to give such person any opportunity or making representation on the penalty proposed: Provided further that this clause shall not apply (a) where a person is dismissed or removed or reduced in rank on the ground of conduct which has led to his conviction on a criminal charge; or (b) where the authority empowered to dismiss or remove a person or to reduce him in rank is satisfied that for some reason, to be recorded by that authority in writing, it is not reasonably practicable to hold such inquiry; or (c) where the President or the Governor, as the case may be, is satisfied that in the interest of the security of the state it is not expedient to hold such inquiry.'

note was accordingly prepared and sent to the cabinet secretariat. Till I left government service on premature voluntary retirement in March 1993, it never came up for discussion.

> For the first time, action against indicted officers was started in 1992, when I was home secretary. In all, 72 officials had been indicted by the Mittal Committee. Of these, 13 had retired and 3 had died. Charge sheets were served on 49 officials allegedly found guilty. In respect of 7, charge sheets could not be served either because of certain directions of the CAT [Central Administrative Tribunal], or because of the stay to the proceedings given by the courts. Prior to the end of 1991, some of the indicted officers were even promoted to higher posts. It was decided with the home minister's approval that none of the indicted officers would be considered for promotion till departmental inquiries against them were decided finally. Thus, at least in a small way, the credibility of the system was established to some extent. (Godbole 1996: 327–29)
>
> These questions have been raised from time to time in Parliament but the government did not take them seriously. Triloki Nath Chaturvedi had raised this matter in the Rajya Sabha on 18 March 1993 and had pointed out that the Court had acquitted nine persons who were charged with crimes in this case. Similarly, 40–45 persons were acquitted earlier due to sloppy police investigation and lack of evidence. In his recent order, Additional Sessions Judge S.S. Bali, gave benefit of doubt to 9 persons accused of looting and burning shops and several vehicles in the Karol Bagh area. The Court had observed that the police had not submitted the case properly which had created doubts on the veracity of the prosecutor's case. (*RSD*, Vol. 166.4, 1993: 330–31)

This question was raised in the Lok Sabha on 16 August 1993 when Jagmeet Singh Brar said that, till then, the government had appointed as many as six committees to investigate the riots. They included the Potti–Rosha Committee, the Jain–Bannerjee Committee and the Jain–Aggarwal Committee. The last-named committee had given a 206-page report to the Lieutenant Governor P.K. Dave. Brar quoted a paragraph from the report which said: 'Indeed, the whole investigation was done in such a casual and mechanical manner that no attempt was made even to find out the witnesses present during the occurrence, if any, much less corroborative evidence in any shape or form.' He said that the committee had suggested action against 298 police officers of Delhi. According to the committee, in three days, 300 people had been killed. He said he had hundreds of affidavits with him. According to Brar, the CBI was not willing to handle the cases because, when it tried to arrest important people, it had not been able to do so. The government itself had admitted to the Jain–Aggarwal Committee that the total number of people killed was 2736. He said that after nine years, only three murder cases had been convicted, involving fifteen accused and twenty deaths. Brar said that, shockingly, the term of the Jain–Aggarwal Committee, which expired on 31 July 1993, was not extended by the government.

L.K. Advani said that the matter raised by Brar was very important and it could be suppressed by adopting a silent attitude to it. Advani underlined that as many as 3000 innocent persons had been burnt alive within three–four days in the capital. He said he did not remember any such abhorrent incident occurring even in 1947. Murders had been committed in those days too, but innocent people had not been charred to death in this manner. He said that Prime Minister P.V. Narasimha Rao was the Minister of Home Affairs at that time and he had stated in the meeting of the consultative committee that, in total, 400 persons were killed. Atal Bihari Vajpayee had written a letter to Rao, indicating that the BJP had identified the names of 2700 victims, from which it can be guessed that over 3000 people had been killed. Later on, a commission, too, had confirmed that more than 3000 persons were killed but nobody had been punished. He further said that he did not hold either the police or the bureaucracy responsible for, 'such kind of heinous crimes cannot be perpetrated without the direct or indirect involvement of some politicians. This question will continue to be raised until the guilty politicians and officers are punished.'

Ram Vilas Paswan said that he was among the eyewitnesses of those riots and narrated how his house was set ablaze. He added:

> I am levelling a direct charge against the government as to why it did not take a decision to impose curfew at that time immediately. Why the curfew was clamped after 7 or 8 hours? The present prime

minister was the minister of home affairs in those days. I have information that the directions were issued from the top from the point of views of [sic] incite riots in any way between the Hindus and Sikhs throughout the country so that the Congress might come back to power again. The dead body of Smt. Indira Gandhi was made a subject of political gain... Whosoever the officers or ministers were responsible for it, action must be taken against them.

Rabi Ray, former Speaker of the Lok Sabha, said, 'The political aspect of the incident becomes more ghastly when the ruling party perpetrates this misdeed. Direct allegations have been levelled against the police department and politicians.' Ray recalled the address delivered by the prime minister from the Red Fort just the previous day (15 August) in which he had talked about protecting the minorities and about the misuse of religion. He urged that all other issues should be set aside and these main issues should be urgently discussed.

Lokanath Choudhury said that the government was confounding the issue. It had not taken any action against the police officers who had been found guilty for not registering the cases against those responsible. He suggested that an all-party meeting should be convened to discuss the subject.

Replying to the debate, Rajesh Pilot, minister of state in the ministry of home affairs, assured the House that the guilty would be punished severely, without any consideration of party or their position in the government. He said that the government would give all information to the House in the next session when it was convened after one and a half months. Guman Mal Lodha said, 'The names of the honourable members of Parliament as have been referred to by the commission should be revealed in the house'. Ram Vilas Paswan said that the report of the commission had not been presented to the Lok Sabha. He asked whether a copy of the report would be made available to the House. Jagmeet Singh Brar wanted to know whether the government would extend the term of the Jain–Aggarwal Committee, which had expired on 31 July and which had done a good job of it. Rajesh Pilot tried to defend this onslaught but was hardly convincing. He merely said, 'The idea is not to go back to history and find faults as to how it has happened'. Jagmeet Singh Brar interjected to say: 'The Mishra Commission has stated that the then-home minister [Rao] did not come out and go to a single place to console the people.' George Fernandes said, 'We want a copy of the report. Is this House going to be denied the report?' Once again, Rajesh Pilot feebly responded: 'About the report, I will come back to the House when we meet in the next session.' (*LSD* Vol. 24, 1993: 262–73)

Lalita Ramdas, in her article, 'Thoughts on 1984: A Fragile Democracy', pointed out that, though years have elapsed since the 1984 Sikh carnage, emotions have mellowed, details have faded and people have moved on, still, the feelings of outrage and the questions remained sharper than ever. She emphasized that the victims and the survivors were:

> ...utterly shattered because, for the most part, they had voted for the Congress, were supporters of Indira Gandhi, and were mourning her death. The names of those who were perceived to be behind the attacks—Dharamdas Shastri, H.K.L. Bhagat, Lalit Maaken, Jagdish Tytler, Sajjan Kumar, and many others—were already common knowledge, and surfaced in statement after statement made to hundreds of volunteers in camps across the city. That the high command of the political parties chose to turn a blind eye is reprehensible to put it mildly.

Ramdas further wrote:

> Already in 1984, the future events of 1992 and Gujarat 2002 were being foreshadowed and scripted. Confidence-building peace marches through crowded gullies where several Sikh families still lay holed up, were challenged on the streets by armed mobs of infuriated trishul-carrying young men who openly asked us if we were Hindus, and why we were supporting disloyal Sikhs. These were the training grounds for militant Hindutva of the next decade. [For those interested, Amitava Ghosh has an evocative piece on the 1984 riots in which he describes this incident ('The Ghosts of Mrs Gandhi'), and which was first published in *The New Yorker*].

Ramdas indignantly wrote:

> Little did one know then that twenty-one years, eight commissions and committees down the line, not one was willing to clearly nail the guilty and to bring them to book...At a loss for words, I can do no better than to quote Siddhartha Varadarajan in his recent insightful essay in *The Hindu* titled, 'Moral Indifference as the Form of Modern Evil', where he has drawn logical parallels between 1984 and the Holocaust, as also with the massacre of Muslims in Gujarat in 2002. He laments that the learned judge (Nanavati) has 'pulled his punches at a time when the country needed a knockout blow to protect itself from a "riot system" that has become so well-entrenched and institutionalized that any ruling party anywhere in the country can use it with impunity'. Varadarajan rightly points out that, although the Nanavati report has all the 'telltale dots of official guilt, the dots are not connected'. (Ramdas *EPW*, 17 September 2005: 4108–10)

Sanjay Suri, who has written the book, *1984: The Anti-Sikh Violence and After*, has asked the question: 'Three thousand murders and no justice. Is this not betrayal?' He said in an interview:

> I have put down in the [above] book that I reported the 9/11 attacks in the US for the *Outlook* magazine. Three thousand killed there in a sudden, violent attack. Three thousand killed in New Delhi in a sudden, violent attack. How have we reacted? How did they react? They said, 'We want justice'. They did not forget it. Why are we being told, 'Forget about it, *chhodo*?' (*IE* 28 July 2015: 4)

The Anti-Brahmin Riots in Maharashtra in 1948

Reference may be made in this context to the parallel case of widespread atrocities committed in 1948 in western Maharashtra against Brahmins, a small minority, merely because Nathuram Godse, Mahatma Gandhi's assassin, was also a Brahmin. Hardly any action was taken in those cases by the provincial government. Vallabhbhai Patel, in his letter dated 22 May 1948, had conveyed to B.G. Kher, chief minister of Bombay, his unhappiness over its policy regarding 'the treatment of the offences committed in the Deccan after the assassination of Mahatma Gandhi'. Kher wrote to Patel on 26 May 1948 saying:

> As I had no idea that the action taken by us would be misunderstood by you, I did not give you the reasons for taking this line of action... I did not approve of even 'the patriotic and heroic actions' of the 1942 saboteurs and could not for a moment approve of or have any consideration for the offenders of 1948. We took the strongest steps possible and succeeded in getting the situation under control in a short time. Hundreds of people were rounded up and cases were promptly registered and investigated. *Soon after the events, the arrests and the strong attitude of the government were bitterly criticized by a section of Congressmen* which was in authority in the Provincial Congress Committee of Maharashtra, and when the Maharashtra Provincial Congress Committee met recently to take stock of the situation, *the Maharashtra Provincial Congress Committee not only did not condemn in clear terms the happenings but wanted a sympathetic attitude to be taken as regards the accused persons.* Shri [N.V.] Gadgil,[7] who took a prominent part in the Maharashtra Provincial Congress Committee deliberations, supported this attitude of compromise. On the other side, the tension between Brahmins and non-Brahmins did not ease and *it was very difficult to get evidence against the offenders on account of fear of future reprisals.* This being so, there were not very bright chances for securing a conviction in cases of arson and looting and even murder. As these actions were a result of mass action, it was necessary to make the masses realize the enormity of their action. This would be possible only if many of the persons responsible for these actions could be convicted and punished severely. *Because of want of courage to give evidence, this did not seem likely. Three cases which were taken to court were acquitted. This had a bad effect... Some non-Brahmin leaders, like Messrs Jedhe and [Shankarrao] More preached that the actions [against Brahmins] were justified* and that the Hindu Mahasabha people deserved all that they got... There was no idea of making a compromise or showing sympathy

---

[7] Minister in the Nehru cabinet and later, governor of Punjab.

towards anybody in this attitude. The step was taken only on account of the stark realities of the peculiar situation of the parts affected and also for considerations of maximum effective action... [Y.B.] Chavan[8] and Tapase[9] also thought this to be the best policy.

Not convinced by what Kher had stated, Patel replied on 5 June 1948:

I regret I am still unconvinced that the action was wise and proper. Fear of further reprisals by perpetrators of evil and wrong-doers can hardly be a justification for treating such wrong-doers with leniency. It has never paid to condone crimes of violence under any so-called repentance. After all, such things are done under a spirit of mass hysteria, and leniency shown at one time is soon forgotten; more particularly, it is ignored when the scene of another mass hysteria sets in. However, although your action places us under a serious predicament in Kolhapur, now that you have already taken action on those lines, I have nothing more to say. (Das 1973: 77–80)

This case is no different from the tragic happenings in Delhi after Indira Gandhi's assassination. Significantly, the attitude of the Congress party was exactly the same in 1984 and thereafter, as it had been in 1948. This is an eloquent commentary on India's commitment to secularism and adherence to rule of law in the country.

The Bombay Riots in 1992 and 1993

Horrendous communal riots raged for a full twenty days in Bombay in December 1992 and January 1993. In December 1992, the death toll was 227, those who reported for treatment in municipal hospitals was 2370. The corresponding figures for riots in January 1993 were 557 deaths and 2309 reported in hospitals. The deaths due to firing in January 1993 were 175. About 60–67 per cent of the riot victims were Muslims though they constituted only 15 per cent of the Bombay population (1981 census). The number of people who fled Bombay during the riots

---

[8]Later, chief minister of Bombay Province and Maharashtra state, and also central minister for a number of years.
[9]Later, central minister and governor of Punjab.

was 1,50,000. The estimated number of people who sought refuge in various relief camps was as high as 1,00,000.

These riots were in retaliation for the demolition of the Babri Masjid. Sadiq Israr Sheikh, who claims to have carried out the bombings with Indian Mujahideen men has admitted: 'I was a nationalist, then Communist, but Babri and riots changed me'. (*IE* 1 October 2015: 7)

Dileep Padgaonkar, a respected journalist and former editor of *TOI*, wrote:

> High-tech terrorism, almost certainly linked to the riots manifested itself in the bomb blasts of March 12, 1993 [referred to earlier]. By April, however, no one could say where crime merged into religion and when the two together made common cause with terrorism provoked, to some degree at least, by forces outside the country. This nexus made it difficult to govern Bombay and the fear was that India as a whole would become ungovernable. (Padgaonkar 1993: xvi, 3)

Darryl D'Monte, in the essay, 'What Bombay Teaches Us', pointedly wrote:

> More than the physical destruction, it was the psyche which took the worst battering. Suddenly, Muslims began to be referred to as 'them', and thought of as 'the other'; stereotypes were conjured up from a varied past…This isolation of the Muslims will be the biggest toll of the Bombay riots…The story was altogether different in January when it was Shiv Sena which grasped the opportunity to bare its fangs. (Padgaonkar 1993: 291, 294–95)

Rajdeep Sardesai, in his highly penetrating and sensitively written essay, 'The Great Betrayal', has brought out the emergence of Shiv Sena in Bombay and its highly deleterious effects on Maharashtra. The essay brings out how the state government was caught napping while Bombay was burning and how the police were unfairly targeted by the politicians. A Janata Dal leader made a statement accusing the police of targeting Muslims. These comments were not entirely without foundation, but 'the timing was disastrous. They only served to exacerbate an already surcharged atmosphere and widen the communal rift. Worse, it pushed the police on the defensive at a time when they were struggling to cope with the escalating conflict...Some leaders, like George Fernandes and V.P. Singh, were guilty of making such accusations without even a study of the riot-hit areas. Police morale was further dampened when two senior Congress observers, Ghulam Nabi Azad and S.S. Ahluwalia, visited the city and made a categorical statement, "During the riots the police were communally biased." When one of these central team observers visited the cabin of a senior police officer, he noticed a statue of Shivaji. "What is that statue doing there?" was the loaded question... To the poisonous brew of a communalized society, a divided government and a vengeful underworld had been added another ingredient—a demoralized police force.'

Sardesai emphasized that, *in the January 1993 riots, the Shiv Sena had effectively taken over Bombay. Its mouthpiece,* Saamna, *added fuel to fire with its headlines like, 'The Nation Must Be Kept Alive', 'The Next Few Days Will Be Ours' and 'Lesson Had Been Taught'.* Prime Minister Narasimha Rao, at his press conference in Bombay on 15 January, 'conveniently side-stepped the Shiv Sena's role in the riots. That morning's *TOI* had a banner headline where the Sena had admitted its role in the riots. Instead of strongly reacting to the news, Rao blandly said that a judicial inquiry would be ordered into the riots. The next morning's papers even had a photograph of Rao discussing the situation with a few Shiv Sena leaders. Sardesai concluded by saying: *'The real tragedy is that there is no one to hold the politicians—the nation's new maharajas—accountable for their actions. A Bal Thackeray can get away by making the most incendiary statements with scarcely the fingernail of the law touching him...Watching this criminal–politician mafia hijack society is the silent majority...In future, they may not prove so submissive.* (Padgaonkar 1993: 179, 187, 191–92, 198–200, 207, 210)

Bal Thackeray's interview in *Time* magazine, given at the time when the riots were on, is shocking, to put it mildly:

Question: Why is Shiv Sena attacking Muslims?
Answer: Muslims started the riots and my boys are retaliating. Do you expect the Hindus to turn the other cheek? I want to teach the

Muslims a lesson. Our fortitude [sic] has gone too far.
Q.: Why are you so angry with the Muslims?
A.: They are not prepared to accept the rules of this land. They don't want to accept birth control. They want to implement their 'Sharia' (Islamic law) in my motherland. Yes, this is the Hindus' motherland.
Q.: But the Muslims are fleeing Bombay.
A.: If they are going, let them go; if they are not going, kick them out...
Q.: Is this a stepping stone towards a Hindu nation?
A.: We don't need stepping stones. This is a *Hindu Rashtra*. (Puniyani 2003: 221)

Kumar Ketkar, a noted journalist, rightly stated:

For various reasons, including the fear psychosis-generated Shiv Sena's violence, the non-Marathi élite gave in to the so-called charms and charisma of Bal Thackeray, and subsequently to even Raj and Uddhav [and now even his son Aditya]. From Amitabh Bachchan to the Ambanis, Pritish Nandy to Sunil or Sanjay Dutt, or even Ratan Tata—they all went to Matoshree, the Bandra residence of the Thackerays. On the political front, Atal Bihari Vajpayee and L.K. Advani, Pratibha Patil and Pranab Mukherjee, Sharad Pawar and George Fernandes, visited Matoshree and saw to it that the photo opportunity was not missed. It is this media-generated hype and awe which spawned a larger-than-life image of the Sena and its leadership. (*India Today* 9 November 2015: 35)

It is important to note that the Bombay riots in December 1992 and January 1993 were spread over an unbelievably long period of twenty days—five days in December 1992 and fifteen days in January 1993. The Srikrishna Commission of Inquiry into these riots was appointed when the Congress government was in power. The Shiv Sena–BJP government came to power in 1995 and it disbanded the commission in January 1996. This was challenged before the Bombay High Court in a Public Interest Litigation (PIL) and thereafter, reluctantly, the commission was revived in May 1996. Its terms of reference were also expanded to cover the chain of bomb blasts which had taken place in Bombay in March 1993. Altogether, 2126 affidavits were filed before the commission—two by the government, 549 by the police and 1575 by members of the public.

Unfortunately, the commission did not go into the larger question of how communal clashes can be averted. Nor did it examine matters relating to the failure of the then Congress government in not taking swift action to control the riots. The commission described the communal violence as 'incurable epileptic seizures'. I find this description inadequate. Communal violence in India can be more appropriately described as a cancer which is threatening to become incurable.

Nalini Gera, in the biography of Ram Jethmalani, wrote that the Congress party, the Samajwadi party and some other organizations had filed a PIL in the Supreme Court, seeking implementation of the report of the Srikrishna Commission of Inquiry, which had indicted the government of the time, namely the Shiv Sena–BJP alliance. Bal Thackeray, the Shiv Sena supremo, was found guilty of inciting the riots through inflammatory editorials. The Maharashtra government gave permission for his arrest and there was concern in all quarters about what might happen if he were arrested. His followers had threatened that if he were arrested, Bombay would burn. Gera's narration of what happened thereafter is shocking. She wrote:

> The prime minister [A.B. Vajpayee] was in a quandary and was under pressure to protect Thackeray as the Shiv Sena was an important ally in the NDA. He asked Ram [Jethmalani] to see if there was a legal way to do so. Ram examined the matter and on 20 July [2000], after meeting the prime minister, made a statement that the case against Thackeray was 'hopelessly time-barred'. 'The law says you cannot file a prosecution after 3 years from the date of commission of the offence,' he said, and added that under Article 162 of the Constitution, the Centre could give executive orders to the state government not to arrest Thackeray, binding the state government to act accordingly. The prime minister asked him to speak to Thackeray...There was an angry outburst from the chief justice who was heading the three-judge bench before whom the matter was being heard: 'Is it open for a member of the cabinet to state something else in the teeth of what had already been stated

in the affidavit filed by the Centre? Saying one thing to the court and stating something else for public consumption is not right.'... He ended by saying that the government seemed to have no notion of collective responsibility. (Gera 2002: 323–24)

It is shocking to see the above opinion suggesting that the Central government could give executive orders to the state government not to arrest Thackeray. This would have been clearly unconstitutional. But it shows the extent to which the NDA government was prepared to go to save Thackeray from arrest. Cases such as these make a mockery of the rule of law in the country. Speaking at a seminar on the salient features of the Srikrishna Commission Report, organized by the People's Union for Civil Liberties (PUCL) in Pune on September 28, 1998, I had stated that Bal Thackeray should have been arrested following Mumbai riots. (*Mid-Day* 29 September 1998: 4)

The phenomenal rise of the Shiv Sena in Maharashtra within a short span of a few years, from its foundation in 1966 in Bombay, has often intrigued political observers. Meena Menon rightly emphasized that the Shiv Sena had enjoyed the confidence of the Congress when it started. The Congress saw the Sena as a check on the Communist parties and what resulted was the nurturing of a cadre that came in handy in 1992. Menon has quoted Jayant Lele, an academic based in Canada, saying: 'The opportunism of the mainstream political parties professing secularism is often blamed for the continuing strength of proponents of Hindutva, such as Shiv Sena. There is ample evidence to show how factionalism within the ruling Congress Party often gave the Sena a new lease of life. (Menon 2012: 231)

Jyoti Punwani, in her essay, 'Police Conduct during Communal Riots: Evidence from 1992–93 Mumbai Riots and its Implications', comprehensively analysed the evidence tendered before the Srikrishna Commission of Inquiry. She invited attention to some provocative slogans which vitiated the atmosphere in Mumbai:

- *Hindustan Hinduonka, nahin kisike baap ka (*Hindustan belongs to Hindus, not to anybody's father)
- *Ayodhya to ek jhaanki hai, Kashi Mathura baaki hai* (Ayodhya

is just a glimpse, Banaras and Mathura are yet to come)
- *Is desh mein rahna hoga, to Hindu banke rahna hoga* (If you want to live in this country, you will have to live like a Hindu)
- *Talwar nikli myan se, mandir banega shaan se* (Now the sword is out of its scabbard, the temple will be built in a grand way)
- *Is desh mein rehna hoga to Vande Mataram kahna hoga* (If you want to live in this country, you will have to recite *Vande Mataram*)

None of the police officers who testified before the Srikrishna Commission found these slogans objectionable. Punwani also gave several instances of highly provocative actions taken by the BJP and its allies like, the VHP, the Bajrang Dal and the Shiv Sena. It was left to Justice Srikrishna to point out that laying down conditions of residence on any citizen, let alone a community, by another group, was not just communal but also fascist. Some other slogans raised by the BJP, the VHP and the Shiv Sena were so offensive that they could not be read out to the commission.

S.K. Bapat, the then police commissioner of Bombay had filed a 172-page affidavit before the commission, presenting his views on the riots. However, according to Punwani, not once did he name the Shiv Sena in the affidavit. Another significant feature of Hindu communal parties was to organize *maha aarti*s (mass prayers). However, no effort was made by the police to stop these aartis. (Shaban 2012: 190–91, 195, 198)

The Godhra Riots in 2002

The carnage that rocked India following the Godhra tragedy on 27 February 2002 was perhaps the worst and most tragic episode of communal violence. It was particularly shameful because it was state-sponsored. More than 2000 persons, mainly Muslims, perished in the violence. The violence is alleged to have begun as a reaction to the torching of a coach of the Sabarmati Express by which karsevaks were returning from Ayodhya. It was alleged that a group of Muslims had deliberately done this. However, there is no unanimity, even among judicial commissions of inquiry, on whether the Muslims were responsible for it. The Concerned Citizens' Tribunal—Gujarat 2002 (CCTG)[10] wrote:

> Having examined the evidence, the Godhra incident of February 27, 2002 does not appear to be a pre-planned or a premeditated one. Our examination of coach S-6, which was burnt, showed that the fire had occurred from within and not from outside. There is no reliable material to say as to who had set fire to the coach. Yet, it appears that the state government rushed to the conclusion that it was a deliberate and pre-planned attack on the *karsevak*s by a particular group of Muslims. This is one of the reasons for the spread of violence in the state.

The tribunal noted that while the nation and the world were condemning violence in Gujarat, senior members of the central NDA government made public statements defending and justifying the role of the state government.

In Annexure 18 of the CCTG Report (Vol. I), the then Prime Minister Atal Bihari Vajpayee's pronouncements on the subject from time to time have been extracted. On 3 March 2002, Vajpayee was quoted on the PMO's website as having said:

> 'From Godhra to Ahmedabad, in so many places, there are so many incidents of people being burnt alive, including helpless women and children. This is a blot on the nation's forehead and has grievously harmed India's image in the eyes of the world.' On 4 April 2002, he was quoted in *Hindustan Times* to have said: 'I do not know what face I will show them (the world) now after the shameful events in Gujarat.' On his visit to Ahmedabad the same day, he was quoted in *Hindustan Times* saying, 'My one message to the chief minister is that he should follow *raj dharma*. A ruler should not make any discrimination between his subjects on the basis of caste, creed and

---

[10] The commission comprised Justice V.R. Krishna Iyer, former judge of the Supreme Court, Justice P.B. Sawant, former judge of the Supreme Court, Justice Hosbet Suresh, former judge of the Bombay high court, Advocate K.G. Kannabiran, Aruna Roy of Majdoor Kisan Shakti Sanghatan, and K.S Subramanian IPS (Retd).

religion.' (CCTG 2002: 9, 248, 252, 299)

The report has quoted the former cabinet secretary, T.S.R. Subramanian, from his statement in *The Indian Express* (10 April 2002) that, 'There is no civil service left in Gujarat... It is a telling indictment... of the collapse of also the police and civil magistracy.' The tribunal unambiguously held Chief Minister Narendra Modi as:

> ...the chief Author and Architect of all that happened in Gujarat after the arson of February 27, 2002. It is amply clear from all the evidence placed before the Tribunal that what began in Godhra could have been, given the political will, controlled promptly at Godhra itself. Instead, the state government under Chief Minister Shri Narendra Modi took an active part in leading and sponsoring the violence against the minorities all over Gujarat...Evidence before the tribunal clearly establishes the absolute failure of large sections of the Gujarat police to fulfil their constitutional duty and prevent mass massacres, rape and arson—in short, to maintain law and order. Worse still is the evidence of their active connivance and brutality, their indulgence in vulgar and obscene conduct against women and children in full public view. It is as if instead of being impartial keepers of the rule of law, they were part of the Hindutva brigade targeting helpless Muslims. (CCTG 2002: 78–79, 81)

A.G. Noorani, a leading jurist, in the article, 'Gujarat Riots: Bringing the Guilty to Court', said that it was time that use was made of the law of torts (civil wrong punishable in damages) against acts of 'misfeasance in public offices'. He invited attention to the observations of the Supreme Court in the judgment delivered on 12 April 2004 (*Zahira Habibullah H. Sheikh v. State of Gujarat and Ors* [2004] 4 SCC 158):

> The role of the state government also leaves much to be desired. One gets a feeling that there was really no seriousness in the state's approach in assailing the trial court's judgment...Criminal trials should not be reduced to mock trials or shadow boxing or fixed trials...Those who are responsible for protecting life and properties and ensuring that investigation is fair and proper seem to have

shown no real anxiety. Large number of people had lost their lives... *The modern-day 'Neros' were looking elsewhere when Best Bakery and innocent children and helpless women were burning, and were probably deliberating how the perpetrators of the crime could be saved or protected.* Law and justice became flies in the hands of these 'wanton boys'. When fences start to swallow the crops, no scope will be left for survival of law and order or truth and justice.

Noorani emphasized that the implications of these observations of the Court were so far-reaching that the Gujarat government applied for their expunction but failed.

During the hearings, the chief justice of India, Justice V.N. Khare said, '*I have no faith left in the Gujarat government.*' After his retirement, he said in an interview to *Hindustan Times* (5 March 2004): 'I tried to give a new dimension to criminal jurisprudence considering the fact that there was total miscarriage of justice in the case.'

Noorani argued that Narendra Modi's prosecution would help evolve the law further in this direction. (Noorani *EPW* 3 July 2004: 2950)

The monthly *Seminar* brought out a special issue titled, 'Society under Siege'—a symposium on the breakdown of civil society in Gujarat. In an article with a telling title, 'Gujarat and Its Bhasmita',[11] Meghnad Desai stated:

> The moral collapse of the government of India over Salman Rushdie's *Satanic Verses* showed that secularism had come to mean equal licence for both [Hindu and Muslim] fundamentalisms... Thus, Muslims are a vote bank and as a matter of practice, religious leaders become the gatekeepers of that vote bank...Gujaratis have turned from being meek and mild and proverbially passive to being macho and aggressive.

---

[11]The author of the article clarified that there is, of course, no such word as *bhasmita*, but *bhasma* is ashes and *asmita* is self-image. The connection should then be obvious.

Upendra Baxi, in his article, 'Notes on Holocaustian Politics', stated: 'Gujarat brings home to us with poignant intensity the consummation of the practices of communalization of governance...The Gujarat carnage sculpts an ominous principle of governance: the democratically elected government owes concrete duties to the dominant majorities to devise ways and means that facilitate communal revenge.'

The *Seminar* special issue listed the several commissions of inquiry on Gujarat which submitted their reports. These include:

> The National Human Rights Commission Report; Report by SAHMAT on Ethnic Cleansing in Ahmedabad; State-Sponsored Carnage in Gujarat: Report of CPI(M)–AIDWA (All India Democratic Women's Association) Delegation; Report of the Independent Fact-Finding Mission titled, 'Gujarat Carnage 2002: A Report to the Nation'; and a report by a Women's Panel sponsored by Citizen's Initiative, Ahmedabad: 'How Has The Gujarat Massacre Affected Minority Women? (*Seminar*, 13 May, 2002: 56, 77, 84–93)

Shreekant Sambrani, in his article, 'Gujarat's Burning Train—India's Inferno?', wrote:

> 'Deranged minds ruled the roost last month. Muslim-owned shops, residences and even trucks and buses were targeted systematically. A respected auto dealer had to run for his life with only the clothes on his back for the crime of building a fancy house in a Hindu area in south Baroda. Retired high court judges faced the same fate in Ahmedabad.' He underlined that *the militant Hindutva bandwagon cannot be wished away for long, nor can it be stopped by moral posturing.* He quoted Salman Rushdie's 'deeply flawed denunciation of the current riots' (*The Washington Post*, 8 March 2002), which leads nevertheless to a correct conclusion: religion is the poison.' (Sambrani *EPW* 6 April 2002: 1306, 1310).

Riaz Ahmad, in his article, 'Gujarat Violence: Meaning and Implications', rightly stated:

> For years to come, the recent communal violence is going to

remain a reference point in identity narratives about the 'self' and 'the other'. According to Ahmad, the violence in Gujarat should be seen in the context of the total crisis sweeping through the Indian political system. Even though there were a few allegations of planned targeting of the Muslim lives and properties during the 1969 [Ahmedabad] riots [referred to elsewhere], by and large, the violence then appeared to be spontaneous. According to *The Gujarat Carnage 2002: A Report to the Nation by an Independent Fact Finding Mission*, the current violence stands out for its planning. But sexual subjugation of the female body as a weapon to humiliate a whole community was seen in 1969 as well as 2002. Ahmad has underlined that commitment to Gandhian values also appears to be declining. The 1969 riots witnessed Morarji Desai and Indulal Yagnik undertaking an indefinite fast, and Ravi Shankar Maharaj, a Sarvodaya leader of Gujarat, going on a *padayatra* (peace march) for the sake of normalcy and peace. In the present case, although some of the leaders awoke to the need of peace marches in Gujarat, nobody has undertaken an indefinite fast for the sake of peace there. Ahmad was prescient when he wrote, 'We may see greater communal polarization. We may witness a more aggressive Hindu religio-cultural nationalism in search of political power. Second, a Muslim political party may be floated...Third, Muslims in general will continue to support political parties that look capable of defeating the BJP in elections...in the face of alienation some Muslims may get involved in political violence including terrorism...' (Ahmad *EPW* 18 May 2002: 1870–73)

Alaknanda Patel, in an article, 'Gujarat Violence: A Personal Diary', related some of her personal encounters in the city of Baroda during the riots and afterwards. Patel graphically described the politics of alienation and the result of 'showing Muslims their place' or 'teaching them a lesson'. As she has written:

The Muslim then withdraws into the world where he has an identity. He displays his faith in his attire and the distinctive beard, in his language with an 'Urduized' Hindi as public means of communication, discarding the Gujarati that he spoke earlier. Ramzan fasts, daily namaaz, religious education, living in segregated areas, become key to his life. On the other side, a more Sanskritized version of Gujarati, religious discourses, observance of fasts, pilgrimages (sometimes organized by political parties), public festivals worshipping different gods, become central to the Hindu life.'

Patel has also brought out that in addition to the large number killed, over 1,00,000 people were rendered homeless. In the crossfire, both communities suffered, whether through loss of lives or income. *The champions of Hindutva had not counted on negative externality*; in its attempt to destroy the Muslims they destroyed the Hindus in a different way. If, for the Muslim community the loss in the riots was Rs 3800 crores, the loss for Hindus was Rs 24,000 crores. The rampage destroyed 1159 Muslim-owned hotels but, in the process, 29,000 people connected with the hotel industry lost their jobs, of these only 700 were Muslims. When, at the Handloom Expo of Ahmedabad in February–March, Muslim craftspeople, possibly about eight, were attacked and the Expo closed down, 325 Hindu artisans from different parts of India lost their business. *Since the riots, in Ahmedabad alone, 27 Hindus have committed suicide because of loss of business and income. This is friendly fire, to use Amartya Sen's term.* (Patel *EPW* 14 December 2002: 4985–87)

Asghar Ali Engineer highlighted the enormity of the Gujarat riots by citing certain instances, such as:

The burning alive of thirty-nine persons, and Ehsan Jafri, an ex-MP of the Congress party, in his bungalow in Chamanpura in Ahmedabad. A Muslim Inspector-General of police, threatened by his own Hindu subordinates, had to take off his police uniform to save himself. A high court judge, not safe in his official residence as he was a Muslim, had to shift under advice from the chief justice of the Gujarat High Court. The worst incident occurred in a slum in Naroda Patiya, a suburb of Ahmedabad, where more than 100 persons, all poor Muslims, were burnt alive in full view of the police force.

Engineer stated that:

> The then-Prime Minister Atal Bihari Vajpayee 'not only failed in controlling the situation but also lost all his credibility by making totally contradictory statements in Ahmedabad and Goa'. While in Ahmedabad, Vajpayee advised Modi to follow *raj dharma*; during his visit to Goa on 12 April, he made a complete about-turn and accused Islam and Muslims of militancy and conflict. He rhetorically asked, 'Who burned the train in Godhra?'

Engineer also said:

> *Thus Vajpayee proved to be as much an RSS* pracharak *as Modi, though he is a crypto variety' while Modi is open… Vajpayee had said at a VHP meeting in Staten Island in New York that the 'RSS is my soul'.* Engineer concluded that the Goa meet had clearly shown that the BJP fully approved of Modi's policies in tackling the communal situation in the state. (Engineer *EPW* 14 December 2002: 5053–54)

Mukul Dube clarified that a riot is necessarily spontaneous, it is blind fury. But what happened in Gujarat was far from blind…The word 'pogrom' has been used to describe the massacre, and the expression 'ethnic cleansing'. (Dube 2004: 33)

Alistair McMillan, in his essay, 'The BJP Coalition: Partnership and Power-Sharing in Government', was forthright when he said:

> The greatest political shock to face the NDA was the Gujarat massacres of 2002. The failure of the BJP government in Gujarat and the leadership in New Delhi to take decisive action against rioters can be seen to have been a key factor in the escalation of communal violence in that state. This was a clear violation of the manifesto commitment of the NDA, yet there was only muted protest from the coalition partners of the BJP. While the TDP [Telugu Desam Party] leader, Chandrababu Naidu, called for the removal of Gujarat Chief Minister Narendra Modi, and Mamata Banerjee boycotted a meeting of the NDA co-ordination committee, there was only one resignation from the government over the issue

(Ram Vilas Paswan (JD (U) [Janata Dal United]). A censure motion in the Lok Sabha on the government's handling of the Gujarat massacres was comfortably defeated (276 votes to 182), despite the abstention of the TDP... The state assembly elections that followed the massacres saw the BJP government return to power in Gujarat, and the 2004 national elections saw little evidence that the events led to a national vote swing against the BJP. (Adeney 2005: 32)

J.B. D'Souza, an illustrious civil servant and former chief secretary of Maharashtra State, in his article, 'A Civil Service Failure: How Can Credibility Be Restored?', pointedly argued that:

...the principal reason for administrative and police failure in Gujarat is the growing power that politicians, and ministers in particular, have assumed over civil and police officers, directly and indirectly, through encouragement and tolerance of inefficiency and misconduct, and by the means of punitive transfers of officials if they act against misbehaving politicians. If [a repetition of] the horrific events of the recent past in Gujarat [is] to be prevented, a sense of the responsibilities under the law should be restored among officials. (D'Souza *EPW* 24 August 2002: 3492–93)

In spite of the highly disturbing narration as above and the observations of the National Human Rights Commission and the Supreme Court regarding the manner in which the riots were handled by the state government, the complicity of the then Chief Minister Modi could not be established in any court of law. At least in the anti-Sikh riots case, Congress President Sonia Gandhi and Prime Minister Manmohan Singh had offered their apologies, though they were not directly in power at the relevant time. In sharp contrast, Modi, though directly concerned, has refused to do so. This must be borne in mind in coming to any conclusions on this horrendous chapter in the history of India.

Communalism and Communal Violence

Jawaharlal Nehru traced in his autobiography the rise of communalism in India:

The rise of the Nationalist Party, or some such party, was inevitable owing to the growing communal temper of the country.[12] On the one side, there were the Muslim fears of a Hindu majority; on the other side, Hindu resentment at being bullied, as they conceived it, by the Muslims. Many a Hindu felt that there was much of the stand-up-and-deliver about the Muslim attitude, too much of an attempt to extort special privileges with a threat of going over to the other side. Because of this, the Hindu Mahasabha rose to some importance, representing, as it did, Hindu nationalism, Hindu communalism opposing Muslim communalism. The aggressive activities of the Mahasabha acted on and stimulated still further this Muslim communalism, and so action and reaction went on and, in the process, the communal temperature of the country went up... (Nehru 1936: 159)

The Bihar communal riots in 1946 had brought out the enormity of the problem and had raised concerns all over the country. Jawaharlal Nehru thought that Hindus had committed excesses against the Muslims and that the riots needed to be put down with a heavy hand. He personally visited Bihar and prevailed on the authorities to take strong action in the matter. In his letter to Vallabhbhai Patel dated 5 November 1946, Nehru wrote, 'As I told you, there is news about their [military] firing on a mob today, inflicting 400 deaths'. (Das Vol. 3, 1972: 166)

In his speech in the British Parliament, Winston Churchill gave credit to Nehru for taking a strong stand in the matter and protecting Muslims.

It is interesting to note that, prior to Independence, the Hindu Mahasabha[13] was interested in joining forces with Congress party for elections in Bengal. Shyama Prasad Mukherjee had met

---

[12]Pandit Madan Mohan Malaviya and Lala Lajpat Rai had formed a new party, called Nationalist Party, to oppose the Swaraj Party and the regular Congress party in the legislature.
[13]A communal organization whose membership was confined to Hindus.

Rajendra Prasad in this connection. Rajendra Prasad had written to Vallabhbhai Patel about it. Patel had replied to Rajendra Prasad saying that, 'The Congress cannot think of any settlement with the Hindu Mahasabha. Besides, there is absolutely no need as the Congress will easily secure all the seats in the Central Assembly so far as non-Muslim constituencies are concerned, except perhaps Dr Shyama Prasad's own seat which, by courtesy, the Bengal Congress Committee may think it proper to allow without contest. (Das 1972: 11–12)

W.G. Joshi, Congress leader from Amravati in Berar province on 26 August 1950, wrote to Vallabhbhai Patel that *'communalism and corruption have now practically become the life blood of the Congress—at least in this province.* (Das 1974: 281)

Banning movies and writings on the pretext of communal sensitivities is a favourite pastime of politicians which has continued right from before Independence.

On 4 August 1947, Vallabhbhai Patel wrote to Morarji Desai, home minister of Bombay, about 'the flare-up in Bombay and the bomb explosion in the cinema'. Morarji Desai replied in his letter dated 6 August, to say: 'I don't think that it has anything to do with the exhibition of *Arab-ka-Sitara*....I have seen that picture myself and have found that the setting of the picture has a historical background regarding the rise of Islam. Some Jews have undoubtedly been shown to have been converted to Islam but there is nothing to show that these were forcible conversions. In any event, the picture contains nothing to which Hindus can legitimately take any objection. The picture, however, has since been banned for one month and the ban will be continued indefinitely in accordance with your advice. (Das 1973: 152–53)

In his letter to Vallabhbhai Patel on 26 March 1950, Jawaharlal Nehru, *inter alia*, expressed his concern at the deteriorating communal situation in the country. He wrote:

Indeed the whole problem is in the nature of communal problem.

We have long stood for discouraging and putting an end to communalism. That has been the Congress policy and it has been repeated and affirmed by Parliament. We talk of a secular state. That of course simply means any normal state today, leaving out the abnormality of Pakistan's Islamic state. We adopted our policy regardless of what the Muslim League or Pakistan might say or do, because we thought that was the only policy, both from the idealistic and practical and opportunist point of view. Any other policy could only lead to disruption and disaster. Certain organizations, notably the Hindu Mahasabha, adopted an exactly contrary policy, that is, contrary to ours, though exactly similar, in reverse, to Pakistan's. *I find that progressively we are being driven to adopt what is essentially the Pakistan or the Hindu Mahasabha policy in this respect.* It may be that the circumstances were too strong for us. (Das 1974: 12)

Vallabhbhai Patel was quite concerned about the perception in certain quarters that he was adopting a communal approach favouring Hindus. In his letter dated 28 March 1950 to Nehru, Patel wrote:

As regards the differences of our approach, as far as I know, there has been none as regards the secular ideals to which we all subscribe and for which we all stand; in fact I have throughout emphasized the need for full protection of minorities in India and condemned violence. At the same time, I have not ignored the basic cause of such violence, namely, what is happening in Pakistan and the bitterness which it engenders in the country...I have also laid stress on the fact that our secular ideals impose a responsibility on our Muslim citizens in India—a responsibility to remove the doubts and misgivings entertained by large sections of the people about their loyalty founded largely on their past association with the demand for Pakistan and the unfortunate activities of some of them. (Das 1974: 19)

The Congress party was no less afflicted with communalism than some other political parties. Matters came to a head on the question of the election of the Congress president at its Nasik session in 1950. Vallabhbhai

Patel had sponsored the candidature of Purshottam Das Tandon, president, provincial Congress committee, though Nehru was totally opposed to it. In his letter to Vallabhbhai dated 27/28 August 1950, Nehru wrote:

> My decision was that I could not serve in the Working Committee if Tandon was president. That held whatever the Congress might decide. That decision was taken for two major reasons: that Tandon had pursued during the past two years and was still pursuing a policy which, to my thinking, was utterly wrong and harmful and his election would undoubtedly give an impetus to this policy, and I must dissociate myself completely from it. Secondly, because the election was becoming more and more a [clash] between varying policies and *Tandon became a kind of symbol of one and was as such being supported widely by Hindu Mahasabha and RSS elements.* To join the working committee for me in these circumstances would be not only some kind of surrender to that policy, however I might explain or limit it, but would also be, in the circumstances, improper and undignified for me. (Das 1974: 221)

Nehru had also written to Tandon earlier on 8 August 1950 to explain to him why he was not in favour of his candidature. Nehru, *inter alia*, had written:

> I think the major issue in this country today, if it is to progress and to remain united, is to solve satisfactorily our own minority problems. Instead of that, *we become more intolerant towards our minorities* and give as our excuse that Pakistan behaves badly...I am most intimately concerned with what happens in India, and this progressive decline in some of the basic things of life is distressing. Unfortunately, you have become to large numbers of people in India some kind of a symbol of this communal and revivalist outlook and the question rises in my mind: *Is the Congress going that way also?*...I would have gladly welcomed your election to the Congress presidentship. But when I look at this matter impersonally and from the larger point of view, I feel that this election would mean great encouragement to certain forces in India which I consider harmful. Hence my difficulty and my distress. (Das 1974: 198)

The data on communal violence in general and riots in particular is not compiled scientifically and systematically by the government and released annually for public dissemination. This information has considerable significance for assessing the working of secularism in the country. As in the case of the recent decision of the central government not to publish the data about the representation of minorities in police, not to publish data on communal violence, and to keep the people in the dark, is the surest recipe for creating public apathy and disinterest in the subject. I would strongly urge urgent reconsideration on these matters, apolitically.

Engineer wrote that several riots took place during the first decade after Independence. Throughout the 1950s, communal violence kept occurring. In 1954, a total of fifty-four riots occurred, in which thirty-four persons were killed and 512 were injured. In fact, there was no year which was free of communal violence. (Engineer 1995b: 95–96)

> In February 1961, serious communal disturbances broke out between the Hindus and the Muslims at Jabalpur, Sagar and a few other places in Madhya Pradesh. In September 1961, serious communal disturbances broke out in Aligarh, Moradabad and several other places in western UP. Referring to these communal riots, *Nehru said that communalism had nothing to do with religion but grew due to the intrusion of politics into the approach of religious groups. It was dangerous because it was easy to rouse people's passions in the name of religion.* (Mullik 1972: 174-6)

On 12 September 1967, the working committee of the All India Muslim Majlis-e-Mushawarat passed a resolution on the communal riots in the country. The resolution, *inter alia*, stated that:

> 'After the bloody riots of 1964, the Majlis arrived at the conclusion that the majority community of this country has failed to create the atmosphere of love, unity, tolerance and sympathy for Muslims of India...As regards the one-sided communal aggression against Muslims in Ranchi, the Majlis is satisfied that Muslims are victims of aggression...To offer effective resistance and fight in self-defence is a right acknowledged by Shariah, law of the land and morality.' Dr Syed Mahmud, who presided over the working committee,

announced in the press conference that *the administration had miserably failed to stop communal riots. The Muslims were suffering from a feeling of insecurity about their life and property.* Now there is a need for Muslims to be prepared for self-reliance and retaliation in self-defence without depending on the government. (Hassnain 1968: 134–35)

For the first time, a call had been given to Muslims all over the country and it showed the desperation on their part.

Matters pertaining to the increasing communal violence continued to agitate Parliament from time to time. In one such case, a 'calling attention' discussion was raised in the Rajya Sabha on 21 November 1978, pertaining to 'increasing trends of communal riots in the country with particular reference to recent incidents in Aligarh'. Since a number of members wanted to participate, a whole day was allotted for the discussion, as an exceptional case and in relaxation of the normal procedure pertaining to a calling attention notice (CAN). A number of speakers alleged that the RSS was responsible for the violence. However, some other members belonging to the BJP contested this and said that Muslim communal organizations were responsible for perpetrating the violence.

Thus, this was a typical example of the blame game, more for public consumption than for any real introspection into the malady of communalism.

In his forthright reply to the debate, the then Prime Minister Morarji Desai *underlined that communal rioting had been the bane of the country right since 1893.* He said:

'There were no Hindu–Muslim riots in this country before 1893. That is the history of this country. It was the Britishers who fomented them in order to serve their purpose and they went on fanning it, and that is how clashes went on taking place and ultimately they culminated in separate electorates which made it still worse. And that is how we acquired this legacy.'

Refuting the charge that communal violence had increased after the Janata government came to power in 1977, Desai cited figures of communal incidents in the decade since 1967: there were 198 incidents in 1967; 346 in 1968; 519 in 1969; 521 in 1970; 321 in 1971; 240 in 1972; 242 in 1973; 248 in 1974; 205 in 1975; 169 in 1976; and 188 in 1977. Desai emphasized that anti-social elements took advantage of the situation and made it communal to exacerbate feelings.

Desai underlined that the Janata government had appointed the Minorities Commission and it was his intention 'to make necessary changes in the Constitution'. He said that when the Janata government came to power, 'there was a question of appointing only a civil rights commission before. But we deliberately made it a minorities commission so that there is more confidence created.' Desai also mentioned that he had asked all the state governments to give full cooperation to the minorities commission whenever they went there. (*RSD* Vol. 107.1, 1978: 167, 207, 218, 303–12)

Lancy Lobo, in his article, 'Adivasis, Hindutva and Post-Godhra Riots in Gujarat', stated that, earlier Hindu–Muslim riots had taken place in tribal areas without involving the tribals. First, communal disturbances involving adivasis in 1990 as a result of Hindutvization which, according to Lobo, is a slightly different process from Hinduiazation. The Hindutvization of adivasis began in the late 1980s. Hindutvization was started by the Sangh Parivar as a planned process. The Sangh Parivar surveyed, selected and targeted villages, planted its men, recruited local people and began its anti-missionary campaigns. Lobo is of the view that the Congress kept the tribals in poverty for forty years and that, lately, the BJP (Hindutva) has introduced hatred among them. Poverty and hatred are a deadly mixture directed towards perceived enemies, the Muslims and Christians. (Lobo *EPW* 30 November 2002: 4844–45, 4849)

Asghar Ali Engineer, in his article, 'Gujarat Riots in the Light of the History of Communal Violence', wrote that *communalism is not the product of religion; it is, in fact, the product of politics of the élite of a religious community. In other words, religion per se does not give birth to communalism, a religious community does.*

As brought out elsewhere, similar was the assessment of Jawaharalal Nehru. However, looking at the rapid increase in communal tempers and tensions in India during the last few years, this is only partly true. It would hardly be correct to say that communalism is only a game played by politicians for their own gain.

Engineer further stated:

'The decade of the 1980s was one in which not only the Nehruvian concept of secularism began to be questioned but communal forces succeeded in consolidating their political base. It was during this decade that a large number of communal riots broke out particularly in north India—Muradabad in 1980; Bihar Sharif in 1981; Baroda and Meerut in 1982; and Nelli in Assam in 1983, in which more than 3000 Bengali Muslims were killed.' The 1969 riots of Ahmedabad further consolidated the position of the BJP in Gujarat. The Ahmedabad riots of 1985 were followed by the Meerut riots of 1987 and the Bhagalpur riots of 1989. Both these riots, reportedly, also saw a great deal of police atrocities and police collusion in killing members of the minority community. Engineer wrote that, in Meerut, the police dragged out 23 young Muslim boys from Hashimpura and shot them dead and threw their bodies into a nearby canal. (Engineer *EPW* 14 December 2002: 5047, 5050–51)

Mukul Dube, in the introduction to his book, *The Path of the Parivar: Articles on Gujarat and Hindutva*, quoted Satyapal Dang from his article in *Mainstream*: 'As regards criticism of Muslim Madrasas, it is possible that some or even many may be teaching fundamentalism. But there are quite a number of educational institutes being run by the RSS which too teach religious fundamentalism. Both deserve to be banned.' (Dube 2004: 29)

In a shocking episode on 24 January 1999, an Australian Christian missionary, Graham Stewart Stains and his two sons were burnt to death in a jeep in Manoharpur village in Orissa. The Bajrang Dal was alleged to have been involved in the incident. There was widespread indignation all over the country. To stem the tide, the government appointed a judicial inquiry commission headed by Justice D.P. Wadhwa of the Supreme Court.

Gopal Krishna's analysis of communal violence brings out that:

The great divide in the history of communal riots in India is 1964... Whereas the total number of reported communal incidents over the period 1950–63 was 1141, giving an average of 81.5 per year, in 1964 it had risen to 2115. Admittedly, 1964 was a particularly bad year for communal violence, but there is no mistaking the fact that it represented a major change in the communal climate in the country. For the seven years between 1964 and 1970 the average number of incidents per year was 1025, as against 81.5 for the preceding 14 years. (Wilkinson 2005: 154)

The data on communal incidents in the country, year after year, is indeed shocking. Leaving aside the holocaust of communal violence immediately preceding and following the Partition of the country, right since 1954 up to 1985, each year is marked by incidents of communal violence. According to official figures, from 1954 to 1985, there were as many as 8449 communal incidents resulting in 7229 deaths and 47,321 persons injured. (Singh 2004: 329–30) This shows the enormity of the problem.

> Reference must be made to the shocking killing of 42 young Muslim men from Hashimpura, a mohalla less than two kilometres away from Meerat city on May 22, 1987, allegedly by men in uniform. However, 16 accused PAC personnel were let off for want of evidence that could nail their complicity in the dastardly act...The 16 policemen are still in service. The accused were never suspended. No departmental action was ever taken. The CID inquiry report submitted in 1994 on the incident was never made public. The annual confidential reports of concerned persons never mentioned charges against them. Some of the accused were also promoted during this period. All accused were released on bail. Between 1997 and 2000, the court issued 23 warrants summoning the accused but nobody appeared in the court. The state government did not consider it important to file an appeal. There was not even a murmur from the Samajwadi Party supremo Mulayam Singh Yadav or his chief minister son Akhilesh Yadav. (*Outlook*, 6 April 2015: 28–36)
>
> A survey undertaken by *The Indian Express* team of police records from Bihar's 38 districts and a journey criss-crossing 18 districts that account for more than 70 per cent of communal

incidents showed a three-fold surge—from 226 between January 2010 and June 2013 to 667 between June 2013 and June 2015. An incident of Eve-teasing, a minor road accident, a cricket match between two local teams, a dispute over a kite or a theft of a buffalo is increasingly likely to become a trigger for a clash between communities in areas where deliberate attempts have also been made earlier to stoke communal faultlines—by dumping carcasses of pigs or beef inside places of worship, defacing idols, tweaking procession routes and exhuming old disputes over the use of common land. (*IE* 26 August 2015: 8)

Ashutosh Varshney, in his analysis of communal violence in India, brought out some significant aspects:

First, communal tensions flare up less in smaller towns, for they lack the relative anonymity of larger towns and allow greater routine interaction between Hindus and Muslims. Or, it may simply be that large towns are extremely difficult places for the police to control violence once it breaks out. Second, arguments about the relation between modernity and communalism or communal violence have long been dominant in intellectual circles. By now, of course, the debate has come full circle. Until the 1960s, modernization was considered a solution to the problem of communalism. Over the last decade or so, however, anti-modernity arguments have acquired unprecedented popularity. India has had strong advocates on both sides. The customary view, a view that is often associated with Nehru and the Indian Left, was that greater modernity would solve the problem of communalism. To the anti-secularist or anti-modernist, however, modernity is a problem, not a solution. Third, he has quoted Amartya Sen who argues that literacy and communal violence are related and that improved literacy will lead to lower communal violence or even its gradual elimination. (Varshney 2002: 106–07)

The Indian experience so far is a mixed one. *Prima facie*, the deep-rooted and long-held distrust between Hindus and Muslims, fanned by fundamentalist elements in both communities in recent years, has been largely responsible for the continuing communal violence in the country. Even a small, insignificant provocation has led to a serious communal conflagration. In the final analysis, reducing the divide between the two communities by conscious efforts, such as mixed housing schemes, and the intermingling of communities in all age groups alone, would help create greater communal harmony and amity. In Chapter 6, I have also elaborated on various steps which need to be taken for a more effective enforcement of the rule of law.

I find it difficult to agree with an influential section of intellectuals who argue that religion as such is not responsible for communalism. Whether it is 'true' religion or otherwise is another matter. Bipan Chandra has argued in his book, *Communalism in Modern India*, that 'religion as such is not responsible for communalism nor does secularism require struggle against religion…' (Chandra 1984: 327). A lot of water has flowed since the time Chandra wrote it. The experience of the last few years shows quite the contrary. The enormity of the problem is illustrated by the *Ghar Wapsi* movement, 'love jehad', the beef ban, agitations for the banning of books and movies, and the communalization of diverse political and social activities.

5

AN INCREASINGLY UNSECULAR SOCIETY

We have just enough religion to make us hate, but not enough to make us love one another.

— Jonathan Swift

For a country to be secular, it is not enough that its Constitution is secular and its government respects all religions alike, or is equidistant from all religions, or does not give the status of a State religion to any one religion. It is equally necessary that its society is secular and its individual citizens are secular. In this chapter, we shall look at some of these aspects. They are:

- Secularism in action;
- Recommendations of three committees or commissions which have looked into the problems of Muslims—India's largest religious minority—namely, the Gopal Singh Committee, the Ranganath Misra Commission, and the Rajinder Sachar Committee;
- The highly disturbing manifestations of alienation; and
- Where are we headed?

Secularism in Action

The experience so far has shown that secularism will succeed only by the creation of a secular society. The events since the BJP's coming to power at the Centre in May 2014 have particularly brought out the importance of this statement.

Even as far back as 1947, Nehru was conscious of the fact that there was a feeling in the country that the central government was following a policy of appeasement towards Muslims. In his letter to chief ministers dated 15 October 1947, he had refuted this charge as:

> ...complete nonsense. There is no question of weakness or appeasement. *We have a Muslim minority who are so large in numbers that they cannot, even if they want to, go anywhere else. They have got to live in India...We must give them security and the rights of citizens in a democratic state. If we fail to do so, we shall have a festering sore which will eventually poison the whole body politic and probably destroy it.* (Guha 2010: 329)

Throughout his tenure as prime minister, Nehru was deeply concerned about the position of minority groups in India which he felt was deteriorating. He referred to this a number of times in his fortnightly letters to the chief ministers. In one such letter, dated 20 September 1953, Nehru wrote:

> I want to share with you a certain apprehension that is growing within me. I feel that in many ways the position relating to minority groups in India is deteriorating... In the Services, generally speaking the representation of the minority communities is lessening. In some cases, it is very poor indeed...In our Defence Services, there are hardly any Muslims left. In the vast Central Secretariat of India, there are very few Muslims. Probably the position is somewhat better in the provinces, but not much more so...This applies to Christians and others also...We have always to remember India as a composite country, composite in many ways, in religion, in customs, in languages, in many ways of life, etc. (Gopal and Iyengar, Vol. I, 2003: 187–88)

In another letter to the chief ministers, dated 20 November 1953, Nehru once again invited their attention to the question of minority communities in the services. He wrote:

> This matter has been causing me grave concern, because, from such partial data as reaches me, I get the impression that, for all practical purposes, the doors of recruitment to minorities for our all-India or state services are largely closed. They are, of course, not closed by any rule or order of government. But in effect that appears to be the case, whether it is the Army, the administrative services, the police, or the many lower services right down to the villages... I think that it would be desirable to collect some data... We cannot tackle the problem unless we know what the problem is. (J.N.M.F., Vol. 24, 1999: 345)

In Appendix 4, I have given the position regarding the employment of Muslims in Uttar Pradesh before Partition. It can be seen therefrom that, in most state services, the Muslim representation was quite substantial and as it also was in the armed forces. It is true that a large number of these Muslims migrated to Pakistan. However, against the background of the pre-Partition period, the substantial reduction in the representation of Muslims in the services and armed forces was particularly striking and was a cause for concern. And this trend has continued all through the years since Independence. It is worth recalling that, when the Rajinder Sachar Committee tried to collect information regarding Muslims in armed forces during the UPA regime, it was resisted by the armed forces as also by the Ministry of Defence on the grounds that it was likely to undermine communal harmony. It is difficult to agree with this stand. No corrective action can be taken unless the factual position on a subject is known.

> Since India is a multi-religious—avowedly secular—country, education had to be kept strictly separate from religion, at least in the State-funded institutions. However, during the last sixty-eight [now sixty-nine] years since Independence, various political parties in power have tried to tamper with this policy. As minister for human resource development during the NDA coalition government of 1998–2004, Murli Manohar Joshi played a key role in the government's manifest attempts to legitimize a saffron version of Indian citizenship: for instance, changing the content

and orientation of school textbooks and enhancing the role of the Saraswati Shishu Mandirs (primary schools) and Saraswati Vidya Mandirs (secondary schools) run by the RSS. (Jeffery 2006: Footnote 3, p. 121)

Subrata Mitra, in his essay, 'The NDA and the Politics of Minorities in India', wrote that, on a sensitive issue such as school prayers, the BJP-led coalition in Uttar Pradesh sought to make the singing of *Vande Mataram* (India's national song) and *Saraswati Vandana* (a Hindu hymn) compulsory in government schools. The songs were considered by the Muslim ulema (clerics) to be idolatrous, and a fatwa (edict) was issued for Muslim parents to withdraw their children from the schools if the state government persisted in its effort. Then, a crucial component of the state's coalition, the Loktantrik Congress party, expressed reservations about forcing students to recite a hymn linked to Hindu nationalism. The then NDA government's home minister L.K. Advani, also took a stand against compulsion.

Prescribing textbooks with a particular slant is not something new or of recent origin. In his letter dated 29 September 1951, to Sampurnanand, governor of UP, Nehru had enclosed a cutting from *The National Herald* which reproduced some sentences found in a Hindi textbook prescribed for VIII Standard students. One sentence read: '*Mere mandir mein Hari rehta, tere masjid mein shaitan*' (God lives in my temple, Satan lives in your mosque). Nehru wrote that 'surely these are hardly suitable for a textbook or for any book. (Godbole 2014a: 144)

V.K. Sinha, in his book, *Secularism in India*, drew attention to the lessons prescribed in a textbook on Indian history for III Standard students in Andhra Pradesh schools with total emphasis only on non-Muslim writings, heroes and characters: Ramayana, Mahabharata, Buddha, Asoka the Great, Vikramaditya, Harsha, Pulakesin II, Pratapa Rudra, Padmini of Chittor, Krishna Deva Raya, Shivaji, Jhansi Lakshmi Bai and Mahatma Gandhi. (Sinha 1968: 98)

Way back in 1996, NCERT [National Council of Educational Research and Training] conducted an evaluation of school textbooks, including those prescribed for the Vidya Bharati schools in the country. It made the alarming discovery that many of the Vidya Bharati textbooks were designed to promote communalism and religious fanaticism in the name of inculcating knowledge of Indian culture in the young generation. (Kuruvachira 2008: 150)

Another contentious issue was a programme which, according to the Left, was intended to rewrite textbooks in a manner so as to glorify Hindu heroes over Muslim rulers. According to T. Wright (2001: 4): 'At the Centre, this took the form of the government packing the governing board of the Indian Council of Historical Research (ICHR) and withdrawing some already written textbooks from publication. However, strident criticism at the state education ministers' conference compelled HRD [Human Resource Development] Minister Murli Manohar Joshi to back down.' In another case, an NDA government ally, M. Karunanidhi, chief minister of Tamil Nadu, objected to the inclusion of material from the Vedas and Upanishads in school curricula, 'which, to his party, smelled of Northern imposition on the South'. (Adeney 2005: 85–86)

Subrata Mitra, in the above book, pointed out that the approaching 1998 general election generated new tactical thinking within the BJP. 'For instance, *one of them concerned circulating the Koran in Sanskrit.*'... The appropriation of the Congress slogan of brotherhood of Hindus and Muslims was further reinforced with a 'guarantee to every Muslim' by Advani of 'security, justice, equality and full freedom of faith and worship'. Going all out to woo the community in the last lap of the party's campaign, he said, 'No BJP government will tolerate any dilution of this guarantee'...This had a follow-up in a long interview to a private television channel by Vajpayee who said that, 'All Muslims should be able to live with self-respect and honour.' (Adeney 2005: 81)

It can be seen how far the BJP, after coming to power at the Centre in 2014, has come from these pronouncements.

John Zavos, in his essay, 'The Shapes of Hindu Nationalism' stated:

In the tribal areas of states such as, Madhya Pradesh and Orissa, the Sangh affiliate, Vanavasi Kalyan Parishad, has been increasingly active, reshaping tribal religious practices within a Hindu framework...In the arena of education, the Sangh now has a network of schools, many run by the Vidya Bharati Akhil Bharatiya Shiksha Sansthan. The Vidya Bharati system supervises over 18,000 schools across India, with 1.8 million students and 80,000 teachers focusing on Sanskrit, moral and spiritual education, yoga and physical development...It is no coincidence that one of the most significant areas of policy development during the NDA's tenure has been in the area of education. From the National Council for Educational Research and Training (NCERT) to the Indian Council of Historical Research (ICHR), Hindu nationalist approaches have been vigorously promoted, further reshaping ideas about Indian history and society in a wide range of schools, colleges and universities. (Adeney 2005: 53)

Marie Lall, in her essay, 'Indian Education Policy under the NDA Government', is another strident critique of intervention by the RSS in the education sector. She stated: 'The first Saraswati Shishu Mandir was established in 1952 by some RSS members, whose aim was to contribute to "nation building" through education. There are now more than 50 states and regional committees affiliated to Vidya Bharati, the largest voluntary association in the country. These coordinate around 13,000 institutions with 74,000 teachers and 1.7 million students. The expansion of the network of RSS schools was a major pillar in this strategy, essentially going against the traditional separation of education and religion. Funds for this expansion have been collected through various means, including charities operating in the West. In fact, according to a recent report published by *Awaaz*, a London-based secular network, almost a quarter of Sewa International's Earthquake Relief Fund, raised from the British public to help Gujarat have been used to build RSS schools. (Adeney 2005: 164)

Niraja Jayal and Pratap Bhanu Mehta have written about how secularism has been eroded over the years. Shortly after her return to power in 1980, Indira Gandhi tended to exploit communal sentiments for political ends: on the one hand, she granted the Muslim University of Aligarh an autonomous status as representing a minority (Graff 1990), and on the other, she made many visits to temples and, in 1983, allowed one of her lieutenants, C.M. Stephen, to state that the political culture of the Congress was 'on the same wavelength' as Hindu culture. The communalization of politics took a new turn under Rajiv Gandhi's government. He, in fact, attempted to balance the ruling made in the Shah Bano affair by deciding to remove the seals from the Ayodhya mosque. (Jayal and Mehta 2010: 212)

After the NDA came to power, one of the first decisions Vajpayee made was to appoint six new governors, five of whom were BJP members. There was nothing unusual in this, considering the series of appointments made by the Congress party while in power. However, it was disturbing to see that the then RSS *sarsanghachalak*, Rajendra Singh, formally addressed top bureaucrats of the UP government in Lucknow. This was a clear attempt to dilute the ostensible civil service political neutrality. In another significant development, ICHR suspended the publication of two volumes of its series titled, *Towards Freedom* by Sumit Sarkar and K.N. Panikkar.

> There is really very little difference between the Congress, which claims to be secular, and parties like the Sena or the BJP. A far cry from the days of Nehru and Gandhi, as Bipan Chandra put it: 'Nehru, for example, would make no compromise with communalism, whatever the electoral consequences. "So far as I am concerned", he was to declare in 1954, "I am prepared to lose every election in India but to give no quarter to communalism or casteism".' (Menon 2012: 237–38)

I have stated elsewhere that the socio-economic and political condition of Muslims has deteriorated over the years. I have given in Appendix IV the figures of representation of Muslims in various services in the Uttar Pradesh government, before Partition. Since then, there has been a sharp decline in their representation, whether at the state level or the Centre. This has been highlighted in a number of important reports, such as the Rajinder Sachar Committee Report in 2006 and the Ranganath Misra Commission Report in 2007. I have referred later in this chapter to the observations of Pranay Gupte, based on the writing of M.J. Akbar, that the representation of Muslims in the private sector is even worse than it is in the government.

> Soumya Shankar, in her article, 'The Takeover: How the Modi Government Has Filled Key Positions in 14 Institutions', wrote that persons close to the BJP or the RSS have been appointed in a number of institutions. These include, among others, the Film and Television Institute of India; Indian Institute of Advanced Study, Shimla; IIT Bombay; IIM Ahmedabad; NCERT, ICHR, ICCR (*Indian Council for Cultural Relations*); IGNCA (Indira Gandhi National Centre for the Arts), and so on. (*The Radical Humanist*, September 2015: 17–19)

This kind of presentation does not really impress me since such appointments—commonly known as the 'spoils system'—are common not only in the governments formed by other political parties in India but also in Western democracies. All that has happened is that persons belonging to the ideology of the ruling party and its affiliate organizations have been appointed in these posts. It is necessary to note that institutions like IGNCA and The Nehru Memorial Museum & Library have been the preserves of the Gandhi–Nehru family all these years. A number of other institutions were also headed by persons closer to the Congress and the leftist ideologies. This is a part of the democratic process and it is high time we got used to it.

The increasing Muslim population has been causing unjustified anxiety to Hindu rightist organizations. In view of the sensitivities of the subject for overall communal harmony, the government of India had made it a point not to publish religion-based cross classification of population, though the National Minorities Commission had asked for this data to be published. For the first time in 2005, data pertaining to the 2001 population census, classified religion-wise, was released by the government, based on the decision taken when the NDA was in power.

The Gopal Singh Committee Report

This committee on the conditions of Muslims, appointed by the government of India on 10 May 1980, submitted its interim report on 31 January 1981, and the second report on 14 June 1983. The reports highlighted a number of features. Some significant findings of the committee were as follows: The enrolment of students at the elementary school stage was only 12.39 per cent. The school drop-out rate at the primary stage was as high as 66 per cent. The percentage of Muslim students in engineering and medical colleges was only 3.41 and 3.44, respectively. The registration of Muslims in employment exchanges was only 6.77 per cent. Muslim representation in public sector undertakings was 10.85 per cent and in private sector enterprises, 8.16 per cent. The representation in government services was only 4.5 per cent in Class I and II and 6 per cent in Class III and IV. There was very poor representation of minorities (particularly Muslims) in the judiciary. There was substantial under-representation of minorities in the state police services, especially in the riot-prone districts and the armed forces. (Puniyani 2003: 145)

According to Mushirul Hasan, the Gopal Singh Committee Report found that a large number of Muslims lived in rural areas, mostly as landless labourers, small and marginal farmers, artisans, craftsmen and shopkeepers. He found that more than half of the urban Muslim population—approximately 35 million out of nearly 76 million—lived below the poverty line. The rest were self-employed. He also discovered that fewer urban Muslims worked for a regular wage or salary than did the members of other religious groups. He has underlined the limited access of Muslims to government-sponsored welfare projects and their small share in private/public employment. (Hasan 2008: 192, Footnote 19)

The Committee recommended that government schools should be opened in predominantly Muslim localities. Fees of colleges and technical institutions should be regulated in accordance with the income of parents in predominantly Muslim areas. Urdu should be declared as the second official language where there is a large concentration of Urdu-speaking people. Adult education facilities and night schools be opened in every Muslim *mohalla* (locality) and Muslims be appointed as teachers. To secure better representation in all-India services and state services, coaching institutions in Muslim areas should be opened. All recruitment boards responsible for recruitment to the Central as well as state level services should have minority representation of not less than 20 per cent. Provincial armed constabulary (PAC) should be made more broad-based and cosmopolitan with a sufficient number of Muslims and other minorities recruited in it. (Puniyani 2003: 146)

The Ranganath Misra Commission Recommendations

On 29 October 2004, the government of India set up a national commission for the socially and economically backward sections among the religious and linguistic minorities. However, the chairman and members were appointed only on 15 March 2005. The commission was headed by Justice Ranganath Misra, former chief justice of the Supreme Court, Dr Tahir Mahmood, former chairperson, National Minorities Commission, and Dr Anil Wilson, principal, St Stephen's College, Delhi, among others. The terms of reference of the commission were: to suggest criteria for the identification of socially and economically backward sections among religious and linguistic minorities; to recommend measures for the welfare of socially and economically backward sections among religious and linguistic minorities, including reservation in education and government employment; and to suggest the necessary constitutional, legal and administrative modalities required for the implementation of their recommendations.

Among the important findings and recommendations of the commission were the following:

- Ideally, there should be no distinction on the basis of caste, religion or class. *There should be a single list of socially and economically backward, including religious and linguistic minorities, based on common criteria. The existing lists prepared on the basis of backwardness of caste or class should cease to exist after the list of socially and economically backward is ready.* The new list of socially and economically backward has necessarily to be family-/household-based. It should be all inclusive and based on socio-economic backwardness.
- Education is crucial for development and enhancement of social and economic status. Equally important is the quality of education.

- The drop-out rate of Muslims is higher at the middle and secondary level.
- *The criterion for reservation should be socio-economic backwardness and not religion or caste.*
- The commission's recommendations should apply to all religious minorities—large or small—including the Hindus in the Union Territory of Lakshadweep and the states of J&K, Meghalaya, Mizoram, Nagaland and Punjab.
- *In matters of criteria for identifying backward classes there should be absolutely no discrimination whatsoever between the majority community and the minorities. The criteria now applied for this purpose to the majority community must be unreservedly applied also to all the minorities.*
- All those classes, sections and groups among the minorities should be treated as backward whose counterparts in the majority community are regarded as backward under the present scheme of things.
- All those classes, sections and groups among the various minorities as are generally regarded as 'inferior' within the social strata and societal system of those communities—whether called 'zat' or known by any other synonymous expression—should be treated as backward.
- All those social and vocational groups among the minorities who, but for their religious identity, would have been covered by the present net of scheduled castes should be unquestionably treated as socially backward, irrespective of whether the religion of those other communities recognizes the caste system or not.
- Those groups among minorities whose counterparts in the majority community are at present covered by the net of scheduled tribes should also be included in that net; and also, more specifically, members of the minority communities living in any tribal area from pre-Independence days should be so included irrespective of their ethnic characteristics.
- At least 15 per cent seats in all non-minority educational institutions should be earmarked by law for the minorities and, of this, 10 per cent should be reserved for Muslims and the remaining 5 per cent for other minorities.

- As in the case with SCs and STs, those minority community candidates who can compete with others and secure admission on their own merit shall not be included in these 15 per cent earmarked seats.
- Select institutions in the country, like the Aligarh Muslim University and the Jamia Millia Islamia, should be legally given a special responsibility to promote education at all levels to Muslim students by taking all possible steps for this purpose. At least one such institution should be selected for this purpose in each of those states and UTs (Union Territories) which has a substantial Muslim population.
- All schools and colleges run by Muslims should be provided with enhanced aid and other logistic facilities adequate enough to raise their standard.
- The Madarsa Modernization Scheme of the government should be suitably revised, strengthened and provided with more funds so that it can provide finances and necessary paraphernalia either (a) for the provision of modern education up to Standard X within those madarsas themselves which are at present imparting only religious education or, alternatively, (b) to enable the students of such madarsas to receive such education simultaneously in the general schools in their neighbourhood. And,
- The rules and processes of the central Wakf council should be revised in such a way that its main responsibility should be educational development of Muslims. For this purpose, the council may be legally authorized to collect a special 5 per cent educational levy from all Wakfs, and (ii) to sanction utilization of Wakf lands for establishing educational institutions, polytechnics, libraries and hostels. (GOI 2007a: 145, 147–51)

These are very thoughtful recommendations which go a long way towards addressing the basic issues pertaining to the deprivation of the minorities in general, and the Muslims in particular. Especially, the recommendation of the commission that categorization as backward must be based entirely on socio-economic criteria and should not be related to either religion, caste or community is noteworthy. The commission categorically recommended that the Constitution (Scheduled Castes) Order, 1950, which originally restricted the scheduled caste net to Hindus and later opened it to Sikhs and Buddhists, thus still excluding from its purview Muslims, Christians, Jains and Parsees, and other religions, should be wholly deleted by appropriate action so as to completely delink the scheduled caste status from religion. Addressing this single issue—as recommended by the commission—would be most crucial in dealing with the problems of minorities. This is particularly relevant in view of the fact that the Constitution (Scheduled Castes) Order, 1950, which had originally declared that no non-Hindu could be a scheduled caste, was later amended to cover Sikhs and Buddhists. As the commission has observed, this was 'wholly repugnant to the letter and spirit of the Constitution'. I have separately recommended that the Constitution should be amended to delete the word 'propagate' from Article 25 (1). If this suggestion is accepted and implemented, there need be no worries that acceptance of the Misra Commission recommendations would lead to uninhibited conversion of persons from Hindu religion to any other religion. Like the recommendations by most of the important commissions of inquiry, this report too has remained without any action being taken and has been consigned to archives. If secularism is to be implemented in the true sense, recommendations, such as those of the Ranganath Misra Commission and the Rajinder Sachar Committee (referred to hereafter) must be resurrected and given serious consideration.

The Rajinder Sachar Committee Recommendations

Justice Sachar, in his report on the social, economic and educational status of Muslims (2005) stated:

> Since the growth of the Muslim population has been above average and is likely to remain so for some time, the question often asked is, whether and if so, when, will the Muslim population become the largest group?... in order to project the share of the Muslim population, projections for the total population are required. Earlier projections assumed that Muslims would reach replacement level fertility ten years later than other communities. *The projections further showed that the share of the Muslim population in India would rise somewhat to just below 19 per cent... and then stabilize*

*at that level. If it should take a longer time for the gap to close, the share of the Muslim population would be correspondingly higher... Broadly, one could say that the Muslim population share is expected to rise from the current level but not expected to be much above 20 per cent by the end of the century...*Contrary to common perceptions, there is a substantial demand for fertility regulation and for modern contraception among Muslims. This calls for the programme to provide better choices to couples. (GOI 2006: 45–47)

According to the essay by P.M. Kulkarni on the demographic profile of Muslims in India, *the population share of the Muslims will stabilize at less than 20 per cent by the end of the century.* Fertility rates among Muslims are higher than average but are declining and converging towards the average. The estimates show that the total fertility rates (TFR) among Muslims declined from about 4.3 to 3.6 in the 1990s, a reduction of about 0.7 points. During the same period, the TFR for the population as a whole declined from about 3.4 to 2.9, a reduction of nearly 0.5 points. *The decline in fertility among Muslims was, therefore, more than average.* Fertility among Muslims varies with socio-economic characteristics, and there are significant inter-regional variations. For example, fertility rates among Muslims in states like Kerala, Tamil Nadu, Karnataka, Jammu and Kashmir and Andhra Pradesh, are much lower than the fertility rates in some of the northern parts of the country for virtually all socio-religions communities. In fact, generally, the gap between average fertility and fertility rates among Muslims is also narrower in these states. The reasons are many. Studies suggest that fertility rates decline with an increase in education, income, and availability of health services. A mix of these factors must be in operation in these states. The main point is that, in states where fertility rates have declined rapidly, the Muslim population has also experienced a relatively faster decline although their fertility rates continue to be somewhat higher than average even in those regions. It has also been seen that Muslims use family planning methods, and the contraception prevalence is about 10 percentage points lower than average. Once again, studies show that differences in education are an important cause of differences in the use of family planning methods. (Basant and Shariff 2010: 7)

A significant finding of the Sachar Committee was that only about 4 per cent of all Muslim students of the school-going age group are enrolled in madarsas. At the all-India level, this works out to about 3 per cent of all Muslim children of school-going age. NCERT data indicate a somewhat lower level of 2.3 per cent of Muslim children aged 17–19 years who study in madarsas. The proportions are higher in rural areas and among males. (GOI 2006: 85)

It is important to take note of these findings as there is a widespread misconception that madarsas are proliferating in the country and spreading fundamentalist and conservative feelings among Muslim children.

Another observation of the Sachar Committee was that, compared to the Muslim majority area, the areas with fewer Muslims had better roads, sewage and drainage, and water supply facilities.(GOI 2006: 149)

This is significant in view of the general ghettoization of Muslims in various urban areas. Lack of infrastructure facilities and of even basic amenities in such areas has been a grievance of Muslim residents for a long time, leading to a feeling of alienation among them.

The Sachar Committee also invited attention to the fact that the share of Muslims in the total funds disbursed by the National Backward Classes Finance & Development Corporation, set up in January 1992, is low: only Rs 23 crores out of Rs 247 crores has been disbursed to Muslim OBCs [Other Backward Classes], *though they constitute 40.7 per cent of the total Muslim population and 15.7 per cent of the total OBC population of the country.* The committee has ascribed this to the lack of Muslim participation in political processes and governance. (GOI 2006: 186–87, 213)

The Sachar Committee stated that, while there is considerable variation in the conditions of Muslims across states, the community exhibits deficits and deprivation in practically all dimensions of development. *An important recommendation made by the committee is to constitute an Equal Opportunity Commission (EOC)* to look into the grievances of the deprived groups. The committee has cited the example of such a policy tool namely, Britain's Race Relations Act, 1976. The committee has also suggested that a carefully conceived 'nomination' procedure should be worked out to increase inclusiveness in governance. (GOI 2006: 240–41)

Another important recommendation of the committee is that a process of evaluating the contents of school textbooks needs to be initiated and institutionalized. In this context, the committee has highlighted that Muslims have the largest percentage share of children in the age group of less than 10 years with 27 per cent falling in this range as compared to the 23 per cent for the country as a whole. However, the current enrolment and continuation rates at the elementary level (though picking up in recent years) are the lowest for the Muslims. The committee has suggested the following:

- Given the fact that a substantial proportion of households in urban settlements lives in one-room accommodation, it is absolutely necessary to create local community study centres for students where they can spend a few hours to concentrate on their studies.
- High-quality government schools should be set up in all areas of Muslim concentration.
- Exclusive schools for girls should be set up, particularly for the 9–12 Standards. This would facilitate a higher participation of Muslim girls in school education. In co-education schools, more women teachers need to be appointed.
- The availability of primary education in one's mother tongue is constitutionally provided for. There is an urgent need to undertake appropriate mapping of the Urdu-speaking population and to provide primary education in Urdu in areas where an Urdu-speaking population is concentrated.
- Working out mechanisms whereby madarsas can be linked with a higher secondary school board so that students wanting to shift to a regular/mainstream education can do so after having passed from a madarsa. (GOI 2006: 244, 248)

The perceptions of common Muslims on their plight, as brought out in the report of the Sachar Committee, are indeed disturbing. The committee stated:

Apparently, the social, cultural and public interactive spaces in India can be very daunting for Indian Muslims...They carry a double burden of being labeled as 'anti-national' and as being 'appeased' at the same time. While Muslims need to prove on a daily basis that they are not 'anti-national' and 'terrorists', *it is not recognized that the alleged 'appeasement' has not resulted in the desired level of socio-economic development of the community.* The committee has brought out that Muslim identity affects everyday living in a variety of ways that range from being unable to rent/buy a house to accessing good schools for their children. In general, Muslims complained to the committee that they are constantly looked upon with a great degree of suspicion, not only by certain sections of society but also by public institutions and governance structures. This has a depressing effect on their psyche. Some women who interacted with the committee informed that, in corporate offices, hijab-wearing Muslim women were finding it increasingly difficult to find jobs. Inadequate representation of Muslims in government jobs, police and paramilitary forces is another major grievance of Muslims. In most of the government departments and public sector undertakings, the share of Muslim workers does not exceed 5 per cent. Fearing for their security, Muslims are increasingly resorting to living in ghettos across the country. This is more pronounced in communally sensitive towns and cities. It was suggested to the Sachar Committee that Muslims living together in concentrated pockets has made them easy targets for neglect by municipal and government authorities. From poor civic amenities in Muslim localities, non-representation in positions of political power and the bureaucracy, to police atrocities committed against them—*the perception of being discriminated against is overpowering amongst a wide cross section of Muslims, particularly among the youth.*

Though the Constitution casts a responsibility on the State to provide education to minorities in their mother tongue at the primary stage, Muslims have a legitimate grievance that there are very few Urdu-medium schools in Muslim localities. Lack of municipal and government primary schools has also forced them to send their children to madarsas.

The Sachar Committee found that Muslims face fairly high levels of poverty. Their conditions on the whole are only slightly better than those of scheduled castes (SCs) and scheduled tribes (STs). While there are variations in the conditions of Muslims across states, the situation of the community in urban areas seems to be particularly bad in relative terms in almost all states except Kerala, Assam, Tamil Nadu, Odisha, Himachal Pradesh and Punjab. Their relative position in rural areas is somewhat better but, here again, in most states, poverty levels among Muslims are higher than in all socio-religious communities, except SCs and STs.

Some of the important recommendations of the Sachar Committee culled out above show that serious thought needs to be given to implementing them expeditiously. They set at rest some of the misconceptions pertaining to the excessively high rate of growth of the Muslim population and to its overtaking the percentage of Hindus in the future.

> For example, [the then] Assam Chief Minister Tarun Gogoi, in a television interview, said, 'You see this [high fertility] is because of low literacy. Most of the Muslims are illiterate. Every family has six, seven, eight, nine, ten members'. Narendra Modi, as chief minister of Gujarat, had evocatively stated, *'Hum do, hamare do, woh paanch, unke pachchis'* (We are two and have two children; they are five and have twenty-five children.) (*Outlook* 24 September 2012: 14)

The VHP has appealed to Muslims to undergo an 'internal reform' for controlling their population growth and follow family planning, 'like other communities in India'. (*IE* 7 September 2015: 7)

BJP's firebrand leader and Gorakhpur MP, Yogi Adityanath, declared that the rise in the Muslim population in the past decade 'is an alarming and dangerous situation for the country'. (*IE* 27 August 2015: 4)

The Sachar Committee Report showed that the Muslim population is expected to stabilize at around 20 per cent of the total and therefore, any such exaggerated fears created deliberately, needed to be given up. By doing so, the prescriptions advocated by some rightist elements that Hindus must start producing four to five children in each family will be jettisoned. Unfortunately, such have been the prejudices in certain sections of society against Muslims that the Sachar Committee Report was largely neglected, not only by Parliament and state legislatures, but also by the media and society at large. As I have urged elsewhere in this book, it will be counter-productive to neglect the socio-economic development of Muslims any longer.

The myth of Muslim population growth has also been brought out by Abusaleh Shariff:

> Muslims have shown a 50 per cent higher decline in the growth rate than Hindus. This positive higher decline of Muslims has been occurring since 1981 and is expected to continue in a manner so that, soon, the Muslim growth rate will be similar to that of the Hindus. The fast pace of decline in Muslims' fertility rate is occurring while they have a much lower mean child-bearing age which, in itself, is evidence that the falling Muslim fertility is choice-based and irreversible in the near future. (*IE* 2 September 2015: 8)

It is not surprising that several prominent Muslim leaders, such as Asaduddin Owaisi, have been expounding the need for Muslims to form a new all-India political party of their own to air their grievances. Syed Ahmed Bukhari has charged that 'the Congress is no longer a secular party.' He has threatened a mass campaign to agitate the grievances of Muslims. (*Tehelka* 8 November 2008: 3).

There are increasing demands for reservations for Muslims in government jobs and institutions of higher learning on the basis of religion. There are also demands that the representation of Muslims in the legislatures should at least be equal to their proportion in the total population (14.2 per cent). These grievances and demands of Muslims are no different from those in the pre-Partition days. The provisions and safeguards embedded in the Constitution do not seem to have made any difference.

The National Crime Records Bureau data show that, as against the Muslim population of 14 per cent as per the 2011 census, Muslims make up for over 21 per cent of all under-trials lodged in jails. In some states with a significant Muslim population, the ratio of percentage of Muslim under-trials in jails to that of the Muslim population is 2:1. (*IE* 5 October 2015: 5)

The data compiled by the government of Maharashtra for the year 2014–15 show that the percentage of minority students in technical and professional courses ranges from 2.1 per cent to 15.3 per cent. The poor representation of minorities is also reflected in overall figures for India, where they account for just 6.6 per cent of the total enrolment in professional courses for 2014–15. (*IE* 19 August 2015: 3)

Lt. General (retd) Zameer Uddin Shah, vice-chancellor of Aligarh Muslim University, has rightly said that Muslims lagged behind in the development race because they kept their women enslaved. 'You have not utilized half of your population. Women remained enslaved. They remained inside home. Muslims have no one else to blame. You enslave women and the result is you are enslaved...Except Turkey and Iran, women remained enslaved in the Muslim world. That is the reason they are backward.' (*IE* 5 October 2015: 6)

This is also brought out by the McKinsey Global Institute Report, 'The Power of Parity: Advancing Women's Equality in India', which shows poor levels of gender parity in India. India's global Gender Parity Score or GPS is 0.48, whereas a score of 1 would be ideal. India's score represents an 'extremely high' level of gender inequality, which compares poorly with 0.71 for Western Europe and 0.74 for North America and Oceania. The report highlights that 'India could boost its GDP by $0.7 trillion in 2025, the largest relative boost of all 10 regions analysed by McKinsey Global. This translates into a 1.4 per cent per year incremental GDP growth for India. About 70 per cent of the GDP increase can happen by raising India's female labour force participation rate by 10 percentage points (*IE* 4 November 2015: 9)

International Monetary Fund Managing Director, Christine Lagarde, had made the same point earlier and stated that India's GDP can expand by 27 per cent if the number of female workers increases to the same level as that of men. (*IE* 7 September 2015: 13)

According to the data released by the census office in June 2016, a massive 11.61 crore Muslims, who make up 67.42 per cent of the

17.22 crore Muslim community, have been listed as non-workers.[1] (*IE* 8 June 2016: 9)

This underlines the importance of doing everything possible to bring Muslims into the mainstream of society and addressing the gender justice and equality issues.

> The UNDP [The United Nations Development Programme], in its Gender Inequality Index for 2014 has ranked India at 132 out of 155 countries. The Human Development Report (HDR) 2015 has also highlighted that on the labour force participation rate for women, Bangladesh is at 57 per cent while India is at 27 per cent. (*IE* 15 December 2015: 7)

The Jefferys, in an article on education in the social and cultural reproductions of Muslims in UP, pointed out that most non-state educational institutions exclude the poor, including most Muslims, rural and urban. They stated:

> Girls are additionally disadvantaged, and Muslim girls even more so. In the UP education sector, gender differentials in school attendance, literacy and educational attainment remain wide… General problems of access to education are exacerbated for Muslim girls because schools are unlikely to be located in Muslim-dominated villages or mohallas. In education, as in other fields, there is a general problem of recruiting and retaining women for rural posts, whether in the government or private sector… Muslim girls were all but absent even in the primary schools in our research villages… However strongly Muslim parents in UP want to provide for their children's education, most have inadequate opportunities to do so. (Hasan 2007: 69–70)

Reference must also be made to a fatwa issued by a cleric asking Muslims not to administer polio drops to their children in Gujarat. The Urdu monthly, *Tameer-e-Hayat*, published from Lucknow, had carried an article in September 2006 issue which questioned the

---

[1] Non-workers are defined as those who do not participate in any economic activity—paid or unpaid, household duties, or cultivation.

effectiveness of polio vaccine and which said it caused infertility. (*IE* 6 November 2015: 9)

Arun Shourie's erudite book on fatwas comprehensively brings out how they are creating a climate against social reforms, education and emancipation of women, and so on. Shourie wrote:

> The ulema have fought hard and long against what most today would consider education. For them, religious education must take priority over modern, technical education…The education of women, in particular their being awakened to new values, their being trained for new professions, their being awakened to their rights—all this is anathema; it is held to be injurious to them, in fact, it is declared to be the way to disrupting society and undermining Islam…[*The fatawa-i-Rahimiyyah* says] it is not permissible to send girls to schools and colleges for acquiring higher education and academic degrees. For there is more harm than benefit in it. (Shourie 1995: 501, 512)
>
> Another religious minority, the Christians, is facing increasing opposition and violence, primarily due to their attempts at conversion of people to Christianity. This has resulted in damage to several churches and injury to some priests and nuns. It is interesting to note that the Supreme Court has asked the Orissa government to be 'generous enough' and relook at its 'secular' policy preventing governments from giving any compensation to any place of worship. (*IE* 23 October 2008).

In the recent past, the Centre had to send advisories from the Ministry of Home Affairs to the governments of Odisha, Karnataka and Kerala to take effective steps to quell violence against Christians and to maintain law and order in the state. However, these can carry weight only if the Centre is able to take the next step of imposition of President's rule under Article 356, if the advice is not heeded by the states. Looking to the composition of the Lok Sabha and the Rajya Sabha, it is certain that the government will find it difficult to get support for any such action.

The Highly Disturbing Manifestations of Alienation

Segregation is not confined only to the lower strata of these communities. As news reports point out from time to time, even well-off Muslim families and public figures find it difficult to get suitable accommodation in metropolitan cities like Mumbai, Pune and Bengaluru. Shabana Azmi has claimed that she and her husband Javed Akhtar could not buy a flat in Mumbai because they were Muslims. She said that Saif Ali Khan had also faced similar prejudice. (*Outlook* 22 September 2008: 88)

In Pune, a housing society in a well-off locality refused permission to one of its members to sell his flat to a Muslim. During the 1993 riots in Mumbai, members of some communal parties were reported to have gone from one building to another to identify and target Muslim residents in the buildings. According to a news report, home-owners in the National Capital Region are seen to be turning away Dalits and Muslims.

Meena Menon has underlined that, 'In Mumbai, it is difficult for Muslims to buy houses…or get houses on rent; housing societies too are known to refuse Muslims flats…Our inclusive philosophy has been narrowed down to such a level of discrimination and things seem to be getting worse…Inherently, there was no bias against Muslims…' (Menon 2012: 237)

> A.G. Noorani, in his article, 'A Home for Equality', has urged that, in the absence of effective legislation against discrimination, courts should step in. He has cited shocking recent cases. Zeeshan Ali Khan, a 22-year-old MBA, was denied a job by a Mumbai firm because he was a Muslim. A 25-year-old public relations professional, Misbah Nayeem Quadir, employed by a consultancy firm, was forced to vacate a flat in Mumbai because she was a Muslim. She was told, 'The building does not allow Muslim tenants in the building.' Things are no different in Delhi. Muslims find it difficult to find a place to rent or buy in up-scale localities…There has been a sharp increase in this kind of discrimination in the last 30-odd years. (*IE* 10 September 2015: 10).

This is borne out once again by the study made by Saugato Datta and Vikram Pathania in the National Capital Region titled

'When the landlord doesn't call back' which shows why the search for a house is longer and more arduous for a Muslim tenant. (*IE* 4 June 2016: 11)

Against this background, it is a welcome development that the government of India proposes to include in the rules under the Real Estate (Regulation and Development) Act, 2016 specific provisions to check bias against religion, sexual orientation and diet. (*IE* 12 June 2016: 1)

Unfortunately, right since Independence, political parties have looked at Muslims as a vote bank. This has meant pandering to the unjustified demands of fundamentalist Muslims, but not addressing their socio-economic problems. M.J. Akbar in his book, *India: The Siege Within*, refers to a survey made of some of India's top private sector companies. The survey found, for example, that in Pond's India Limited, only one of the corporation's 115 senior executives was a Muslim; at DCM [Delhi Cloth Mills], the figure was two out of 987; at Brooke Bond, fourteen out of 673; at ITC [India Tobacco Company], seventeen out of 966; at JK Synthetics, five out of 536; at Ambalal Sarabhai, five out of 628. (Gupte 1989: 214)

Pranay Gupte wrote:

'The ordinary Muslim has been left out of India's economic and political mainstream,' George Fernandes, one of India's leading labour leaders and a former member of the cabinet told me, 'And he faces a bleak future. Muslims don't get ordinary jobs so easily. The Muslim is not wanted in the armed forces because he is always suspect—whether we want to admit it or not, most Indians consider Muslims as a fifth column for Pakistan. The private sector distrusts him. A situation has been created in which the Muslim, for all practical purposes is India's new untouchable.' (Gupte 1989: 214)

It is frightening to see that the disenchantment with secularism has led to both the Muslims and Hindus (and in the decade of the 1990s, the Sikhs) turning to terrorism. It is shocking to see that many of the persons involved in such acts are well educated and highly motivated. This is a unique case of alienation felt by all religious communities in the country!

Not long ago, all terrorist acts used to be routinely ascribed to Pakistan's ISI (Inter-Services Intelligence) and terrorist organizations in Bangladesh. Thereafter, it was found that terrorism was increasingly home-grown and that Indian Muslims were largely responsible for it. Now, even Hindus have joined the fray, with Hindu religious leaders taking the initiative in supporting or organizing acts of terror. The involvement of some serving and retired officers of the armed forces—which represent the best traditions of secularism in the country—shows the depth to which the poison of communal feelings and disenchantment with secularism has spread. It would be disastrous to overlook this phenomenon as a mere aberration. The long-term implications of this development for the unity, integrity and even survival, of the country are horrendous and must not be lost sight of. Rajnath Singh, the then president of the BJP and now the union home minister, had gone to the extent of saying that, if the Hindu terrorism card were overplayed by the Congress and the UPA, it would lead to a civil war in the country. It would be wrong to look at the issue in such a partisan way and as being merely one of law and order. It is imperative that the root cause, namely, the feeling of alienation, injustice and discrimination, is addressed with a sense of urgency.

Secularism, which is a part of the basic structure of the Constitution, is too serious a matter to be neglected any longer. This is underlined by the futile deliberations and outcomes of the meetings of the National Integration Council (NIC) held over the years. Holding these meetings has become a meaningless ritual.

> Looking at the way the governments have been conducting their affairs, Hindu religion is being seen as a state religion, much against the precepts of secularism. Some years ago, when Uma Bharti was the chief minister of Madhya Pradesh, her office had all the look of a typical Hindu home, with framed photos of gods and goddesses. (*Outlook* 29 December 2003: 13)

It is quite common to see the Satyanarayan Pooja being performed in police stations, and the Ganesha festival with its daily pooja and *aarti*s done in government offices. The super-computer developed by C-DAC in Pune was inaugurated by performing a pooja with all rituals.

The foundation-laying ceremony of the new capital, Amaravati, of Andhra Pradesh was held in early 2015 with all the Hindu rituals. According to a news item, beginning 23 December 2015, the new Telangana state is going to hold a five-day *Ayuta Chandi Yagna*—a thanksgiving ritual to the goddess Durga for granting the wish for a separate state. This is estimated to cost up to Rs 3 crores. The *Yagna* would require 50 quintals of ghee made from cows' milk and 10 tons of firewood. About 4000 priests and 1500 *ritwik*s would chant the *Durga Saptashati* mantras 2000 times a day for 5 days. (*India Today* 14 December 2015: 14)

Undeterred by the raging fire that engulfed a section of the thatched canopy at his Rs 7-crore Ayutha Chandi Yagna, Chief Minister K. Chandrasekhara Rao is preparing to follow-up with an even grander ritual. He plans a *Prayutha Chandi Yagam* to mark the implementation of programmes initiated by his government. (*India Today* 11 January 2016: 14)

The actions of state governments, from time to time, have created doubts in the public mind about whether India is really secular. For example, the Akhilesh Yadav government in UP, which is a Socialist party government, has sanctioned a grant of Rs 5.50 crores to Kashi Vishwanath Temple for its beautification. The state government has also decided to regularize the services of the temple's 40 staff members, including priests and other employees involved in handling the daily chores in the temple. (*IE* 19 May 2015: 2)

The takeover by state governments of a number of important Hindu temples and their management by government officers has created the impression of Hinduism being the official religion of the state. This impression is further strengthened by orders passed by the concerned high courts from time to time regarding the administration and management of places of worship. For example, the Madras High Court has prescribed in December 2015 that police should ensure the observance of a dress code for people entering temples in Tamil Nadu and the mandated dress code should be implemented from January 2016. (*IE* 11 December 2015: 10)

For whatever purpose the temples may have been taken over, this step has clearly been counterproductive in terms of its adverse implications for India's secularism. There is no reason why, if the managing committee of a particular trust has mismanaged its affairs, it cannot be superseded. It would be best to appoint in its place a new managing committee of persons of integrity with a clean public image. The time has come to take a policy decision that the government will not take over any temple or place of worship, and that it would be left to society to manage such institutions by formulating detailed guidelines for the purpose.

Where Are We Headed?

Given below are some significant recent events that indicate which way the winds are blowing. They hold up a mirror to show how India's image is changing, and also, how the world at large looks at us. If India has any aspirations of becoming a world, or even a regional, power these pointers cannot be overlooked.

Nandini Sunder stated: If the European Parliament's working group report on religious freedom places India in the lowest category as a 'country of particular concern', the fault must surely lie with those who attack churches, conduct '*ghar wapasi*' programmes, vandalize cinema halls, and so on. (*IE* 28 February 2015: 9)

The BJP Member of Parliament, Chinayya Shetty, has moved a private member's bill seeking to amend the Constitution by substituting the word 'India' by the word 'Hindustan' in the Constitution. (*IE* 3 March 2015: 6)

Mohan Bhagwat, RSS chief, has said that India is a Hindu Rashtra and there is a need to organize all Hindus in the country, for which this is a 'favourable time'. (*IE* 10 February 2015: 5) Bhagwat has said that the map of India can change at any time. (*Sakal* 5 June 2015: 12)

General secretary of the RSS, Bhayyaji Joshi, has said that *Vande Mataram* can be declared as a national anthem as it was widely used in the freedom movement, much earlier than the *Jana Mana Gana* and makes a fervent appeal for patriotism. (*Loksatta* 2 April 2016: 1)

The VHP has demanded that Himachal Pradesh be declared a Hindu State on the grounds that non-Hindus comprise just 5 per cent of the population. This has provoked others into questioning whether the Hindutva fringe wants states in the Northeast declared Christian or

J&K Muslim. (*Outlook* February 23, 2015: 20
    The Shiv Sena, which is an ally of BJP in the central government, has demanded that the word 'secular' should be deleted from the Constitution as India is a Hindu nation. (*IE* 29 January 2015: 3) It has also demanded that India should be declared a Hindu Rashtra.
Sadhvi Prachi, VHP leader, has said that now that the mission of making India Congress-free has been achieved, it is time to make India Muslim-free. (*IE* 8 June 2016: 5)
    Hours before winding up his three-day visit to India, with a striking departure from well-accepted protocol, US President Barack Obama, in a farewell message said that religious tolerance, diversity and protection of the weak and the little are fundamental values that form the bedrock for India's future. Invoking Article 25 of the Constitution, Obama cautioned India against efforts to divide society on 'sectarian lines'. (*IE* 28 January 2015: 1)
    The brutal killing of Mohammad Akhlaq and the critically injuring of his 22-year-old son in Dadri in Uttar Pradesh on September 28, 2015, on mere suspicion of his having killed a cow and eaten and stored the beef, shocked the country. It is believed that this was a deliberate act to spread terror and to create a fear complex among Muslims. The police have filed in December 2015 a charge sheet against 15 people. It names the son of a local BJP leader and his cousin as the main conspirators, who led the mob to Akhlaq's house and assaulted the family. The forensic tests have shown that the meat in Akhlaq's home was not beef but goat meat! (*Loksatta* 29 December 2015: 9)

> Several days after nationwide criticism of this atrocious act, Prime Minister Modi finally broke his silence and spoke on October 8, 2015, the day after President Pranab Mukherjee had spoken about the need for tolerance, but Modi talked only of the incident being 'sad' and 'not desirable'. It was hardly the speech befitting the occasion. He had let down his high office. However, he was able to create a sense of confidence among the people with his speech in Delhi on February 17, 2015, when he categorically stated, 'My government will not allow any religious group belonging to either the majority or minority to incite hatred against others, overtly or covertly. We cannot accept violence against any religion on any

pretext and I strongly condemn such violence.' (*IE* 18 February 2015: 9)

Terrorising people in the name of ensuring ban on eating of beef, vigilante groups have continued to harass people. In one such incident, a right-wing activist group stormed the general compartment of the Kushinagar Express on 13 January 2016 to check the luggage of passangers on suspicion that they were carrying beef, though nothing was found. Naseema Bano and her husband, who, among others, were mal-treated, was, however, reluctant to file a police complaint. 'I thought we were alive, why file a complaint and invite harassment?,' she said. (*IE* 16 January 2016: 1)

It is very unusual for the president of India to make a statement on the current political situation in the country. The atmosphere of intolerance in the country has become so overwhelming that President Pranab Mukherjee expressed his anxieties and unhappiness on this score more than once. The president said, '*We should not allow the core values of our civilization to wither away*. Over the years, our civilization has celebrated diversity, plurality, and promoted and advanced tolerance.' For the second time in a fortnight, on October 19, 2015, Mukherjee expressed the 'apprehension whether tolerance and acceptance of dissent are on the wane in the country'. He underlined that 'humanism and pluralism should not be abandoned under any circumstances'. (*IE* 20 October 2015: 1)

For the third time in less than a month, President Mukherjee spoke out against the rising intolerance, asserting that India had thrived despite all its diversities because of '... assimilation and tolerance. Our pluralistic character has stood the test of time.' (*IE* 1 November 2015: 1)

Except for the time when Shankar Dayal Sharma, as President of India, had issued a strong statement about his uneasiness with the events following the demolition of the Babri Masjid, this is the only other time that a President has publicly given vent to his feelings.

Speaking at the Jammu University convocation, Vice-President Hamid Ansari urged the Supreme Court to clarify the contours within which secularism and composite culture should operate so as to remove ambiguities. He also wondered whether a more complete separation of religion and politics might not better serve Indian democracy. Any public discourse on India being a 'secular' republic with 'composite culture' cannot overlook India's heterogeneity, Ansari said. He added that a population of 1.3 billion comprising over 4,635 communities had religious minorities totalling 19.4 per cent of the total. (*IE* 3 April 2016: 1) Ansari was severely criticized by a section of the RSS, VHP and the right-wing affiliates of the BJP for his communal uttarances! Fali Nariman in his article 'Say it again' (*IE* 5 April 2016: 10) had underlined that what was said by Vice-President Ansari needed to be reiterated as we are living in critical times.

> In fact, these times have been so unusual that even the governor, Reserve Bank of India, Raghuram Rajan, expressed his unhappiness on October 31 at the atmosphere in the country when he called for 'tolerance and mutual respect'. Rajan reiterated on November 4, 2015 that India would be 'crazy to lose' its biggest advantage and emphasized the 'need to keep an open society' and 'resist all attempts at closing it down'. (*IE* 5 November 2015: 1)

To justify the statement, he said that, unless corrective action were taken, foreign investment would be adversely affected. This certainly must be the only instance of the governor, RBI, making such a political statement. As if on cue, Moody's, the US-based rating agency, came out with a report that flagged 'the belligerent provocation of various Indian minorities'.

> This was also the only occasion when scores of writers and artists expressed their strong feelings over the 'vicious assault' on 'India's culture of diversity and debate', the prevailing climate of intolerance, and returned their highly coveted awards. Nayantara Sahgal, renowned writer and niece of Jawaharlal Nehru, who returned the Sahitya Academy award, declared, 'There are times in history when you have to stand up and be counted. This is one of them.' (*IE* 11 October 2015: 9)

Mahesh Sharma, culture minister, struck back saying, 'If they say they are unable to write, let them first stop writing. We will then see.' Meenakshi Lekhi, MP, criticized them as 'intellectual mercenaries'. It is true that no such step had been taken by the writers to protest against major calamitous events such as, the Emergency, the anti-Sikh riots in Delhi, the demolition of the Babri Masjid, the Gujarat pogrom, and so on. However, it is never too late for a civil society to become a watchdog for the public conscience and to help create pressure of public opinion for early corrective action.

Aamir Khan, the prominent Hindi actor, spoke against the prevailing atmosphere of intolerance in the country. Expressing his alarm at the rise in such cases during the previous six to eight months, he said that his wife, who is a Hindu, had asked him if 'We should not move out of India'. He was fiercely attacked by the BJP, the RSS and the Shiv Sena, among others, and was rightly hurt by remarks against him and asked, 'If I must represent anyone, why just Muslims?' (*IE* 25 November 2015: 8) It is interesting to note that Aamir Khan's contract as a brand ambassador for *Atulya Bharat* (Incredible India) campaign has not been renewed! (*IE* 7 January 2016: 5) At a Parliamentary standing committee meeting, BJP MP Manoj Tiwari, who is a popular Bhojpuri singer, is learnt to have called Aamir Khan a traitor and said, 'he should be thrown out [of the country].' (*IE* 9 January 2016: 1) Aamir has also been relieved of his responsibility as a brand ambassador of the road safety campaign. (*Loksatta* 11 January 2016: 10)

Shah Rukh Khan, another well-known Hindi actor, too, had to face strident criticism from the BJP and its affiliate organizations and allies when he expressed his unhappiness at the increasing intolerance in the country.

AIMIM (All India Majlis-e-Ittehadul Muslimeen) president, Asauddin Owaisi, was blunt when he said, 'Iftar parties, skull caps don't work now, Muslim youths want real issues addressed'. (*IE* 27 September 2015: 7)

This is a welcome development. It was long overdue and will go a long way towards making political parties come to grips with the real problems of Muslims.

These times have witnessed several other firsts. Pakistani cricketer-turned-politician Imran Khan, during his visit to India, referred to the problem of the plight of minorities in India with Prime Minister Modi and publicly talked about it. (*IE* 14 September 2015: 4)

The Pakistani singer, Ghulam Ali, had to cancel his music concert in Mumbai due to the threat by the Shiv Sena to disrupt it. Referring to the news that Mamata Banerjee, chief minister of West Bengal, was going to host Ghulam Ali, Taslima Nasreen, the well-known Bangladeshi writer, said, 'But she banned me in West Bengal. Why different treatment? Because Muslim fanatics hate me, not hate Ghulam Ali?' (*Loksatta* 9 October 2015: 6)

The book launch of Pakistan's former Foreign Minister Khurshid Mahmud Kasuri in Mumbai gained notoriety and it had to be conducted with full police protection after Sudheendra Kulkarni, organizer of the programme, had had to undergo the ordeal of having his face blackened by Shiv Sena activists the previous day. The Legislative Assembly of Punjab Province in Pakistan has passed a resolution that United Nations should declare the Shiv Sena as a terrorist organization (*Loksatta* 20 October 2015: 1)

A senior UP minister, Azam Khan, has sought the intervention of the United Nations to look into the 'miseries' of minorities in India. In a letter to UN Secretary-General Ban Ki-moon, Khan accused the RSS of planning to convert 'secular and pluralistic India' into a 'majoritarian theocratic nation as Hindu Rashtra'. (*IE* 6 October 2015: 5)

There were riots in Karnataka when the state government decided to celebrate the birth anniversary of the eighteenth-century warrior, Tipu Sultan. The VHP and the BJP opposed the celebrations, saying Tipu had conducted several atrocities against Hindus. Girish Karnad, Jnanpeeth awardee, said that, if Tipu had been born a Hindu, he would have been a hero in Karnataka, as Shivaji is in Maharashtra. The rightists were so incensed with the comparison that Karnad had to apologize.

The Shiv Sena has demanded through its mouthpiece, *Saamana*, that, since Muslims are used as a vote bank, their voting rights should be scrapped. (*IE* 13 April 2015: 1). A former chief election commissioner has rightly said that there is a case to look into the registration of the Shiv Sena as a political party, as, when a party is registered, it swears by the Constitution. 'A strong commission can send a notice to the Sena, get them to reply or apologize. The EC [Election Commission]'s powers can be used as a deterrent', he suggested. (*Outlook* 27 April 2015: 32)

Sarto Esteves, in his essay, 'Violence against the Cross', wrote that there have been numerous instances, particularly since 1998, when the various offshoots of the RSS— the VHP, the BD [Bajrang Dal], the BJP, etc.—have been giving orders to the Christian community to leave the country by a fixed date; the Christians have been called 'traitors', 'foreigners', 'thieves', 'second-class citizens'; they are asked to win the 'goodwill' of the Hindu community if they wish to continue to live in India; they are denied the full right to avail of the freedom of religion given to the citizens of India in Article 25...The minister of state for home informed the Lok Sabha on August 28, 2001 that there were 417 attacks on Christians in India since 1999 in which 33 persons were killed and 283 were injured...In the months and years after the statement referred to above...the attacks have increased and multiplied, and are occurring in every part of the country. Bombs have been planted for the first time in the history of Christianity in India in its churches in Karnataka, Andhra Pradesh and Goa...Above all, what has been happening in Gujarat since 1997, the murderous attacks on the Christians and their institutions on December 25, 1998 is what even primitive races were not known to be resorting to. The entire holocaust has been documented in all its details in innumerable reports, books, articles in national and foreign press, and in a report prepared with meticulous care and precision by the citizens' commission on the persecution of Christians in Gujarat in 1998–99... (Puniyani 2005: 278, 281)

Outlook magazine did a cover story on 'Christians and Conversion' in which it listed incidents involving attacks on Christians since April 2014, by classifying them as churches vandalized; pastors attacked; diktats issued on missionary schools; Sunday service, carols disrupted; entry of Christians banned in villages; inadequate supplies of public distribution grains to 52 Christian families in Chhattisgarh, and so on. (*Outlook* 29 December 2014: 25)

With religious fundamentalism raising its head all round, Christians too cannot be left far behind. The synod of the Kerala-based Syro-Malabar Catholic Church has directed its priests to use their Christian names, which is a mark of their Christian identity. The directive is being seen as an indirect message to the young Catholic priests to drop their Hindu names. (*IE* 4 September 2015: 6)

Muslims in India are not far behind in their acute intolerance, when it comes to any criticism of their religious customs and practices, even by their own co-religionists. The newly renovated studio of a Muslim videographer in Kerala was torched and destroyed by Muslim fanatics for his having expressed his view on his 'WhatsApp Islam' that a lot of malpractices were being committed in the name of using purdah. (*Loksatta* 29 December 2015: 9)

The 'infection' of hate-speech-making is spreading across political parties. The inflammatory speeches made by some Congressmen in Shamli district of UP have led to communal tension. Police have filed FIRs (First Information Reports) under sections 153 and 153A of IPC against responsible persons. (*IE* 31 December 2015: 1)

These actions and reactions contain seeds of communal conflagration and are matters of concern.

The Dharma Jagran Samanway Samiti, an RSS affiliate, has resolved to put a stop to the conversion of Hindus by the year 2020 and to continue Ghar Wapsi (reconversion) vigorously so that the Hindu population increases by the next census in 2021.

Under the rules of conduct, government servants are barred from joining any political organization or political party. For the first time, in January 2000, the BJP government in Gujarat issued orders relaxing this restriction and permitted state government servants to become members of the RSS. Similar orders were issued by the Chhattisgarh government to its staff in March 2015. (*Outlook* 16 March 2015: 16)

Reportedly, serious thought is being given to relax the ban on recruitment in the government services of members of RSS. (*Loksatta* 11 June 2016: 4)

A number of senior functionaries in the RSS have been appointed as Governors. Tripura Governor Tathagat Roy has defended his attending the RSS Shakhas and has said 'other Governors also visit RSS *Shakhas*'. (*IE* 10 April 2016: 1) Incidentally, it must be noted that during the Congress party regime, too, some governors claimed to be Congressmen and acknowedged their loyalty to the Congress, even while in the office. This raises the larger question of keeping party loyalty and ideology distinct from the responsibilities of a Constitutional office.

Possibly for the first time, V.K. Saraswat, a member of the National Institute for Transforming India (NITI) Aayog, attended, as chief guest, the Dussehra function organized by the RSS, in Nagpur on 22 October 2015.

> Mukul Dube lamented the fact that, though Ustad Faiyaz Hussain Khan's composition is played in Hindu temples, it made no impression on those who destroyed his statue in Baroda. All that mattered was that he was a Muslim. Faiyaz Khan is the man whose *Vande Nandakumaram*, a composition in *raga Kafi*, has been played in Krishna temples. It was immaterial that the well-known classical singer, Pandit Srikrishna Narayan Ratanjankar, had learnt his *gayaki* from Ustad Faiyaz Khan. (*EPW* 18 May 2002: 1885–86)

A committed high-level *pracharak* (functionary) of the RSS was appointed adviser to the chief minister of Madhya Pradesh with the rank of a minister. The BJP chief minister of Maharashtra, Devendra Fadanvis, has appointed an RSS functionary in the chief minister's personal office.

Ram Naik, governor of UP, has defended the arms-training being imparted to the members of Bajrang Dal. (*IE* 25 May 2016: 5) It may be mentioned that this organization had often come to adverse notice in the past, including its alleged role in the demolition of the Babri Masjid.

Noorani stated that the then Minister for Human Resource Development in the NDA government from 1999 to 2004, and also a former BJP president, Murli Manohar Joshi, had asked Muslims to call themselves 'Mohammedia Hindus', in short, Hinduize themselves. (*EPW* 18 March 2000: 969)

The assassination of three well-known rationalists and writers, two in Maharashtra and one in Karnataka and—the inability of the police and even the CBI to make a successful breakthrough in the crimes, has led to large-scale adverse comments. Sanatan Sanstha, a radical

Hindu organization, is a suspect in at least one of the murders. The Congress government in Maharashtra in 2011 had sent a proposal to the UPA (United Progressive Alliance) government at the Centre to ban the organization but it was not agreed to. Uddhav Thackeray, Shiv Sena chief, has publicly supported the Sanatan Sanstha and criticized the murdered rationalist, Govind Pansare, as *'dharma virodhi'* (one opposed to religion).

Surya namaskar (yogic exercise) is being propagated in schools in various states, but Muslims are opposed to it. When the matter was taken to the Madhya Pradesh High Court, it directed that the exercise cannot be made compulsory. The All India Muslim Personal Law Board has declared that performing yoga and *surya namaskar*, is a 'big sin' for Muslims.

> Asghar Ali Engineer, in his article, 'BJP Government and Minorities' has written that the BJP faced stiff opposition from the Opposition secular parties when it tried to introduce *Saraswati Vandana* (a prayer to the goddess Saraswati) in a conference of education ministers of states in Delhi in 1999. The education ministers belonging to secular parties staged a walkout when the conference was to begin. The Opposition parties raised the issue in Parliament and there were heated exchanges. The BJP government in UP also faced tough opposition when it sought to make *Saraswati Vandana* compulsory in all government schools, along with the singing of *Vande Mataram*. The matter went to such an extent that Maulana Abul Hasan Nadvi asked Muslim parents to withdraw their children from schools if it were made compulsory. The stiff opposition to these measures by minorities on one hand, and by secular parties on the other, brought considerable embarrassment to the BJP government at the Centre. The government had to retreat. Engineer has also invited attention to attacks mounted on Christians, particularly in Gujarat and Orissa. He has underlined that communalization touched new heights in this period, with more than 629 communal riots during 1988, in which about 207 lives were lost. (*EPW* 22 May 1999: 1245–46)

The question of imposing a meat ban during *Paryushan Parva*, the annual holy period of the Jains, became a highly emotive and controversial issue in 2015, though some ban orders applicable for this period used to be issued in some cities and states in the past. The *Indian Express* rightly commented editorially that 'The individual is the only proper arbiter of what he or she should eat or should not.' (*IE* 14 September 2015:10).

The Bombay High Court stayed the ban announced by the government of Maharashtra on the sale of meat on 17 September 2015 in Mumbai. When the matter was raised before the Supreme Court, it said a ban could not be forced down somebody's throat (literally!), and that the 'spirit of tolerance was paramount.' As usual, the Shiv Sena and the Maharashtra Navanirman Sena (MNS) made some offensive and intemperate comments such as, 'the writ of Gujaratis will not be permitted to run in Mumbai'. The Jains naturally reacted strongly in the matter.

The Rajasthan High Court order, declaring *santhara* (fasting to death) illegal has agitated the Jain community as interference in their religious practices. The Supreme Court has stayed the Rajasthan High Court order pending a decision on the appeal. This brings forth once again issues pertaining to the sanctity of religious practices.

International Yoga Day was celebrated in Delhi with big fanfare with Prime Minister Modi as the chief guest. As a result, keeping in view the protocol, Vice-President Hamid Ansari was not invited to the function but, such is the intrinsic distrust of Muslims that Ram Madhav, BJP general secretary and a senior RSS functionary, tweeted that Ansari had not attended the programme as he, being a Muslim, was opposed to yoga. This was shocking indeed and the government apologized to the Vice-President, but it showed the lengths to which even senior functionaries of the BJP and the RSS are prepared to go. Madhav's apologizing later was futile.

Speaking at the golden jubilee celebration of All India Muslim Majlis-e-Mushawarat on August 31, 2015, the vice president of India, Hamid Ansari, had underlined that the commendable official objective of *sabka saath, sabka vikas* was for the inclusive development of all, for which, a prerequisite was affirmative action. He listed the principal problems confronting India's Muslims as identity and security; education and empowerment; an equitable share in the largesse of the State; and a fair share in decision-making. There was nothing in this statement which could be objected to. In fact, the evaluation committee, headed by Amitabh Kundu, in its report submitted in June 2015, for examining the extent to which the Sachar Committee's recommendations had been acted upon, had brought out that between 2004–05 and 2011–12, the poverty levels for Muslims were higher than the national average and their percentage in government services too was very low. (*Loksatta* 2 September 2015: 7)

It is shocking to see that, since Ansari is a Muslim, not only was his statement criticized but he was also personally attacked by Hindu rightist elements. An article in the RSS mouthpiece, *Panchjanya*, criticized him as a 'communal Muslim leader'. It added: 'Islam and modernity are two poles that can never meet. But leaders like Ansari never make them understand this.' (*IE* 15 September 2015: 5) The VHP called Ansari's statement communal and said that it was not befitting the vice president. (*Loksatta* 2 September 2015: 4)

The BJP government in Haryana has asked the school council for educational research and training to suggest which shlokas (stanzas) from the *Bhagwat Gita* can be introduced in the school curriculum. (*IE* February 2015: 1)

K. Chandrasekhar Rao, chief minister of Telangana state, wants to convert Yadagirigutta Temple into Telangana's equivalent of Venkateswar Temple in Tirumala. Land is being acquired for expansion. This is estimated to cost Rs 500–600 crores. (*IE* 26 August 2015: 10)

> The Malayalee literary critic, M.M. Basheer, has been writing a series of newspaper columns on the Hindu epic, the Ramayana. But he had to stop after writing five columns because of a sustained campaign on the telephone by a set of unnamed persons, who upbraided him for writing on Rama when he was a Muslim. Seventy-five-year-old Basheer regretted that he had been reduced to being just a Muslim. (*IE* 4 September 2015: 4)
>
> The All India Muslim Personal Law Board [AIMPLB] has come out openly against what it calls the rising influence of 'Brahmin

Dharma' and Vedic culture, that are out to harm Islamic beliefs by all means. The AIMPLB has asked for constant vigil against attacks on Islam's teachings. It has also targeted the Central government for propagating yoga, *surya namaskar* and *Vande Mataram*, 'which are part of the Brahmin Dharma and are against the ideology of Muslims'. (*IE* 23 June 2015: 1) Interestingly, Mehbooba Mufti, president of the People's Democratic Party (PDP), which is an ally of the BJP in J&K, has equated the Hindu fringe elements 'misusing the name of Hinduism' with the IS 'misusing the name of Islam'. (*IE* 6 December, 2015: 6)

Both Houses of Parliament were rocked by the Opposition parties targeting the BJP and the RSS over the alleged forced conversion of fifty-seven Muslim families in Agra, and accusing the government of following the Hindutva agenda. (*IE* 11 December 2015: 6)

In November 2015, members of the VHP blackened the faces of two Ajmer municipal corporation officials over the death of two cows and three calves at a corporation-run shelter for stray cows.

Intemperate and questionable statements are being made, not just by the fringe elements of the BJP and its affiliate organizations, but also by those holding responsible positions. One of them is Haryana Chief Minister, Manohar Lal Khattar, who said that Muslims can live in this country, but they will have to give up eating beef. Later, he denied making such a statement and said that he was misquoted. But, in this electronic age when every statement made by important functionaries is recorded and played on TV, no one believes in such denials. In response to Karnataka Chief Minister Siddaramaiah's open challenge that nobody could stop him from eating beef if he wanted to, a local BJP leader from Karnataka's Shimoga district was arrested for threatening to behead the chief minister if he dared to eat beef. (*IE* 4 November 2015: 6)

Uttarakhand Chief Minister Harish Rawat has said that those who killed cows had no right to stay in this country. (*Loksatta* 21 November 2015: 1)

It was interesting to see that, days after the minister for minorities affairs in GOI, Mukhtar Abbas Naqvi, said that those who eat beef should go to Pakistan, Minister of State for Home Kiren Rijiju, said, 'his colleague's statements were "unpalatable".' 'I eat beef, I am from Arunachal Pradesh, can somebody stop me?' said Rijiju. (*IE* 27 May 2015: 1)

Assam Governor P.B. Acharya stated on 21 November, 2015 that 'Hindustan is for Hindus'. Assam Chief Minister Tarun Gogoi has written to the President of India, Pranab Mukherjee, that the Governor had converted the Guwahati Raj Bhavan into 'an annexe of the BJP office' and that the governor should be removed from office. (*IE* 29 November 2015: 4)

The Speaker of the legislature is expected to create confidence in his non-partisan approach in conducting the business of the House. However, these niceties are no longer considered important. The Speaker of J&K Assembly, Kavinder Gupta, announced that he is a 'proud RSS man' when the National Conference and Congress MLAs shouted slogans: RSS Speaker, *hai hai* (Down with the RSS Speaker). (*IE* 6 October 2015: 6)

Cow slaughter has been banned in most states in the country. The Supreme Court has upheld this ban though the merits thereof are difficult to fathom. The functionaries of the BJP and its rightist organizations seem to be taking the law into their hands to enforce the ban in their own ways. The Goshamahal BJP MLA, T. Raja Singh, had announced that he would not allow the beef festival planned by students of Osmania University in Hyderabad on December 10, 2015. He claimed that he would 'kill or be killed to protect cows'. (*IE* 3 December 2015: 5)

This 'one-point programme' has gone to the extent where the central government has decided to set up a laboratory at the Mumbai port to check the export of beef.

The forcible inspection of tankers carrying buffalo tallow by cow-vigilante groups in Punjab have forced at least one soap unit in the state running for the past thirty-one years to shut down. Several other units are expected to follow suit.

The banning of books on the grounds that they offend the religious sensitivities of one religious group or the other has been a routine response of the government of India and the state governments, all these years. One of the more celebrated of such cases is the banning of Salman Rushdie's book, *Satanic Verses*, by the Rajiv Gandhi government. After keeping quiet all these years, P. Chidambaram, former home and finance minister in several Congress governments, said in 2015 that it was a wrong decision. Fortunately, in several cases, the decisions to ban books have been reversed by the high courts and the Supreme Court. The latest example of intolerance is the protests by Catholic Secular Forum for a ban on the play, *Agnes of God*. Fortunately, the government of Maharashtra turned down the request. The play opened to cheers and applause in Mumbai on 5 October 2015. (*IE* 6 October 2015:4)

> Prashant Kumar has written about the passage of the Uttar Pradesh Regulation of Public Religious Building and Places Act amid loud protests during the BJP rule in the state in January 2000. After Rajasthan, which passed a very similar legislation 46 years ago, UP is the first state to regulate the use of private property for public religious purposes. It is feared that the UP law is likely to target Muslim places of worship and learning while leaving intact Hindu temples. (*EPW* 18 March 2000: 977)

Soli Sorabjee, in his weekly column on 'Growing Intolerance' way back in 2008, well before the current wave of intolerance rose to its unbelievable height wrote:

> The worst manifestation was when the prestigious Bhandarkar Institute in Pune was vandalized by bigots, and invaluable manuscripts were destroyed because the American author, James Lane, who had made some unpalatable remarks about Chhatrapati Shivaji in his biography, had worked at the institute...The latest shocking incident of intolerance is the call given by the All India Ulema Council, which has asked the Muslim community to boycott all Godrej products unless the company's chairperson, Adi Godrej, apologizes for hosting writer Salman Rushdie. This call has perturbing implications. What right has any person or body of persons to dictate to and intimidate any Indian citizen about his wish to invite or host a reception for a person of his or her

choice because the invitee is disliked by some fanatical members of a particular community...If these trends are not repressed urgently and severely, bigotry and intolerance will destroy our democratic social fabric. (*IE* 20 January 2008: 7)

Intolerance in any form and by any functionary—whether of the government or a political party/organization—must be deprecated and condemned. Widespread misuse of the IPC provision pertaining to sedition (section 124A) by the police has become a cause for serious concern. This provision has been derived from the original provision in Macaulay's Draft Penal Code, 1837. It was later included in the IPC in 1870 and reflected the concerns of the British rulers. It is meant to take action for bringing hatred or contempt, or exciting or attempting to excite disaffection towards the government established by law in India. All that was done in 1948 was to substitute the words 'British India' by the word 'India'. In fact, the provision ought to have been removed after Independence, or at least amended to suit the democratic governance which India has given to itself. Unfortunately, it has continued on the statute book in its original form and is being profoundly misused. The Maharashtra police had filed charges against some young Naxal workers for espousing the cause of the tribals. There have been similar cases in Delhi, West Bengal, and so on. In another case, the Tamil Nadu police have slapped sedition charges against persons who were agitating for imposition of a ban on sale of liquor. (*Outlook* 16 November 2015: 25)

The RSS membership is stated to be growing at 10,000 to 15,000 recruits every month, and is reported to have reached all districts in the country, except J&K. (*IE* 17 August 2015: 9) Reference must also be made to a massive show of strength organized by the RSS in an impressive get-together, named Shiv Shakti Sangram, near Pune on 3 January 2016, in which over 1.5 lakh *swayamsevak*s (volunteers) participated. The RSS has launched a new strategy of spreading its wings among persons of all castes, creeds and religions to give it a mass base. This will have important implications for the future of politics in the country.

The widespread violence indulged in by Muslim rampaging mobs and the demonstrations by over a lakh of Muslims in the Malda district of West Bengal in January 2016, in response to some intemperate statement made by a VHP functionary, is a matter of serious concern. (*Loksatta* 7 January 2016: 9)

> It was perhaps for the first time in recent years that Muslims have come out in protest in such huge numbers. India is becoming like a tinderbox and even a small communal comment can lead to unimaginable consequences. Equally disconcerting was the news report that the MHA had decided to withdraw the prosecution under the National Security Act of a Bajrang Dal leader, who beat up and paraded a Muslim man through a market in Shamli in UP after blackening his face. (*IE* 7 January 2016: 1)

This disturbing narration should make anyone uneasy about India's future. There is a saying in Marathi that you can wake up someone who is asleep but not one who is pretending to be asleep.

6

THE WAY AHEAD

It always seems impossible until it's done.

—Nelson Mandela

The thrust of this chapter is on operationalizing secularism. To begin with, attention has been invited to suggestions made by some commissions and commentators on how to deal effectively with the problem of communalism. Attention has also been invited to some interesting suggestions made in the Constituent Assembly, which showed the far-sightedness of the members. As for the operationalization of secularism, I have discussed in this chapter some important proposals, which include the creation of a constitutional commission on secularism, the separation of religion from politics, amendment of the Constitution to strengthen its secular precepts, two important electoral reforms, and a number of suggestions for strengthening the rule of law. The series of thoughtful suggestions could go a long way towards making India a truly secular nation.

Some Prescriptions

Over the years, concerned with the deteriorating communal situation in the country and its serious implications for the dilution of secularism, perceptive observers and commentators have made a number of suggestions for dealing with the future.

In a hard-hitting article on the 1984 riots in Delhi, quoted earlier in Chapter 3, Lalita Ramdas said:

'It was not enough for the prime minister to apologize to the Sikhs and to the nation, no matter how sincere the apology. It is much too late for that kind of apology to make an impact. It is time for statesmanship, not gamesmanship. Several commentators, including Siddharth Varadarajan, have suggested a number of steps to deal with the recurrent communal clashes in the country. These include the reopening of all the cases left untouched from the 1984 riots; setting up special courts; drawing up a tight legislation on genocide, as well as laws which must enshrine the principles of "vicarious criminal and administrative liability" as well as the "doctrine of command responsibility".' (Ramdas *EPW* 17 September 2005: 4111)

However, Ramdas believes that, if our national institutions are to be subjected to a process of rigorous audit and detoxification, this must go hand in hand with our own version/adaptation of a Truth and Reconciliation Commission, which alone might have a possibility of assuaging the feelings of the people.

The Concerned Citizens' Tribunal Gujarat, 2002 recommended that:

A Standing National Crimes Tribunal be established, forthwith, to deal with all cases of crimes against humanity and all pogroms; offences in the nature of genocide; cases of mass violence; cases of riots and incidents, where there has been large-scale loss of lives and destruction of property; caste, religious, linguistic, regional, ethnic and racial violence. A suitable statute should be enacted by Parliament. The tribunal also recommended that law enforcement be made impartial, effective and humane. The social composition of all law enforcement agencies should be diverse, wherein at least 25 per cent of the personnel should be from among the minorities and women.

According to the tribunal, the extremely partisan role of the law enforcement agencies has been generally attributed to the following four factors:

- A culture of governance, which makes the police function as a subordinate body, carrying out orders and directions of the

political executive.
- Deeply entrenched communal prejudices in the minds of a section of officials and police personnel.
- The social composition of the police and of the other wings of the law enforcement and criminal justice system, wherein minorities are persistently under-represented.
- The lack of training in humane and effective mob control by the police. This is a state of affairs that needs to be rectified quickly. The tribunal noted with anguish and concern that no political party has ever paid heed to the urgent need for radical police reforms. The tribunal recommends that this matter be debated and legislated upon with the utmost urgency. Let not more carnages take place that are condoned by the political class, simply because it lacks the moral courage to initiate and push for an independent police authority in the country.

Finally, among the recommendations of the tribunal, is an important suggestion: 'Mixed localities, housing complexes, housing societies, clubs, educational and recreational institutions should be promoted, and social intercourse and interactions including voluntary inter-caste, inter-religious marriages should be encouraged. Common festivals and festivities should be organized not only on national occasions but also to celebrate the special occasions of all religious groups. (CCTG 2002: 176–81)

As brought out earlier in Chapter 4, A.G. Noorani, in the context of the terrible Gujarat riots of 2002 and the state government's alleged complicity therein, suggested that the law of tort needs to be invoked to ensure the accountability of the State and its functionaries. It is time this proposal was examined in depth and pursued.

Upendra Baxi, in his article in *Seminar* (referred to in Chapter 4) has recalled that:

> V.S. Mani, writing in *The Hindu*, had suggested a specific legislation enacting the crime of genocide. Baxi has also suggested that the granting of bail in such cases should be exception rather than a norm. He has also suggested that Autonomous Rapid Action Legal Task Force should be established in each state for speedy investigation and prosecution of communal offenders. His other

suggestions include: People found guilty should be debarred, as a part of punishment, from holding any public position, including positions as political party officials and agents. Any person charged with acts of commission and omission in the performance of public duties should be disabled during the pendency of judicial proceedings from contesting elections or otherwise occupying any public office. The Penal Code provisions concerning incitement to religious enmity and hatred and creation of public mischief should be further expansively developed. The burden of proof should be reversed in specific situations now cruelly represented by the Gujarat carnage. (Baxi *Seminar* 513, May 2002: 83)

V.V. Singh, in his study on communal violence in Uttar Pradesh, highlighted the role of religious extremism in such conflicts. Among his conclusions are: communal disturbances are the result of reinforced polarization and that the cure of communal riot is much beyond the role of the police. At best, it can only inhibit, if it takes measures in advance, by anticipating trouble. (Singh 1993: 168–69)

Some Interesting Amendments Which Could Have Made a World of Difference

Tajamul Husain moved an amendment in the Constituent Assembly to the effect that in Article 19, it may be added that 'No person shall have any visible sign or mark or name, and no person shall wear any dress whereby his religion may be recognized'. Clarifying the point Husain said:

> ...in civilized countries, people have family names, namely, Disraeli or Birkenhead. From these names, you cannot say that Disraeli was a Jew and Birkenhead was a Christian. If you hear the name of Lord Reading, you cannot say to what religion he belongs. There was a man in England whose name was Lovegrove. You cannot say to what religion he belongs, though I know he was a Muslim. There are many Christians in England who have become Muhammadans. So, in those countries you cannot find out to what religion a man belongs simply by his name. In this country, of course...from a person's name you can find out his religion...in England there was

a time when there was no uniformity of dress but the Honourable Law Minister will agree with me that an Act was actually passed in Parliament by which there was uniformity of dress...We should not, being a secular state, be recognized by our dress. If you have a particular kind of dress, you know at once that so and so is a Hindu or a Muslim. This thing should be done away with. (*CAD* Vol. VII, Book 2, 2009: 818–19)

Husain himself stated, 'I know I am 100 years ahead of the present times.'

I find this amendment particularly attractive, keeping in view the other extreme to which the world seems to be moving. It would be recalled that after the Godhra riots, establishing and retaining one's identity as a Hindu or a Muslim became very important. In fact, India has become an outstanding example of identity politics. Every issue is looked at from the point of view of one's religion and even caste. The use of a burqa or purdah, for example, instead of being considered anachronistic, is being supported by even educated Muslim women's groups. The headscarf too has become equally an identity symbol. It is not uncommon to come across news items saying Muslims or non-vegetarians are not admitted as members of housing societies nor given tenancy. It may be recalled that, during the communal riots in Mumbai in December 1992–January 1993, Shiv Sainiks made efforts to target Muslim residents of buildings based on their surnames.

Husain's amendment would have gone a long way towards addressing these issues, though it is impossible to translate it into reality in this continent-sized country, keeping in view its strong regional preferences in respect of attire.

H.V. Kamath moved an important amendment in the CA to say: 'The state shall not establish, endow or patronize any particular religion. Nothing shall however prevent the State from imparting spiritual training or instruction to the citizens of the Union.' The amendment sought to separate religion from the State. Kamath said: 'Personally, I believe that because Asoka adopted Buddhism as the state religion, there developed some sort of internecine feud between the Hindus and the Buddhists, which ultimately led to the overthrow and the banishment of Buddhism from India.

Therefore, it is clear to my mind that if a state identifies itself with any particular religion, there will be a rift within the State. After all, the State represents all the people who live within its territories, and, therefore, it cannot afford to identify itself with the religion of any particular section of the population... But to my mind a secular state is neither a godless state nor an irreligious nor an anti-religious state. (*CAD* Vol. VII, Book 2, 2009: 824–25)

I believe that this amendment should have received serious attention from the Constituent Assembly but it was rejected. It is important to note that the Supreme Court, in its observations in the *Bommai* case, had made precisely this point and had held that a political party should not be permitted to profess any religion since, if such a party comes to power, the religion professed by that party is perceived as a State religion. This is exactly what has happened after the BJP has come to power at the Centre with a clear majority in the general elections held in 2014. As in the case of the uniform civil code, the Congress party, deliberately or otherwise, decided not to address this issue and, in a way, created a permanent problem for the Indian polity. With the present political alignments in the country, it is unlikely that any consensus can be built to address this issue in the near future.

The National Anthem and the National Song

Muslims in India have often incurred the wrath of the majority community for their refusal to treat the national song *Vande Mataram* with respect or even to sing it when the occasion demands. A common person is often unaware of the exact status of the *Vande Mataram* in relation to the national anthem. In this context, the statement made by Dr Rajendra Prasad, in the Constituent Assembly on 24 January 1950 needs to be noted:

The composition consisting of the words and music known as *Jana Gana Mana* is the National Anthem of India, subject to such alterations in the words as the government may authorize as occasion arises;[1] and the song *Vande Mataram*, which has played a historic part in the struggle for Indian freedom, shall be honoured equally with *Jana Gana Mana* and shall have equal status with it. (Applause). I hope this will satisfy the Members.

The concept of secularism has become somewhat controversial because of instances where, in the name of one's religion, some persons have even failed to show respect to the National Anthem or the National Song. The decisions of the courts supporting such action have also been frowned upon by people. In 1986, a two-judge bench of the Supreme Court ruled in *Bijoe Emmanuel v. State of Kerala* ([1986] 3 SCC 615; *AIR* 1987 SC 748) that Jehovah's Witnesses constitute a religious denomination. Compelling a student belonging to Jehovah's Witnesses to join in the singing of National Anthem despite his 'genuine, conscientious religious objection', would contravene the rights guaranteed by Articles 19 (1) (a) and 25 (1). The Court has noted that Jehovah's Witnesses wherever they are (England, USA) do not sing the National Anthem, though they show respect to it by standing up whenever it is sung. They truly and conscientiously believe that their religion does not permit the singing of the National Anthem. The Court has said: 'The question is not whether a particular religious belief or practice appeals to our reason or sentiment but whether the belief is genuinely and conscientiously held as part of the profession or practice of religion. If the belief is genuinely and conscientiously held, it attracts the protection of Article 25 but subject, of course, to the inhibitions contained therein.' (Jain 2010: 1322–23)

I feel that a line must be drawn regarding religious sensitivities and, wherever matters pertaining to the national honour are concerned, they

---

[1] There has been a demand that the word 'Sind' should be deleted from the national anthem as it is no longer a part of India. This demand has been rejected on the grounds that the national anthem is sacrosanct and no change can be made therein. However, the above quoted statement of the president of the Constituent Assembly shows that there is no such bar to making any suitable changes. Whether such changes should be made or not is another matter which would have to be decided on the basis of political consensus on the subject.

should prevail over individual rights.

It was reported that in August 2014, the police in Kerala slapped IPC section 124A (sedition) on seven people, including two women, after they had failed to stand when the national anthem was being played in Thiruvananthapuram theatre. (*IE* 1December 2015: 9)

These days, the police in various states are prone to branding offences as sedition in a routine manner, making a mockery of law. Some recent cases of this type include: a case filed against Aseem Trivedi, a cartoonist (2012), Arundhati Roy and Hurriyat leader Ali Shah Geelani for their anti-India speeches at a seminar (2010), Binayak Sen for supporting Naxalites (2007) Simranjit Singh Mann for raising pro-Khalistan slogans (2005) and VHP leader Praveen Togadia for an attempt to wage a war against the State (2003). (*India Legal* 15 April 2016: 61) I would strongly suggest that an amendment of IPC may be undertaken to make the position clear and also to ensure that, in the process, the important principle of freedom of religion and conscience is not permitted to be compromised in any way.

A heartening development must be noted. India's largest Islamic seminary, Darul Uloom Deoband, has issued directions to all madrasas and establishments related to Muslims in the country to celebrate Independence Day with zest and fervour by hoisting the national flag at these places. All Muslim households have also been directed to hoist the tri-colour on their houses. 'Why is someone isolating us? This is our country, our land, our place. We want to clear any misconception about our integrity towards the country', said the press secretary, Darul Uloom Deoband (*IE* 14 August 2015: 5)

An Overdue Relook at the Constitution

From one point of view, sixty-nine years since Independence is not a long period in the life of a nation but, looked at from another point of view, it is certainly long enough to take stock of the nation's successes, failures and concerns. Unless lessons are learnt from experience, we may be repeating the same mistakes. Specific mention may be made of the direction of the Supreme Court that, since secularism is a part of the basic structure of the Constitution, Parliament will not be competent to dilute its provisions in any way. However, what is proposed hereunder are steps to strengthen secularism, not to weaken it.

It would be pertinent to refer to what Dr Ambedkar told the Constituent Assembly in his speech on 25 November 1949. Ambedkar said that Jefferson, the great American statesman who played so great a part in the making of the American Constitution, expressed some very weighty views which makers of constitutions (and their implementers) can never afford to ignore. In one place, he said: 'We may consider each generation as a distinct nation, with a right, by the will of the majority, to bind themselves, but none to bind the succeeding generations, more than the inhabitants of another country.'

In another place he (Jefferson) said:

…Our lawyers and priests generally inculcate a doctrine, and suppose that the preceding generation held the earth more freely than we do; had a right to impose laws on us, unalterable by ourselves, and that we, in like manner, can make laws and impose burdens on future generations, which they will have no right to alter; *in fine, that the earth belongs to the dead and not the living.* (Rao 1968a: 940)

There can be no better guideline to consider some important amendments of the Constitution as suggested hereafter to equip India to meet with the challenges ahead.

A. Creating a commission on secularism

As brought out in Chapter 4, the Supreme Court has done a great service to the country by declaring that secularism is a part of the basic structure of the Constitution. But this declaration has remained on paper and no steps have been taken so far to translate it into reality, except for its becoming a part of the political rhetoric in the country. Some of the other features of the basic structure recognized by the Supreme Court, are parliamentary democracy, independence of the judiciary, freedom of the press, and so on. For each one of these, over the years, an institutional and legal framework has been established to make sure that they are carefully nurtured and safeguarded. For example, the Election Commission of India has been sufficiently empowered to ensure that there are free and fair elections in the country and electoral malpractices are put down with a heavy hand. The Indian Parliament is vigilant about safeguarding its independence, privileges and supremacy. The judiciary, after its shocking experience of being undermined during the Emergency in 1975–77, has been vigilant in guarding its turf. In fact, since then, the Indian judiciary has emerged as the world's most powerful judiciary with even matters pertaining to the appointments of high court and Supreme Court judges coming entirely under the Supreme Court. This is the only case of its kind in the world. In 2015, the Supreme Court declared unconstitutional the law unanimously passed by Parliament to appoint a National Judicial Commission for the purpose. The institutions of the Supreme Court and the Election Commission have emerged as the most respected institutions in the country, enjoying the highest credibility. This is no mean achievement.

Against this background, it is particularly unfortunate that no steps have been taken by the government to ensure a proper implementation of secularism and to give it credibility. The discussion in this book shows that, in fact, secularism has lost all credibility in the country since it has become a plaything in the hands of political parties, irrespective of the hues and colours to which they belong. At the same time, it needs to be emphasized that secularism will decide how India will emerge over the years. We have seen how, in the decade of the 1980s, the fringe and extremist elements in the minuscule religious minority of Sikhs—just about 1.5 per cent of India's total population—held the country to ransom for nearly a decade, and led to the shocking alienation of Sikhs, not only those living in India but also those residing abroad.

By comparison, the Muslim population in India is already a little over 14 per cent. Based on certain assumptions, it is projected to stabilize at around 20 per cent in the next few years. Most Muslims in India are highly tolerant and peace-loving, but there are fringe and extremist elements which cannot be overlooked. Particularly, in view of external forces, such as the ISIS, Al-Qaeda and the ISI, it would be in India's interest to ensure that home-grown terrorist forces are not permitted to emerge. But this is only the negative side of it. It is necessary that the issue should be addressed in a positive manner so as to bring Muslims into the mainstream of society. In this context, the atmosphere in the country since the beginning of 2015, brought out in Chapter 5, is one of serious concern.

The issues pertaining to secularism emerge in diverse sectors of society. As seen earlier, these relate to attempts to rewrite history, communalization of academic and research institutions, rewriting of textbooks, circumscribing artistic freedom and so on. At present, these issues can be agitated primarily before the higher judiciary since Parliament has become largely dysfunctional. And whatever is raised in Parliament inevitably becomes highly politicized and is looked at on the basis of party loyalties and strategies.

The experience of raising issues pertaining to secularism by way of a Public Interest Litigation (PIL) has also been far from happy. Strictly speaking, a PIL is supposed to be a non-adversarial litigation. Both parties are expected to look at the issues constructively to arrive at a workable and acceptable solution to the problem in hand. However, the experience has been quite the contrary. Practically in every case, the government has taken an adversarial position and contested even reasonable proposals put forth by petitioners. Second, as brought out in my book, *The Judiciary and Governance in India* (2008), the process of getting a PIL admitted is somewhat opaque, and the outcome can hardly ever be predicted. Third, it takes an unduly long time to get the final decision of the court. For example, in the PIL pertaining to the appointment of a Lokpal, due to resistance from successive governments, the case was heard on nearly twenty-nine occasions and was finally closed due to lack of response from the central government. In the case of a PIL pertaining to the non-implementation of the recommendations of the National Police Commission regarding modalities for appointment, and so on, of police officers, it took over twelve years for the Supreme Court to give a final decision. It was the same as regards PILs pertaining to the Haj subsidy, the proliferation of Shariat courts as a parallel judicial system, the RJB–BM dispute, and so on. With this background, taking recourse to a PIL does not appear to be an alternative to the setting up of any independent institution for deciding matters pertaining to secularism.

B. Commission on secularism

Clearly, the time has come to create a new institution, namely, a commission on secularism (COS) for ensuring adherence to the constitutional mandate on secularism. I had propounded this idea while discussing the lessons of Partition in my book, *The Holocaust of Indian Partition: An Inquest* (2006). To be effective, such a commission must be appointed by an amendment of the Constitution and should be presided over by a former chief justice of India, with five other members drawn from among eminent jurists, former judges of the Supreme Court, chief justices of the high courts, and other public figures of the highest integrity and reputation. The term of the members should be five years or attainment of the age of seventy-two years, whichever is earlier. The commission should be covered by the provisions of the Contempt of Court Act. The selection of the chairman and members of the COS should be transparently apolitical. The Selection Committee may comprise the Vice President of India, the prime minister, the Speaker, the chief justice of India, the union home minister and the leaders of the Opposition in the Lok Sabha and the Rajya Sabha.

Such a commission would be able to take a holistic view on all matters pertaining to secularism, and even intervene in matters coming up before the high courts and the Supreme Court. Reference may be made in this context to the very laudable role played by the National Human Rights Commission (NHRC), which had intervened in cases pertaining to the Godhra pogrom before the Supreme Court, and which has become an important moral voice to reckon with. At a time when there are only a few national leaders of stature left in the country with any moral authority and credibility who command universal public respect, the commission on secularism would be ideally suited to fill the vacuum.

The COS will be best equipped to create public awareness on secularism. Its open hearings will provide an opportunity to all political parties, intellectuals, religious leaders, NGOs, and concerned citizens to argue their points of view, either in person or through an advocate, in a free and fair manner. Keeping in view the basic purpose of setting up the COS, it is suggested that the hearings of the commission should be televised. It is only through such a public discourse that the values of secularism enshrined in the Constitution can be translated into reality.

The commission should have the responsibility of pronouncing judgments on all declarations, actions and programmes of political parties, public institutions, state and central governments, electronic and print media, and others, so far as their impact on secularism is concerned. The commission may take cognizance of such actions *suo moto* or on an application from any individual or organization. The decision of the commission should be binding on all concerned, unless it is set aside or modified by the Supreme Court. Thus, inevitably, the powers and authority of the COS would have to be much wider than those of the NHRC, whose recommendations are not binding on the government. It may be relevant in this context to recall that the often-violent agitations for the ban on cow slaughter subsided when the matter went before the high courts and later, the Supreme Court, irrespective of the merits of their decisions. Similarly, the highly emotive and explosive issues pertaining to the implementation of secular policies need to be depoliticized by entrusting them to a constitutional commission on secularism. It may be recalled that Turkey's ruling Justice and Development Party (AKP) faced a serious battle for survival in 2007 when the country's constitutional court reviewed a case to ban the party for its alleged anti-secular activities in violation of the Turkish Constitution.

The reports of all commissions and bodies set up by the government have to be submitted by them to the government which, in turn, submits them to Parliament. Often, there is considerable delay in the process and the government chooses the time politically most convenient and opportune for the purpose. Looking to the special position proposed to be accorded to the COS, it is suggested that the annual or any special reports of the commission may be submitted by the commission directly to Parliament and the government, and released simultaneously to the media and the public.

Secularism is a precious fundamental right of each citizen, and the COS would ensure that it becomes a reality. I am aware that such a step will be resisted by vested interests, but if the pressure of public opinion is built up, its establishment would make a significant difference to the way India is governed. The question which remains is, whether there will be statesmanship and political will to support this far-reaching and over-due political reform. A national campaign needs to be launched to prevail upon all political parties to initiate and support steps for a constitutional amendment to set up a commission on secularism.

C. Separating religion from politics

The serious problem of communalism and communal violence was discussed earlier in Chapter 4 It is interesting to see from Nehru's fortnightly letter to chief ministers as far back as 3 September 1954 that the nature or the intensity of the communal problem has not changed even after sixty-two years since then, underlining the importance once again of separating religion from politics. Nehru wrote that:

> There are some Muslims in some centres who might be prone to mischief. There are one or two Muslim organizations that have been carrying on objectionable activities...The Hindu communal organizations are definitely aggressive and they can play on the religious or other feelings of the majority community... Agitations like the anti-cow slaughter one are also used for this purpose. I have no doubt that many people who participate in this agitation are influenced by political or like motives and not so much by religious ones. The RSS utilizes this for its own purposes. (Gopal and Iyengar Vol. I, 2003: 190–91)

I have brought out earlier in Chapter 4 how the issue of separating religion from politics—which is so crucial for the success of secularism—has been totally neglected. In fact, the Constituent Assembly (Legislative) was forthright in passing the resolution in 1948 itself to separate religion from politics. This was the first major resolution adopted by that body. Jawaharlal Nehru had lent full support to it. This must have been on his mind when he wrote his fortnightly letter to the chief ministers of states on 5 February 1948, in which he reiterated:

> There is a strong opinion in the country, with which I sympathize, that no political-religious organization or rather no organization confined to a particular religious group and aiming at political ends, should be allowed to function. We have suffered enough from this type of communalism whether it is Muslim or Hindu or Sikh...I do not want, of course, to suppress any legitimate political activity. But the combination of political activity with a religious group is a dangerous one as we know from experience. You will have to give

thought to this matter as to what should be done. (Parthasarathi 1985: 60)

Sadly, during his long term of seventeen years as prime minister, Nehru failed to take any further action. Successive governments thereafter similarly put this issue on the back-burner. It was only when the Babri Masjid was demolished that the Narasimha Rao government decided to make a show of taking action, and introduced in 1993 the Constitution (Eightieth) Amendment Bill and a bill for amendment of the RPA (The Representation of People Act). As discussed earlier, both these bills failed to get any support and had to be withdrawn.

I firmly believe that, unless this issue is addressed with sufficient political resolve so as to carry through a suitable constitution amendment, it will be futile to talk about India as a secular nation. On the basis of past experience and to meet with the concerns expressed by some political parties during the debate on the Constitution (Eightieth) Amendment Bill in 1993 regarding the likely misuse of the enactment, I would suggest that the amendment bill should be confined only to the deregistration of a political party which has religious links, and the restraining of such a political party from contesting elections at any level in the country. A political consensus needs to be built up among political parties for the purpose. If political parties—such as the BJP, the Akali Dal, the Shiv Sena, the Muslim League, the All India United Democratic Front (AIUDF) (headed by Maulana Badruddin Ajmal) in Assam, and the All India Majlis-e-Ittehadul Muslimeen (AIMIM) (headed by Asauddin Owaisi)—are not prepared to join in the consensus, a strong public opinion will have to be created nationally to isolate them, and to go ahead with the constitution amendment, disregarding their opposition. Some persons may consider this a tall order but there is no getting away from such a surgical operation, if the patient is to be saved.

D. Other measures for strengthening secularism

The Supreme Court, while declaring secularism as a part of the basic structure of the Constitution, has laid down that Parliament will not be competent to dilute secularism in any way. But this also implies that Parliament is fully competent to take steps to strengthen it. In the light of the exhaustive discussion in the previous chapters, it is evident that the Constitution needs to be amended to bring out the following:

- **Defining the word 'secular'.** This exercise has eluded all the efforts made so far. At the same time, unless the word is unambiguously defined, it will be impossible to translate it into reality. The definition of secularism as understood in Western democracies will not be suitable for India, in view of the preponderant role which all religions play in public life. In connection with the debate on intolerance in the country, Union Home Minister Rajnath Singh has asserted in Parliament that the true meaning of the word 'secular' was '*panth nirapeksha*' and not '*dharma nirapeksha*'. (*Loksatta* 27 November 2015: 4) Unless a definition which would be acceptable to all sections of people is evolved, it would be difficult to get their unstinted cooperation in its implementation.
- **Defining the word 'minority'.** The Constitution does not define this word. The Supreme Court has looked at the question of minorities in numerical terms and has said that a group or community whose percentage of population is less than 50 per cent of the total, depending on the context of whether the country or the state or the district, and so on, would have to be considered a minority. On this basis, Muslims, who are the largest minority in the country constituting a little over 14 per cent of the total population, are a minority. Technically, they will continue to be a minority till they cross 50 per cent of the population. It is another matter that the Muslim population may not reach this level at any time. It is also relevant to take note that the current Muslim population in India is the second largest in the world. It is only on historical basis that the Muslims have come to be classified among the minorities from the British days. It is high time a proper definition of the term minorities was evolved and incorporated in the Constitution. It may be advisable to lay down the maximum percentage of the total population up to which a community would be eligible to be considered a minority. This would be in addition to the other criteria, such as their having a distinct language, script or culture.

- **Right to propagation.** Apart from allowing freedom of conscience and permitting free profession and practice of religion, Article 25 gives freedom of propagation of religion. There was considerable controversy about giving this right, and that, too, as a fundamental right. Several members in the Constituent Assembly spoke against giving such a right but their objections were overruled on the specious plea that it was necessary to give this right in accordance with the compromise which was arrived at with the Muslims and the Christians, who had argued that propagation was a duty cast on them by their religion. I have brought out, earlier, the recommendations of the Niyogi Committee on the subject.

  There are a number of decisions of the high courts and the Supreme Court, according to which *the right to propagation is not a right to conversion*. The activities of Muslims and Christian missionaries in some parts of the country have led to serious law-and-order problems. The Ghar Wapsi movement undertaken by Hindu organizations has also led to communal tensions and agitations in various places. It is high time this problem was nipped in the bud by amending Article 25 to delete the word 'propagation' in it.

- **Doing away with protection to minority educational institutions.** Articles 25 to 29 of the Constitution are really the crux of secularism, except for the word 'propagation' as discussed earlier. Article 30 (1), which gives minorities the right to establish and administer educational institutions is, in one sense, an appendage and need not have been there at all. But this too, was inserted, particularly at the instance of Christians and Anglo-Indians, who had a number of educational institutions. There was considerable opposition in the Constituent Assembly to this article, but the Congress party wanted to be generous to the minorities, disregarding the likely long-term implications of encouraging separate identities and undermining the spread of secular education. For the reasons discussed in Chapter 3, there is no justification for continuing this right of the religious minorities. If at all, it could be retained for the linguistic minorities. But, considering the rapid spread of English as a medium of instruction across the country, including in the rural areas, due to the forces of globalization and the spread of information technology, even for minorities, it is no longer necessary to give this right.

- **Deleting the provision for the prohibition of cow slaughter.** Article 48, though a part of the directive principles, has now been elevated in public discourse to the level of a fundamental right. The marginal note of this article is innocuously worded as 'organization of agriculture and animal husbandry'. However, the sting is really in the sentence which asks the State to prohibit the slaughter of cows and calves and other milch and draught cattle. I have discussed at length in Chapter 3 the pros and cons of the issue. The basic question is whether such a total ban on the slaughter of cows and their progeny is justified on any grounds at all except that of the religious sentiments of Hindus. But even in regard to them, there is no universal demand for a total ban by all Hindus. Most importantly, such a ban is not in keeping with secularism. As I have brought out elsewhere, the Indian Constitution is a mix of several compromises, particularly in so far as its proclaimed secular ideology is concerned.

Particularly after the BJP government came to power at the Centre in 2014, the demand for banning cow slaughter has gained strength. Effectively, 'Ban the Beef' has become the national motto and yet another potent instrument in the hands of extremist elements for disturbing the peace, tranquillity and communal harmony in the country. Jawaharlal Nehru had stoutly opposed the demand for banning cow slaughter during his term and had even staked his prime ministership thereon. Thereafter, the stand of the Congress party has changed completely and now it seems to be as much in favour of a total ban as the BJP and the Shiv Sena. It is time to consider seriously whether India can sustain its claim as a secular nation by resorting to such populist measures. I am firmly of the view that all well-meaning people in the country should come forward to oppose strongly the present moves on the subject.

Two basic electoral reforms

1. Making voting compulsory

Secularism in India has remained at the margin, mainly because people have not looked at it as their fundamental right. In fact, it is considered an important ingredient of vote-bank politics. Unless all eligible voters participate in elections, the accountability of the political parties cannot be established fully. The government of Gujarat took the initiative in the matter by enacting a law for making voting compulsory for elections to village panchayats. The governor had reserved the bill for the President's approval. In many instances in the past, the central government has looked at a number of proposals received from the state governments in a partisan manner. This bill was one of them and was kept pending by the UPA government for a long time. A private member's bill to make voting compulsory had been introduced in Parliament during the UPA period, but it was not supported by the government.

> Voting has been made compulsory at least in 30 democracies around the world. They are among others, Argentina, Australia, Austria, Belgium, Bolivia, Brazil, Costa Rica, Cyprus, Fiji, Greece, Luxembourg, Peru, Singapore, Switzerland and Uruguay. Compulsory voting was introduced in Australia in 1924, when the voter turnout was just about 58 per cent in the elections in 1922. Now Australia consistently boasts of a voter turnout of over 90 per cent. Compulsory voting in Belgium dates back to 1893. Currently, the voter turnout in Belgium is over 90 per cent. (Godbole 2014b: 174–75, 248–49)

As can be seen, the results achieved are quite striking. The objections raised against making voting compulsory are hardly convincing. For example, it is argued that a person cannot be forced to vote if he does not want to. The law can provide that a person would have the option to go to the polling station and mark his preference on the ballot paper in a separate box showing his disinclination to vote. Another objection—which has been raised—is that it would be administratively impossible to deal with hundreds and thousands of cases where people default and do not vote. Even this objection is not sustainable since such cases can be dealt with by post by conveying to the person that he would have to pay a designated fine for contravention of the law for compulsory voting. Even announcing on a notice board—in the case of village panchayats—and in newspapers—in other cases, the names of persons who have not voted, could serve the purpose of *shaming the persons*. Particularly in a case like India, where the day of voting is declared a public holiday, there is no justification for not voting. *In the final analysis, the question is whether absentee democracy is what we are aiming at.* If all minorities, for example, make it a point to go and vote, their political leverage will increase by leaps and bounds, and their voice will no longer be ignored by the political parties. When the voting age was reduced by the Rajiv Gandhi government from twenty-one years to eighteen years, lots of doubts were raised about its advisability, but we have seen what a difference it has made to the political life in the country in terms of empowering the youth, bringing their concerns to the forefront in political debate and so on. Similarly, now, voting needs to be made compulsory for elections to the local bodies, state legislatures and Parliament.

2. Making 50 per cent plus 1 vote necessary to win

The first-past-the-post system adopted in India since the British times—though simple to administer—suffers from some striking deficiencies. It is seen that, in most cases, the winning candidate gets negligible votes, at times just 20 to 30 per cent of the total, which is a mockery of representative democracy. In the elections to the UP Assembly held in 2007, 96.53 per cent of the winners polled less than 50 per cent of the votes cast. The corresponding figures were 89.71 per cent in Bihar (2005), 88.89 per cent in Bihar (2006), 81.63 per cent in Tamil Nadu (2006), 93.84 per cent in Jharkhand (2005), and so on. In the Lok Sabha elections in 2004, the corresponding percentage was 59.85. (Gopalaswami 2007: 196)

The National Commission to Review the Working of the Constitution (NCRWC) also invited attention to this matter and stated:

The multiplicity of political parties, combined with our Westminster-based first-past-the-post system, results in a majority of legislators and parliamentarians getting elected on a minority vote. In other words, they usually win by obtaining less than 50 per cent of the votes cast, that is, with more votes cast against them than in their favour. There are states where 85 per cent to 90 per cent of the legislators have won on a minority vote. At the national level, the proportion of MPs who have won on a minority vote is over 67 per cent at an average for the last three Lok Sabha elections. In extreme cases, some candidates have won even on the basis of 13 per cent of the votes polled.

But more importantly in this system, the winning candidate often confines his propaganda to his own caste, creed, language or religious group. Particularly in a country like India, which is a multi-religious, multi-racial, multi-linguistic and multi-ethnic society, a system must be devised which would make it as representative of this diverse community as possible. This can be done only by ruling that a winning candidate must get a minimum of 50 per cent of the votes plus 1 vote. To be able to achieve this, a candidate would necessarily have to appeal to a broad spectrum of his constituency. This will be especially important for minorities since they are often neglected and overlooked in the present election campaigns.

It has been argued that this would prolong the election process and would be administratively impossible to implement. However, this objection is clearly not based on any in-depth understanding of the issues. With the adoption of the electronic voting system, it should not be difficult to hold a second round of voting among the two top candidates who had received the maximum votes. The Election Commission has favoured this suggestion and has said that it sees no difficulty in its implementation. The NCRWC had also recognized 'the beneficial potential of this system for a more representative democracy'. The commission has recommended that the government and the Election Commission of India should examine this issue in all its aspects, consult various political parties and other interests that might consider themselves affected by this change, and evaluate the acceptability and benefits of this system. The Commission recommended a careful and full examination of this issue. (GOI 2002: 91–92)

If secularism is to be strengthened in the country, I strongly believe that this electoral reform is absolutely necessary and needs to be implemented as soon as possible.[2]

Centre–State Relations and the Bogey of Federalism

During the last few years, a number of critical issues facing the country have got bogged down due to the fears expressed by the states about federalism getting adversely affected. This cry of 'federalism in danger' is as dangerous as the cry of 'religion in danger'. This has affected policies in various areas, such as enacting a model law for Lokayuktas, the enactment of a central legislation for the CBI, the reorganization of the Railway Protection Force, the setting up of a federal police agency (discussed later in this chapter), and so on. When the Constitution was prepared, the problems of law and order, terrorism, Naxalism, organized crime, and crimes with international ramifications were not serious enough and, therefore, the subjects, 'public order' and 'police' were put in the State List. Ideally, both these should have been put in the Concurrent List, as is the case in a number of Western democracies. As a result, states have been objecting to the role of the central government in these matters. But this has not prevented them from relying on the deployment of central paramilitary forces whenever the occasion demanded. But, restricting the role of the central government has led to cases such as the Ayodhya debacle, the Godhra riots and major communal riots in a number of states. The time has, therefore, come to take a serious view of the amendment of the Constitution. Needless to say, federalism will be relevant only if the country survives.

At the same time, it is essential that the central government and the political party in power at the Centre give up their overbearing attitude when dealing with the states. The Modi government is often criticized on this account but the treatment given to the states by successive Congress

---

[2]According to Nepal's ambassador to India, Deep Kumar Upadyay, Nepal's newly promulgated Constitution is the most progressive in South Asia with its provisions of 33 per cent reservation for women. It also has both first-past-the-post system and proportional representation. This combination of the two ensures that the minorities' representation is taken care of. (*IE* 24 September 2015: 1)

prime ministers and even by the general secretary of the Congress party, Rajiv Gandhi, was equally overbearing and, at times, even insulting. To cite a few instances: it started with Nehru removing Gopichand Bhargava as chief minister of Punjab in 1951 in spite of Bhargava's clear majority support in the legislature party; the unceremonious removal of N.T. Rama Rao as chief minister of Andhra Pradesh by Governor Ramlal at the instance of Indira Gandhi in 1984; the selection of Babasaheb Bhosale as chief minister of Maharashtra in a highly arbitrary manner which was indelibly inked in the public mind by R.K. Laxman's well-known cartoon, which showed Indira Gandhi pointing at Bhosale—the new chief minister—standing in a line of supplicants, waiting respectfully to receive her at the airport; Rajiv Gandhi insulting the then Chief Minister Anjaia of Andhra Pradesh during his visit to the state, which was seen as an insult to Telugu *atmagauravam* (self-respect). N.T. Rama Rao came to power the next year, riding on that sentiment.

Prime ministers declaring economic packages during their visits to states are reminiscent of the days of the princely states. We have abolished the princely states but not the mindset, which still continues to be highly feudalistic. The settling of political scores with the states which were being ruled by parties other than those ruling at the Centre was also a common grouse of the states. This included starting fresh CBI inquiries or closing them down as convenient. Even basic courtesies—such as consulting the chief minister before the appointment of a governor or removing a governor from a state—have not been observed. This high-handed attitude of the central government has gone to the extent where a bill sent for obtaining the President's approval before its introduction or after its passage by the legislature has been held up, not just for months but in some cases even for years together. To this long list must be added a disturbing development which came to light during the elections of the Bihar legislature in 2015, when personal attacks were made by Prime Minister Modi, Nitish Kumar and Lalu Prasad Yadav against each other. In doing so, even common civilities and courtesies were not observed. This certainly cannot help to create a proper climate for amiable Centre–state relations. If the constitution amendments given above are to be undertaken, the states will need to have confidence that they will be treated fairly, judiciously and with respect, whichever political party is in power at the Centre. Any such constitution amendment will require a two-third majority in both Houses of Parliament and its ratification by state legislatures. This would be possible only by building a national consensus on the subject. The ruling party at the Centre will have to make concerted efforts for the purpose. This looks next to impossible in the present confrontationist climate and fragmented polity in the country.

These issues are particularly relevant if communal violence and communal riots are to be dealt with effectively. The experience so far shows that unless the central government is enabled to take an active role in the matter, merely making available to the states central paramilitary forces and intelligence inputs from central agencies will not be adequate. It will be recalled that, in the national catastrophic situation pertaining to the RJB–BM agitation in November–December 1992, nearly 20,000 persons of several paramilitary forces were stationed in and around Ayodhya. This was the single largest mobilization of central forces for such an operation since Independence. The contingency plan prepared by the Ministry of Home Affairs covered all the logistics, such as movement of the central forces by air, rail and road, supplies, tent accommodation, food and weapons. However, since the BJP government in UP refused to deploy these forces around Babri Masjid for its protection, this gigantic effort of the government of India served no purpose. The founding fathers of the Constitution cannot be blamed for not having imagined such irresponsible conduct on the part of a state government. Experience has shown that several state governments have been equally lax in dealing with serious communal riots. This is as true of the state governments headed by the BJP as it was of the Congress party, the CPI (M), the DMK or other political parties. The issue, therefore, needs to be considered dispassionately and institutionally, keeping aside political baggage and rhetoric.

It is time we realized that the first prerequisite of secularism in a country is to make sure that there is communal amity and harmony, and that the life and property of persons belonging to all religions are protected. The minimum that a common person wants is a peaceful life for his family and himself. Looking to the atmosphere of hate, intolerance, religious strife, the targeting of not only the minorities but also the intellectuals, rationalists, writers and artists, serious doubts arise as to whether India can qualify as a secular state. If the present highly unsatisfactory and disturbing situation on this score is to be remedied, fresh thinking will have to be done on a number of issues. One of these is the re-demarcation of the role of the state governments and the Centre.

After the Kargil War in 1999, the government decided to review India's security management system, particularly in the areas of intelligence, internal security, border management and defence management. The government appointed four task forces to look into these areas. I was the chairman of the task force on border management. The recommendations of the task forces—which were to be submitted within three months of their constitution—were expeditiously processed by the cabinet secretariat, and placed before a group of ministers (GOM) comprising L.K. Advani, Minister of Home Affairs, George Fernandes, Minister of Defence, Jaswant Singh, Minister of External Affairs, and Yashwant Sinha, Minister of Finance. The recommendations of the GOM were finalized in record time and placed before Parliament in February 2001.

Particular attention may be invited to the recommendations of the GOM on constitutional provisions. The group noted that:

> The Union government's ability to deal with situations caused by grave threats to internal security has eroded over the years and needs to be strengthened. This capability should flow from the Constitution. One way to do this is to strengthen the emergency provisions under Articles 352 and 359. The other way is to exploit the vast untapped constitutional potential between the power to issue directives under Articles 256 and 257 on the one hand and the power to proclaim Emergency under Article 352, on the other. The source of this potential lies in Article 355 which casts upon the Union the responsibility to protect every state against internal disturbances and to ensure that the government of every state is carried on in accordance with the provisions of the Constitution.
>
> It would be both appropriate and timely, if the provisions contained in Article 355 are made use of pro-actively. To do so, supporting legislation will have to be enacted to, *inter alia*, cover the following:
>
> (a) *Suo moto* deployment of central forces, if the situation

prevailing in the states so demands; the legislation will spell out situations in which such deployment may take place, as also its consequences.

(b) Defining powers, jurisdiction, privileges and liabilities of the members of central forces, while deployed in states, in accordance with Entry 2-A of the Union List.

(c) Specifying situations construed as failure/break-down of constitutional machinery in a state, in which the central government can intervene to advise or direct, as the case may be, a state government, and violation of these advisories/ directions would invite action under Article 365/352.

Accordingly, the following action may be taken with regard to the proposed legislation under Article 355:

(a) The matter be taken to the Inter-State Council (ISC) and a small group of members of the council be constituted to examine the issue in all its dimensions.

(b) The matter be discussed with the leadership of all political parties to generate consensus.

Simultaneously, a comprehensive reference may be made to the Law Commission on the question of strengthening Articles 352 and 359, without compromising the spirit of democracy and federalism which guides the Constitution. (GOI 2001: 43–44)

It may come as a surprise to see the stand of the BJP government now on these important issues since it is diametrically opposite to the stand taken by the BJP during the RJB–BM agitation in 1992, as brought out in my memoir, *Unfinished Innings: Recollections and Reflections of a Civil Servant*, referred to in Chapter 4. Even the stationing of 20,000 central paramilitary forces by the central government at a distance of 8 kilometres from Ayodhya was stoutly opposed by Kalyan Singh, the then-chief minister of UP. The state government had also opposed any move on the part of the central government to use Articles 355 and 356 of the Constitution (to protect the state from internal disturbance). But it is good to see that finally, wisdom has dawned on the BJP as can be seen from the recommendations of GOM quoted above. It is never too late. Obviously, the world looks different when seen from the North and South Blocks in Delhi than from street agitations. But, even though these recommendations of the GOM were made in February 2001, no follow-up action was taken by the NDA government till the end of its term in 2004. Now that the BJP is in power once again at the Centre, I hope it will take an active interest in pursuing these recommendations of the GOM and developing an all-party consensus to amend the Constitution suitably. By doing so, at least future contingencies—such as threats of the takeover of mosques in Varanasi and Mathura, or communal riots such as Godhra and Mumbai—could be dealt with more effectively.

The GOM had also referred to the proposal of the MHA:

> ...for setting up a federal agency to deal with grave offences which have inter-state and nation-wide ramifications. This was opposed by the states on the plea that it infringed on their constitutional right to maintain law and order. Considering the worrisome internal security scenario in the country, the states may be approached again, at an appropriate time, to agree to this proposal, since it may become increasingly difficult for the state governments to handle such crimes entirely on their own. (GOI 2001: 45)

No follow-up action was taken on this recommendation by the NDA government till it demitted office in 2004. Now that it has come back to power, let us hope that this matter will be pursued vigorously by the government.

The Welfare of Minorities

Among the minorities, the most sensitive subject has been that of Hindu–Muslim relations over the years. The Partition of the country and the creation of Pakistan, accompanied by a holocaust of unimaginable proportions, have added a new dimension to the problem. At the same time—as I have mentioned earlier—Muslims constitute over 14 per cent of India's population, and this percentage is expected to stabilize at about 20 per cent. If underlying assumptions in this projection change, this percentage may even increase. Therefore, any inclusive development cannot possibly exclude such a large proportion of the Indian population.

Successive reports by independent observers have emphasized the enormity of the problem. Unfortunately, any discussion on this subject is looked at purely from a political perspective and is branded as wooing the minorities or as vote-bank politics. It is time the political discourse on the subject got out of these narrow confines and looked at the problem in a broader perspective.

It cannot be denied that Muslims have lagged behind in several vital spheres such as, education, health, literacy, employment, and so on. The British policy of communal electorates and reservation in matters of employment, and so on have been so catastrophic that most sections of Hindu society are not inclined to look at the problem apolitically.

Restructuring Police Departments

Experience has shown that the weaknesses and inadequacies of the police have been largely responsible for starting or escalating communal violence. The root cause of this is the politicization and communalization of police in various states. Several judicial commissions of inquiry appointed on major communal riots have strongly brought out this point. The misuse of the police during the Emergency of 1975–77 reached such shocking proportions that the Shah Commission of Inquiry had passed severe strictures. After the Janata government came to power in 1977, it was decided that structural changes would have to be made in police departments, if similar situations were not to recur in the future. Accordingly, the National Police Commission (NPC) was appointed by the central government under the chairmanship of Dharm Veer, former cabinet secretary. The commission comprised senior, experienced and respected police officers. The commission submitted eight reports by 1981, by which time Indira Gandhi had come back to power. Though the commission had chalked out a plan for its further work, it was peremptorily wound up by the government. In fact, the reports of the commission were also consigned to the archives and they were resurrected only when the United Front government came to power. The then Home Minister Indrajit Gupta wrote a personal letter to the chief ministers to expedite the implementation of the reports. Unfortunately, due to the vested political interests of all political parties which were in power in one state or another, the reports were not acted upon.

Finally, several PILs were filed in the high courts and the Supreme Court with a prayer that the government should be directed to take an expeditious follow-up action. The Supreme Court was reluctant to admit the PILs, but finally agreed to do so, and also directed that all other PILs filed in the high courts should be transferred to the Supreme Court. The final decision of the Court came only in September 2006, nearly twelve years after the filing of the PILs. Though inordinately delayed, the Supreme Court laid down guidelines for the reorganization of police departments in the states and at the Centre. Nearly a decade has elapsed since the decision of the Supreme Court, but most major state governments have not implemented the Court orders.

> The data collected by the Bureau of Police Research and Development (BPR&D) for the year 2013 shows that almost 80 per cent of Superintendents of Police (SPs) in districts across the country were transferred within two years of their tenure in a district. More than 50 per cent were transferred in less than a year. According to the data, UP has been the worst offender in terms of transferring officers before their two-year tenure is complete. Even officers senior to SPs have not been spared. As per the data, in 2013, 114 range DIGs (Deputy Inspectors of Police) faced transfers within a year of their tenure. As many as 48 were transferred within two years. (*IE* 29 November 2015: 7)

For some strange reason, the Supreme Court has been reluctant to haul up the defaulting states for contempt of court.

If the guidelines laid down by the Supreme Court had been followed, the appointments of Directors General of Police would have become more apolitical. They would have been given a fixed tenure of two years. The appointment of other senior officers in the state would also have been based on the recommendations of the establishment boards set up for the purpose. All field officers would have been given a fixed term of two years. An institutional mechanism would have been created for looking into the complaints about and grievances against the police. All this would have made a significant difference to the handling of the law-and-order situation in general and communal violence in particular. No words are strong enough to condemn the situation in which even the orders of the highest court in the land get overlooked. The Modi government at the Centre has been emphasizing its commitment to ushering in good governance. However, maintaining law and order and communal harmony must be a prerequisite of good governance. Regrettably, there are no signs of this yet.

Communalization of the police has been a matter of serious concern right since the Independence of the country. During the RJB–BM agitation it was found that the UP police had been communalized. Therefore, the home ministry had made specific suggestions to the BJP government in UP that central paramilitary forces should be stationed in close proximity of the masjid. But the state government was reluctant to do so. The Uttar Pradesh Provincial Armed Constabulary (UP-PAC) was believed to be communally oriented. Union Home Minister S.B. Chavan, had expressed his apprehensions on this account. This was also prominently seen during the 1984 anti-Sikh riots in Delhi, the riots in Mumbai in December 1992 and January 1993, the assessment of the Srikrishna Commission thereon, and the Godhra riots in Gujarat in 2002.

Meena Menon rightly underlined that, after the riots in Mumbai in 1992:

> The entire government machinery is working to keep policemen out of the purview of punishment. The [Shiv] Sena defends the police every time, saying taking action will demoralize the police force. The government too is quite chummy with the Sena and has no intentions of prosecuting Bal Thackeray or any of the *Sainiks* involved in the riots. (Menon 2012: 241)

In this connection, special mention must be made of the statements of L.K. Advani, who had spearheaded the RJB-BM agitation. He has written in his autobiography, *My Country My Life*:

> I recall vividly an experience en route from Ayodhya to Lucknow [on 6 December 1992 after the demolition of Babri Masjid]. In spite of strict security all along the 135-kilometre journey, I could see people engaged in celebrations everywhere. Within half an hour of our departure from Ayodhya, our car was stopped by the police.

On seeing that the car carried Pramod Mahajan and me, a senior officer of the UP government walked up to us [and] said, 'Advaniji, *kuch bacha to nahin na? Bilkul saaf kar diya na?*' (I hope nothing of the structure is surviving and that it has been totally razed to the ground.) I am recounting this incident only to highlight the general mood of the populace, including employees and officials of the state government, after the tragic development in Ayodhya—that of jubilation. (Advani 2008: 402)

The NPC, in its eighth and concluding report submitted in May 1981, made two significant recommendations:

One, the term of office of the Director General (DGP)/ Inspector General of Police (IGP) [as was the position of the head of police in a state at that time] appointed under the [Police] Act shall be four years from the date of his appointment. Two, an officer who has functioned as the DGP/IGP, after his retirement from service, shall not be eligible for any employment under the government of India or under the state government or in any public undertaking in which the GOI or the state government has a financial interest. (GOI 1981: 52)

This is a critical recommendation which ought to have been acted upon much earlier. There have been any number of instances where senior police officers who had obliged the political party in power during the communal riots have been handsomely rewarded. One can cite dozens of instances to support this. I would suggest that even now it is not too late to accept this recommendation. I wish to suggest only one amplification of this: such officers will not be given party tickets to contest elections during a cooling-off period of three years.

If a sense of confidence is to be created amongst the minorities that they will be treated fairly, justly, and that their life and property will be safeguarded, all-out efforts will have to be made to deal with the communal bias in the police. Some of the subjects which need to be included in the syllabus of police training institutes are the precepts of secularism, safeguarding the interests of the minorities and the importance of human rights. Actual case studies of communal riots, and the findings of official inquiries or judicial commissions of inquiries, must be placed before field police officers and constabulary for discussion in the refresher courses organized for them. Knowledgeable representatives of minority communities could also be called for interaction with the police personnel in the training sessions. Unfortunately, this important aspect has been totally lost sight of.

It is necessary to give sufficient representation to minorities in the police services. In this context, the example of the Rapid Action Force of the central government, which is often deployed during communal riots is noteworthy. Conscious efforts have been made by the central government to give representation to minorities in this force. This example needs to be replicated in similar forces raised by the states.

One indication of how the winds are blowing since the BJP's coming to power at the Centre in 2014 is the recent instructions issued by the home ministry to the National Crime Records Bureau (NCRB) not to publish the data on Muslims in police. The publication of such data first began sixteen years ago. This is the first time that such a ban has been imposed. (*IE* 30 November 2015: 1)

Such efforts are really counter-productive for the success of secularism. It is interesting to see that the NCRB report for 2013 showed that there were 1.08 lakh Muslim police who accounted for 6.27 per cent of the total strength of 17.31 lakh police in the country, as compared to their percentage of 7.55 in 2007. Public pressure must be brought on the government to revise this decision and to ensure that data on Muslims in police is published each year.

The Rule of Law and Reality

Even if police departments are restructured as above, and other changes suggested herein are effected, unless the rule of law is established in the country, nothing substantial can be achieved. This is particularly true in dealing with an important and sensitive subject like secularism.

In this context, reference must be made to the statement made by Rohini Salian, special public prosecutor in the 2008 Malegaon blast case. She said that, after the new government came to power at the Centre in 2014, she was told to deal softly with the Hindu extremists involved as accused in the case. (*IE* 25 June 2015:1)

Later, on being questioned by the media, she even gave the name of the officer of the National Investigation Agency (NIA) who had made this suggestion to her. According to news reports, the other cases involving Hindu terror are the Malegaon blasts, 2006; the Ajmer Sharif blast, 2007; the Mecca Masjid blast in Hyderabad, 2007; the Samjhauta Express attack, 2007; and the Modasa explosion in 2008. Unless these cases are pursued vigorously and justice is not only done but is seen to have been done, it will be difficult to sustain confidence in India's secularism.

It is shocking to see the reversal of its stand by the NIA in the Malegaon bomb blast case regarding the role of Hindu extremist elements. Three investigating agencies—the state anti-terrorism squad (ATS), CBI and NIA—have investigated the case at some time or the other. The NIA has now decided to give a clean chit to Sadhvi Pragya Singh Thakur as an accused in its charge sheet filed in the Mumbai court and has also decided to drop charges under the stringent Maharashtra Control of Organised Crime Act (MCOCA) against Colonel Purohit and all other accused. (*IE* 13 May 2016: 1) This has created a serious credibility gap regarding the authenticity and integrity of police investigation in such sensitive cases, highlighting the importance of ensuring that the police organizations are kept away from political interference.

I have referred earlier to how important provisions of sections 153-A and 153-B of the Indian Penal Code (IPC) have largely remained on paper. Section 153-A deals with promoting enmity between different groups on grounds of religion, race, place of birth, residence, language, among others, and doing acts prejudicial to the maintenance of harmony. It came into effect on 4 September 1969 and has been comprehensively worded to take care of all kinds of actions which may disturb public tranquillity. The offences under this section are punishable with imprisonment which may extend to three years, or with a fine, or with both. The offence under this section is cognizable, non-bailable, non-compoundable and triable by a first class magistrate. Subramanian Swamy has challenged the validity of this section in the Supreme Court. I sincerely hope that its validity will be upheld by the Court as it is crucial for maintaining communal harmony in the country.

Section 153-B was inserted in 2005 and deals with imputations and assertions prejudicial to national integration. The offence is punishable with imprisonment, which may extend to three years, with a fine, or with both. However, if the offence is committed in any place of worship or in any assembly engaged in the performance of religious worship or religious ceremonies, it is treated more seriously and is punishable with imprisonment, which may extend to five years and will also be liable to a fine. The offence under this section is also cognizable, non-bailable, non-compoundable and triable by a first class magistrate.

> Reference must be made to the commendable efforts made by Meena Menon to get information under the Right To Information (RTI) Act from December 2004 regarding the fate of cases filed by the police against Bal Thackeray, the founder and chief of the Shiv Sena, during the riots in Mumbai of 1992–93 and earlier. The appendix to her book published in 2012 shows how much pains she had to take to get this crucial information from police records. The replies to her RTI queries started coming in only from 18 January 2011, seven years after the filing of the application. Of the fourteen cases mentioned in the communication dated 18 January 2011, three cases were closed under A Summary (case closed for filing a false or baseless FIR), two cases were closed on 31 December 1991, and one was closed on 26 December 1991. In four cases, Thackeray was acquitted by the court on 18 October 1996. Three more cases were closed after C Summary (no evidence in the case). The same was the fate of, most of the cases filed in other police stations. In several cases no information could be made available to the applicant. In spite of Menon pursuing this matter relentlessly the government continued to deny information on the other pending cases for one reason or another. (Menon 2012: 243–48)

This is an eloquent—but by no means unusual—example of the disregard of the important provisions of CrPC and IPC for dealing effectively with the communalization of public life. As can be seen, no appeals were filed in cases where Thackeray was acquitted and, amazingly, several cases were closed by following summary procedures on the grounds that either they were false or there was no evidence. This is the 'majesty of law' about which a common citizen hears, time and again. It is often said that, 'howsoever high you may be, the law is above you'. This is certainly not true so far as the high and mighty in public life are concerned. For example, the UP government withdrew eleven cases filed against Agra BJP corporator Kundanika Sharma in 2016 for making hate speeches during the last few years, before she joined the Socialist Party. (*IE* 4 May 2016: 1)

Senior police officers need to be given full powers to directly prosecute persons infringing on these provisions, without the necessity of obtaining approval of the state government. Experience has shown that the state governments look at this question entirely from a political point of view and withhold approval for prosecution or even totally reject the proposal. It has been seen that cases filed under these sections are often withdrawn later at the behest of the government for political ends. If secularism is to be translated into reality, communalism will have to be put down with a firm hand. And this would be possible only by ensuring that the above provisions of IPC are made effective. The NCRWC has also said that 'effective implementation of laws is lacking. This deserves the highest degree of attention.' (GOI 2002: 87)

Towards this end—as recommended by the second administrative reforms commission—the provisions contained in section 196 CrPC requiring prior sanction of the union or state government or the district magistrate for initiating prosecution of offences under sections 153A, 153B, 295A (deliberate and malicious acts, intended to outrage the religious feelings of any class by insulting its religion or religious beliefs); and of Section 505 (statements conducing to public mischief); Sub-sections (1) (c) (with intent to incite, or which is likely to incite, any class or community of persons to commit any offence against any other class or community), (2) (statements creating or promoting enmity, hatred or ill-will between classes) and (3) (offences under sub-section (2) committed in place of worship, for example), of IPC, be deleted. It has also rightly suggested that the punishment for communal offences be enhanced, and special courts be set up for speedy disposal of the cases. I fully agree with the recommendation of The Second Administrative Reforms Commission (SARC) that a separate law to deal with communal violence is not required. The UPA's proposal in this regard had led to a bitter confrontation between the states and the Centre and also the political parties which were in opposition then. Strengthening the provisions of the IPC and the CrPC will be adequate to deal with the situation.

The last sixty-nine years since Independence have not only seen repeated incidents of communal violence—as brought out in this book—

but, regrettably, some of these riots literally turned into massacres. To recall, a few of these were the Jabalpur riots during Nehru's time in 1961; the Ahmedabad riots in 1969; the anti-Sikh riots in Delhi in 1984; the Mumbai riots in 1992–93; and the Godhra riots in 2002. Against this background, it is necessary to make a special provision to deal with genocides such these: The law should provide to make such offences cognizable and non-bailable, with much stricter punishment extending up to life imprisonment. Fear of law must be inculcated unambiguously, and anti-social elements—which generally take advantage of these situations—and the government functionaries—who either connive at them or even support them—must be dealt with severely. The law should permit class-action suits to be filed and provide for special courts to be set up for speedy trials.[3]

Unusual times call for unusual solutions. Experience has shown that hardly any worthwhile action has been taken so far against government functionaries who were handling these situations and who failed miserably. The time has come to examine whether the provisions of the law of torts should not be extended to all those remiss in handling genocides. Class-action suits need to be initiated in such cases, as it would be impossible for individual victims to file cases against the concerned powerful politicians and police functionaries. It is only by applying the provisions of the law of torts that they would become seriously aware of their responsibilities.

Another legislation which has wholly remained on paper is the Religious Institutions (Prevention of Misuse) Act, 1988. The Rajiv Gandhi government must be given credit for enacting this legislation but it has remained only as a showpiece. During the Punjab agitation, it was seen that there was large-scale misuse of gurdwaras by terrorists for preaching their ideology. In Jammu and Kashmir, the separatists have been using Friday namaaz gatherings to launch their ideological offensive against the central government and its organizations. Hardly

---

[3] In the Gulberg Society case in the Godhra riots in 2002, in which sixty-nine people, including ex-Congress MP Ahsan Jafri was burnt alive, the decision was announced by the court on 2 June 2016. The court convicted twenty-four persons and acquitted thirty-six. (*IE* 3 June 2016: 1) Now the appeals will go on for several years to come.

any action has been taken in these cases. I had referred earlier, in Chapter 4, to the Places of Worship (Special Provisions) Act, 1991 which, too, has not been acted upon.

> In recent months, the Sanatan Sanstha has been in the news for its radical philosophy as regards the Hindu religion and also because it is alleged to have been involved in the assassination of Comrade Pansare in Kolhapur in Maharashtra. Former chief minister of Maharashtra, Prithviraj Chavan, stated that, in 2011, the Maharashtra government had sent all required documents and evidence to the Central government, seeking a ban on the Sanatan Sanstha. However, the home ministry had failed to act on it. (*IE* 24 September 2015: 3)

Sushilkumar Shinde, who was the then union home minister, has tried to defend himself by saying that this proposal was never brought to his notice. It is necessary to note that decisions on matters of banning an organization do not depend on who heads the home ministry. It has to be a case properly made out and legally sustainable not only before a tribunal but also before the high court and the Supreme Court, before whom it invariably gets challenged. But the important point is that in such cases, excessive secrecy must be avoided and if, for any reasons, a proposal sent by the state government is found to be weak, the reasoning must be made public to create a proper understanding of the issues in society at large.

I have brought out separately how communal speeches made by candidates have not been adequately dealt with under the provisions of the Representation of People Act, 1951. I have also referred therein to the observation of the Supreme Court in one of the cases that, as long as communal political parties are not banned from participating in the political life of the country, there is very little that the courts can do to restrain this. Reference must also be made to the recommendation of the NCRWC in this regard. The commission recommended:

> Any election campaigning on the basis of caste or religion and any attempt to spread caste and communal hatred during elections should be punishable with *mandatory imprisonment*. If such acts

are done at the instance of the candidate or his election agents, these *would be punishable with disqualification*. (GOI 2002: 87)

The Adoption of an Inquisitorial System

The experience of investigation of crimes in communal riots—whether it be the Godhra riots or any other major communal riots in the country—has raised serious questions. There is a widely prevalent view that such cases are not investigated vigorously or objectively, and the police often act under political pressure or in a communal manner, favouring one community or another. It may be recalled that, in some cases, a plea was made to the high courts and the Supreme Court that a special investigation team (SIT) be appointed by the Court, and that the investigation also be carried out under its supervision. Such petitions were agreed to by the Supreme Court in the Godhra cases, but obviously this cannot be done in every case, considering the workload of the high courts and the Supreme Court. It is, therefore, time to consider whether, in cases involving large communal riots, the French model of 'police judiciare' should be adopted.

> R. Deb wrote that, as far back as 1962, the Royal Commission on Police in the U K had recommended that 'the investigation of cases is a part of the judicial process and that the police must be entirely independent in the discharge of functions which are judicial or quasi-judicial.' He also pointed out that there was likely to be stiff opposition from the police establishment itself to any scheme of total separation of the investigating police from the law-and-order police. (*Journal of Indian Law Institute* [henceforth *JILI*] 1992: 271–73)

P.M. Bakshi, in his article, 'Continental System of Criminal Justice', wrote:

> Under the inquisitorial system, [as opposed to the accusatorial system prevalent in India] the court and its adjuncts (the examining magistrate and the public prosecutor) exercise full control over the preliminaries, that is to say, the investigation and also the presentation of the case at the trial. The offender, once formally accused, is the central party in the investigation, in the sense that

he and his counsel are entitled to see all statements of witnesses and exhibits amassed by the police and examining magistrate, and also to suggest further leads to be investigated. The victim of the offence is also a full party, in the sense that he may (with counsel of his own) intervene as a *partie civile* [civil party] in the pre-trial investigation and in the trial, and have his claim to the civil relief (arising out of the crime) adjudicated in the criminal proceedings. The court exercises an affirmative role, rather than the role of an umpire in the conduct of the prosecution. As compared to the above, in the accusatorial or adversary system, the accused (and his counsel, if any) are outside the preliminary investigation and have little right to any disclosure in advance of the prosecution evidence. At the trial, the court functions more as an umpire, leaving the presentation of the official case to the prosecuting attorney, and the responsibility of presenting the evidence on behalf of the accused is that of the accused and his counsel. (Bakshi *JILI* 1994: 420–21, 428)

The Justice Malimath Commission Report on Reforms in Criminal Justice System noted that:

The inquisitorial system is certainly efficient in the sense that the investigation is supervised by the judicial magistrate which results in a high rate of conviction. The committee, on balance, felt that a fair trial and, in particular, fairness to the accused, are better protected in the adversarial system. However, the committee felt that some of the good features of the inquisitorial system can be adopted to strengthen the adversarial system and to make it more effective. This includes the duty of the court to search for truth, to assign a pro-active role to the judges, to give directions to the investigating officers and prosecution agencies in the matter of investigation and leading evidence with the object of seeking the truth and focusing on justice to victims. (GOI 2003: 265–66)

B.K. Nehru, former civil servant, diplomat and governor, in his book, *Thoughts on Our Present Discontents*, drew attention to the fact that:

In a country where telling lies in a court of law is not regarded as immoral, and where the police are unfortunately not always above manufacturing evidence and extorting confessions, a system of this kind [inquisitorial] would...be definitely more suitable to our needs than our present procedures. As a result of a thorough magisterial investigation already made, the onus to prove his innocence lies heavily on the accused. This will shock our lawyers who have inherited Anglo-Saxon prejudices along with their system, but there is reason to believe that there are fewer miscarriages of justice under the continental system and much greater enforcement of the law than is prevalent in India today. (Nehru 1986: 111–12)

Justice V.R. Krishna Iyer, former judge of the Supreme Court, in his article in *The National Herald* in 2003, emphasized the arcane procedures of the adversarial system, modeled mainly on the colonial paradigms, making litigation a difficult project, at once expensive and endless, through appeals, reviews, revisions, and myriad interlocutory intricacies. So much so, that for an indigent and illiterate, agrestic and proletarian community, the search for judicial justice is 'a riddle wrapped in mystery inside an enigma'. The whole law of evidence, pleadings, hearings and intermediate wrangles is primitive and untouched by technology or modern management skills. (Iyer *The National Herald* 8 October 2003)

The Law Commission of India, in its seventy-seventh report submitted in 1978, recommended that 'Although we have adopted the accusatorial system, the trial judge should not play an altogether passive role, but must take greater interest and elicit such information as may be helpful in finding the truth. (GOI 1978: 157)

In spite of these valid arguments, there are many legal luminaries who are strongly opposed to any change-over from the existing system. In my book, *The Judiciary and Governance in India* (2008), I had examined these facets in the light of experience in a number of cases. I had stated:

This touching faith in the present state of the Indian criminal justice system is difficult to understand. Even a cursory look at the data regarding the conviction rate should be instructive in this regard. In

1968, the conviction rate was 70 per cent. In 1999, it came down to below 40 per cent and in 2003, it was 35 per cent. In 2006, it was estimated to be below 30 per cent. According to the then-Chief Justice of Bombay High Court, M.B. Shah, in 1998 the conviction rate was just 5 per cent. I had suggested that a trial should be given to the inquisitorial system by adoption on a pilot basis in selected districts. (Godbole 2008: 440–44)

This has assumed new urgency in the context of increasing threats to secularism. In all major cases with a bearing on secularism in recent years, namely, the anti-Sikh riots in Delhi in 1984, the demolition of the Babri Masjid in 1992—which led to horrendous communal riots in Mumbai and elsewhere in the country in December 1992 and January 1993—the Godhra riots in 2002, the Muzzafarpur riots in UP, and so on, it has come to light that the police investigation and convictions leave much to be desired. This has created a great sense of insecurity among the victims of these riots most of whom belonged to minorities. I, therefore, believe that the time has come to take a decision that, at least in cases of communal riots, to begin with, the inquisitorial system should be adopted. This one single step will go a long way in reassuring the minorities that the government is serious about the implementation of secularism.

Recommendations of the Second Administrative Reforms Commission

Reference must be made to some important recommendations of the Second Administrative Reforms Commission (SARC) in its fifth report submitted in June 2007. I propose to discuss only those recommendations which have a bearing on the issues pertaining to secularism.

> SARC has invited attention to the Communal Violence (Prevention, Control and Rehabilitation of Victims) Bill, 2005. This bill, prepared by the UPA government, met with stiff resistance and was criticized by all sections of public opinion. One of the main reasons for this was that the bill was placed by Sonia Gandhi before her advisory council, at whose instance several amendments were made in the bill. The states had opposed the provisions of the bill, which gave

special powers to the Union government to deal with communal violence in certain cases. In terms of clause 55 of the bill, the Central government was to be given power to give directions to the state government in case of communal disturbances, to issue notifications declaring any area within a state as a communally disturbed area, and to deploy armed forces wherever necessary. Where it was decided to deploy armed forces, an authority known as unified command was to be constituted for the purpose of coordinating and monitoring such deployment. Every such notification would be placed before both Houses of Parliament. It was also provided that such notification shall specify the period for which the area will remain so notified which shall not exceed in the first instance, 30 days. The Central government was also to be empowered to extend this period by notification, but the period during which an area could be notified as a communally disturbed area was not to exceed a total continuous period of 60 days.

It is mainly these clauses pertaining to the proposed involvement of the central government that were considered objectionable by the states. We have earlier discussed the need to amend the Constitution to bring the two subjects, namely, 'police' and 'public order' into the Concurrent List. There is no getting away from this necessity any longer. This is particularly important in the context of the growing and imminent threats of terrorism and attempts from external sources such as the ISIS, the ISI and Al-Qaeda, to the security of the country. Concerted efforts will have to be made to build a national consensus on this subject. As can be seen from the Draft Communal Violence Bill, 2005, drafted by the UPA and the recommendations of GOM cited earlier, both the Congress and the BJP were essentially in favour of enlarging the role of the central government. As I see it, this was the first major breakthrough. This consensus needs to be built upon for taking further steps expeditiously. Once this is done, it should not be difficult to demarcate and agree upon the modalities and the institutional arrangements for the central government's role.

Attention must be invited to some other significant recommendations of SARC. I find that some of these are particularly relevant in the context of the growing and widespread communal violence in the country.

- As seen in a number of cases, the state governments have not hesitated to issue instructions to the police on how to deal with communal riots. At times, these have extended even to the 'obstruction of justice'. SARC has, therefore, suggested that, 'No government functionary shall issue any instructions to any police functionary which are illegal or mala fide.' It also suggested that obstruction of justice should be defined as an offence under the law. Both these are eminently timely recommendations and need to be acted upon without any loss of time.
- As far as possible, the deployment of police personnel in police stations with a significant proportion of religious and linguistic minorities should be in proportion to the population of such communities within the local jurisdiction of such police stations.
- Another very important recommendation is that no sanction of the union government or a state government should be necessary for prosecution under section 153 (A). Section 196 CrPC should be amended accordingly. Experience so far has shown that, due to political influence-peddling, section 153 (A) has become practically a dead letter. There have been hardly any prosecutions under this section and convictions are even rarer. In the context of the increasing communal tensions and animosities, this section needs to be used extensively and forcefully. Similar recommendations have been made in the past but have not been acted upon. Acceptance of this recommendation and immediate follow-up action will go a long way in creating an atmosphere of communal harmony.
- Yet another recommendation of SARC's is that prosecution in cases related to rioting or communal offences should not be allowed to be withdrawn. This recommendation, too, is overdue. The experience of communal riots in Mumbai referred to in Chapter 4 showed that a number of cases against Shiv Sena activists were withdrawn by the state government. So also, the cases filed against the then Shiv Sena supremo, Bal Thackeray.
- SARC's recommendation that commissions of inquiry into any major riots/violence should give their report within one year is also very important. I have shown in Chapter 4 how the Liberhan Ayodhya Commission of Inquiry took an incredible

seventeen years to complete its deliberations. The Srikrishna Commission of Inquiry into the Mumbai riots was not permitted to function by the then Shiv Sena–BJP government for quite some time. The experience of commissions of inquiry in the Godhra riots has been no different. In the ultimate analysis, it is the commitment of the government to public accountability which matters. Another disturbing factor which was responsible for delays in the functioning of some commissions—such as the Liberhan Commission—was the stays granted by the high courts of UP and Delhi more than once. I had, therefore, strongly urged in my book, *The Judiciary and Governance in India* (2008) that the high courts and even the Supreme Court must lay down for themselves a guideline that in no case would a stay granted by a court be continued for more than three months.

- Another suggestion of SARC's is that: 'The recommendations made by a commission of inquiry should normally be accepted by the government, and if the government does not agree with any observations or recommendation contained in the report of the commission, it should record its reasons and make them public'. Such a recommendation has been made a number of times in the past but has not been taken note of by the governments, whether at the Centre or the states. In fact, the number of commissions whose recommendations have been acted upon can be counted on the fingers of—maybe just one hand. Finally, therefore, it is a question of whether the government is serious about its professed commitment to secularism.
- SARC suggested that all riots should be documented properly and analysed so that lessons could be drawn from such experiences. This, too, is a very valid point. In connection with the research for my previous books, I found that even in the library of Parliament, reports of a large number of commissions of inquiry in communal riots were not available. Most of the reports are not available as public documents to a researcher.

The following recommendations of SARC regarding the obligations of the union and the states deserve careful consideration:

- A law should be enacted to empower the union government

to deploy its forces and even to direct such forces in case of major public order problems which may lead to the breakdown of the constitutional machinery in a state. However, such deployment should take place only after the state concerned fails to act on a 'direction' issued by the union under Article 256 of the Constitution. All such deployments should be only for a temporary period not exceeding three months, which could be extended by another three months after authorization by Parliament.
- The law should spell out the hierarchy of the civil administration which would supervise the forces under such circumstances.

SARC also suggested the creation of a new category to be called federal crimes, which would have inter-state or national ramifications. The commission recommended that a new law should be enacted for the purpose, and the following offences should be included in this category:

- Organized crime
- Terrorism
- Acts threatening national security
- Trafficking in arms and human beings
- Sedition
- Major crimes with inter-state ramifications
- Assassination of (including attempts on) major public figures
- Serious economic offences.

SARC suggested the enactment of a new law to govern the working of the CBI. This law should stipulate its jurisdiction, including the power to investigate the new category of crimes. (GOI 2007b: 242–44, 253, 264, 267–68, 274–75)

The recommendation pertaining to the enactment of a law for the CBI is directly related to the subject of this book, as several major cases pertaining to communal riots have been handed over to the CBI from time to time. As can be seen, a number of recommendations of SARC converge with those of GOM on the Kargil War and the discussions in Chapters 3 and 4 of this book. It is important to note that *section 43 of the Forty-second Amendment Act inserted a new Article 257A in the*

Constitution empowering the central government to send any armed force or other force of the union for dealing with any grave situation of law and order in any state. Such force would act in accordance with the directions of the central government and not be subject to the control of the state government. Also, the new article empowered Parliament to specify, by law, the powers, functions and liabilities of the members of any such force deployed in a state. Unfortunately, this provision was deleted when the Janata government came to power in 1977. This was the outcome of the tremendous anger and frustration of the states with the Indira Gandhi government's style of functioning, particularly during the Emergency. If this article had been permitted to remain on the statute book, the Babri Masjid may not have been destroyed, and the communal riots in Mumbai and Godhra could have been avoided. Thus, India is paying a price for the short-sightedness of its political leadership.

Since then, for years together, some of these questions have been evaded by successive political establishments. The time has come when patch-work solutions are no longer going to be of any avail. If secularism is to be a part of the basic structure of the Constitution—as declared by the Supreme Court—in the real sense of the term, ways will have to be found without any further delay to make it a reality.

Safeguarding the Future of Secularism

In 1964, the government of India had appointed a high-level education commission under the chairmanship of D.S. Kothari, the then chairman of University Grants Commission (UGC). The commission comprised fifteen eminent educationists from India and abroad. On 29 June 1966, it submitted a comprehensive report on a whole gamut of issues pertaining to the education sector to the Minister for Education, M.C. Chagla. One of the items discussed by the commission was 'secularism and religion'. Given below are the recommendations of the commission so far as the subject matter of this book is concerned:

> It would not be practicable for a secular state with many religions to provide education in any one religion. It is, however, necessary for a multi-religious democratic state to promote a tolerant study of all religions so that its citizens can understand each other better and

live amicably together. It must be remembered that, owing to the ban placed on religious instruction in schools and the weakening of the home influences which, in the past, often provided such instruction, children are now growing up without any clear ideas of their own religion and no chance of learning about others. In fact, the general ignorance and misunderstanding in these matters are so widespread in the younger generation as to be fraught with great danger for the development of a democracy in which tolerance is rated as a high value. We suggest that a syllabus giving well-chosen information about each of the major religions should be included as a part of the course in citizenship or as part of general education, to be introduced in schools and colleges up to the first degree. It should highlight the fundamental similarities in the great religions of the world and the emphasis they place on the cultivation of certain broadly comparable and moral and spiritual values. It would be a great advantage to have a common course on this subject in all parts of the country and common textbooks which should be prepared at the national level by competent and suitable experts available on each religion. When these courses have been prepared, it would be worthwhile to have them scrutinized by a small committee of eminent persons belonging to different religions to ensure that nothing is included in them to which any religious group could take legitimate objection. (GOI 1966: 20–21)

These are highly thoughtful recommendations. I fully agree with them and find that they are as relevant today. Unfortunately, though fifty years have elapsed since the submission of the report, nothing has been done by the government so far. If follow-up action had been taken, the complaints of saffronization of textbooks during the BJP rule and their secularization under the leftist and the Congress rule would not have become such a contentious issue. It is also necessary to ensure that these issues are not politicized. If a constitutional commission on secularism—as suggested above—is appointed, any grievances on this subject can be referred to it.

In this context, a reference may be made to the recommendations of the S.B. Chavan Committee in its report submitted to Parliament in February 1999. It, *inter alia*, recommended: 'Another significant factor that merits urgent attention now is religion. Although it is not the only source of essential values, it certainly is a major source of value generation. *What is required today is not religious education but education about religions, their basics, the values inherent therein and also a comparative study of the philosophy of all religions.*' The committee strongly urged *education about religions as an instrument of social cohesion and religious harmony.* (Apte 2005: 177)

In *Aruna Roy v. Union of India* ((2002) 6 SCALE 408), the Supreme Court ruled that the concept of secularism is not endangered if the basic tenets of all religions all over the world are studied and learnt. Value-based education will help the nation to fight against fanaticism, ill-will, violence, dishonesty and corruption. These values can be inculcated if the basic tenets of all religions are learnt. (Jain 2010: 1317)

The Right to Freedom of Religion

A number of Sikh and Buddhist institutions had suggested to the NCRWC certain changes in Article 25 (2) which reads as follows: '(2) Nothing in this article shall affect the operation of any existing law or prevent the State from making any law–

(a) Regulating or restricting any economic, financial, political or other secular activity which may be associated with religious practice;
(b) Providing for social welfare and reform or the throwing open of Hindu religious institutions of a public character to all classes and sections of Hindus.

Explanation I. The wearing and carrying of kirpans shall be deemed to be included in the profession of the Sikh religion.

Explanation II. In sub-clause (b) of clause (2), the reference to Hindus shall be construed as including a reference to persons professing the Sikh, Jaina or Buddhist religion, and the reference to Hindu religious institutions shall be construed accordingly.

As can be seen, Explanation II to Article 25 provides that reference

to Hindus in sub-clause (b) of clause (2) should be construed as including a reference to Sikhs, etc. The commission, without going into the larger issue on which the contention is based, was of the opinion that the purpose of the representation would be served if Explanation II to Article 25 were omitted and sub-clause (b) of clause (2) of that article reworded as follows:
'(b) providing for social welfare and reform or the throwing open of Hindu, Sikh, Jaina or Buddhist religious institutions of a public character to all classes and sections of these religions.' (GOI 2002: 67)

This recommendation is yet to be acted upon by the government. It should be recalled that this grievance of the Sikhs figured as a part of the demands during the Khalistan agitation in the 1990s. There is no reason why such minor irritants should be permitted to vitiate the atmosphere and raise doubts about India's commitment to secularism.

The Ranganath Misra Commission for Religious and Linguistic Minorities candidly commented:

We cannot understand that if, according to any indication in the Constitution, Sikh, Buddhist and Jain faiths were akin to Hinduism, why did the Constitution (Scheduled Castes) Order, 1950, initially declare that no non-Hindu could be a scheduled caste—thus excluding even the Sikhs, Buddhists and Jains? Why did it take the Sikhs six long years and the Buddhists fourteen years to get themselves included in the scheduled caste net? And why are the Jains even now excluded from it? *It seems that the scheduled caste net was initially restricted to Hindus for some supra-Constitutional reasons, and seeking support from the Constitution for later extending it to the Sikhs and Buddhists was an afterthought—which, however, is wholly repugnant to the letter and spirit of the Constitution.* (GOI 2007a: 169)

The issue raised by the commission is of considerable importance and clearly, the decision to bring Sikhs and Buddhists into the scheduled castes' net must have been due to political compulsions. Since this issue will be relevant for any decision on extending the same treatment to

Muslims as proposed by the Ranganath Misra Commission, it may be advisable to have an authoritative opinion on the subject by making a reference to the Supreme Court under Article 143 of the Constitution.

The State Must Be Equidistant from All Religions

In the light of the definition of secularism as *'sarva dharma samabhav'* (equal respect for all religions), a questions is often asked about whether the Indian State has remained equidistant from all religions. The Hindu religion has received the maximum attention from the government and the courts so far. This is evident from the number of enactments passed by the states and the Centre for reforming the Hindu religious customs and practices. The intervention by the courts has gone to the extent of deciding what religion is and which customs and practices are intrinsic to the religion. The recent decision of the Rajasthan High Court in respect of *'santhara'* in Jainism is similarly viewed and has been challenged in the Supreme Court. The Hindu law has been codified, overriding serious, vocal and persistent opposition. But the same does not hold true in regard to the other religions. For example, in spite of repeated suggestions, the government has desisted from doing anything to bring about reforms in the Muslim personal law, its customs and traditions. The government has consciously overlooked the demands made by liberal elements in the Muslim community, so as not to displease the orthodox, conservative and fundamentalist minority among the Muslims.

The government has also adopted a hands-off policy in regard to the Christian religion. Illustratively, reference may be made to the demand made by an enlightened section of the Christians for a law governing church property. Justice K.T. Thomas, a retired judge of the Supreme Court, in the speech delivered at a meeting organized by the Goa Cultural and Social Centre on 28 July 2009, invited attention to the fact that enactments had been passed in respect of properties of important Hindu temples such as the Tirupati Temple and the Guruvayur Temple, namely, the Tirumala Tirupati Devasthanam Act; the Travancore–Cochin Hindu Religious Institutions Act; the Madras Hindu Religious and Charitable Endowments Act 1951. 'A division bench of the Kerala High Court is conferred jurisdiction to review the auditing of the accounts of all temples falling under the purview of the said enactments. I remember,

I too was a member of that division bench for a certain period along with Mr Justice Paripoornan...All these enactments were passed on the strength of Article 26 of the Constitution of India.'

Similar is the position in respect of Sikh religious properties and wakf properties. Under the relevant legislations, their activities are subject to a judicial scrutiny apart from public auditing and so on. Justice Thomas rightly asked why the different denominations of the Christian religion were unwilling to have a law enacted for administering church properties. A draft bill for the administration of church properties and institutions was prepared by the organizers of the Joint Christian Council, Kerala and forwarded to the chief secretary, government of Kerala, on 9 July 2012. However, due to opposition from church interests, no action was taken thereon. This is a glaring instance of the State's reluctance to address the issue.

I had earlier referred to the recommendation of the Hindu Religious Endowments Commission (1962) that there should be 'no insuperable difficulty or complication in enacting a uniform legislation dealing with the religious endowments of all communities in India... Such legislation should of course incorporate such special provisions as may be considered necessary for the endowments of individual religions or communities.' I also referred earlier to the demand made by a section of the Christian community that a law should be enacted to ensure proper management of church properties. All these cases underline the need for enacting a comprehensive central legislation to cover endowments pertaining to all religions in India. There is enough evidence of the State's not being equidistant from all religions. Long-overdue action taken on this matter will strengthen the confidence of the common person in the concept of secularism.

I have also brought out earlier the gross and widely prevalent mismanagement of wakf properties. This major problem has still not been adequately addressed either by the states or by the Centre due to apprehensions of hurting the sentiments of Muslims. According to a decision of the Supreme Court in December 2015, the state governments have been directed to appoint, within four months, three-member tribunals for speedy disposal of cases pending before the wakf tribunals. (*Sakal Today* 20 December 2015: 1).

Tahir Mahmood, former chairman of the National Minorities

Commission and ex-member, Law Commission, in his article, 'Repeal This', suggested that 'The archaic concept of Wakf for the settler's limitless generations is out of tune with the social and economic circumstances of our time. The institution was abolished by law in Syria, Egypt, Libya and the UAE, in 1949, 1952, 1973 and 1980, respectively. (*IE* 1 August 2015: 10)

Such a decision will not be easy in India!

On 29 September 2009, the Supreme Court had given directions that unauthorized places of worship should be removed expeditiously. However, state governments and local bodies are dragging their feet in complying with this order. When the matter was brought to the notice of the Bombay High Court in so far as Maharashtra was concerned, the court has directed the State once again to take prompt action and to submit a full report to the court. (*Loksatta* 9 October 2015: 1)

It remains to be seen what action is taken by the government.

To Sum Up

In a pluralistic society such as that of India, secularism was expected to be the unifying force for building bridges between the religious communities. Instead, secularism itself has become a divisive force. As seen, all efforts made so far to ban communal parties and organizations, and to prohibit them from entering the political life of the country have been unsuccessful. The scope of these efforts was also restricted to the laws relating to elections to Parliament and state legislatures. While these are no doubt important objectives, they, by themselves, are not adequate. Secularism has to become a way of life, and mechanisms need to be established to translate it from a constitutional precept into an integral part of governance and public life. I trust this book will go some way towards achieving this aim.

APPENDIX I

DECLARATION ON THE RIGHTS OF PERSONS BELONGING TO NATIONAL OR ETHNIC, RELIGIOUS AND LINGUISTIC MINORITIES

Adopted by General Assembly resolution 47/135 of 18 December 1992

Art. 1

1. States shall protect the existence and the national or ethnic, cultural, religious and linguistic identity of minorities within their respective territories and shall encourage conditions for the promotion of that identity.
2. States shall adopt appropriate legislative and other measures to achieve those ends.

Art. 2

1. Persons belonging to national or ethnic, religious and linguistic minorities (hereinafter referred to as persons belonging to minorities) have the right to enjoy their own culture, to profess and practise their own religion, and to use their own language, in private and in public, freely and without interference or any form of discrimination.
2. Persons belonging to minorities have the right to participate effectively in cultural, religious, social, economic and public life.
3. Persons belonging to minorities have the right to participate effectively in decisions on the national and, where appropriate, regional level concerning the minority to which they belong or the regions in which they live, in a manner not incompatible with national legislation.
4. Persons belonging to minorities have the right to establish and maintain their own associations.
5. Persons belonging to minorities have the right to establish and maintain, without any discrimination, free and peaceful contacts with other members

of their group and with persons belonging to other minorities, as well as contacts across frontiers with citizens of other States to whom they are related by national or ethnic, religious or linguistic ties.

Art. 3

1. Persons belonging to minorities may exercise their rights, including those set forth in the present Declaration, individually as well as in community with other members of their group, without any discrimination.
2. No disadvantage shall result for any person belonging to a minority as the consequence of the exercise or non-exercise of the rights set forth in the present Declaration.

Art. 4

1. States shall take measures where required to ensure that persons belonging to minorities may exercise fully and effectively all their human rights and fundamental freedoms without any discrimination and in full equality before the law.
2. States shall take measures to create favourable conditions to enable persons belonging to minorities to express their characteristics and to develop their culture, language, religion, traditions and customs, except where specific practices are in violation of national law and contrary to international standards.
3. States should take appropriate measures so that, wherever possible, persons belonging to minorities may have adequate opportunities to learn their mother tongue or to have instruction in their mother tongue.
4. States should, where appropriate, take measures in the field of education in order to encourage knowledge of the history, traditions, language and culture of the minorities existing within their territory. Persons belonging to minorities should have adequate opportunities to gain knowledge of the society as a whole.
5. States should consider appropriate measures so that persons belonging to minorities may participate fully in the economic progress and development in their country.

Art. 5

1. National policies and programmes shall be planned and implemented with due regard for the legitimate interests of persons belonging to minorities.

2. Programmes of cooperation and assistance among States should be planned and implemented with due regard for the legitimate interests of persons belonging to minorities.

Art. 6

States should cooperate on questions relating to persons belonging to minorities, *inter alia*, exchanging information and experiences, in order to promote mutual understanding and confidence.

Art. 7

States should cooperate in order to promote respect for the rights set forth in the present Declaration.

Art. 8

1. Nothing in the present Declaration shall prevent the fulfilment of international obligations of States in relation to persons belonging to minorities. In particular, States shall fulfil in good faith the obligations and commitments they have assumed under international treaties and agreements to which they are parties.
2. The exercise of the rights set forth in the present Declaration shall not prejudice the enjoyment by all persons of universally recognized human rights and fundamental freedoms.
3. Measures taken by States to ensure the effective enjoyment of the rights set forth in the present Declaration shall not *prima facie* be considered contrary to the principle of equality contained in the Universal Declaration of Human Rights.
4. Nothing in the present Declaration may be construed as permitting any activity contrary to the purposes and principles of the United Nations, including sovereign equality, territorial integrity and political independence of States.

Art. 9

The specialized agencies and other organizations of the United Nations system shall contribute to the full realization of the rights and principles set forth in the present Declaration, within their respective fields of competence.

Source: Durga Das Basu, *Constitutional Law*, Vol. 3, 2008, pp. 3574–77.

APPENDIX II

THE CONSTITUTION (EIGHTIETH AMENDMENT) BILL, 1993
BILL NO. 73 OF 1993
(INTRODUCED IN LOK SABHA ON 29 JULY 1993)
A BILL FURTHER TO AMEND THE CONSTITUTION OF INDIA

Be it enacted by Parliament in the Forty-fourth Year of the Republic of India as follows:

1. **Short title and commencement** (1) This Act may be called the Constitution (Eightieth Amendment) Act, 1993.

   (2) It shall come into force on such date as the Central Government may, by notification in the Official Gazette, appoint.

2. **Insertion of new article 28A: State to have equal respect for all religions:**
   In Part III of the Constitution, after Article 28 and before the heading, 'Cultural and Educational Rights', the following article shall be inserted, namely:
   '28A. The State shall have equal respect for all religions.'

3. Insertion of new Article 35A: Legislation to declare certain associations as banned on certain grounds:
   In Part III of the Constitution, after Article 35, the following article shall be inserted, namely:
   '35A. Notwithstanding anything in this Constitution–
   (a) Parliament may, by law, provide that any association or body of individuals be banned, if it, by words, either spoken or written, or by signs or by visible representations or otherwise, promotes or attempts to promote disharmony or feelings of enmity, hatred or ill-will between different classes of citizens of India:
   (i) on grounds of religion; or

(ii) on grounds of race, place of birth, residence, language, caste or community;
(b) the law referred to in clause (a) may make provisions for the forfeiture of property, movable or immovable, of the banned association or union and such other incidental or consequential provisions as Parliament may think fit;
(c) The Supreme Court shall, to the exclusion of any other court, have jurisdiction in respect of any matter arising under the law referred to in clause (a)'.

4. **Amendment of Article 102**: In Article 102 of the Constitution, in clause (1), after sub-clause (d), the following sub-clauses shall be inserted, namely:
    '(da) if he, after making and subscribing the oath or affirmation in accordance with the form set out for the purpose in the Third Schedule for election to Parliament, makes use of religion, including religious symbols, for the purposes of the said election;
    (db) if he promotes or attempts to promote feelings of enmity or hatred or ill-will between different classes of citizens of India on grounds of religion, race, caste, community or language.'
5. **Amendment of Article 191**: In Article 191 of the Constitution, in clause (1), after sub-clause (d), the following sub-clauses shall be inserted, namely–
    '(da) if he, after making and subscribing the oath or affirmation in accordance with the form set out for the purpose in the Third Schedule for election to the Legislature of a state, makes use of religion, including religious symbols, for the purposes of the said election;
    (db) if he promotes or attempts to promote feelings of enmity or hatred or ill-will between different classes of citizens of India on grounds of religion, race, caste, community or language.'
6. **Amendment of Article 226**: In Article 226 of the Constitution, in clause (1), after the word and figures 'Article 32', the words, brackets, letters and figures 'but subject to the provisions of clause (c) of Article 35A,' shall be inserted.
7. **Amendment of Ninth Schedule**: In the Ninth Schedule to the Constitution, after entry 257 and before the Explanation, the following entry shall be inserted:
    '258. The Religious Institutions (Prevention of Misuse) Act, 1988 (Central Act 41 of 1988).'

Statement of Objects and Reasons

The Constitution provides for the establishment of a secular state for the governance of the country. This principle was reaffirmed by the Constitution (Forty-second Amendment) Act, 1976, by which the word 'secular' was incorporated in the Preamble to the Constitution.

2. Despite the safeguards provided in the Constitution, communalism is taking root and unless effective measures are urgently taken to curb it, it may become a threat to the secular and democratic ideals on which our society is based.
3. It has, therefore, become necessary to further amend the Constitution–
   (a) to provide that the State shall have respect for all religions;
   (b) to confer power on Parliament to ban any association or body of individuals if it promotes or attempts to promote disharmony or feelings of enmity, hatred or ill-will between different classes of citizens of India on grounds of religion, race, place of birth, residence, language, caste or community;
   (c) to provide in Articles 102 and 191 that making use of religion, including religious symbols, for the purpose of getting elected to Parliament or to State Legislature or promoting or attempting to promote feelings of enmity, hatred or ill-will between different classes of citizens of India on grounds of religion, race, caste, community or language would be a ground for disqualification;
   (d) to amend the Ninth Schedule to include therein the Religious Institutions (Prevention of Misuse) Act, 1988;
   (e) to make certain consequential amendments in Article 226.
4. The Bill seeks to achieve the above objects.

New Delhi;
The 25th July 1993.   S.B. Chavan

Annexure

Extract from the Constitution of India
226. Power of High Courts to issue certain writs:

(1) Not withstanding anything in article 32, every High Court shall have power, throughout the territories in relation to which it exercises jurisdiction, to issue to any person or authority, including in appropriate cases, any Government, within those territories

directions, orders or writs, including writs in the nature of *habeas corpus*, *mandamus*, prohibition, *quo warranto* and *certiorari*, or any of them, for the enforcement of any of the rights conferred by Part III and for any other purpose. (Kashyap 1993: 74–77)

APPENDIX III

THE REPRESENTATION OF THE PEOPLE (AMENDMENT) BILL, 1993
BILL NO. 74 OF 1993
(INTRODUCED IN LOK SABHA ON 29 JULY 1993)
A BILL FURTHER TO AMEND THE REPRESENTATION OF THE PEOPLE ACT, 1951

BE it enacted by Parliament in the Forty-fourth year of the Republic of India as follows:

1. **Short title:** This Act may be called The Representation of the People (Amendment) Act, 1993.
2. **Amendment of section 29A:** In section 29A of the Representation of the People Act, 1951 (hereinafter referred to as the principal Act) –
   (i) in sub-section (7), for the existing proviso, the following proviso shall be substituted, namely:
   'Provided that no association or body shall be registered as a political party under this sub-section, if –
   (a) The association or body bears a religious name; or
   (b) The memorandum or rules and regulations of such association or body do not conform to the provisions of sub-section (5);'
   (ii) for sub-section (8), the following sub-section shall be substituted, namely:
   '(8) Not withstanding anything contained in any other provision of this Act or in any other law for the time being in force, an appeal shall lie to the Supreme Court from any decision of the Commission under this section:
   Provided that every appeal under this section shall be preferred within a period of thirty days from the date of the decision of the Commission:
   Provided further that the Supreme Court may entertain an appeal after

the expiry of the said period of thirty days if it is satisfied that the association or body had sufficient cause for not preferring the appeal within such period.'

3. **Insertion of new section 29B: de-registration of political parties:** In Part IV A of the principal Act, after section 29A the following section shall be inserted, namely:

'29B. (1) Where, –

(a) Any political party bears a religious name; or

(b) The memorandum or rules and regulations of the political party no longer conform to the provisions of sub-section (5) of section 29A; or

(c) The activities of the political party are not in accordance with its memorandum or rules and regulations referred to in sub-section (5) of section 29A,

its registration as a political party under section 29A shall be liable to be cancelled by an order of the High Court within whose jurisdiction the main office of that political party is situate.

(2) On receipt of a complaint that there is sufficient cause for cancelling the registration of a political party under sub-section (1), the High Court may call upon the political party affected by notice in writing to show cause, within thirty days from the date of the service of such notice, why the registration of the political party should not be cancelled:

Provided that where the High Court is not satisfied that there is sufficient cause for cancelling the registration of the political party, it may summarily reject the complaint.

(3) After considering the cause if any, shown by the political party or office-bearers or members thereof, the High Court may, after holding such inquiry as it may deem fit and after calling for such information as it may consider necessary from the political party or from any office-bearer or member thereof, decide whether or not there is sufficient cause for cancelling the registration and make such order as it may deem fit either dismissing the complaint or cancelling the registration of the political party.

(4) No complaint under sub-section (2) shall lie to the High Court within a period of ninety days from the commencement of the Representation of the People (Amendment) Act, 1993 on the ground specified in clause (a) of sub-section (1), if the political party changes its religious name

within the said period.'

Statement of Objects and Reasons

Democracy and secularism are the two pillars of our State. They represent the basic features of the Indian constitutional polity. The principle of equality is the very foundation of both democracy and secularism. Under the Constitution, all the citizens of India enjoy equal rights and privileges without any discrimination and no section of people is competent to usurp the rights of another section. One of the menaces which our country faces today is that of communalism. It fragments the society and holds a threat to the unity and the integrity of India.

In view of above, it has become necessary to strengthen the provisions of section 29A of the Representation of the People Act, 1951 relating to registration of political parties. It is proposed to further amend that section so as to provide that no association or body shall be registered by the Election Commission as a political party under that section if the association or body bears a religious name, since such a religious name could be said to contain an appeal to vote for the political party on the ground of religion which would be detrimental to the cause of secular democracy. An appeal is proposed to be provided against the decision of the Election Commission to the Supreme Court. Further, a new section 29B is proposed to be inserted in the said Act, whereunder a complaint can be made to the High Court within whose jurisdiction the main office of a political party is situate, for cancelling the registration of a political party where such political party bears a religious name or the memorandum or rules and regulations of the political party no longer conform to the provisions of the sub-section (5) of section 29A or the activities of the political party are not in accordance with the said memorandum or rules and regulations. It is also proposed to lay down a time limit of ninety days within which political parties with religious name would be required to change such names and conform to the new law.

The Bill seeks to achieve the above objects.

New Delhi   H.R. Bhardwaj

Annexure

Extract from the Representation of the People Act, 1951
(43 of 1951)
PART IV A
Registration of Political Parties

29A. Registration with the Election Commission of associations and bodies as political parties:

(5) The application under sub-section (1) shall be accompanied by a copy of the memorandum or rules and regulations of the association or body by whatever name called, and such memorandum or rules and regulations shall contain a specific provision that the association or body shall bear true faith and allegiance to the Constitution of India as by law established, and to the principles of socialism, secularism and democracy, and would uphold the sovereignty, unity and integrity of India.

(6) The Commission may call for such other particulars as it may deem fit from the association or body.

(7) After considering all the particulars as aforesaid in its possession and any other necessary and relevant factors and after giving the representatives of the association or body reasonable opportunity of being heard, the Commission shall decide either to register the association or body as a political party for the purposes of this Part, or not so to register it; and the Commission shall communicate its decision to the association or body:

Provided that no association or body shall be registered as a political party under this sub-section unless the memorandum or rules and regulations of such association or body conform to the provisions of sub-section (5).

(8) The decision of the Commission shall be final. (Kashyap 1993: 78–83)

APPENDIX IV

THE POSITION OF MUSLIMS IN UP BEFORE PARTITION

UP Muslims led the way for the Partition of India. Their argument was that Congress rule in 1937–39 had been unfair to them and that they could not expect a just and fair treatment in a united free India. On 11 January 1939, Pandit Govind Ballabh Pant, the then-Prime Minister of UP, met with the UP Press Consultative Committee and placed the following factual position before them:

> ...The Muslims formed about 14 per cent of the population. Generally, the Muslim representation in services is far in excess of what it should be on the population basis. Take for example some important services. In the provincial executive service, the Hindus are 52.5 per cent and the Muslims 39.6; among the tahsildars, Hindus 54.9 and Muslims 43.6; among naib tahsildars, Hindus 55.9 and Muslims 41.1; in the provincial judicial service, Hindus 72 and Muslims 25; among deputy superintendents of police, Hindus 56 and Muslims 28; among police inspectors, Hindus 46.4 and Muslims 30; among sub-inspectors, Hindus 54.2 and Muslims 43.8; among head constables, Hindus 35.3 and Muslims 64.4; in the UP agricultural service – Class I, Hindus 64 and Muslims 21; in the UP agricultural service – Class II, Hindus 76 and Muslims 12; in the subordinate agricultural service, Hindus 73 and Muslims 25; among veterinary inspectors, Hindus 24 and Muslims 52; among veterinary assistant surgeons, Hindus 35 and Muslims 58; among gazetted officers of the cooperative department, Hindus 62.5 and Muslims 37.5; in the UP forest service, Hindus 57 and Muslims 19; among forest rangers, Hindus 80.5 and Muslims 18.5; among

deputy rangers, Hindus 74.4 and Muslims 25; among assistant excise commissioners, Hindus 57 and Muslims 14; among excise inspectors, Hindus 65 and Muslims 31; in the UP educational service—Class I, out of 15 posts, 4 are held by Muslims... I claim that what we have done is not only just but even generous... (Malkani 1993: 173–74)

Note: During the British period, the percentage of Muslims in the Indian army was 29. The Nizam's police force and the army of 42,000 men was mainly recruited from the Muslim community.

ABBREVIATIONS

AICC	All India Congress Committee
AIDWA	All India Democratic Women's Association
AIMPLB	All India Muslim Personal Law Board
AMU	Aligarh Muslim University
BD	Bajrang Dal
BHU	Banaras Hindu University
BJP	Bharatiya Janata Party
BPR&D	Bureau of Police Research and Development
CA	Constituent Assembly
CAD	Constituent Assembly Debates
CALD	Constituent Assembly (Legislative) Debates
CAN	Calling Attention Notice
CAT	Central Administrative Tribunal
CBI	Central Bureau of Investigation
CCPA	Cabinet Committee on Political Affairs
CCTG	Concerned Citizens Tribunal Gujarat
CJI	Chief Justice of India
CID	Criminal Investigation Department
COS	Commission on Secularism
CPI(M)	Communist Party of India (Marxist)
CrPC	Criminal Procedure Code
DGP	Director General of Police
DIG	Deputy Inspector General (of Police)
DMK	Dravid Munnetra Kazagam
EOC	Equal Opportunity Commission
EPW	Economic and Political Weekly
ET	Economic Times
GDP	Gross Domestic Product

GOI	Government of India
GOM	Group of Ministers
GOMP	Government of Madhya Pradesh
HM	Home Minister
HLC	Hindu Law Committee
HT	Hindustan Times
IB	Intelligence Bureau
I & B	Information and Broadcasting
ICCR	Indian Council of Cultural Relations
ICHR	Indian Council of Historical Research
IE	Indian Express
IGNCA	Indira Gandhi National Centre for Arts
IGP	Inspector General of Police
IIM	Indian Institute of Management
IIT	Indian Institute of Technology
INC	Indian National Congress
IPC	Indian Penal Code
ISC	Inter-State Council
ISI	Inter-Services Intelligence (of Pakistan)
ISIL	Islamic State of Iraq and the Levant
ISIS	Islamic State of Iraq and Syria
J	Journal
J and K	Jammu and Kashmir
JILI	Journal of Indian Law Institute
JNMF	Jawaharlal Nehru Memorial Fund
LAD	Legislative Assembly Debates
LSD	Lok Sabha Debates
MHA	Ministry of Home Affairs
MLA	Member of Legislative Assembly
MNS	Maharashtra Navanirman Sena
MP	Member of Parliament
NCERT	National Council of Educational Research and Training
NCM	National Commission for Minorities
NCRB	National Crime Records Bureau
NCRWC	National Commission to Review the Working of the Constitution
NDA	National Democratic Alliance

NHRC	National Human Rights Commission
NIA	National Investigation Agency
NIC	National Integration Council
NITI	National Institution for Transforming India
NPC	National Police Commission
NWFP	North West Frontier Province
OBC	Other Backward Classes
OUP	Oxford University Press
PAC	Provincial Armed Constabulary
PIL	Public Interest Litigation
PM	Prime Minister
PMO	Prime Minister's Office
PUCL	People's Union for Civil Liberties
PUDR	People's Union for Democratic Rights
RBI	Reserve Bank of India
RJB-BM	Ram Janma Bhoomi- Babri Masjid
RPA	Representation of People Act
RSD	Rajya Sabha Debates
RSS	Rashtriya Swayamsevak Sangh
SARC	Second Administrative Reforms Commission
SC	Scheduled Castes
SCC	Supreme Court Cases
SGPC	Shiromani Gurudwara Prabandhak Committee
SIT	Special Investigation Team
SP	Superintendent of Police
ST	Scheduled Tribes
TIFR	Tata Institute of Fundamental Research
TOI	Times of India
UGC	University Grants Commission
UP	Uttar Pradesh
UPA	United Progressive Alliance
UT	Union Territory
VHP	Vishva Hindu Parishad

BIBLIOGRAPHY

Abdullah, Hasan, 'Minorities, Education and Language', *Economic & Political Weekly* (henceforth, *EPW)*, 15 June 2002.
Adeney, Katharine, and Lawrence Sáez, (eds), *Coalition Politics and Hindu Nationalism*, London and New York: Routledge, 2005.
Advani, L.K., 'Transgressing Boundaries of Gender and Identity', *EPW*, 7 September 2002.
——, *My Country My Life*, New Delhi: Rupa & Co., 2008.
——, *As I See It: LK Advani's Blog Posts*, New Delhi: Rupa & Co., 2011.
Ahmad, Riaz, 'Gujarat Violence: Meaning and Implications', *EPW*, 18 May 2002.
Aithal, Rajani V., 'Freedom of Religion Bill 2006 in Himachal Pradesh', *The Radical Humanist*, October 2007.
Akbar, M.J., *India: The Siege Within: Challenges to a Nation's Unity*, New Delhi: Penguin Books, 1984.
——, *Nehru: The Making of India*, London: Penguin–Viking Books India, 1988.
Ambedkar, B.R., *Thoughts on Pakistan*, Bombay: Thacker and Company, 1941.
An-Na'im, Abdullahi Ahmed, *Islam and the Secular State: Negotiating the Future of Shari'a*, Harvard University Press: Cambridge, Massachusetts, and London, England, 2008.
Apte, Bal, (ed.), *Supreme Court on Hindutva: Extracts and Comments*, New Delhi: India First Foundation, 2005.
Bachal, V.M., *Freedom of Religion and the Indian Judiciary: A Critical Study of Judicial Decisions 26-1-1950 to 26-1-1975*, Poona: Shubhada Saraswat, 1975.
Baird, Robert D., (ed.), *Religion in Modern India*, New Delhi: Manohar Publications, 1981.
Bakshi, P.M., 'Continental System of Criminal Justice', *Journal of Indian Law Institute* (henceforth, *JILI)*, October–December 1994.
——, *The Constitution of India: Selective Comments*, Delhi: Universal

Law Publishing Co., 1998.

Banerjee, A.C., *The Constituent Assembly of India*, Calcutta: A. Mukherjee & Co., 1947.

Banerjee, Sikata, 'The Saffron Wave: The Eleventh General Elections in Maharashtra', *EPW*, 4 October 1997.

Banerjee, Sumanta, 'Need of the Hour: Beyond "Detoxification"', *EPW*, 5 June 2004.

Banerjee, Vikramjit, and Sumeet Malik, 'Changing Perceptions of Secularism', *The Supreme Court Cases, Journal Section*, Vol. 7, 1998.

Basant, Rakesh, and Abusaleh Shariff, (eds.), *Handbook of Muslims: Empirical and Policy Perspectives*, New Delhi: Oxford University Press (henceforth, OUP), 2010.

Basu, Durga Das, *Constitutional Law of India*, Vol. 3, 8th edition, New Delhi: LexisNexis Butterworths Wadhwa, 2008.

———, *Introduction to the Constitution of India*, Gurgaon: Lexis Nexis, 2013.

Baxi, Upendra, *Inhuman Wrongs and Human Rights: Unconventional Essays*, New Delhi: Har-Anand Publications, 1994.

———, 'Notes on Holocaustian Politics', *Seminar* 513, May 2002.

———, 'The Second Gujarat Catastrophe', *EPW*, 24 August 2002.

Berlinerblau, Jacques, *How to be Secular: A Call to Arms for Regional Freedom*, Boston, New York: Houghton Mifflin Harcourt, 2012.

Beteille, Andre, 'Secularism and the Intellectuals', *EPW*, 5 March 1994.

Bhargava, Rajeev, 'Giving Secularism Its Due', *EPW*, 9 July 1994.

———, (ed.), *Secularism and Its Critics*, Delhi: OUP, 1998.

Bharatiya, V.P., 'Minorities Commission: Constitutional Metamorphosis?', *JILI*, Vol. 29, 1979.

Bilgrami, Akeel, 'Two Concepts of Secularism: Reason, Modernity and Archimedean Ideal', *EPW*, 9 July 1994.

Chagla, M.C., *Roses in December: An Autobiography*, 11th edition, Mumbai: Bharatiya Vidya Bhavan, 2000.

Chandhoke, Neera, *Beyond Secularism: The Rights of Religious Minorities*, New Delhi: OUP, 1999.

Chandra Bipan, *Communalism in Modern India*, second revised edition, Vikas Publishing House, New Delhi, 1984.

Chapalgaonkar, (Justice) Narendra, *Secularism in India: Meaning and Practice*, Yashwantrao Chavan Memorial Lecture, 14 May 2010, Mimeo.

Chatterjee, Partha, 'Secularism and Toleration', *EPW*, 9 July 1994.

———, (ed.), *State and Politics in India*, Delhi: OUP, 1997.

Chauthaiwale, Vijay, Shreekant Katdare, and Saiyed Purujit, (eds.), *Hindutva in Present Context*, Ahmedabad: Bharat Vichar Manch, 2010.
The Complete Works of Swami Vivekananda, Vol. I, Calcutta: Advaita Ashrama, 1989.
Concerned Citizens' Tribunal – Gujarat 2002, *Crime against Humanity*, Vols I & II, Mumbai: Citizens for Justice and Peace, 2002.
Constituent Assembly of India Debates (CAD), Vols IV–VI, 1947–48, New Delhi.
———, Vol. XI, November 1949.
———, Vols I–VI, Book No. 1, 2009.
———, Vol. VII, Book 2, 2009, New Delhi.
———, Vols X–XII, Book 5, 2009.
Constituent Assembly of India (Legislative) Debates, Vol. I, No. 1, 1947, New Delhi.
———, Vol. V, No. 1, 1948, New Delhi.
———, Vol. V, No. 1, 1949, New Delhi.
———, Vol. VI, 1949, New Delhi.
———, Vol. VI. 1949, New Delhi.
Constituent Assembly of India (Legislative), *Report of the Select Committee on the Hindu Code Bill*, New Delhi, August 1948.
Dalwai, Hamid, *Muslim Politics in India*, Bombay: Nachiketa Publications, 1968.
D'Souza, J.B., 'A Civil Service Failure: How Can Credibility be Restored?' *EPW*, 24 August 2002.
Das, Durga, (ed.), *Sardar Patel's Correspondence, 1945–50*, Vol. 2: 'Elections to Central and Provincial Legislatures; Direction of Congress Campaign', Ahmedabad: Navajivan Publishing House, 1972.
———, (ed.), *Sardar Patel's Correspondence, 1945–50*, Vol. 3: 'Guidance to Ministries; Constituent Assembly Problems; Interim Government Deadlock; Reforms in Indian States', Ahmedabad: Navajivan Publishing House, 1972.
———, (ed.), *Sardar Patel's Correspondence, 1945–50*, Vol. 5: 'Control over Congress Ministries; Indian States' Accession,' Ahmedabad: Navajivan Publishing House, 1973.
———, (ed.), *Sardar Patel's Correspondence, 1945–50*, Vol. 6: 'Patel–Nehru Differences; Assassination of Gandhi; Services Reorganized; Refugee Rehabilitation' Ahmedabad: Navajivan Publishing House, 1973.
———, (ed.), *Sardar Patel's Correspondence, 1945–50*, Vol. 9, Political Controversies, Refugees from East Bengal, Territorial Integration of Princely States, Ahmedabad: Navajivan Publishing House, 1974.

———, (ed.), *Sardar Patel's Correspondence, 1945–50*, Vol. 10: 'Acute Power Struggle; Triumph of Mutual Accommodation; Warning against China', Ahmedabad: Navajivan Publishing House, 1974.

Das, S.C., *The Biography of Bharat Kesari D. Syama Prasad Mookerjee with Modern Implications*, New Delhi: Abhinav Publications, 2000.

Deb, R., 'Need for Placing Investigating Police under Judiciary', *JILI*, Vol. 34, 1992.

Derrett, J. Duncan M., *Religion, Law and the State in India*, London: Faber and Faber, 1968.

Desai, Meghnad, 'Gujarat and Its Bhasmita', *Seminar* 513, May 2002.

Deshpande, G.P. (GPD), 'An Occasion for the RSS', *EPW*, 25 March 2006.

Dharmadhikari, (Justice) C.S., 'Criminal Justice System and Tribes in India', *All India Reporter* (henceforth, *AIR*) *(Jour)* 1988.

Dhavan, Rajeev, *The Amendment: Conspiracy or Revolution*, Allahabad: H. Wheeler & Company, 1978.

———, 'The Ayodhya Judgment: Encoding Secularism in the Law', *EPW*, 26 November 1994.

Dhavan, Rajeev, and Thomas Paul, (eds), *Nehru and the Constitution*, New Delhi: Indian Law Institute; Bombay: N.M. Tripathi, 1992.

Diwan, Paras, *Abrogation of Forty-Second Amendment: Does Our Constitution Need a Second Look*, New Delhi: Sterling Publishers, 1978.

———, *Indian Constitutional Amendments: From First to Forty-fourth*, New Delhi: OUP and IBH Publishing Company, 1980.

Dube, Mukul, 'The Vedic Taliban', *EPW*, 18 May 2002.

———, *The Path of the Parivar: Articles on Gujarat and Hindutva*, Gurgaon: Three Essays Collective, 2004.

Economic & Political Weekly, 'Another Sati' (editorial), 17 August 2002.

Elst, Koenraad, *Decolonizing the Hindu Mind: Ideological Development of Hindu Revivalism*, New Delhi: Rupa & Co., 2001.

Engineer, Asghar Ali, (ed.), *The Shah Bano Controversy*, New Delhi: Orient Longman, 1987.

———, (ed.), *Problems of Muslim Women in India*, New Delhi: Orient Longman, 1995a.

———, *Communalism in India: A Historical and Empirical Study*, New Delhi: Vikas Publishing House, 1995b.

———, 'Sacred and Secular: False Divide', *EPW*, 18 October 1997.

———, 'Communal Violence', *EPW*, 26 December 1998.

———, 'Resolving Hindu–Muslim Problem: An Approach', *EPW*, February 1999.

———, 'BJP Government and Minorities', *EPW*, 22 May 1999.
———, 'Gujarat Riots in the Light of the History of Communal Violence', *EPW*, 14 December 2002.
———, *Communal Challenges and Secular Response*, Delhi: Shipra Publications, 2003.
———, 'Abolishing Triple Talaq: What Next?', *EPW*, 10 July 2004.
———, *Muslim Minority: Continuity and Change*, New Delhi: Gyan Publishing House, 2009.
Engineer, Asghar Ali, and Uday Mehta, (eds), *State Secularism and Religion: Western and Indian Experience*, New Delhi: Ajanta Publications, 1998.
Farouqui, Ather, 'Urdu Language and Education: Need for Political Will and Strategy', *EPW*, 22 June 2002.
Gajendragadkar, (Justice) P.B., *The Constitution of India: Its Basic Philosophy and Basic Postulates*, Bombay: OUP, 1969.
———, *Secularism and the Constitution of India*, Kashinath Trimbak Telang Endowment Lectures, University of Bombay, 1971.
———, *To the Best of My Memory*, Bombay: Bharatiya Vidya Bhavan, 1982.
Galanter, Marc, 'Secularism, East and West', *Comparative Studies in Society and History—An International Quarterly*, Vol. VII, Nov.1-October 1964, The Hague, Netherlands: Mouton & Co.
———, (ed.), *Law and Society in Modern India*, Delhi: OUP, 1989.
Gandhi, Rajmohan, *Patel A Life*, Ahmedabad: Navajivan Publishing House, 1990.
Gandhi R.M., *Dr Durga Das Basu: Comparative Federalism*, 2nd revised edition, Nagpur: Wadhwa Books, 2008.
Gera, Nalini, *Ram Jethmalani: The Authorized Biography*, New Delhi: Penguin–Viking Books India, 2002.
Ghai, Rajat, 'United by Dharma, Divided by Law', http://www.business-standard.com/article/opinion, 21 January 2014.
Gill, S.S., *The Dynasty: A Political Biography of the Premier Ruling Family of Modern India*, India: HarperCollins, 1996.
Goa, Daman and Diu Advocates' Association, *Family Laws of Goa, Daman and Diu*, Vol. I, Vasco Da Gama, Goa: Devi Shreevani Education Society, 1989.
Godbole, Madhav, *Unfinished Innings: Recollections and Reflections of a Civil Servant*, New Delhi: Orient Longman, 1996.
———, 'Madarsas: Need for a Fresh Look', *EPW*, 13 October 2001.
———, *The Holocaust of Indian Partition: An Inquest*, New Delhi: Rupa & Co., 2006.

———, *The Judiciary and Governance in India*, New Delhi: Rupa & Co., 2008.

———, *India's Parliamentary Democracy on Trial*, New Delhi: Rupa & Co., 2011.

———, *The God Who Failed: An Assessment of Jawaharlal Nehru's Leadership*, New Delhi: Rupa & Co., 2014.

———, *Good Governance Never on India's Radar*, New Delhi: Rupa & Co., 2014.

Gopal, S., (ed.), *The Collected Essays*, Ranikhet: Permanent Black, 2013.

Gopal S., *Jawaharlal Nehru—An Anthology*, , New Delhi: OUP, 1980.

Gopal, S., and Uma Iyengar, (eds), *The Essential Writings of Jawaharlal Nehru*, Vol. I, New Delhi: OUP, 2003.

———, (eds), *The Essential Writings of Jawaharlal Nehru*, Vol. II, New Delhi: OUP, 2003.

Gopalaswami, N., 'Political Parties and Elections: Some Issues', *Journal of Constitutional and Parliamentary Studies*, Vol. 41, Nos 3–4, New Delhi, July–December 2007.

Gore, M.S., *Secularism in India*, Bombay: Vindhya Prakashan, 1991.

Government of India, Legislative Assembly Department, *Report of the Joint Committee to Amend and Codify the Hindu Law Relating to Intestate Succession*, New Delhi, 1943.

———, *Report of the Hindu Law Committee*, New Delhi, 1947.

———, Ministry of Home, *Report of the Dargah Khwaja Saheb (Ajmer) Committee of Enquiry*, New Delhi, 1949.

———, Ministry of Information and Broadcasting, *Independence and After: A Collection of the More Important Speeches of Jawaharlal Nehru from September 1946 to May 1949*, New Delhi, 1949.

———, Ministry of Law, *Report of the Hindu Religious Endowments Commission (1960–1962)*, New Delhi, 1962.

———, Ministry of Education, *Report of the Education Commission 1964–66*, New Delhi, 1966.

———, Ministry of Law, Justice and Company Affairs, *Wakf Inquiry Committee: Interim Report*, New Delhi, 1973.

———, Ministry of Law and Justice, *Law Commission of India, Seventy-Seventh Report on Delay and Arrears in Trial Courts*, New Delhi, 1978.

———, Ministry of Home Affairs, *Eighth and Concluding Report of the National Police Commission*, New Delhi, 1981.

———, *White Paper on the Punjab Agitation*, New Delhi, 1984.

———, Cabinet Secretariat, *Reforming the National Security System: Recommendations of the Group of Ministers*, New Delhi, 2001.

———, *Review of the Working of the Constitution, Report of the National Commission to Review the Working of the Constitution*, Vol. II, Book 1, New Delhi, 2002.

———, Ministry of Home Affairs, *Report of the Committee on Reforms of Criminal Justice System (Justice V.S. Malimath Committee)*, Vol. I, New Delhi, 2003.

———, Cabinet Secretariat, *Prime Minister's High Level Committee on Social, Economic and Educational Status of the Muslim Community of India: A Report*, New Delhi, 2006.

———, Ministry of Administrative Reforms & Personnel, Second Administrative Reforms Commission, *Public Order*, Fifth Report, New Delhi, 2007.

———, Ministry of Minority Affairs, *Report of the National Commission for Religious and Linguistic Minorities*, New Delhi, 2007.

Government of Madhya Pradesh, *Report of the Christian Missionary Activities Enquiry Committee (Niyogi Committee), Madhya Pradesh*, Vol. I, 1956.

Government of United Provinces, Local–Self-Government Department, *Report of the Muslim Public and Charitable Waqf Committee*, Allahabad, 1932.

Granville, Austin, *Working a Democratic Constitution: The Indian Experience*, New Delhi: OUP, 1999.

Grover, Verinder, (ed.), *Gandhi and Politics in India*, New Delhi: Deep & Deep Publications, 1987.

———, (ed.), *Political Thinkers of Modern India: Jawaharlal Nehru*, Vol. 10, New Delhi: Deep & Deep Publications, 1990.

Guha, Ramachandra, *Makers of Modern India*, New Delhi: Penguin–Viking Books India, 2010.

———, 'Death by a Thousand Cuts', *The Radical Humanist*, June 2015.

Gupta, Madan Gopal, *Aspects of Indian Constitution*, Allahabad: Central Book Depot, 1960.

Gupte, Pranay, *India: The Challenge of Change*, London: Methuen—Mandarin, 1989.

Hardy, P., *The Muslims of British India*, Cambridge: Cambridge Press, 1972.

Hasan, Mushirul, (ed.), *Living with Secularism: The Destiny of India's Muslims*, New Delhi: Manohar Publishers and Distributors, 2007.

———, *Moderate or Militant: Images of India's Muslims*, New Delhi: OUP, 2008.

Hassnain, S.E., *Indian Muslims: Challenges and Opportunities*, Bombay:

Lalvani Publishing House, 1968.
Hepburn A.C., ed., *Minorities in History*, Edward Arnolds, London, 1978.
Huntington, Samuel P., *The Clash of Civilizations and the Remaking of World Order*, New York: Simon & Schuster, 1996.
Hussain, Muzaffar, *Insight into Minoritism*, New Delhi: India First Foundation, 2004.
Islam, Mohammed Nazrul, 'Medical Secularism vs Religious Secularism: A New Era of Ayurveda in India', *The Indian Journal of Social Work*, Vol. 75, Issue 2, April 2014.
Islam, Shamsul, *Golwalkar's We or Our Nationhood Defined: A Critique with the Full Text of the Book*, New Delhi: Pharos Media, 2006.
Ittyipe, Minu et al., 'Their Cross to Bear: The Christian Community Is in Mortal Fear As the Sangh Parivar Steps Up Attacks over "Conversions"', *Outlook*, 29 December 2014.
Ivekovic, Rada, 'The Veil in France: Secularism, Nation, Women', *EPW*, 13 March 2004.
Jacobsohn, Gary Jeffrey, *The Wheel of Law: India's Secularism in Comparative Constitutional Context*, New Delhi: OUP, 2003.
Jagmohan, *Reforming Vaishno Devi and a Case for Reformed, Reawakened and Enlightened Hinduism*, New Delhi: Rupa & Co., 2010.
Jahanbegloo, Ramin, *India Revisited: Conversations on Contemporary India*, New Delhi: OUP, 2008.
Jahagirdar, (Justice) R.A., 'Apostasy in Islam' *The Radical Humanist*, October 2007.
——, 'Burkqa: A Needless Controversy', *The Radical Humanist*, February 2010.
——, 'Secularism Revisited', *The Radical Humanist*, February and March 2015.
——, 'Secularism Revisited', *The Radical Humanist*, May 2015.
——, 'Secularism in India—The Inconclusive Debate', *The Radical Humanist*, February 2016.
Jain, M.P., *Indian Constitutional Law*, 6th edition, Nagpur: LexisNexis Butterworths Wadhwa, 2010.
Jamil, Javed, '"Ghar Wapsi"': A Ploy to Push Anti-conversion Bill and the Second Round of Privatisation', *The Radical Humanist*, February 2015.
Jawaharlal Nehru Papers, The Nehru Memorial Museum & Library, New Delhi, in *Muslim India*, August 2008.
Jayal, Niraja Gopal, and Pratap Bhanu Mehta, (eds), *The Oxford Companion to Politics in India*, New Delhi: OUP, 2010.
Jeffery, Patricia, and Roger Jeffery, *Confronting Saffron Demography*,

Gurgaon: Three Essays Collective, 2006.
Jaffrelot, Christophe, *The Hindu Nationalist Movement in India*, New Delhi: Penguin–Viking Books India, 1996.
Jha, Shefali, 'Secularism in the Constituent Assembly Debates, 1946–1950', *EPW*, 27 July 2002.
Jhingran, Saral, *Secularism in India: A Reappraisal*, New Delhi: Har-Anand Publications, 1995.
Juergensmeyer, Mark, *Religious Nationalism Confronts the Secular State*, Delhi: OUP, 1998.
Kagzi, M.C.J., *The Kesavananda Case*, Delhi: Metropolitan Book Company, 1973.
Kamath, M.V., *Nani A. Palkhivala: A Life*, New Delhi: Hay House India, 2007.
Kanungo, Pralay, *RSS's Tryst with Politics from Hedgewar to Sudarshan*, Delhi: Manohar Publishers and Distributors, 2003.
Karandikar, M.A., *Islam in India's Transition to Modernity*, Bombay: Orient Longman, 1968.
Kashyap, Subhash C., *Delinking Religion and Politics*, New Delhi: Vimot Publishers, 1993.
———, *Our Constitution*, New Delhi: National Book Trust, India, 1994.
———, *History of the Parliament of India*, Vol. 2, Delhi: Shipra Publications, 1995.
———, *History of the Parliament of India*, Vol. 3, Delhi: Shipra Publications, 1996.
———, *History of the Parliament of India*, Vol. 4, Delhi: Shipra Publications, 1997.
———, *History of the Parliament of India*, Vol. 5, Delhi: Shipra Publications, 1998.
———, *History of the Parliament of India*, Vol. 6, Delhi: Shipra Publications, 2000.
———, *Constitution Making Since 1950: An Overview*, Delhi: Universal Law Publishing Co., 2004.
———, *Concise Encyclopedia of Indian Constitution*, New Delhi: Vision Books, 2009.
Khan, Mohamad Raza, *What Price Freedom: A historical survey of the political trends and conditions leading to Independence and the birth of Pakistan and after*, Madras: The Nuri Press, 1969.
Khan, Shafaat Ahmad, *What Are the Rights of the Muslim Minority in India?*, Allahabad: The Indian Press Limited, 1928.
Khanna, (Justice) H.R., Supreme Court Judgment on Article 356, *AIR*

(Journal) 1994.
Khilnani, Sunil, *The Idea of India*, Delhi: Penguin Books, 2004.
Kogekar, S.V., *Revision of the Constitution*, R.R. Kale Memorial Lecture, 1976, Gokhale Institute of Politics and Economics, Poona, 1976.
Kripalani, J.B., *My Times: An Autobiography*, New Delhi: Rupa & Co., 2004.
Kumar, Ajay, 'Enforcement of Secularism in India', *AIR, 2002*, Journal Section.
Kumar, Arun, *Cultural and Educational Rights of the Minorities under Indian Constitution*, New Delhi: Deep & Deep Publications, 1985.
Kumar, Virendra, 'Towards a Uniform Civil Code: Judicial Vicissitudes', *JILI*, Vol. 47:24, 2000.
Kurukshethra Prakasan, *M.S. Golwalkar: His Vision and Mission*, Kochi, 2008.
Kuruvachira, J., *Politicisation of Hindu Religion in Post-Modern India*, Jaipur: Rawat Publications, 2008.
Kutty, M.P.K., 'Justice Wadhwa Committee Report: A Test for Nation's Secularism', The *Times of India*, 13 September 1999.
Larson, Gerald James, *India's Agony over Religion*, Delhi: OUP, 1997.
Legislative Assembly Debates, Vol. V, No.1, 1 April 1946, New Delhi.
———, Vols VII–VIII, October–November 1946, New Delhi.
———, Vol. IV, No. 1, 25 March 1947 to 9 April 1947, New Delhi.
Limaye, Madhu, *Musings on Current Problems and Past Events*, Delhi: B.R. Publishing Corporation, 1988.
Lobo, Lancy, 'Adivasis, Hindutva and Post-Godhra Riots in Gujarat', *EPW*, 30 November 2002.
Lok Sabha Secretariat, *Dr. Syama Prasad Mookerjee*, Eminent Parliamentarians Monograph Series, New Delhi, 1990.
———, *Lok Sabha Debates*, Vol. 62, 1976, New Delhi.
———, *Lok Sabha Debates*, Vol. 65, 1976, New Delhi.
———, *Lok Sabha Debates*, Vol. 19.1, 1993, New Delhi.
———, *Lok Sabha Debates*, Vol. 19.2, 1993, New Delhi.
———, *Lok Sabha Debates*, Vol. 20.1, 1993, New Delhi.
———, *Lok Sabha Debates*, Vol. 21.1, 1993, New Delhi.
———, *Lok Sabha Debates*, Vol. 23.1, 1993, New Delhi.
———, *Lok Sabha Debates*, Vol. 23.2, 1993, New Delhi.
———, *Lok Sabha Debates*, Vol. 23.2, 1993, New Delhi.
———, *Lok Sabha Debates*, Vol. 24, 1993, New Delhi.
———, *Lok Sabha Debates*, Vol. 25, 1993, New Delhi.
———, *Lok Sabha Debates*, Vols 26–27, 1993, New Delhi.

Luthera, Ved Prakash, *The Concept of Secular State and India*, Bombay: OUP, 1964.
Madan, T.N., *Secularism and Fundamentalism in India: Modern Myths, Locked Minds*, Delhi: OUP, 1997.
———, *Images of the World: Essays on Religion, Secularism and Culture*, New Delhi: OUP, 2006.
Mahajan, Gurpreet, *Identities and Rights: Aspects of Liberal Democracy in India*, Delhi: OUP, 1998.
Mahajan, Vidya Dhar, *Chief Justice Gajendragadkar: His Life, Ideas, Papers and Addresses*, New Delhi: S. Chand & Co., 1966.
Mahmood, Tahir, *Muslim Personal Law: Role of the State in the Subcontinent*, Bombay: Vikas Publishing House, 1977.
———, 'Walking Away from the Code', The *Indian Express*, 20 October 2015.
Malhotra, Inder, *India: Trapped in Uncertainty*, New Delhi: UBS Publishers' Distributors, 1991.
Malik, Kenan, *From Fatwa to Jihad: The Rushdie Affair and Its Legacy*, London: Atlantic Books, 2009.
Malkani, K.R., *The RSS Story*, New Delhi: Impex India, 1980.
———, *The Politics of Ayodhya and Hindu–Muslim Relations*, New Delhi: Har-Anand Publications, 1993.
Massey, James, *Minorities in Democracy: The Indian Experience*, New Delhi: Manohar Publishers and Distributors, 1999.
Mathur, Shubh, *The Everyday Life of Hindu Nationalism: An Ethnographic Account*, Gurgaon: Three Essays Collective, 2008.
McGuire, John and Ian Copland, (eds), *Hindu Nationalism and Governance*, New Delhi: OUP, 2007.
Menon, Meena, *Riots and After in Mumbai: Chronicles of Truth and Reconciliation*, Delhi: Sage Publications, 2012.
Mohd. Ahmed Khan v. Shah Bano Begum and Others, (*1985*) *2 Supreme Court Cases 356*.
Mohd. Hanif Quareshi and Others v. State of Bihar, *AIR 1958 SC 731*, 23 April 1958.
Mullik, B.N., *My Years with Nehru 1948–1964*, New Delhi: Allied Publishers, 1972.
Mushir-ul-Haq, *Islam in Secular India*, Indian Institute of Advanced Study, Simla, 1972.
Nanda, B.R., (ed.), *Mahatma Gandhi: 125 Years*, New Delhi: New Age International Publishers and ICCR (Indian Council for Cultural Relations), 1995.

Naqvi, Saba, 'Numerocracy: Will the Majoritarian Project Subvert the Very Democratic Tradition That Has Brought the BJP to Power?', *Outlook*, 25 August 2014.

Narain, Iqbal, *Secularism in India*, Jaipur, Delhi: Classic Publishing House, 1995.

Nariman, Fali, 'Lecture on *Minorities at Crossroads: Comments on Judicial Pronouncements*', 12 September 2014.

National Commission for Minority Educational Institutions, http://ncmei.gov.in/index.aspx?clt=1 and http://www.ncmei.gov.in/index.aspx?clt=16

National Commission for Minorities, https://en.wikipedia.org/wiki/National_Commission_for_Minorities

National Minorities Development & Finance Corporation: Overall Achievements, http://119.18.54.23/-nmdfc/financial-physical-achievements/

Needham, Anuradha Dingwaney, and Rajeswari Sunder Rajan, (eds), *The Crisis of Secularism in India*, Ranikhet: Permanent Black, 2007.

Nehru, B.K., *Thoughts on Our Present Discontents*, Delhi: Allied Publishers, 1986.

Nehru, Jawaharlal, *An Autobiography*, New Delhi: OUP, 1936.

———, *The Discovery of India*, Jawaharlal Nehru Memorial Fund, New Delhi: OUP, 1981.

———, *Selected Works of Jawaharlal Nehru*, Second Series, Vol. 24, Jawaharlal Nehru Memorial Fund, New Delhi, 1999.

———, *Selected Works of Jawaharlal Nehru*, Second Series, Vol. 29, Jawaharlal Nehru Memorial Fund, New Delhi, 2001.

Niyogi Committee Report on Christian Missionary Activities, 1956, https://en.wikipedia.org/wiki

Noorani, A.G., *The RSS and the BJP: A Division of Labour*, New Delhi: LeftWord Books, 2000.

———, 'Protecting Minority Rights', *EPW*, 18 March 2000.

———, *Constitutional Questions in India*, New Delhi: OUP, 2000.

———, *Savarkar and Hindutva: The Godse Connection*, New Delhi: LeftWord Books, 2002.

———, *Citizens' Rights, Judges and State Accountability*, New Delhi: OUP, 2002.

———, 'Gujarat Riots: Bringing the Guilty to Court', *EPW*, 3 July 2004.

———, *Destruction of the Babri Masjid: A National Dishonour*, New Delhi: Tulika Books, 2014.

———, 'A Home for Equality', The *Indian Express*, 10 September 2015.

PSM, 'UP Crisis: United Front in Political and Ethical Disarray', *EPW*, 15

November 1997.
Padgaonkar, Dileep, (ed.), *When Bombay Burned*, New Delhi: UBS Publishers' Distributors, 1993.
Pancholi, N.D., 'Judgment in Hashimpura Massacre (1987): A Travesty of Justice', *The Radical Humanist*, April 2015.
Parliament of India, House of the People, *The Muslim Wakfs Bill, 1952, Report of the Select Committee*, New Delhi, 1954.
———, Rajya Sabha Secretariat, *The Hindu Succession Bill, 1954, Report of the Joint Committee*, New Delhi, 1955.
———, Rajya Sabha Secretariat, *Report of Joint Parliamentary Committee on Wakf*, New Delhi, 2008.
Parthasarathi, G., (ed.), *Jawaharlal Nehru: Letters to Chief Ministers 1947–1964*, Vol. I, Jawaharlal Nehru Memorial Fund, New Delhi, 1985.
Patel, Alaknanda, 'Gujarat Violence: A Personal Diary', *EPW*, 14 December 2002.
Professional's Marriage and Divorce Laws, Delhi: Professional Book Publishers, 2015.
Puniyani, Ram, *Communal Politics: Facts versus Myths*, New Delhi: Sage Publications, 2003.
———, (ed.), *Religious Power and Violence: Expression of Politics in Contemporary Times*, New Delhi: Sage Publications, 2005.
———, 'Ambedkar's Ideology: Religion, Nationalism and Indian Constitution', *The Radical Humanist*, June 2015.
Pawar, Prakash, (ed.), *Yashwantrao Chavan Reflects on India: Society and Politics*, Pune: Diamond Publications, 2015.
Rajinder Sachar Committee, 'Report: Community on the Margin', *Frontline*, 2–15 December 2006.
RSS Resolves...: Full Text of Resolutions from 1950 to 1983, Karnataka: Rashtriya Swayamsevak Sangh, 1983.
Raghavan Srinath, ed., *Sarvapalli Gopal: The Collected Essays*, Permanent Black, Ranikhet, 2013.
Rahman, S. Ubaidur, 'Minorities Commission Should Be Disbanded', *The MilliGazette*, http://www.milligazette.com/Archives/01062002/0106200248.htm
Rajan, Radha, *Eclipse of the Hindu Nation: Gandhi and His Freedom Struggle*, Kolkata, New Delhi, Ernakulam: New Age Publishers, 2009.
Rajya Sabha Secretariat, *Report of the Joint Committee: The Hindu Marriage and Divorce Bill, 1952*, November 1954.
Rajya Sabha Secretariat, *Rajya Sabha Debates*, Vol. 15, 1956, New Delhi.
———, *Rajya Sabha Debates*, Vol. 104.1, 1978, New Delhi.

―――, *Rajya Sabha Debates*, Vol. 106.1, 1978, New Delhi.
―――, *Rajya Sabha Debates*, Vol. 106.3, 1978, New Delhi.
―――, *Rajya Sabha Debates*, Vol. 107.1, 1978, New Delhi.
―――, *Rajya Sabha Debates*, Vol. 107.2, 1978, New Delhi
―――, *Rajya Sabha Debates*, Vol. 166.2, 1993, New Delhi.
―――, *Rajya Sabha Debates*, Vol. 166.3, 1993, New Delhi.
―――, *Rajya Sabha Debates*, Vol. 166.4, 1993, New Delhi.
―――, *Rajya Sabha Debates*, Vol. 167.1, 1993, New Delhi.
―――, *Rajya Sabha Debates*, Vol. 167.3, 1993, New Delhi.
―――, *Rajya Sabha Debates*, Vol. 168.2, 1993, New Delhi.
―――, *Rajya Sabha Debates*, Vol. 168.3, 1993, New Delhi.
―――, *Rajya Sabha Debates*, Vol. 169.1, 1993, New Delhi.
Ramdas, Lalita, 'Thoughts on 1984: A Fragile Democracy', *EPW*, 17 September 2005.
Rangan, Pavitra S., 'This Ain't No Homecoming: in Western UP, It's a Baleful Season ... a Festival of Fear, *Outlook*, 29 December 2014.
Rao, B. Shiva, (ed.), *The Framing of India's Constitution: Select Documents*, Vol. I, Bombay: N.M. Tripathi Private Limited, 1966.
―――, (ed), *The Framing of India's Constitution: Select Documents*, Vol. II, Bombay: N.M. Tripathi Private Limited, 1967.
―――, (ed.), *The Framing of India's Constitution: Select Documents*, Vol. III, Bombay: N.M. Tripathi Private Limited, 1967.
―――, (ed.), *The Framing of India's Constitution: Select Documents*, Vol. IV, Bombay: N.M. Tripathi Private Limited, 1968a.
―――, (ed.), *The Framing of India's Constitution: A Study*, Bombay: N.M. Tripathi Private Limited, 1968b.
Rao, P.V. Narasimha, *Ayodhya 6 December 1992*, New Delhi: Penguin–Viking Books India, 2006.
Raz, Mohamood Alam, 'Muslims in Public Service: A Comment', *EPW*, 9 March 2002.
Religious census: Narendra Modi government releases religious census, Muslim population rises 24 per cent in India. http://www.financialexpress.com/article/miscellaneous/narendra-modi,
Rodrigues, Valerian, *The Essential Writings of B.R. Ambedkar*, New Delhi: OUP, 2002.
Roy, M.N., 'The Practice of Fascism', *The Radical Humanist*, June 2015.
Saberwal, Satish, and Mushirul Hasan, *Assertive Religious Identities: India and Europe*, New Delhi: Manohar, 2006.
Salam, Dr Md. Abdus, 'The Struggle beyond Committees and Commissions', *TwoCircles.Net*, http://twocircles.net/2012jun03/ struggle_beyond_

committees_and_co.
Samagra Savarkar Vangmaya, vol. 6, Part II, Savarkar Rashtreeya Smarak Prakashan, Mumbai, 2001. (Marathi)
Samaj Prabodhan Sanstha (Institute of Social Renaissance), *Secularism and the Maharashtra Élite: A Symposium*, Bombay: Nachiketa Publications, 1969.
Sambrani, Shreekant, 'Gujarat's Burning Train: India's Inferno?', *EPW*, 6 April 2002.
Sapru, Tej Bahadur, *Constitutional Proposals of the Sapru Committee*, Bombay: Padma Publications, 1945.
Sathe, S.P., *Judicial Activism in India: Transgressing Borders and Enforcing Limits*, New Delhi: OUP, 2002.
Savarkar, V.D., *Hindutva*, Bombay: Veer Savarkar Prakashan, 1923.
Sen, Amartya, *The Argumentative Indian*, London, England: Allen Lane, 2005.
Sen, Ronojoy, *Articles of Faith: Religion, Secularism and the Indian Supreme Court*, New Delhi: OUP, 2010.
Seervai, H.M., *Constitutional Law of India*, 4th edition, Silver Jubilee Edition, Vol. 1, New Delhi: Universal Law Publishing Co., 2011a.
———, *Constitutional Law of India*, 4th edition, Silver Jubilee Edition, Vol. 2, New Delhi: Universal Law Publishing Co., 2011b.
Setalvad, M.C., *Secularism*, Patel Memorial Lectures, Publications Division, Ministry of Information & Broadcasting , Government of India, New Delhi, 1967.
———, *My Life—Law and Other Things*, Bombay: N.M. Tripathi Private Limited, 1970.
Shaban, Abdul, (ed.), *Lives of Muslims in India: Politics, Exclusion and Violence*, London, New York, New Delhi: Routledge, 2012.
Shah, A.B., *Challenges to Secularism*, Bombay: Nachiketa Publications, 1969.
Shahabuddin, Syed, 'Minority Identity and its Discontents', *EPW*, 9 April 1994.
Shariff, Abusaleh, 'Myth of Muslim Growth', The *Indian Express*, 2 September 2015.
Sharma, G.S., (ed.), *Secularism: Its Implications for Law and Life in India*, Bombay: N.M. Tripathi Private Limited, 1966.
Sharma, Arvind, 'Debates on Religion', *EPW*, 13 March 2004.
Sharma, Pranay, 'A State under the Swastika', *Outlook*, 24 August 2015.
Smith, Donald E., 'Secularism in India', *Comparative Studies in Society and History—An International Quarterly*, Vol. VII, Nov. 1-October 1964,

The Hague, Netherlands: Mouton & Co.

Shourie, Arun, *Religion in Politics*, New Delhi: Roli Books International, 1987.

———, *Indian Controversies: Essays on Religion in Politics*, New Delhi: ASA Publications, 1993a.

———, *A Secular Agenda*, New Delhi: ASA Publications, 1993b.

———, *The World of Fatwas or the Shariah in Action*, New Delhi: HarperCollins India, 1995.

———, *Worshipping False Gods: Ambedkar and the facts which have been erased*, New Delhi: ASA Publications, 1997.

Shourie, Arun, et al., (eds), *The Ayodhya Reference: Supreme Court Judgment and Commentaries*, New Delhi: Voice of India, 1995.

Siam-Heng, Michael Heng, and Ten Chin Liew, (eds), *State and Secularism: Perspectives from Asia*, London: World Scientific, 2010.

Singh S., *Dr Ambedkar on Minorities*, New Delhi: India First Foundation, 2005.

Singh, G.B., '"Bill of Rights"' in the Constitution of India Updated', *The Radical Humanist*, June 2015.

Singh, R.P.N., *Islam and Religious Riots: A Case Study: Riots and Wrongs*, New Delhi: India First Foundation, 2004.

Singh, Karan, *India and the World*, New Delhi: Har-Anand Publications, 1995.

Singh, Kharak, 'On Sikh Personal Law: An Abstract', http://www.sikh-history.com/sikhhist/archivedf/feature-aug2001.html

Singh, Perneet, 'After 3 Decades, Sikh Demand for Separate Status Gains Force Again', *The Tribune*, 17 December 2014.

Sinha V.K., (ed.), *Secularism in India*, Bombay: Lalvani Publishing House, 1968.

———, (ed.), *Secular Values in a Liberal Democracy*, Mumbai: Indian Secular Society, 2003.

Sinha, Chitra, *Debating Patriarchy: The Hindu Code Bill Controversy in India (1985–1956)*, New Delhi: OUP, 2012.

Sitaramayya, Pattabhi, *The History of the Indian National Congress*, Vol. I (1885–1935), Bombay: Padma Publications, 1946.

———, *The History of the Indian National Congress*, Vol. II (1935–1947), Bombay: Padma Publications, 1947.

Smith, Donald Eugene, *India as a Secular State*, London: Princeton University Press; Bombay: OUP, 1963.

Socialist Party, *Draft Constitution of Indian Republic*, Suresh Desai, Secretary, Socialist Party, Bombay, 1948.

Srikrishna, (Justice) B.N., 'Skinning a Cat', (2005) 8 SCC (Jour) 3.
———, 'Secularism under Our Constitution', V.M. Tarkunde Memorial Lecture, *The Radical Humanist*, October 2007.
———, *Judicial Activism*, Lalit Doshi Memorial Lecture, Mumbai, 2012.
Srinivasan, T.N., (ed.), *The Future of Secularism*, New Delhi: OUP, 2007.
The Swaran Singh Committee Report, 1976.
Tahmankar, D.V., *Sardar Patel*, London: George Allen and Unwin, 1970.
Tandon, B.N., *PMO Diary I: Prelude to Emergency*, New Delhi: Konark Publications, 2003.
———, *PMO Diary II: The Emergency*, New Delhi: Konark Publications, 2006.
Thakur, C.P., and Devendra P. Sharma, *India under Atal Bihari Vajpayee: The BJP Era*, New Delhi: UBS Publishers' Distributors, 1999.
Thomas, (Justice) K.T., *Should There be a Law for Governing Church Property*, Speech delivered at Goa International Centre, Panaji, on 28 July 2009, Indian Institute of Christian Studies, Kottayam.
Tope, T.K., and H.S. Ursekar, *Why Hindu Code?* (*A Historical, Analytical and Critical Exposition of the Hindu Code Bill*), Lonavala, District Poona: Dharma Nirnaya Mandal, 1950.
Tulzapurkar, (Justice) V.D., 'Uniform Civil Code', *AIR (Jour)*, 1987.
Tyabji, Nasir, *Political Economy of Secularism: Rediscovery of India*, EPW, 9 July 1994.
Tyagi, Ruchi, *Secularism in Multi-Religious Indian Society*, New Delhi: Deep & Deep Publications, 2001.
Vanaik, Achin, 'Situating Threat of Hindu Nationalism: Problems with Fascist Paradigm', *EPW*, 9 July 1994.
———, *The Furies of Indian Communalism: Religion, Modernity and Secularization*, New York: Verso, 1997.
Varshney, Ashutosh, *Ethnic Conflict and Civic Life: Hindus and Muslims in India*, New Delhi: OUP, 2002.
Vijay, Tarun, *Saffron Surge: India's Re-emergence on the Global Scene and Hindu Ethos*, New Delhi: Har-Anand Publications, 2008.
———, *India Battles to Win*, New Delhi: Rupa & Co., 2009.
Vivekanandan, B., (ed.), *Echoes in Parliament: Madhu Dandavate's Speeches in Parliament (1971–1990)*, New Delhi: Allied Publishers, 1995.
Vohra, Ranbir, *The Making of India: A Historical Survey*, London: M.E. Sharpe, 1997.
Wani, M. Afzal, 'Freedom of Conscience: Constitutional Foundations and Limits', *JILI*, Vol. 47:24, 2000.
Wilkinson, Steven I., *Critical Issues in Indian Politics: Religious Politics*

and Communal Violence, New Delhi: OUP, 2005.

Williams, Rina Verma, *Postcolonial Politics and Personal Laws: Colonial Legal Legacies and the Indian State*, New Delhi: OUP, 2006.

Yaqin, Anwarul, *Constitutional Protection of Minority Educational Institutions in India*, New Delhi: Deep & Deep Publications, 1982.

Zakaria, Rafiq, *Rise of Muslims in Indian Politics,* Bombay: Somaiya Publications, 1970.

———, *Indian Muslims: Where Have They Gone Wrong?*, Mumbai: Bharatiya Vidya Bhavan in collaboration with Popular Prakashan, 2004.

ACKNOWLEDGEMENTS

At the outset, I must place on record the excellent library support I received while researching for this book. I am obliged to N.A. Chaudhari, Librarian of the Gokhale Institute of Politics and Economics, Pune, Manjiri Joshi, Librarian in the Indian Law Society's Law College, Pune, and Chaya Mangsulkar, Librarian in the Indian School of Political Economy, Pune. I am thankful to Shri Pradeep Rawat, former member of Parliament, for making available extensive material from his personal library.

My daughter Meera Godbole-Krishnamurthy was a constant source of encouragement with solicitous inquiries about the progress of the book. My grand-daughter, Taarini, ten years old, staying in far away Hawaii, was ever curious about the process of writing a book, how far I had come, how many pages it was going to be, and what it was going to say. These queries kept me on my toes!

As usual, my biggest debt of gratitude is to my wife, Sujata, who this time, also took the trouble of typing most of the manuscript. It was her ever-smiling disposition, understanding and encouragement which helped me finish the book expeditiously.

I am indebted to Shri Kapish Mehra for bestowing his personal attention on the manuscript and ensuring its speedy publication. I am grateful to my editors Shreya Mukherjee and Sayantan Ghosh for taking keen interest in giving finishing touches to the manuscript. I do not know how to adequately thank the Rupa team headed by Ritu Vajpeyi-Mohan for bringing out yet another of my books so promptly and elegantly.

Madhav Godbole
Pune

INDEX

Abhiram Singh v. C.D. Commachen and Ors, 67
Abhiram Singh v. C.D. Conmachen, 63
accommodative pluralism, 56
Acharya, P.B., 325
Adityanath, Yogi, 303
The Adoption of Children Bill, 1972, 105
Advani, L.K., 15, 225, 245, 255, 353, 358
Agnes, Flavia, 171
Agrawal, Justice, 61
Ahluwalia, S.S., 222
Ahmad, Naziruddin, 130, 147
Ahmad, Riaz, 270
Ahmadi, Justice, 61
Ahmedabad riots, 1969, 364
Ahmedabad St. Xaviers College Society v. State of Gujarat, 60
Aiyar, Dr C.P. Ramaswami, 111
Ajmer Sharif blast, 2007, 361
Akali Dal, 96
Akbar, M.J., 6, 83, 292
India: The Siege Within, 309
Akhand (united) Bharat, 24–25
Akhil Bharat Krishi Goseva Sangh v. Mirzapur Moti Kureshi Kassab Jamat, Ahmedabad, and Others, 214–215
Al-Aqsa incident, 13–14
Alexander, P.C., 252

Ali, Ghulam, 317
Aligarh Muslim University (AMU), 104
All-India Conference of Indian Christians, 71
All-India Hindu Mahasabha, 71
All-India Liberal Federation, 71
All-India Muslim League, 71
All India Muslim Personal Law Board, 107, 162, 164, 166, 321, 323–324
All-India States' People's Conference, 71
Alva, K.L. Nagappa, 221
Ambedkar, B.R., 7, 31–32, 78, 88, 126, 129, 152, 158, 174, 176, 186, 200
political democracy, 14
Thoughts on Pakistan, 80–81
Ambedkar, Prakash, 97
Anand Marriage Act, 97
Anand Marriage Validating Act, 1909, 138
Aney, M.S., 71
An-Na'im, Abdullahi Ahmed, 14
Ansari, Hamid, 314–316, 322
Anthony, Frank, 31, 44, 90
anti-Brahmin riots in Maharashtra, 1948, 258–260
anti-casteism, 61
anti-Sikh riots, 1984, 250–258, 364, 369

1984: The Anti-Sikh Violence and After (Sanjay Suri), 258
Articles of Indian Constitution
  Article 14, 203, 213
  Article 19, 149–151, 332
  Article 25, 95–96, 203, 213, 345
  Article 25 (1), 298
  Article 26, 113
  Article 29, 190, 345
  Article 30, 187, 190–193, 195
  Article 30 (1), 184, 345
  Article 35, 148
  Article 44, 112, 134, 150, 157, 162
  Article 48, 27, 51, 202, 207, 346
  Article 54, 142
  Article 107, 232
  Article 143, 242
  Article 292, 73
  Article 294, 73
  Article 296, 73
  Article 355, 248
  Article 356, 248, 307
  Article 25 (a), 182
  Article 35-A, 228–229
  Article 51A, 27
  Article 257A, 373
  Article 290 A, 51
  Article 25(2) (b), 51
  Article 19(1) (g), 27, 203, 213
  Article IV, 72
Aruna Roy v. Union of India, 376
Aurobindo, Sri, 10
Austin, Granville, 40
Ayyangar, M. Ananthasayanam, 90, 173, 219
Ayyar, Alladi Krishnaswami, 151–152
Azmi, Shabana, 308

Babri Masjid demolition, 2, 15–16, 62, 64, 222, 237–250, 320, 369
Bachal, V.M., 113
Badrudduja, Syed, 15
Bahadur, Mahboob Ali Baig Sahib, 94, 148
Bahadur, Pocker Sahib, 148
Bajrang Dal, 162
Bakshi, P.M., 366–367
Banaras Hindu University (BHU), 104
Banerjee, Vikramjit, 60
Bapat, S.K., 266
Basheer, M.M., 323
Basu, Chitta, 233
Basu, Durga Das, 157
Baxi, Upendra, 331–332
  definition of secularism, 54–55
  Gujarat carnage, 270
  Muslim Women's Bill, 170
  'The Constitution (Eightieth) Amendment Bill: Politics as Religion,' 228
Bhagat, H.K.L., 253
Bhagwat, Mohan, 24, 249, 312
Bhalla, Surjit, 212
Bharathi, L. Krishnaswami, 176
Bharatiya Janata Party (BJP), 1–2, 11, 69, 98, 162, 205, 317
  cow slaughter, prohibition of, 205–206
  rise and fall in electoral politics, 3–4, 19
Bhargava, Pandit Thakur Das, 124, 132, 135, 198, 202
Bhargava, Rajeev, 17
Bhargava, Thakur Das, 209
Bharucha, Justice, 62
Bhave, Vinoba, 207
Bhushan, Shanti, 49–50, 105–107
Bihar communal riots, 1946, 275–276
Bombay Prevention of Excommunication Act, 1949, 66
Bombay riots, 1992 and 1993, 260–266, 364

Bose, Ajoy, 170
Bose, Subhas Chandra, 71
Brar, Jagmeet Singh, 254
Buddhists in Maharashtra, 97
Bukhari, Syed Ahmed, 304

cabinet committee on political affairs (CCPA), 243, 253
Carson, Ben, 26
Cattle Preservation and Development Committee, 213
Central Khilafat Committee, 71
centre–state relations, 350–355
Chagla, M.C., 52, 94, 156–157, 179, 374
Chand, Dr Bakshi Tek, 135
Chandhoke, Neera, 52–53
Chandrachud, Justice Y.B., 60, 169–170
Chatterjee, Somnath, 226, 244–245
Chaudhri, Kamala, 137
Chaudhuri, Rohini Kumar, 130
Chavan, S.B., 227, 244
Chavan, Y.B., 18
Chennithala, Ramesh, 232
Chidambaram, P., 326
Child Marriage Restraint Act, 1929, 124–126
The Child Marriage Restraint Act, 1929, 105
Child Marriage Restraint (Amendment) Bill, 105, 124
Choudhury, Lokanath, 256
Chunder, Pratap Chandra, 104
Code of Criminal Procedure (CrPC), 172, 362, 363
  section 125, 166–168, 172
  section 196, 363, 371
  section 295 A, 210
Commission on Marriage and Family Laws, 160
commission on secularism (COS), 337–341

Communal Award, 87
communalism and communal violence, 274–285
  All India Muslim Majlis-e-Mushawarat's resolution, 279
  as a game played by politicians, 282–283
  Gopal Krishna's analysis of, 283
  in India, 275–277
communalization of the police, 358
Concerned Citizens' Tribunal Gujarat, 2002, 81–82, 330–331
Congress party, 4, 35, 50, 103, 105–107, 141, 170, 277
  Babri Masjid demolition, 240
  communalism in, 5
  election manifesto, 1971, 38
Constituent Assembly, 88, 131, 173, 201
  composition of, 30–36
  debates, 35
  Husain's amendment, 333–334
Constituent Assembly (Legislative), 1948, 219–220, 342
Constitution (Eightieth) Amendment Bill 1993, 221, 343, 384–387
Constitution of India, 336–337
  amendments suggested, 337–346
  Constitution (Eightieth Amendment) Bill, 51
  Constitution (Forty-fifth Amendment) Bill, 1978, 49
  Constitution (Forty-sixth Amendment) Bill, 1978, 115
  controversial amendments, 38–44
  Gokhale's contention on 1976 amendment, 41
  rights of minorities, 44–46, 52–53
  as secular, 36–51
  use of the term 'secularism,' 37–38, 42, 45–46
Constitution (Scheduled Castes)

Order, 1950, 297
cow slaughter, prohibition of, 5, 12, 27, 195–213, 346
  agitations for, 207
  in China, 198
  Constitutional provision, 202–203
  difficulties with, 212–213
  Hindu sentiment in, 196
  and Hindu Vedic scriptures, 198–199, 206–207
  Nehru's understanding, 197–198, 206–208, 210–211, 217–218
  observations of Mahatma Gandhi, 199, 204
  religious point of view, 201
  Report of the National Commission on Cattle, 215
  Supreme Court pronouncements, 213–218
CPI (Communist Party of India), 35, 226

Dalton, Dennis, 25
Darul Uloom Deoband, 336
Das, Justice S.R., 191
Das, Mahant Nrutya Gopal, 249
Das, Seth Govind, 199–201, 207, 209
Dasgupta, Swapan, 50
Datta, Saugato, 308
Dayal, Rajeshwar, 252
Declaration on the Rights of Persons Belonging to National or Ethnic, Religious and Linguistic Minorities, 76, 381–383
Delhi State Congress Committee, 6
Desai, Meghnad, 18–19, 269–270
Deshmukh, Dr G.V., 120–121
Dharma Jagran Samanway Samiti, 319
Dhavan, Rajeev, 46, 66
Dhote, Jambuvant, 44
Dhulekar, R.V., 200

Directive Principles of State Policy, 202
Dispensation of Property Act, 136
D'Monte, Darryl, 261
Draft Constitution in the Constituent Assembly, 88–91
Drafting Committee, 31–35, 88, 92, 186, 201
Draft Preamble, 36
Dr Ramesh Yeshwant Prabhoo v. Prabhakar Kashinath Kunte, 68
D'Souza, J.B., 274
Dube, Mukul, 273, 282

Ebrahim Sulaiman Sait v. M.C. Muhammad and Anr, 67
educational institutions, protection of minority, 184–195, 345–346
  admissions guidelines, 193–194
  amendments, 186
  experience of states in the implementation of Article 30, 187, 191–193, 195
  National Commission of Minorities guidelines, 187–188
  Ranganath Misra Commission for Religious and Linguistic Minorities, 193
  right of administration, 195
  rights pertaining to language and culture, 190–191
  St. Stephen's College Society case, 189–190
electoral reforms, 347–350
Emergency period, 38–39
Enactment of Muslim Women (Protection of Rights on Divorce) Act, 166–172
  critics, 170–172
Engineer, Asghar Ali, 16, 20–21, 23, 170, 272–273, 279, 281, 321
Esteves, Sarto, 318

Fernandes, George, 225
Fernandes, John F., 222–223
Firdaus Amrut Higher Secondary School, Ahmedabad v. M.M. Dave, 187
Foreign Contribution (Regulation) Act (FCRA), 183
Forty-fourth Amendment Bill, 1978, 38, 40, 48
Franklin, E.W., 178
'freedom of religion' clause, 173

Gadgil, N.V., 125
Gajendragadkar, Chief Justice P.B., 13, 55, 67, 119, 152
  ban on the slaughter of cows and calves, 210–211
  Reflections On Hindu Law, 145
  religious conversions, 183
Ganapati festival, 23
Gandhi, Indira, 1, 44, 106, 153, 291, 351
Gandhi, Mahatma, 10, 36, 223
  on prohibition of cow slaughter, 199, 204
Gandhi, Rajiv, 1, 155, 167–168, 234, 351
Gandhi, Sonia, 274
Geelani, Ali Shah, 336
gender justice and equality issues, 306
Gera, Nalini, 264–266
Ghai, Rajat, 97
Ghar Wapsi movement, 183–184, 285
Godhra riots, 2002, 266–274, 364, 366, 369
Godse, Nathuram, 258
Gokhale, H. R., 41, 106
Gole, P.B., 125
Golwalkar, M.S., 10, 116
  about 'Hindutva and Secularism,' 10–11

Gopal, S., 196
Gopal Singh Committee Report, 293–295
Goswami, Dinesh Chandra, 42
Gupta, Indrajit, 42, 226
Gupte, Pranay, 250, 292, 309
Gwyer, Sir Maurice Linford, 45

Harijan Temple Entry Act, 1947, 103
Harinarayanan, Swami, 111
Hasan, Mushirul, 294
Hepburn, A.C., 79
Hindu Adoptions and Maintenance Bill, 1956, 143
Hindu Code Bill, 5, 119–146, 163
  age of marriage, 131
  on child marriage, 124–126
  on divorce, 123–124
  enactments, 142–146
  history of improvements in, 135–136
  and joint family system, 132
  objections to, 123
  personal laws, 122
  prohibition of polygamy, 122–123
  rights of property, 129–133
  social customs of Hindus, 121
  succession act, 143
  translations, 122
  women's right to property, 120, 129
Hinduism, 2, 16–18, 63, 67–69, 82
Hindu law, 102. *see also* Hindu Code Bill
Hindu Law Committee, 122
Hindu Mahasabha, 5–7, 31
The Hindu Marriage Act, 1955, 105
Hindu population *vs* Muslim population, 19–20, 319
Hindu Rashtra, 20
Hindu religion, 28
Hindu Religious Endowments

Commission (1960–62), 111
Hindu Succession Bill, 1954, 142
Hindutva ideology, 53, 63, 68–69, 324
  origin and spread, 2–13
Hindutva Judgment, 62
The Holocaust of Indian Partition— An Inquest (Ram Madhav), 24
Huntington, Samuel P., 25
Husain, Tajamul, 174, 332
Hussain, Muzaffar, 84–85, 95, 186

Ibrahim, Dawood, 246
Imam, Ali, 71
Imam, Hussain, 149
India as a Secular State (Donald Smith), 5
The Indian Christian Marriage Act, 1872, 105
Indian Muslims, 13
Indian Penal Code (IPC)
  section 124A (sedition), 336
  sections 153-A and 153-B, 361–362
India's secularism, assessment of, 13–25
Indra Sawhney v. Union of India, 61
inflammatory speeches, 319
inquisitorial system, adoption of, 366–369
Insight into Minoritism (Muzaffar Hussain), 84–85
Intelligence Bureau (IB), 1–2
intolerance, 316–328
ISIS (Islamic State of Iraq and Syria), 26–27, 80–81, 83
Islam in India's Transition to Modernity (M.A. Karandikar), 15
Ismail Faruqui v. Union of India, 62
Iyer, Justice V.R. Krishna, 368

Jabalpur riots, 1961, 364

Jahagirdar, Justice R.A., 46, 55–57
  'Secularism in India—The Road Behind and The Road Ahead,' 57
Jain, Ajit Prasad, 34
Jain, Jinendra Kumar, 223
Jain, M.P., 188
Jain–Aggarwal Committee, 254
Jain–Bannerjee Committee, 254
Jain community, 103
  issues pertaining to sanctity of religious practices, 322
Jainism, 82
Jain Law, 102
Jamil, Javed, 183
Janata Party, 59
  election manifesto of, 48
Jan Sangh, 6
Jayakar, M.R., 8
Jayal, Niraja, 291
Jefferys, 306
Jha, D.N., 209
Jhingran, Saral, 84
Jinnah, Mohammad Ali, 8, 83, 124
John, V.K., 75
Justice Malimath Commission Report on Reforms in Criminal Justice System, 367–368

Kamath, H.V., 89, 176
Kant, Krishan, 47
Kanungo, Pralay, 12, 17
Karandikar, M.A., 15
Karemuddin, Kazi Syed, 93
Kargil War, 1999, 353
Karnad, Girish, 317
Kashyap, Subhash, 140
Kasuri, Khurshid Mahmud, 317
Kaur, Rajkumari Amrit, 55, 77, 88, 101, 142, 146, 173–174, 195
Kerala Education Bill, 1957, 74, 188, 191–192
Kesavananda Bharati v. State of Kerala, 60

INDEX ♦ 423

Ketkar, Kumar, 263
Khaliquzzaman, Chaudhri, 92
Khan, Aamir, 316
Khan, Arif Mohammad, 167, 170
Khan, Azam, 317
Khan, Khurshed Alam, 107
Khan, Saif Ali, 308
Khan, Shafaat Ahmad, 71
Khan, Shah Rukh, 316
Khanna, Justice H.R., 65, 235
Kher, B.G., 103, 258–260
Khilafat movement, 13
Khurana, Madan Lal, 241
Khurshid, Salman, 216
Khusro, A.M., 81
Kogekar, S.V., 40
Kothari, D.S., 374
Kripalani, J.B., 137, 145–146, 155
Krishna, Gopal, 282
Krishnamachari, T.T., 31, 99, 176
Kultar Singh v. Mukhtiar Singh, 67
Kumar, Nitish, 116
Kumar, Sajjan, 253

Lagarde, Christine, 305
Lall, Marie, 291
Lari, Z.H., 92–94, 200
The Lawyers Collective, 66
Laxman, R.K., 351
Lekhi, Meenakshi, 315
Liberhan Ayodhya Commission of Inquiry, 247
Limaye, Madhu, 82, 231
Lobo, Lancy, 281
Lodha, Guman Mal, 226

M. Ismail Faruqui v. Union of India, 242
MacDonald, Ramsay, 87
Madhav, Ram, 24, 322
Madras Congress Resolution, 1927, 71
Mahajan, Sumitra, 154–155

Maharashtra Control of Organised Crime Act (MCOCA), 361
Mahmood, Dr Tahir, 159–161, 295
Maitra, Lakshmi Kanta, 175
Malaviya, Pandit Madan Mohan, 124–125
Malegaon bomb blast case, 361
Malik, Sumeet, 60
Malkani, K.R., 10, 233
Man, Sardar Bhopinder Singh, 90
Mann, Simranjit Singh, 336
Manoharan, K., 44
Manohar Joshi v. Nitin Bhaurao Patil and Anr, 68
Marumakkathayam Law, 152
Masani, M.R., 142, 146, 158
Mathew, Justice, 60
Mathew, Justice K.K., 182
Mathur, Justice A.K., 215
McMillan, Alistair, 273
Mecca Masjid blast, 2007, 361
Mehta, Hansa, 31, 55, 91, 101, 130, 142, 146
Mehta, Om, 208
Mehta, Pratap Bhanu, 291
Menon, Meena, 308, 358, 362
minorities, 344. see also educational institutions, protection of minority; religious conversions/religious propagation
  AMU as a minority institution, 104–105
  Aurangzeb's '*jaziya* tax,' 97
  comments on use of term, 99–101
  in Constitution, 101–108
  and fundamental rights, 75
  and identity politics, 105–106
  interpretation of, 70–86
  Jain community, 102–104
  Kerala Education Bill, 74
  'miseries' of, 317
  Nehru Report, 71–72
  official recognition in India, 86–98

problem of, 89–90
protection of minority educational institutions, 118, 185–196
Rajkumari Amrit Kaur's memorandum on, 77, 101–102
Ranganath Misra Commission recommendations, 295–298
Rau committee on Hindu law, 102
religious endowments, 108–114
right to freedom of religion, 98–101
Sikhs, entitlement, 72
UN General Assembly Resolution related to protection and welfare of, 76–77
welfare of, 355–356
Minorities in History (A.C. Hepburn), 79
Minto, Lord, 86
Misra, Lokanath, 175
Mitra, Subrata, 289–290
Mitter, Dr Dwarkanath, 122
Modasa explosion, 2008, 361
Modi, Narendra, 10, 19, 212, 249, 268-269, 273–274, 303, 313, 316, 322, 350, 351
Mohani, Maulana Hasrat, 93
Mukherjee, Samar, 208
Mukherjee, Shyama Prasad, 11, 31, 98, 139-140, 275–276
Munshi, K.M., 78, 150–152, 154, 176, 185
Mushir-ul-Haq, 21
Muslim brotherhood, 13
Muslim League, 5, 31, 65, 71, 77, 154, 156, 221, 226, 235–237, 277, 343
Muslim Personal Law (Dr Tahir Mahmood), 159
Muslims, 82, 103, 293
Alienation, manifestations of, 308–312
attitude towards forces of secularization, 21
Enactment of Muslim Women (Protection of Rights on Divorce) Act, 118, 166–172
Gopal Singh Committee Report on conditions of, 293–295
and growing intolerance, 314–328
identity for, 71
increase in population, 19–20
Lucknow as cultural centre for, 82–83
as minority, 5, 15, 17, 287
misconceptions pertaining to the high rate of Muslim growth, 303–304
Muslim–non-Muslim conflict, 25–26
personal laws of, 94, 147–151, 155–156, 161–166
'political importance' of, 70
population, 19–20, 355–356
Rajinder Sachar Committee recommendations, 298–307
reservations in government jobs and institutions of higher learning, 304
rights of Mussulmans, 147
separate national state for, 80–81
and *Surya namaskar* (yogic exercise), 321
under-trials in jails, 304
Muslim terror and fundamentalism, spread of, 25
Muslim Wakfs Bill, 1952, 109–111
Mustafa, Seema, 168
Mysore Constituent Assembly, 100
My Years with Indira Gandhi (P.C. Alexander), 252

Naidu, K. Venkataswami, 111
Naik, Ram, 226, 320
Nair, M.N. Govindan, 208
Narain, Govind, 252

Narayan, Jayaprakash, 185–186, 195
Nariman, Fali S., 2, 66, 85, 115, 190–191, 194, 315
National Commission for Minorities (NCM), 2
  guidelines for determining minority status, 187, 193
  objects and reasons of, 115
National Commission to Review the Working of the Constitution (NCRWC), 348
National Human Rights Commission (NHRC), 98, 166, 274, 340
National Minorities Commission (NMC), 70, 114–117, 195, 293, 295
National Police Commission (NPC), 356–357, 339
Nehru, B.K., 367
Nehru, Jawaharlal, 1, 4–6, 9, 11, 14-15, 24-25, 36, 53, 58, 72, 74, 127–128, 132, 137, 139, 141–143, 146, 153, 177–178, 180, 195-197, 209, 237–239, 278, 287, 343
  communalism in India, 275–276
  on growing communalism, 5–6
  Hindu law, 119
  on the Hindu Rashtra, 6–7
  idea of secularism, 54
  Muslim problem in India, 72–73
  Objectives Resolution, 74–75
  religion from politics, importance of separation of, 220, 342–343
  secularism of, 14–15
  understanding in cow slaughter prohibition, 197–198, 207–208, 210–211, 217–218
Nehru, Motilal, 71, 87
Nehru Report, 71–72
Nepal, 25, 350
Noorani, A.G., 8, 249, 268–269, 308, 320, 331

Objectives Resolution, 74
Owaisi, Asaduddin, 304, 316, 343

Padgaonkar, Dileep, 261
Palkhivala, Nani, 46
Pandeya, Dr Laxminarayan, 50, 231
Pant, Govind Ballabh, 75, 174, 185, 239
The Paradox of American Power (Joseph S. Nye), 28
Paswan, Ram Vilas, 226, 243, 255–256
Pataskar, H.V., 133-134, 143
Patel, Alaknanda, 271
Patel, Vallabhbhai, 9, 15, 75, 82, 84, 92, 100, 103, 173–174, 237, 258, 275–278
  Report of the Advisory Committee on Minorities, 77
Pathania, Vikram, 308
Patil, S.K., 221
personal laws, 147–151
Places of Worship (Special Provisions) Act, 1991, 232, 239, 365
police departments, restructuring, 356–360
Potti–Rosha Committee, 255
Powathil, Archbishop Emeritus Joseph, 193
Pradhan, G.R., 71
Prasad, Dr Rajendra, 36, 126–128, 137, 141, 196, 276
Prasad, Mahabir, 111
proselytization, 13
public interest litigation (PIL), 162, 339, 357
PUDR/PUCL reports on rioting, 250
Punjab Agitation, 1980s, 95–96
  White Paper on, 95–97
Punwani, Jyoti, 265

Purie, Aroon, 212
Purohit, Col., 361

Qasim, Syed Mir, 221
Qureshi, Mohd. Hanif and Others, 197, 213, 217
Qureshi, Shuaib, 71

Radhakrishnan, S., 10, 58, 74
Rahman, S. Ubaidur, 117
Rahmani, Maulana Mohammad Wali, 162
Raja, C. Kunhan, 198
Rajagopal, O., 223
Rajinder Sachar Committee, 288, 298
Rajinder Sachar Committee recommendations, 298–307
Rajinder Sachar Committee Report, 292
Rajya Sabha Joint Parliamentary Committee on Wakf, 111
Ram, Jagjivan, 31, 174
Ram, Pandit Sita, 210
Ramakrishna Mission, 186, 195, 198
Ramaswamy, Justice, 61, 63
Ramdas, Lalita, 257–258, 329
Ramesh Yeshwant Prabhoo v. Prabhakar K. Kunte, 62
Ram Janma Bhoomi case. see Babri Masjid demolition
Ranganath Misra Commission for Religious and Linguistic Minorities, 193–194, 377
  recommendations, 295–298
  report, 292
Rao, Jagannath, 43
Rao, K. Chandrasekhar, 311, 323
Rao, M. Chalapathi, 239
Rao, N.T. Rama, 351
Rao, P.V. Narasimha, 224, 229, 240–241, 243, 247–251, 255, 262, 343

Rasul, Begum Aizaz, 130
Rau, Justice B.N., 55, 99, 101, 122, 133, 185
Rau, P. Kameswara, 111
Rau Committee, 102, 123
Rawat, Harish, 324
Ray, Rabi, 256
Reddi, K.C., 100
Reddy, Justice B.P. Jeevan, 61, 64
Religion and Public Life, 28
Religion from politics, importance of separation of, 219–237, 342–343
  communal parties, need to ban on, 221–222
  Constitution (Eightieth) Amendment Bill, opposition to, 225–237
  public debate, 225
  support and opposition, 223–227
Religious conversions/religious propagation, 172–185, 345
  attempts by Christian missionaries, 180–181
  constitutional issues, 181–182
  Niyogi Committee recommendations, 178–180
  reconversion, 183–184
Religious endowments, 108–114
Religious Institutions (Prevention of Misuse) Act, 1988, 364
Representation of the People Act (RPA), 1951, 68, 222-224, 229, 343, 365
Rev. Stanislaus v. State of Madhya Pradesh and Ors, 180
Right to freedom of religion, 98–101, 376–378
Roy, J.J.M. Nichols, 202
Roy, M.N., 51
Roy, Tathagat, 319
RSS, 162, 183, 249, 280, 318, 322
  ban on, 9–10

concerns about activities of, 4
Ghar Wapsi movement, 183–184
ideology, 17–18
Lok Sabha elections in 2014, role in, 10
membership, 327
resolutions and policies passed, 11–12
Tamil Nadu government's ban on the Hindu conference, 13
RSS Resolves, 11
rule of law, 360–366
Ruthnaswamy, M., 85, 172, 185

Saadulla, Muhammad, 92
Sa'adulla, Syed Muhammad, 33
Sachar Committee, 114
Sahay, Ram, 200
Sahib, B. Pocker, 92
Sahib, Muhammad Ismail, 149–150
Sahu, Lakshminarayan, 138
Saiadulla, Syed Muhammad, 201
Sait, Ibrahim Sulaiman, 46–47, 226, 243
Saksena, H.P., 143
Saksena, Mohan Lal, 109
Saksena, Shibban Lal, 33, 200
Saleem, Mohammad Yunus, 114
Salve, N.K.P., 174
Sambrani, Shreekant, 50, 270
Samjhauta Express attack, 2007, 361
Samy, V. Narayana, 224
sanatan dharma (Vaidic dharma), 4
Santhanam, K., 34, 133
Sapru, Tej Bahadur, 71
Sapru Committee, 73
Saran, Sankar, 111
Saraswat, V.K., 320
Sarda Act, 136
Sardar Syedna Taher Saifuddin Saheb v. State of Bombay, 66
Sardar Taheruddin Syedna Saheb v. State of Bombay, 60

Sardesai, Rajdeep, 261–262
The Satanic Verses (Salman Rushdie), 108
Savarkar, Vinayak Damodar, 4, 7
definition of a Hindu, 8–9
distinction between Hindutva and Hinduism, 9
Fatherland *(pitrubhoomi)* and Holy Land *(Punyabhoomi)*, 9
Sawant, Justice, 64
Second Administrative Reforms Commission (SARC), 369–374
secularism, 310
in action, 286–293
commission on, 337–341
Constitution as secular, 36–51
India's, assessment of, 13–25
interpretations of Supreme Court, 60–69
Jawaharlal Nehru's idea of, 53
as a legal concept, 52
national anthem and national song, singing of, 334–336
in Nepal, 25
problems of defining, 51–59, 344
problems of implementing, 20
safeguarding the future of, 374–376
secular state, essential requisites of a, 54
as *sui generis*, 111
tolerance to other religions, 47, 62
Upendra Baxi's definition of, 54
V.M. Tarkunde Memorial Lecture on, 53–54
by way of public interest litigation (PIL), 339
Secularism and Its Critics (Rajeev Bhargava), 17
Secularism in India (V.K. Sinha), 289
Seervai, H.M., 45, 54, 182
Sen, Amartya, 20
Sen, Binayak, 336

Sen, K.C., 111
Sen, P.K., 37
Sen, Ronojoy, 66
Setalvad, M.C., 58
  My Life—Law and Other Things, 58–59
Seth, Damodar Swarup, 186
SGPC (Shiromani Gurdwara Parbandhak Committee), 96
Shaban, Abdul, 19–20
Shah, A.B., 204–205
Shah, K.T., 88, 138, 174
Shah, Lt. General (retd) Zameer Uddin, 305
Shahabuddin, Syed, 50
Shah Bano case, 155, 159, 164, 166, 167
Shah Commission of Inquiry, 356
Shankar, Soumya, 293
Shariat Act of 1937, 152
Shariff, Abusaleh, 304
Sharma, Kundanika, 362
Sharma, Mahesh, 315–316
Sharma, Shankar Dayal, 58, 314
Shayara Bano case, 163
Sheikh, Sadiq Israr, 261
Shenoy, P.R., 42
Shetty, Chinayya, 312
Shinde, Sushilkumar, 365
Shiv Sena, 69, 162, 211, 223, 235, 237, 249, 261–266, 313, 316–317, 321–322, 343, 346, 358, 362
Shourie, Arun, 103, 221–222, 307
Shree Ahimsa Army Manav Kalyan Jeev Daya Charitable Trust v. Mirzapur Moti Kureshi Kassab Jamat, Ahmedabad, and Others, 214
Shukla, Ravi Shankar, 177–178
Sikh fundamentalism, 103
Sikhism, 82
Sikh personal law, 162

Sikh religion, 95
Sikhs, 98–99, 103
Sikri, S.M., 252
Sindhi, Ahmed Bakhsh, 221
Singh, Dr Ramji, 208
Singh, Harnam, 98
Singh, Jaswant, 143, 353
Singh, Justice Kuldip, 64
Singh, Kameshwar, 137
Singh, Karan, 82, 245
Singh, Manmohan, 274
Singh, Mohan, 233
Singh, Rajendra, 292
Singh, Rajnath, 310, 344
Singh, Sardar Hukam, 34, 138
Singh, Sardar Mangal, 71
Sinha, Chief Justice, 66–67
Smith, D.E., 23
Smith, Donald, 5–6, 209
Socialist party, 35–36
Sorabjee, Soli, 230, 326
Special Marriage Act III of 1872, 142
Special Marriage Amendment Bill, 121
Special Marriage Bill, 1954, 142
spoils system, 293
S.R. Bommai v. Union of India, 53, 61–63, 64, 235
Srikrishna, Justice B.N., 53–54, 161–162, 169, 242
Srikrishna Commission of Inquiry, 263
Srinivasavaradan, T.C.A., 252
St. Stephen's College, etc. v. the University of Delhi, 188
Stains, Graham Stewart, 282
State of Gujarat v. Mirzapur Moti Kureshi Kassab Jamat, Ahmedabad, and Others, 214
State of Orissa and Ors v. Mrs Yulitha Hyde and Ors etc., 180
The Story of My Life (M.R. Jayakar), 8

Sub-committee of the Constituent Assembly on Minorities, 78
Subrahmaniam, K., 50
Subramanian, T.S.R., 268
Sunder, Nandini, 312
Suri, Sanjay, 258
Swamy, Subramanian, 361
Swaraj Constitution for India, 71
Swaran Singh committee, 38, 43

Tandon, B.N., 153, 163, 235
Tandon, Purshottam Das, 278
Thackeray, Bal, 262
Thakur, Sadhvi Pragya Singh, 361
Thoughts on Pakistan (Ambedkar), 7
Tilak, Lokmanya, 223
T.M.A. Pai Foundation v. State of Karnataka, 191
Togadia, Praveen, 336
Trived, Aseem, 336
Tully, Mark, 16
Tulzapurkar, Justice V.D., 159
two-nation theory, 9
Tyabji, Badr-ud-din, 252

Umesh and Others v. State of Karnataka and Others, 214
U.N. Sub-Commission on Prevention of Discrimination and Protection of Minorities, 85
Uniform Civil Code, 146–166
and Muslim personal laws, 146–151, 155–156, 161–167
United Nations General Assembly Resolution 47/135, 1992, 76–77
Unlawful Activities (Prevention) Act, 237
UPA (United Progressive Alliance) government, 97, 163, 321, 347, 369

Vaishampayen, S.K., 105
Vajpayee, Atal Bihari, 227, 255, 263-264, 267, 273, 292
Varma, Veena, 144
Varshney, Ashutosh, 284
Veer, Dharm, 356
Vidyasagar, Ishwar Chandra, 135
Vishva Hindu Parishad (VHP), 162, 249, 266, 303, 312, 317–318, 324
Vivekananda, Swami, 2, 198

Wadhwa, Justice D.P., 282
Wakf Enquiry Committee, 110
Wani, Dr M. Afzal, 182
Weiner, Myron, 79
Widow Remarriage Act, 102, 135, 140
Wilson, Dr Anil, 295
Wirth, Louis, 79
Worshipping False Gods: Ambedkar, and the facts which have been erased (Arun Shourie), 31
Wright, T., 79, 290
Wright Jr., Theodore P., 85

Yadav, Shyam Lal, 106
Yadav, Surya Narayan, 227
Yajee, Sheel Bhadra, 221

Zahira Habibullah H. Sheikh v. State of Gujarat and Ors, 269
Zakaria, Fareed, 16-17
Zakaria, Rafiq, 56, 83
Zavos, John, 290
Ziyauddin Burhanuddin Bukhari v. Brijmohan Ramdass Mehra, 59–60